GOTREK & FELIX
CITY OF THE DAMNED

More Warhammer from Black Library

· GOTREK & FELIX ·

GOTREK & FELIX: THE FIRST OMNIBUS
William King
(Contains the novels: *Trollslayer, Skavenslayer* and *Daemonslayer*)

GOTREK & FELIX: THE SECOND OMNIBUS
William King
(Contains the novels: *Dragonslayer, Beastslayer* and *Vampireslayer*)

GOTREK & FELIX: THE THIRD OMNIBUS
William King & Nathan Long
(Contains the novels: *Giantslayer, Orcslayer* and *Manslayer*)

GOTREK & FELIX: THE FOURTH OMNIBUS
Nathan Long
(Contains the novels: *Elfslayer, Shamanslayer* and *Zombieslayer*)

ROAD OF SKULLS
Josh Reynolds

GOTREK & FELIX: LOST TALES
An anthology edited by Laurie Goulding

GOTREK & FELIX: THE ANTHOLOGY
Edited by Christian Dunn

CITY OF THE DAMNED
David Guymer

SLAYER OF THE STORM GOD
An audio drama by Nathan Long

CURSE OF THE EVERLIVING
An audio drama by David Guymer

· ULRIKA THE VAMPIRE ·
Nathan Long

Book 1: BLOODBORN
Book 2: BLOODFORGED
Book 3: BLOODSWORN

· THANQUOL & BONERIPPER ·
C.L. Werner

Book 1: GREY SEER
Book 2: TEMPLE OF THE SERPENT
Book 3: THANQUOL'S DOOM

A WARHAMMER NOVEL

DAVID GUYMER

GOTREK & FELIX

CITY OF THE DAMNED

BLACK LIBRARY

A BLACK LIBRARY PUBLICATION

First published in Great Britain in 2013 by
Black Library,
Games Workshop Ltd.,
Willow Road, Nottingham,
NG7 2WS, UK

10 9 8 7 6 5 4 3 2 1

Cover illustration by Phroilan Gardner
Map by Nuala Kinrade.

© Games Workshop Limited 2013. All rights reserved.

Black Library, the Black Library logo, Warhammer, the Warhammer Logo, Time of Legends,
the Time of Legends logo, Games Workshop, the Games Workshop logo and all associated
brands, names, characters, illustrations and images from the Warhammer universe are either
®, TM and/or © Games Workshop Ltd 2000-2013, variably registered in the UK and other
countries around the world. All rights reserved.

A CIP record for this book is available from the British Library.

UK ISBN13: 978 1 84970 528 8
US ISBN13: 978 1 84970 529 5

No part of this publication may be reproduced, stored in a retrieval system, or transmitted
in any form or by any means, electronic, mechanical, photocopying, recording or
otherwise, without the prior permission of the publishers.

This is a work of fiction. All the characters and events portrayed in this book are fictional,
and any resemblance to real people or incidents is purely coincidental.

See Black Library on the internet at
www.blacklibrary.com

Find out more about Games Workshop
and the world of Warhammer at
www.games-workshop.com

Printed and bound by CPI Group (UK) Ltd, Croydon, CR0 4YY

This is a dark age, a bloody age, an age of daemons
and of sorcery. It is an age of battle and death, and of the
world's ending. Amidst all of the fire, flame and fury
it is a time, too, of mighty heroes, of bold deeds
and great courage.

At the heart of the Old World sprawls the Empire, the
largest and most powerful of the human realms. Known for
its engineers, sorcerers, traders and soldiers, it is
a land of great mountains, mighty rivers, dark forests
and vast cities. And from his throne in Altdorf reigns
the Emperor Karl Franz, sacred descendant of the
founder of these lands, Sigmar, and wielder
of his magical warhammer.

But these are far from civilised times. Across the length
and breadth of the Old World, from the knightly palaces
of Bretonnia to ice-bound Kislev in the far north, come
rumblings of war. In the towering Worlds Edge Mountains,
the orc tribes are gathering for another assault. Bandits and
renegades harry the wild southern lands of
the Border Princes. There are rumours of rat-things, the
skaven, emerging from the sewers and swamps across the
land. And from the northern wildernesses there is the
ever-present threat of Chaos, of daemons and beastmen
corrupted by the foul powers of the Dark Gods.
As the time of battle draws ever near,
the Empire needs heroes
like never before.

North of Here Lie The Dreaded Chaos Wastes.

Here Be Trolls...

' Claws

Erengrad.

Praag.

Kislev

Kislev.

middle mountains,

enheim.

Wolfenburg.

Talabheim

The Empire

Altdorf.

Karak Kad

Nuln.

The Moot.

Sylvania.
Dracken -hof.

Zhufbar.

Averheim.

Black Water.

ains.

Karak Norn.

Black fire Pass.

'I have a recurring dream.

'Always it awakens me with chills, my spirit returning from a place that the sun cannot touch, and on that count, at least, this night differs little. I leave Gotrek snoring soundly in the pallet opposite and, in the quiet light of moon and stars from the tavern's little window, I write.

'My hands shake, for never before has it come so clearly. For the first time I think I remember how it ends. I consider waking Gotrek. But I fear to. I fear that he will only confirm what I already now suspect. That this was no mere dream. That Gotrek and I did encounter a monster of a kind I have never before seen, and that we did then pursue it to its lair; a ruined city, deep in the darkest wolds of wild Ostermark.

'I feel the residue of this nightmare lifting from me, some curative in the familiar act of scratching paper with sharpened quill. I must continue, commit these images to permanence and order ere they fail me again. As I arrange my thoughts, a lingering shard of dread makes my heart race. I had hoped the mundanity of words would rob the visions of their power, but they now seem only more plausible, not less.

'For perhaps it was only a matter of time before Gotrek and I journeyed to the City of the Damned…'

– From *My Travels with Gotrek*, Vol. VI,
By Herr Felix Jaeger

PROLOGUE

The priest's sermon echoed within the hollow belly of the cathedral, an ugly wooden ceiling surmounting limestone walls and columns of pale Totenwald pine. In rough-spun woollen robes of white and red, Arch-Lector Hans-Jorgen Gramm snarled from his pulpit like a wolf in a cage. Hammered into the high wall above the altar, the majesty of Ghal-maraz, the hammer of the man-god Sigmar, overlooked the congregation. Its handle was varnished oak, its head tin and plated brass that the ignorant might mistake for gold. The priest turned to it often as he spoke, grasping for the acclaim of his god.

Men and women in grubby woollen smocks packed the cathedral, spilling through the open doors into the square beyond. They listened in mute devotion. The priest's High Classical meant little, but something in his vehemence touching their shared faith. Lay clergy walked the ranks of devotees in the Kirchplatz, relaying his words like living echoes. The fog that smothered the entire township seeped through the open threshold and into the cathedral where it took on a remarkable, shifting colouration before the great circular window of stained glass set above the lintel. The gathered penitents sniffled and shivered, submerged to the knees in a frigid rainbow of misdirected light.

Such was all to the good.

To live was to devote oneself to Sigmar.

To devote oneself to Sigmar was to suffer.

Pages in white linen smocks, their hair cropped short, walked the aisles bearing candles. The flames spat valiantly against the encroaching fog, releasing a hiss of brimstone, casting the memorial stones and plaques that adorned the walls into densely shadowed relief. Heroes, martyrs, their names outliving their frail bodies: Albrecht, who fought in the Great War alongside Magnus the Pious himself; Thesen, who gave his life defending this most holy site from the dread von Carsteins; Gottlieb who helped break the siege of Osterwald and rout the army of Azhag the Slaughterer; Golo, his son, who came closer than any before to purging the Ostermark Moors of its taint.

There were others, their names and deeds no less worthy, two hundred years of the von Kuber line. Reliefs of their likenesses glowered by candlelight from the long walls. The artistry was provincial, edging rough, figures lacking in symmetry. But it had been done with faith.

Baron Götz von Kuber sat in the front row, hunched before the altar as if in deep contemplation. He was a tall man, handsome, his likeness a reflection of those portrayed in stucco upon the walls. He was garbed for temple in his finest, a sombre grey doublet with padded sleeves, the linen overlayer embroidered with devotional symbols in threads of silver and black. But for him, the pew was deserted, a long stretch of bare wood reserved for the great and the good. Reserved for him.

He was only half listening to the sermon.

'Gramm will not approve.'

A powerfully built man in the stark grey livery of the von Kuber barony leaned forward from the pew behind to hiss in his baron's ear. He shared his lord's dark hair, complemented by a thick, horseshoe moustache. Götz had found Konrad Seitz as a fierce young lad in a Sigmarite orphanage in Kielsel. His common stock was no barrier here, and he had served in Götz's household guard since he had first mastered the horse and memorised the catechisms of devotion. There was none more loyal, none more intransigent in their faith.

Götz did not turn, made no other gesture to indicate that he had heard. Head bowed and nodding with the priest's words, his eyes flicked up. Gramm was lost in a froth of exhortation, veritably clawing at his wooden pulpit, and with no attention to spare his noble benefactor. 'Magnus tasked my line with this duty,' Götz whispered, 'not his. Gramm will be returning to Osterwald tomorrow and will likely not return until spring. Don't worry about him.'

'It's not him I worry for, lord.'

'Then what? Of all men, I believed I could count on you, brother?'

'To the end of days, lord. But I worry that if the clergy turn against you…'

Götz silenced the man with a single shake of the head, still observing the service faithfully. 'The faithful believe as we do. Chaos cannot be allowed this foothold in our lands. It is an affront to the Empire bequeathed us by holy Sigmar.'

Konrad said nothing. Götz took his silence as blessing.

'Promise me, Konrad, that should anything befall me you will continue this work. Promise me that you will burn this sore from the face of Ostermark.'

'What's this talk?' Konrad hissed. 'Has the white lady approached your dreams as she has others?'

'No, praise Sigmar, his faith in me doesn't waver.'

Konrad exuded relief. Oblivious to the conversation beneath

his nose, the priest continued to rage. 'I'm glad. Even Father Gramm has been struck by nightmares. The darkness of the city grows.'

'Containing this evil so long has only granted it time to grow strong. Violence is all the forces of night understand.' Götz was silent a moment as Gramm turned his way to exalt the champion who kept the tide of Chaos at bay. Götz took the praise coldly. 'I'm the last of my line. It is just that the city we have watched all these generations should die with me. Promise me. Promise me that it will soak in a river of blood.'

Before Konrad could answer, a minor commotion broke out from the cathedral doors. Götz took the excuse to look around. A soldier was squeezing through the packed congregation, attracting the unspoken ire of the lay clergy. They chastised him with sharp eyes and pointed looks. They were wasting their time. No one gave less of a damn for anyone else than Caul Schlanger. The newcomer nudged aside a chanting page and quick-marched the length of the aisle, then made a crab-wise shuffle along the penultimate pew, past the knees of rapt soldiers in the baron's grey, before finally squeezing in next to Konrad Seitz. Konrad afforded a spartan nod in greeting.

The preacher admonished the interruption with a glare without breaking the stream of rhetoric. Götz clasped hands between his knees and returned his eyes to the arch-lector.

Caul leaned over the back of Götz's pew, hanging his head as though in prayer. 'Another sighting of the Beast, lord,' he hissed, breath warm on Götz's neck. 'Reliable this time. One of our own patrols.'

Götz digested that ambiguous news. 'How many dead?'

'Thirty bodies found. We burned them to be on the safe side.'

Götz nodded. Caul Schlanger was almost everything that Konrad Seitz was not. He was gristle on bones, eyes a reptilian green, thin lips stuck in a knowing sneer. Where he came from was just another piece of the enigma; some said Averheim, others Luddendorf, while still others insisted his extraction was Kislevite. Götz had even heard it rumoured that Caul was not the man's real name, that he had shortened it out of frustration with superfluous letters. It would not be the oddest tale, and the man harboured idiosyncrasies aplenty to render it plausible. All Götz knew for a fact was that Caul was a murderous bastard, spared the hangman's noose in Waldenhof by a baron's good word and a meagre sum of coin. But on the one value of consequence, Konrad and Caul both stood equal.

The shared conviction of faith.

'We lost the creature on the moors,' Caul hissed. 'But we are certain it was headed for the city.'

The city. It irked no end how they all skirted its name, avoiding mention even of the coded allusion that had long ago replaced it. The City of the Damned. Götz considered 'The von Kuber curse' to be a name more apt. For two hundred years it had blighted Götz's antecedents, but no more. His father, Golo, had made inroads, but it would be him, Baron Götz von Kuber that finally brought this long war to a close.

'This is why the City of the Damned must be purged,' he murmured. He kept his voice flat and his face down, lest the arch-lector see his lips move. 'Evil begets evil. It must be cast down, damnation take the naysayers and the hidebound who say otherwise. Rivers of blood, my brothers. It will be glorious.'

Caul regarded him strangely.

'Do you doubt our path?' Götz pressed. 'Do you believe the heathen and the heretic undeserving of our mercy?'

'No lord. Death by righteous hands is a justice they scarce deserve.'

'But…?'

'But the city is damned. The Pious himself let it lie. Do you really think it can be saved?'

Baron Götz von Kuber closed his eyes and allowed the elegy of Hans-Jorgen Gramm to sweep him away, through visions of blood and glory and destinies soon to fall.

'Leave salvation to the Sisters of Shallya, brothers. We are warriors, and I will see this end. One way or another.'

CHAPTER 1

The Beast of the Ostermark Moors

Felix Jaeger shivered in the autumnal chill that ghosted through the silent village. Wedged into the crease between two hills, the wind washed over in occasional gusts, coming and going with spits of rain from the grim, mid-afternoon sky. It was a tiny place, probably not large enough to earn its own point on a map, just a single cobbled lane of low, grey walled houses. Their doors were bolted and barred, their windows boarded, iron hammers nailed into the walls. Felix counted maybe nine or ten houses on each side, colourless uneven stone and grey mortar, each separated from the next by walled yards that sheltered tough-looking vegetables from the worst of the wind. On the village's outskirts stood a sad little garden of Morr marked by a weather-pitted stone hammer. A goat picked its way around unmarked memorial slabs. It ignored Felix entirely as he walked by. A bronze bell around its neck tinkled as it bent to crop at a clutch of dandelion stalks.

'Do you think they heard that we were coming?'

Gotrek scanned the row of houses with his one good eye.

His enormous axe rested against one shoulder, its broad runic blade spattered with raindrops. He grunted, whether in amusement or acknowledgement, Felix never could say. 'I didn't start that fight, manling. All I wanted was ale and some answers. Is it my fault that folk hereabouts have no manners?'

'These are the moors, Gotrek. I doubt whether anyone here has encountered a dwarf outside of a priest's sermon. You can't blame them for not knowing how to... er...' He hesitated, not wanting to earn the Slayer's ire for himself. 'How to behave around one.'

Gotrek grumbled and returned his eye to the road. 'If I told that lot the elves had left, they'd probably have a parade.'

Felix felt the tug of a smile at that. The people around here were certainly isolated. And superstitious too. This landscape bred strange ideas in people's hearts. Every nook and valley had a capricious spirit that needed appeasing, every gurgling brook played host to the shade of some tragic and hopelessly romantic heroine. But of every myth spouted in the alehouses of Osterwald, surely the most egregious was that of – and here the drunken farm boys and goatherds would widen their eyes and speak in hushed growls as though in some awful student production of a Detlef Sierck melodrama – *the Beast of the Moors*.

A missing person in one village, a broken seal on a family crypt in the next, strange sightings and animal howls on the moors. To Felix's mind, it was all little more than glorified sheep rustling and banditry dressed up as some subhuman horror to frighten outsiders, children and the overly credulous. Not that that ruled out many of the folk of Ostermark. He sighed. Or Trollslayers in search of a glorious doom, for that matter.

'This Beast of theirs has put the fright up them, that's for sure,' said Gotrek, uncaring for Felix's thoughts. 'I just hope this time we didn't miss it.'

Felix chose to say nothing, looking instead to the far end of the street just as a sudden breeze made his long hair and red Sudenland cloak snap out behind him. He turned his jaw side-on, a slap of drizzle to the face. He was bone weary. He tried to remember exactly when it was that he had started to have difficulty sleeping. It was after departing from Oster-wald, he was reasonably certain, recalling his last night in the airless attic above the playhouse with an unexpected fond-ness. It was this blasted moor. His nights within it had been restless, his dreams visited by fog and anguished souls. Some nights he saw a lady in white. She never spoke, just watched, watched as her black-walled city burned. Just remembering it made him shiver.

The Ostermark Moors was desolate country and the road had been as uneventful as it had been in dire need of care. These routes, if his history served, had been built to bear the armies of Emperor Magnus as they purged the northern provinces of Chaos in the aftermath of the Great War and had likely not been touched since. Derelict shrine posts marked the road-side with a neglectful infrequency. Felix had counted perhaps two or three each day, but it varied. Hewn from single lumps of grey limestone into the rough form of a hammer, heads carved with classical script weathered to obscurity, devotion bowls gouged into the stony hafts. A week or so back, Felix had found a couple of verdigrised pfennigs behind a skein of cobwebs. He had left them. Even he and Gotrek were not yet hungry enough to steal from Sigmar. The best those recesses had offered their god since had been a nesting magpie that had squalled like a jilted harlot the moment they came near. Even Gotrek had gritted his teeth and left the bird in peace.

Two weeks out of Osterwald with nothing but dry-stone walls, empty hills, and Gotrek's complaints of sore feet, even Felix was starting to itch for some excitement. Gotrek may not have started that brawl in the last village but he had taken to it with an equal mix of enthusiasm and shame, as a man despairing of thirst might throw himself onto a muddy puddle. It had only lasted a minute; half a dozen goatherds that had thought to make light of Gotrek's short stature and tattoos all beaten unconscious, the interior of the tavern turned upside down, Gotrek himself stood in the middle of it looking strangely downcast that there was no watch to drive him out of town. Like a child who'd ruined his bed and now had to sleep in it.

There was no watch here, no militia, no sign whatsoever of Emperor Karl Franz's rule, or whatever baron levied troops and tax in his name. That village had been three days ago, and in that time they had not passed another living soul.

'The Beast, I'm telling you,' said Gotrek, hefting his axe easily in one ham-like fist. It rattled on its chain like a leashed hound.

Felix peered through the crudely nailed slats that blocked the window of what smelled like a smokehouse. Smoke pumped fitfully from its chimney. Felix stared at the smokehouse chimney, jerking damp locks from his forehead. The smoke moulded into twisted shapes, dragged up by the wind like a chain from a well.

For a moment, the eddies in the smoke had resembled a figure.

Gotrek smoothed his thumb around the blade of his axe until blood welled in a scarlet bead. 'A long time it's been coming, too. I'm due a half-decent scrap.'

Felix moved his own hand to the dragonhead hilt of his sword. He gave it a short tug to ease it from the leather grip of its scabbard. Journeying with Gotrek Gurnisson, it paid to be cautious.

'Do you think they're still inside?' he said, turning his back with some difficulty on the smoky phantasm and nodding towards the boarded windows.

'Aye, manling. Even your kind aren't foolish enough to keep a fire going untended.'

'Unless they fled in a hurry.'

'Oh, they're here,' Gotrek answered with a grin absent of several teeth. He waved over the abandoned street. Felix took in the boarded windows, the reinforced doors. 'This wasn't done in a hurry.'

Felix looked over the sharply angled slate rooftops to the low hills ranged up on either side. A stretch of dry-stone wall petered out into a pile of rubble about halfway up the rightward slope. The hill on the other side boasted nothing so grand to mark it. Heathers and brambles scratched a living from the thin topsoil. The flora here was not even green, but rather an off-putting kind of purplish brown. Like an old bruise.

'Come out, you beardless cowards!' Gotrek suddenly roared, making Felix start. 'We'll not harm you.' The Slayer turned to Felix and gave a gravelly chuckle, then muttered under his breath, 'Probably.'

'Gotrek,' Felix breathed, stilling his companion with a gloved finger on his arm.

Gotrek looked up, then followed Felix's nod, just catching the shadow of movement from behind a boarded window. It had come from the larger, two-storey building that overlooked the far end of the street. Even without any kind of sign or welcome, Felix had enough experience of the taverns of this world to recognise another. Its construction was of the same grey stone that characterised the region with a pair of wide, covered, windows either side of a sturdy oak double door. A quiescent chimney stack poked between the slate tiling of its tall, sloping roof, black tiles that the cawing blackbirds sheltering under its eaves had pebbled white. The street's cobbles marched directly on that front door before veering around, edging slightly up the rightward hill, and coming about into what looked like a coaching yard at the rear. Weeds choked the cobbles. Felix doubted a coach had stopped here since the road had been laid. If then.

Gotrek cackled and stomped off in that direction, warming his muscles with a slow swing of his axe. The runes hummed as it bit into the wind. Felix bit his lip and hurried after him. He looked over his shoulder and shivered.

He could feel eyes on him.

From the tavern doors, there came the scrape of a heavy crossbar being removed and then slowly, as if acting under great duress, one half of the double door edged wide. A heavy-set man with a bald scalp, dressed in a sleeveless woollen smock and greasy overalls, nudged aside the door on the fat of his left arm. A blond-haired lad in a padded jerkin appeared at his back with a spear and doing his darnedest to look anything other than terrified.

He was not having a great deal of success.

Felix froze in his tracks, slowly removing his hands from his belted blade. Held into the crook of the bigger man's arm was a flared-muzzled handgun of a kind that Felix had not seen outside of the Imperial Gunnery Museum in Nuln. He took a careful step back and raised his hands. If he were to be riddled with buckshot in the middle of nowhere on the Slayer's latest nihilistic quest, then the knowledge that he had been killed by a weapon at least a century out of date would come as scant consolation. Gotrek kept nonchalantly on, as though he had seen nothing.

'Gotrek,' he hissed.

The dwarf took another couple of paces before he stopped too. He swung back his axe to rest against his shoulder, for all the world like a lumberjack at the start of a shift. 'A welcome as warm as your ale, eh barkeep?'

Felix saw the man's bare arms pucker in the wind, the antique blunderbuss trained on Felix before it swung down to target Gotrek. Not that it really mattered what he aimed at,

Felix thought with alarmingly sound reasoning. A weapon like that could probably spray the whole street.

'Who are ye?' The bald man barked in a rough Ostermark drawl.

'Just travellers,' Felix called back, before Gotrek could contrive a way to get them both riddled with birdshot. Felix thought he saw the man smirk.

'Oh aye? Travellers, yer say?' He jabbed his blunderbuss threateningly at Gotrek. 'Travelling where?'

'Wherever we bloody well like,' Gotrek growled.

For a moment, the man was taken aback by Gotrek's fierceness, and the weapon drooped slightly before snapping back up. 'Yer travelin' nowhere lessen I say so, yer hear?'

Gotrek thrust out his chin and took a step forward. The blunderbuss tracked him, deadly orifice gaping like a maw to the netherworld. 'Think you can stop me?'

'Gotrek,' Felix murmured, a stage whisper that carried. 'Please don't get me shot.'

'Hah!' Gotrek barked. 'Is that what's worrying you, manling?'

Felix eyed the large gun. 'At present, yes.'

'Shut yer mouths,' the man said. His finger trembled on the trigger.

'Um, Gotrek...'

Some itch at the roof of his spine had made Felix turn. The door to the smokehouse creaked open and a large man with red eyes and a soot-stained smock appeared in the doorway. He had a meat saw clutched in one hand, gristle hanging from the teeth. A woman, similarly begrimed, followed him onto the street, a shovel held close to her breast in both hands. Further down the lane, there came the sound of bolts being withdrawn and wooden hinges grinding open, the street slowly filling with silent, drably-garbed peasants, dirty hair ruffled by the wind. There must have been a good dozen, faces blending into a frightened, grimy mass. They said nothing, just afforded each other nods as they advanced, shoulder to shoulder, goat hooks, peat shovels and sticks waving over their heads. They stared at him, blank and afraid, and he stared back.

Just what we need, thought Felix, forgetting the tavern-keeper's blunderbuss as his hands dropped instinctively to his scabbard. An angry mob.

Felix eyed the villagers warily. They held their distance for now, but terror did odd things to a man's courage and it did not look like it would take much to provoke a charge. He glanced over at Gotrek, the Slayer stood with pursed lips, regarding them impassively. His axe had not shifted from its perch against his shoulder.

'What's this, Gregor? Found some other way to bring the Beast on our heads?' The accusation came from somewhere within the mob, Felix did not see where, but the jeers that followed told him it was a conviction shared.

The man, Gregor, swung his blunderbuss to cover the street. It did not cow them in the slightest. Or rather, Felix thought, they were already far too afraid of something else. The blond-haired boy at Gregor's back, gripped his spear with white knuckles and pressed closer to the larger man, sweeping the crowd with wide white-filled eyes.

'Back to yer homes,' Gregor growled. 'I'll not tell yer twice.'

'Yer'll see us all dead!' shouted the same man. Felix got a good look at him this time, dark hair and dark eyes, goats' wool jerkin muddy and indistinguishable from any other. 'Is that what yer want, Gregor? You want this land for yerself, like that witch o' yers?' More shouts, even angrier this time. Someone threw a stone, it whisked inches over Felix's head and struck the wall by the tavern-keeper's arm, making the large man duck and pull his gun away to shield himself.

'Quiet down,' said Gregor, the strain of trying to be heard without shouting pulling his voice thin. 'Yer'll bring the monster onto us, fer sure.'

That gave the mob pause, or at least another source of superstitious terror to dilute their attention. Felix felt the tension, like a bowstring ready to be unleashed. They scanned the hilltops with quiet fear.

'Let's all be calm,' said Felix, taking the opportunity to fill the silence with his father's most reasonable mercantile tone. He was not sure how he and Gotrek managed to walk into these things; he just hoped to be able to diffuse it before Gotrek lost his patience. 'I fear we're all the victims of some misunderstanding. We really are nothing more than innocent travellers.'

For a moment or two there was silence, then a thrown stone struck his wrist. He gasped and clutched it to his belly. That was not exactly the response he had been hoping for. He edged back from the mob, closer to Gotrek and the tavern-keeper.

'No closer, *travellers*,' Gregor snarled. 'We've all heard stories of the Beast.' He regarded Gotrek suspiciously, his eyes hard. 'And I don't like the look o' thissen. He looks wild enough. And if that were not proof enough, the last village we heard hit was Taalsveldt just back yonder way. Maybe *he's* the Beast.'

Felix winced as Gotrek hefted his axe and growled. 'Pick your next words with care, barkeep, and remember that a dwarf won't soon forget an insult.'

'They...' the lad behind the tavern-keeper spoke up, his voice catching. He took a hard swallow before continuing. 'They don't look much like beasts, pa.'

'Hush, Thomas,' Gregor whispered. 'Ain't no tellin' that fer sure.'

'The Beast is taller, Gregor, you big oaf.' The call came from the crowd, swiftly joined by a babble of others.

'Aye, like an ogre.'

'And its claws are longer.'

'Not an ogre, Heinrich, like a troll.'

'Cold, grey flesh.'

'Eyes of daemonfire.'

'Claws like knives.'

'Grey skin, aye, like a troll I said.'

Felix nodded, spreading his arms as if a glimpse up his sleeves would offer the final proof of his humanity. 'It's true, see. We've never even seen your Beast.'

'More's the pity,' Gotrek grumbled under his breath.

'He said he's a dwarf,' Thomas whispered into his father's ear, eyes fixed on Gotrek. He lowered his spear. 'Didn't Father Gramm say to always do right by dwarfs? I don't want no trouble with the baron.'

'Too right,' said Gotrek. 'Now put down that lump of rust. It'll never fire and everyone here with half an eye knows it.'

Gregor clutched the firearm so tight that Felix thought it might bend out of shape. 'This… this is the weapon my ancestors used to purge the moors of Chaos!'

'Should have given it better care then, shouldn't you?'

'That's it, Beast!' Gregor aimed his blunderbuss at Gotrek and squeezed down on the trigger. The villagers took a collective gasp and threw themselves to the ground. Felix went down a half second later, leaving only Gotrek standing. There was a click and then nothing. Gregor shook the blunderbuss angrily, then depressed the trigger twice more, summoning two more clicks. 'Sigmar's grief,' he swore.

'Damp in the powder chamber,' Gotrek explained. 'Look at that rust around the lock.' The man sagged and held up the wheel-lock mechanism for inspection.

'So then,' said Gotrek, already stomping towards the tavern doors. 'Now we're all friends, how about an ale? I'm thirsty and I get irritable when I'm thirsty.'

The villagers were pulling themselves to their feet, holding to each other for support and glaring hatefully at Gregor and his son. The tavern-keeper backed away from them, pushing the lad, Thomas, through the door and gripping his blunderbuss like a truncheon. He still looked unconvinced that Gotrek and

Felix were who they claimed to be, but did not seem to know what to do about it given his useless firearm. He glared at Felix in indecisive fear before the angered murmurings of the mob made his mind up for him.

'Fine. Come on in.' He took a quick step onto the street to clear the door but sidestepped hurriedly to the left to keep his back to the wall. He peered up at the hilltops. The wind made the heather wave. 'We'll deal with this out of sight. And the rest of you!' This was hissed down to the knot of villagers. 'Back to your homes. Quick, before you're seen.'

The peasants did not move. They stared at the tavern-keeper, and at Felix, with a bitterness born of terror. He did not know what had angered them so, but it would only take the smallest spark to inflame that anger into something more deadly. Felix's gaze found its way back to the cemetery at the edge of town. The gnarled old stone hammer stood bent in the wind. There was no sign of the goat. He supposed one of the villagers must have taken the opportunity to bring it indoors.

'Hurry,' urged Gregor with a nervous eye on the crowd. 'You don't want to be out when the sun sets.'

Felix looked first to the tavern-keeper and then to the sky. It was a miserable blue-grey, but sunset was several hours away at least. 'What happens at night?'

'The Beast hunts.'

'Back! Back, beast!'

Felix ducked under the lintel behind Gotrek, just as a rough-shaven man made a grab for a sword where it lay on a table. His hand shoved the blade off, sending it across the floorboards with a dull clatter. He swore and staggered from his stool, struggling to pull a knife from his britches while simultaneously tugging on the straps that flapped from his unbuckled leather cuirass.

'Peace, Rudi,' said Gregor, entering behind Felix with young

Thomas in tow. 'Nowt but a pair on the road.'

Rudi threw up his hands and gasped for breath. 'Rhya's tears, you… you fat old fool.' He kneaded his temples, as though possessed by the suspicion that some darkness lurked there. 'What happened to hiding? Hmm? To holding out for the baron?' The man was raving. The lad, Thomas, ran across to him, but Rudi shouldered past him. 'You can't just… you just can't let strange folk in. What if the Beast has been following them?'

'My brother has seen it,' Thomas explained, still trying to get close enough to calm him.

'Has he now?' asked Gotrek, suddenly interested.

Rudi pulled clear of his brother's attentions and was struggling to rid himself of his armour, working himself into a state as he yanked at the single fastened tie at his left hip. At last it relented, the whole piece dragging over his head. He let it fall. He crossed his arms, still breathing heavily. He was a strapping young man, hard-earned muscles trembling in departing panic against his woollen undershirt. He glared at Gotrek and, for a moment, Felix feared he was about to do something foolish, but then he sagged. He and Gregor shared a look and, without another word spoken, bent to collect his armour and turned away, heading for a back door.

'Rudolph saw nothing,' said Gregor as the door eased shut. Felix heard the tramp of feet on wooden slats as the man headed upstairs. 'Ain't nobody seen the Beast and lived.'

'I think I like it here, manling,' Gotrek remarked. Rudi's fallen blade had tangled between the legs of a stool. Gotrek toed it aside, then dragged the stool back. The snarl of wood on wood worked the tension in the room like a blunt knife across iron. If Felix were feeling less charitable, he would think Gotrek did it on purpose. The dwarf swung himself over the stool and sank down. He rapped on the tabletop with the knob of his axe before setting it down where Rudi's sword had been with a stamp of metal. He set to unscrewing its chain from his bracer. 'Ale. And don't think I'm paying for it after that nonsense in the street.'

Gregor started at the dwarf's voice. The man looked anxious, distracted, as if their simply being there was making him nervous. He gave a curt bow and did as he was bid, circuiting around and behind a bar that was ranked with dusted barrels and ran the wall on Felix's left.

Felix followed the dwarf to the table, ducking under a crude hammer of Sigmar that had been fashioned from a pair of twisted horseshoes and hung by a cord from the rafters. His passage set it swaying. He stilled it between thumb and forefinger.

The room was spacious, three or four long tables with stools scattered around them and a couple of private snugs in the far corners. It held a dank air of neglect, like sour meat and wet fur. And it was dark. An unlit hearth mouldered softly within the back wall. What little sunlight strained through the grey mesh of clouds found its way into the tavern rudely barred as Thomas pulled the door closed and reset the heavy crossbar. Moths butted their heads dumbly at the window boards, their wing beats a staccato stutter as they sought out the slivers of illumination that gleamed between the joins. Slowly, Felix's eyes began to adapt to the gloom.

'That lot outside don't seem too fond of you, barkeep,' said Gotrek.

'They're scared,' said Gregor. He had paused under a brass plaque on the wall behind the bar. A pair of hooks protruded from it. He sighed and returned the antique blunderbuss back to its mount. 'My great, great, great…' He trailed off and closed his eyes, shook his head when the answer would not come. 'Blood of Magnus,' he said, signing the hammer with a pudgy finger. 'He were a pilgrim, like most folks were back when, settled after the Great War were won.'

'Faster with that ale. And tell me more of your boy's run-in with the Beast.'

'Poor Rudolph,' said Gregor with a sigh, rummaging under the bar for a tankard partway clean. He held it under one of the tapped kegs, blew dust from the tap and opened it. Golden-brown froth sputtered from the nozzle, hissing into a shuddering stream.

'Doing good business out here, are you?' asked Gotrek, eyeing the filling tankard with a healthy distaste.

Gregor kept his thoughts to himself, half an eye on Thomas as his youngest joined him briefly behind the bar. Gregor closed off the tap and hastened to Gotrek's table with the dwarf's beer. He set it on the table and retreated back to the bar.

Gotrek gathered the vessel into one meaty fist. Shoving off against the table leg, he forced his stool back along the floorboards, kicked off his boots, and planted his bare feet onto the table beside his axe with a sigh of deep gratification. Stretching out his toes, he took a whiff of ale. His face scrunched but he took a swallow anyway. He sat back.

'Orc-spit,' he muttered. 'Bloody orc-spit.'

Felix pulled up a stool of his own and sat. He noticed Thomas wandering the perimeter of the room, crumbling lumps of subtly discoloured suet along the length of the skirting.

Gregor saw his quizzical look. 'Black hellebore,' he explained. 'For the rats.'

'Got some right big'uns,' Thomas added with pride, brushing fatty grey spigots from his fingers.

'Aye,' Gregor agreed, shooing the lad away. 'Go wash yer hands in the stream. And don't tarry visiting yer mother, run right back. It'll be dark in a couple of hours.' Thomas hurried off, following his elder brother's path out the back door. Gregor watched him go, wringing his own hands through his apron. He returned to Felix. 'Sometimes you see packs of 'em, particularly over yonder hill.' He gestured vaguely south-west. 'Sylvania way. Big enough to bring down a ram, oftentimes.'

Felix shuddered at the mention of that benighted province. The shadows suddenly seemed a little bit darker, and he did not think it would necessarily kill anyone for Gregor to start a fire.

'Good meat on 'em though,' Gregor continued.

Felix looked up, horror creased into the lines of his face. 'You eat them?'

'We ain't animals. But come winter, ground up in grain, the goats won't turn their noses.'

And who then eats the goats, Felix wondered? He knew he should not judge poor folk for finding food wherever and however they were able, but even a starving man should think twice before considering the meat of a giant rat from the corrupted fields of Sylvania. Perhaps their forebears had been more wise, before generation after generation on the threshold of evil had softened their minds to its dangers. He regarded the tavern-keeper warily. He despised himself for the sudden wash of moral indignation. It reminded him so much of his father, and of the priests the old man had paid to school him and his brother, but Felix was all too familiar with the pernicious influence of Chaos. Without realising it, he found himself scanning Gregor's body for any outward symptom of mutation.

He pulled his gaze away and cleared his throat nervously. 'Why is it that the villagers think you will bring the Beast here?'

'Aye!' said Gotrek, slamming his fist on the table. 'I'd hear more of this monster before I kill it.'

'Kill it?' said Gregor, incredulous. He shook his head slowly, eyes closed. Felix felt pity for him then. These people had lived so long under a cloud they could not believe there might be light behind it. 'No one has gotten a good look at it, nor knows what it is or why its come. I'll say no more. It knows, they say, and it'll hunt down any that see its face or speak its name.'

Felix looked Gregor in the eye. 'Is that why the villagers are afraid? Did Rudi see the creature? Do they fear it will come after him?'

Gregor had turned white.

Gotrek cackled into his ale. 'It must be some creature, to have snatched the spine from so many.'

'It is that, master dwarf, that and much worse.' Gregor gulped, head sweeping from side to side as though he feared the walls were closing in. 'Near every village I know has been hit bar thissen. There's been word from nowhere for nigh on a month. Not unusual for the time o' year, but no good neither.' He leaned forward, resting his forearms on the bar. 'Now, I see yer're hunting this beast, so yer can stay this one night, but come morning I want yer gone. Yer're right, Rudolph was with the baron's men when they ran the Beast to ground on the borders of the Totenwald. Do you know how many men survived?'

Gotrek fingered the golden links of his nose chain thoughtfully. 'So it makes its lair in the forest, you think?'

Gregor pushed himself from the bar with an angry scowl. He would say no more, however Gotrek goaded, and busied himself filling a second tankard which he then slammed onto the table in front of Felix. Its contents splashed over Felix's hand. He licked the spillage from his fingers, wincing at the unexpected sourness.

He drank anyway. The long road had bred into him a craving for ale, however foul.

Thomas returned from his errand, but stayed only a moment to share a whisper with his father before departing to secure the back door and join his elder brother. Gregor came and went to replenish their ales and, though not asked, Felix gave the man his last two coppers. They were Bretonnian, about a hundred years old, salvaged from some barrow or other. He smiled ruefully at the ungodly places Gotrek had dragged him through since that night in Altdorf when he had sworn an oath to record the Slayer's doom. Gregor moved on, ignorant of Felix's reminiscences, getting down onto hands and knees to stack fresh wood within the fireplace. After a few minutes of scraping and muttering, Felix felt warmth on his back.

Somehow the crackling glow afforded the tavern no additional cheer, serving if anything merely as highlight to the gloom.

'Forget this den of cowards,' said Gotrek. 'First thing in the morning, we head for the forest.' His chuckle was hollow. 'It's good to have a direction at last. I can take my own measure of this creature.'

Felix took another sip, deep in thought. Something that Gregor had said was troubling him. He had said that Rudi encountered the Beast as part of a deliberate engagement of the baron's troops. And if the baron himself was treating such rumours seriously...

He forced himself to swallow his mouthful of ale before it could grow any staler.

It could only mean there was some truth to the wild tales. Perhaps there truly was a Beast after all. It was not a reassuring notion.

In spite of his troubled thoughts, Felix felt his eyelids grow heavy. The road had been long, and heat and ale were a potent alliance that his tired body could not resist. His body ached at the thought of a straw pallet in the coaching yard, much less a proper bed in an actual room.

'Meinen herr,' Felix began, forcing his eyes to stay open. 'This baron you all speak of, is he a good man?'

'An educated one like yerself might not think so, but I'd say aye.' Gregor nodded to the bent little hammer mobile that twisted slowly above the door. 'We do right as men of Sigmar, and der Kreuzfahrer will do right by us.'

'What do you mean?'

Gregor's gaze lingered on the icon of Sigmar, his attention distracted by whatever he could see through the gaps in the blocked out window. Felix wondered if the village-folk were still out there. 'The baron has Sigmar in his gut; eats, drinks, and sleeps it. He never slacks from scouring the moors of evil. He'll not be idle while the Beast lives. Not von Kuber. If nowt else, we can sleep easier for that.'

'Tomorrow,' Gotrek repeated, downing his vile brew in one long draw. His tone brooked no dissent. 'We'll show this baron of yours how it's done.'

The sun sank behind the hills, burnishing the west-facing slopes a ruddy amber. On the roof of the smokehouse, cloaked in the effluvia of its chimney stack, a bird that was not a bird emitted a shrill, off-key whistle. The call was copied and carried. A hooded spectre looked up from a freshly killed goat and crept into the lengthening shadows of the graveyard. It bared its bloodied fangs and voiced its own cry.

Within their homes, villagers hugged their children near and together trembled as the eerie dusk chorus spread.

On the darkened eastern hill overlooking the village, unwitnessed by man or star, dark creatures heard the signal and keened their excitement. Blades were brandished. Bellies growled. They slunk downhill, a sussurant whisper of lowered voices and black cloaks, converging on the gloom that pooled amongst the drab stone structures of the valley floor. From the rooftop, one more cry burst out, and then was silent. There they waited, pressed against walls and under covered windows, impatient, eager, silent as death itself.

Soon.

But something did see. What appeared at first nothing but a boulder, crouched from the sun under the lee of a gorse-strangled outcropping of rock and thin soil, slowly shifted. Knifelike claws drew back from eyes that burned a volatile red and conjured simulacra from the night; shades from the aethyr that swarmed the valley's rare constancy like a rash of blisters.

The Beast directed his notice from his followers and to the village below, a penumbral wash of impermanence and illusion.

'Master. It is time.'

The speaker hunched before him. It was small, temporary, a mural in fractured glass. It came with others, all on one knee and cloaked in black, eyes averted. The Beast cinched his own cloak tight.

Do not look at me!

The thought arrived in his throat, a bass rumble that rattled the bowels of those gathered. They trembled but did not dare flee.

'It… it is time.'

Time.

The fools should know better. Soon it could be over. Except soon would never come.

Not for one of the Damned.

Ever ephemeral, his thoughts dispersed, ugly flakes of self that spiralled into divergent streams of subconsciousness. It was maddening. Some atavistic core of intellect bellowed and raged, grasping at the glimmering foil of madness with conceptual claws. Stiffly, his body one that no sane god had ever intended to move, he rose. Bones ground as his horrendous form pulled free of its earthen cocoon. His minions fell back with startled cries.

The world was broken. It flickered and shimmered and swam before eyes filled with hurt. He saw the village, as it had been and how he would remake it. A growl rose from his belly as he strode. It was a word, a name, his name, all that he still knew to be true.

'Huurrrlk.'

CHAPTER 2

The Shadow of the Beast

Felix snapped free of his doze. Momentarily confused by the unfamiliar surrounds, he pulled himself upright, rubbing his knuckles against his eyelids to clear them of sleep. He paused mid-motion and set his palm over his forehead. His head felt as though some manner of creature had crawled into his ear to lay eggs. He groaned with feeling.

Gotrek was sitting across from him, still drinking, tattoos twisting under the dying light of the hearth.

'You were dreaming, manling. Like a dog.' The dwarf's ugly face creased into a grin. 'It looked like you were killing.'

Felix massaged his temples. 'Dying would be more like it,' he croaked.

'Did you hear it?' whispered Gregor. 'Is that what woke you?' The tavern-keeper was crouched by the nearest window, eye pressed to the gap between the boards, as though straining to squeeze it through. Sweat glazed his smooth pate.

'Hear what?' Felix asked.

'Bah,' said Gotrek, then belched, dribbling a trickle of ale beard. 'He soils his britches over a squawking bird.'

Now that Felix listened he could hear what sounded like harsh calls. A raven or a jay, perhaps, though he had always been more interested in fencing and poetry than natural philosophy as a boy and he really did not have a clue.

Gregor was not listening either way. He shivered as though the fire's embers had turned frosty. 'Maybe birds sing at night where yer're from, but here they do it at dawn.'

Felix frowned. That did make an unpleasant kind of sense.

'It's the Beast,' Gregor breathed, wilting to the floor. 'It's come for us!'

Gotrek smeared spilled ale unhurriedly over his chin on the back of his trunk-like arm and then rose, only a little unsteadily. 'Typical manling courage. Sooner shoot a thirsty dwarf in the street than offer ale, but a gibbering wreck when a pack of winged rats start yapping. I tell you, manling–'

A deep, animal, roar set the hammer mobile hung from the ceiling to tinkling. Gregor covered his ears and whimpered. Gotrek broke off from what he was about to say and grinned.

'Gotrek, I don't think that that was a bird.'

The dwarf was already tugging on his boots and reaching for his axe. He gave a sharp laugh and bolted the weapon to his bracer. He sniffed the rim of the axe blade lustily. 'If it is, manling, then it's one I'd like to meet.'

'Are you both mad?' Gregor crawled on hands and knees to the door, blocking it with his own quavering body. There was another bellow, and this time a child's scream. Gregor scrunched his eyes tight and buried his face into his apron. 'It's the *Beast*. It's going to kill us all.'

'Move aside,' Gotrek growled, his axe menacing.

'I won't.'

'You picked a strange spot to finally take a stand.'

Gotrek swung his axe. Gregor screamed. At the same moment, another wail of pain sounded from without, and the axe whisked over the man's head to thunk into the door. Chips flew where the runic blade bit. Gotrek twisted and pulled, the door's cheap panelling coming away as he wrenched the axe free.

'Get him out of my way, manling,' he spat in Felix's general direction. 'I'm going round him or over him, and I'm not greatly minded which.'

Felix dragged the limp tavern-keeper aside as Gotrek shortened his grip on his axe and smashed the door's lock to flinders. The double doors bowed out under the blow but the crossbar held them shut. Gotrek gave the heavy beam a kick from beneath that knocked it from its bracket, then put his boot through the doors to send them crashing wide. Felix stiffened at the sudden gust of cold.

'Please, master dwarf,' Gregor sobbed, skin clammy in spite of the cold. 'Don't let it have Rudi.'

Gotrek rounded on the two men.

'I'm going to feed the monster's neck to my axe! What it does next is *its* business. Coming, manling?'

Without waiting for Felix's answer, Gotrek ran into the street, axe leading, bellowing a string of insults to whomever it was that might be listening. Felix rushed to the door, staring into the grey embers of twilight.

It was chaos.

While the majority of dwellings remained locked and barred, a dozen or more men and women with their makeshift weapons had flooded the street in response to those initial screams. He saw Gotrek's orange crest forging through an anarchic swell of men and livestock. From his vantage at the far end of the long street, Felix caught a shadow of something on the rooftops, of several somethings, sinister patches of darkness that seemed to merge and split and dart from point to point without ever deigning to transition the space between. He began to see a pattern to their movements: they were fanning into a ring to corral the milling villagers.

Just as this revelation came the air was torn by a tremendous whine. He shouted a warning to Gotrek and the villagers to get down, but it was too late.

Blood gouted from impact craters in skulls, chests, backs. Bodies fell, some wailing agony, others already dead, to be crushed into the cobbles by their animals. The survivors screamed and ran, but there was no order to it, no plan, and another volley of unseen hail sent more bodies flapping to their deaths. In the midst of the massacre, Gotrek bellowed a war cry, but there was nothing in reach of his axe. His frustrated roars were answered with a redoubled barrage from the rooftops.

Felix scanned the sloping roofs in desperation. It was possible he could scale the uneven walls to reach them, but he was not sure what he would do once he got there. The mystery assailants were almost themselves a part of the darkness, like ghosts. And that was all assuming nothing tried to fire at him the minute they saw him trying.

A bowel-twisting bellow of primal bloodlust rent the night. For a brief instant, the attention of all was diverted to the far end of the street. Felix looked too, almost unwilling to believe his own eyes as they fixed on the brooding monstrosity that prowled the verges of the village's graveyard. It stood massive in the distance, almost as tall at the shoulder as the house that abutted the garden of Morr.

The Beast.

It was surrounded by more industrious scraps of shadow, but they were too far away for Felix to make out what they were up to. Gotrek unleashed a torrent of curses and started to shove his way through the crowd in that direction. The rooftop attackers unleashed another salvo, throwing the surviving villagers into a frenzied rush for safety. Gotrek swore as they barged into him from all sides, running amongst the stampeding villagers with his axe held high. With dawning horror, Felix realised that they were being herded like sheep; right down the throat of the Beast. The rooftop shadows kept up their attack. Felix saw a bullet strike the back of the Slayer's head. The dwarf staggered, but kept on going, falling further to the rear of the longer-legged humans with every stride as more and more of the deadly rain became focused on him.

Felix dropped down to Gregor's side, gripping the man's shoulder tightly enough for the pain to distract him from his terror. 'Find somewhere safe, friend, and stay there. Trust me that my companion is fearsome as he is belligerent.' Karaghul slid from its scabbard and he swept back his cloak to free his right arm.

Felix darted from his shelter, took a deep breath, and broke into a sprint.

Most of the shadows had followed after Gotrek, but from the nearest rooftops where the streets had been purged of the living, he saw a few descend from the eaves as though on wings. They bore pitchers of oil that they cast over doors, boarded windows, and other wooden parts of those houses where people still hid inside and then, with shrill calls and demented laughter, they hurled their torches.

The houses went up like tormented daemons, windows ablaze like roiling eyes, doorway mouths screaming with heat. Felix tried to drown out the cries as women and children roasted in their homes. He charged for the nearest shadow-creature, but its alertness was superhuman and it was scaling the wall more swiftly than Felix could run over level ground. Flames consumed the house's frontage and he recoiled from the heat. There was nothing he could do to save it.

He left it to its death and hurried after Gotrek.

There were more dead bodies lying in the street, but no longer so many screams. He ran, eyes burning from the fire. Smoke pumped into the street like blood. The hellish light had robbed the attackers of their ethereal illusion. They were solid enough, draped in all-encompassing cloaks of midnight blue and black. He saw them silhouetted against the flames. He could not count how many. Shadows ran over rooftops on either side of him in pursuit, sprinting with ease along treacherous slate roofs, leaping acrobatically from roof to roof to keep pace. There was a whir and snap as one of them let loose with a slingshot. Its aim was poor. Felix did not even hear the bullet miss.

He saw the Beast ahead.

Huge from a distance, it was frighteningly immense up close, a pair of vicious red eyes burning from the depths of a tightly cinched cowl. Other than that, its features were impossible to discern, swaddled as it was in rags that looked as if they had been worn when it crawled from its grave. The headstones around it had been turfed over and cloaked figures stood knee-deep in pits dug with their own bound hands. Only the stone hammer of Sigmar remained standing, powerless in the shadow of the Beast. Bones and fragments of bones littered the disturbed earth. Dark shapes ran between the diggers to gather every piece and stuff them into black wool sacks.

The Beast emitted a continuous rumble of noise, aiming a crack of its twin-tailed whip, barbed with what looked like bone, over the heads of its toiling charges. Mindless with fear, the villagers let themselves be driven towards it. Most were cut down by flashes of rusted metal amongst the shadows that swarmed about the Beast's feet, but two were unlucky enough to make it through.

It did not even look as if the giant had noted their existence until an arm like a stone column dashed the first to pulped meat sent careening over the graveyard and into a wall. The body fell, leaving a flowering of blood splatters on the lumpen stone. The second was still coming to terms with his horror when, almost too swift for Felix to follow, that massive arm splayed open to reveal five knifelike claws that lanced through the villager's scalp. It launched into another harrowing roar, some abominable melding of beast and man. There was a flash of teeth within the creature's hood and the villager's screams were abruptly silenced. Blood spattered the Beast's cowl as the man's jugular spurted crimson. Still holding its whip, the Beast took the man by the collar and, with a sickening crunch of vertebrae, snapped his neck like a wishbone. The Beast upended the shattered body, head twisted and pinioned between its own shoulder blades, blood sputtering from its neck as though it were some monstrous gourd. Sticky fluids painted the Beast's hood as the monster guzzled its fill.

Felix felt a sickness in his gut, but gripped his sword two-handed and took courage from Gotrek's presence.

Gotrek powered into the graveyard, scattering the ghostly creatures before him like grass. Felix roared a war cry of his own and charged in at the Slayer's back. The ground under their feet was treacherous, and more than once the Slayer stumbled over a shallow grave or lost his footing in loose earth. Fresh bodies lay splayed over the opened graves, their blood draining into the soil.

The Beast turned at Gotrek's approach, its warm feast still in its grip. It regarded Gotrek for a long time, almost as if to convince itself that the dwarf really did dare to attack it, then flung the villager with a casual underarm sweep. Gotrek barked a curse and tried to duck, the two bodies colliding with a meaty slap. Something else broke within the once-living missile and the pair of them toppled back into an open grave.

'Gotrek!' Felix shouted, trying to force his way through the earth and bodies to the dwarf's aid.

The Beast emitted a chorus of breathy pants, bobbing its head in time. Felix got the impression that it was laughing. It uncoiled its whip and cracked it once, tensing its muscles and snarling something that sounded almost like speech.

'Huurrrlk!'

Sickly ropes of bloody drool swayed from its hood and it gesticulated up at the roof of the house that abutted one side of the graveyard. It clenched its fist and yanked it down, up and down, as though it were a mallet aimed at Gotrek's head. Felix swung to look up the steep angle of the roof behind him. There was not a single bare tile. Shadows jostled for purchase, loaded sling cords beginning to whir above their heads like an angry horde of cicadas.

Felix's throat felt suddenly dry. Gotrek was pulling himself out of the hole, shaking earth from his crest and spitting curses.

'Gotrek, stay down!'

With a barrage of whines and cracks, a hail of sharpened rocks beat the earth around Gotrek's shelter, forcing the dwarf deeper into the shallow trench. Felix jumped back and out of the line of fire. Mail struck stone. He pressed himself as tight as he could feasibly get into the uneven stone wall. The creatures could not draw a bead on him under the overhanging eaves. Not that that was any help to Gotrek. Their slings had the dwarf pinned under a relentless hail of fire.

The Beast stalked through the barrage as though it were nothing, growling unintelligible sounds and making sweeping gestures with its claws over the ruined graveyard. The cowardly shadow-creatures that Gotrek's charge had driven off flowed back, using their monstrous master for cover where they could and snatching up the last few bones that still littered the bloodstained earth. Felix saw one of them struck by a bullet in the chest. Its arms flared and it fell back, hood and sleeves venting green-black smoke, its body dissolving before Felix's eyes. All that hit the ground was a chemically charred cloak.

'Manling! What's going on?'

Gotrek ducked back as the creatures on the roof renewed their efforts to put him down.

The grave robbers were peeling away, their shoulders laden

with knobbly sacks, and dashing back into the burning village in the direction of the tavern. The Beast threw Felix one last look of semi-intelligent evil, emitting a wheeze of panting laughter before turning its bulk and chasing after its minions. The creatures on the roof did not follow, maintaining a persistent rate of fire that kept Gotrek, only his crest visible, hunkered down.

'Do something, manling! I'll not be found cowering in some dead man's grave!'

Felix parted himself from the wall long enough to steal a glance over the lip of the roof. Gnarled, tumescent claws curled over the guttering, like hideously mutated birds settling for the night to roost, calling to each other with that deadly leather-strap whir.

'Make a diversion, manling. Draw their fire.'

'How?'

Gotrek spluttered as he ducked a fresh volley, driving his face into the muck. 'You went to university. Think of something!'

Felix clutched his sword to his chest. He had read history and classics, hardly the stuff that heroes were made of. He moved to the edge of the wall and peered around the corner. The tavern was ablaze along with half of the village. The Beast and its minions had already reached it, gathering up more of the shadow-creatures in its wake and bearing right into the hills. Felix set his jaw.

Oh well, here goes.

He leapt as high as he could, roaring himself hoarse as his body corkscrewed and he drove an arm around the guttering. When his hand grazed those misshapen claws, his first burning instinct was to snap it back, but he fought it. Its touch was vile: rotten flesh that gave beneath the pressure of his fingers, brittle stalks of hair that prickled his skin like a dead man's whiskers, odd protuberances of bone that had no rightful place on a living beast. Suppressing his nausea, he grabbed one of the creature's ankles. There was a squawk of surprise and then a thump as gravity reasserted its will and Felix began to fall. The creature's body struck the roof and slid, Felix's weight dragging it down. Claws shrieked against the tiles and then, just as black robes flared over empty space, bit into the lip of the guttering to arrest its fall.

It kicked out with its free leg, battering Felix about the head and catching him a stinging blow to his eye that had it immediately puffing up with tears. He ignored the battering and tackled its writhing shape in a bear hug, lifting his own feet from the earth. Suddenly holding far more than its own skinny weight, the monster screamed a very man-like scream and the pair of them dropped the short way together. Felix held on as his back hit the ground and drove the wind from his lungs. The creature landed on top, scrabbling furiously with head, feet, elbows, and claws. Unable to hold on, Felix let go. It sprang up, blindingly quick, long knives sprouting organically from its sleeves. It pounced, but Felix was ready for it and threw up his sword.

The creature impaled itself with a piercing wail. To Felix's horror, that did not stop the creature struggling. It jerked as if hoping to pull itself free, but the action only slid it further down the blade. Felix recoiled, bracing it on his boot to drive it back. There was a fizzing sound and the thing's body gave as though its robe were suddenly hollow. Acidic green-black foam dribbled from its hood, fizzing darkly and leaving black burns where it landed on Felix's armour. After a few seconds, all that was left impaled on Felix's sword was a steaming strip of black rag.

Felix lay on his back, panting with shock and disgust. A mass of eyes peered down at him over the eaves. They glowed like witchfire, mismatched; reds, greens, blues, weird hues that railed against the ordered strictures of visible spectra. An angry snarl started up somewhere within the pack and spread. Slingshots whirred above the shadow-creature's heads.

'Gotrek! They're distracted, Gotrek!'

'Keep at it, manling.'

Felix gasped, incredulous. Sometimes he honestly believed that the Slayer would not be satisfied until Felix joined him in whatever doom he found for himself. He rolled his head back to watch, upside down, as Gotrek waded through the soil towards the stone monument of Sigmar's hammer that leaned from the earth in the middle of the graveyard. Gotrek set his enormous hands to either side of the great hammer's haft and pressed in. His shoulders bulged as he strained to tear it from the ground. Gotrek was mad! The hammer was as tall as Felix and solid stone. Gotrek was undoubtedly the strongest dwarf Felix had ever encountered, but even he had limits.

One of the creatures shrilled a note of alarm and the others shifted their aim from Felix and back towards the greater threat. They let loose. Missiles pattered off the stone bulk of the hammer but, shielded in its lee, Gotrek suffered only grazes. With a scream of effort Gotrek wrenched the hammer free, its haft streaming soil and fibrous strings of root. Its weight drove Gotrek back before he could set himself against it. Muscles pulled hard as Gotrek held the monolithic weapon steady and then, madly, started to spin. The mighty warhammer swung out to its full length, around and around, faster and faster, thumping through the air like a steam-powered piston until its head began to blur and, with a dwarfish war cry, Gotrek let go.

Gotrek's aim was true and the night reignited with fresh screams as the giant missile crashed through the wall of the building. There was an implosion of loose stone as the wall failed to offer even token resistance and crumbled. The roof bucked and, suddenly finding nothing beneath it, began to topple, shedding black slate and shrieking figures into the ruined interior before the rest of the roof and three more walls collapsed in on top of them, blasting the graveyard with a wash of pulverised masonry.

Felix stood and dusted himself off. He coughed, regarding Gotrek with a wary respect and a healthy amount of fear. Gotrek stooped to gather his axe, the weapon almost flying from his hands such was the awesome reduction in weight by comparison. The Slayer panted as he pulled his way across the graveyard. Every so often, a muscle twitched, the only outward indication of his exertions.

'Right then. Let's have after the big one.'

Hurrlk loped ahead of his minions. They could outrun a horse over short distances, but even they could not match his awesome stride. Burning hovels were reduced to pleasing ruin on either side. His body reported heat, but his mind would accept none. He passed through a ghost town, as it had been once and as he would remake it again.

With a vague awareness, he noted the destruction unfolding at his back. He was curious, a maddened core of him just itching to face that which could inflict such damage. He suppressed it. He was too close to give in to those urgings now, however unlikely it was that a dwarf and a man could ever stop him.

He could not be bested.

Not then, not now, not ever.

That was truly maddening.

He snarled and ran. The tavern roared in the unholy grip of an inferno, shadows cast onto a struggle on its doorstep. Three skulking shadows dragged a corpulent man from the fire. One held him from behind, pinning his arms in its own as another stabbed him over and over in the chest with a serrated knife. Blood blossomed in ink spot patterns on his clothing. Another voice screamed. He ignored it. The mortals died and they were luckier for it. They died because the world was saner for their loss. They tangled the mind, made it torpid and angry; easier to eradicate them all, relieve the world of its burden and let quiet ghosts lie.

They died, but he was not here to kill.

He followed the road to the right and up the valley slope to where it terminated. Plants snapped and fell dead as they sought to scratch at his calves. He crashed through the brittle fauna and again, through a dry-stone wall that had not for one scintilla ever threatened to slow his path.

The Master will rise, has arisen, will arise again.

There was but one treasure yet unclaimed.

The Master would be pleased.

Rudi screamed and stabbed his knife at the shadow-creature's face. It was so ungodly quick! His wrist was caught in its hands and a clawed foot slammed into his kidney before he even began to see it move. Pain exploded in his side and he collapsed to one knee. He drove an elbow toward the thing's belly, only to see it blocked by a blur of dark rag.

'Thomas!' He choked with pain and inhaled fumes. His brother had bolted out the back way as the tavern front had gone up in flames. Then their father had charged out the front door and left Rudi a decision.

He hoped Thomas had got out safely.

Another creature was circling behind him. Too quick for him to act to stop it, it grasped him by both shoulders and bit down into the meat of his neck. He screamed, flailing his pinned wrist, jerking against the creature at his back. But they had him. Rudi's screams bled into a whimper, strength floundering, skin peeling from the burning tavern. A third creature rose from his father's corpse and licked its blade clean, face still concealed beneath a grubby cowl. It froze, tongue sticking out, staring over Rudi's shoulder.

There was a roar, then the slick note of meat separating before metal and the pressure on Rudi's wrist eased. An axe flashed before his eyes. A head dropped from the creature's shoulders and rolled. Rudi caught a glimpse of scabs and weeping sores before both body and head dissolved into a stinking green juice that seeped through its cloak and ran between the cobblestones. The second creature released his neck and yelped like a kicked dog as a rune-scrawled longsword spit through its chest. It flared down into gloop before the man behind it could pull the weapon free. He shook the steaming rags from his sword with a look of disgust.

'Come on, manling. It's getting away.'

The dwarf made an abortive effort at chasing after the third and final creature, but gave up after just a few steps as it accelerated out of the village and out of sight.

Rudi accepted the hand that the tall, blond-haired man offered and let himself be hauled to his feet. His saviour's mail was brilliant in the pyre that had been his home.

'Thank you, Herr…'

'Felix. And…' The man looked down to the eviscerated body that had been Rudi's father, eyes hooded. Felix seemed genuinely affected. A rare enough quality in a stranger. 'I'm sorry for your father. And for all of this.'

The returning dwarf grunted, non-committal.

Rudi hung his head. 'It's my fault,' he breathed.

'You fought, friend,' said Felix. 'You could have done nothing more'

'No!' Rudi roared, throwing off Felix's consoling arm. He stared hard at his father's body. 'The Beast came for me. It came because I saw. I tried to hide and now my home is ashes.' He clutched at his head, fingernails burrowing into his scalp and pulling at his hair until white roots showed. The smell of burning hung like a mantle. Somehow, despite the fire, the wind still gusted cold and he shivered.

'Don't be such an idiot,' said the dwarf. His tattoos were frightening, covered with dirt and the occasional gobbet of hissing green slime. 'Take a look around. This monster doesn't care a damn about you.'

'But… but,'

'It's true,' said Felix. 'It came for your graveyard, not you.'

Rudi released his taut scalp. Palms flat to his cheeks, he directed his unwilling face toward the path of crushed heathers that marked the trail of the Beast. 'The… graveyard?'

'Yes,' said Felix. 'Why? What's buried there that a monster like that could want?'

Rudi did not answer right away. He bent to collect his knife and sword, then rolled his father onto his front with a quiet prayer that the earth accept him.

'Speak up,' said the dwarf. 'Or we'll leave you behind and have after it ourselves.'

'I don't know what it hopes to find.' Rudi stood, applying pressure to his bruised side. He looked out onto the darkened moors, nodding his head in grim acknowledgement to some unspoken promise. 'But I know where it's going.'

CHAPTER 3

The Morning After

Felix panted from the effort of climbing. Brambles scored pale tracks into his long-suffering boot leather and more than once he had had to snatch his cloak from taloned branches he had not seen in the receding glow of the dying village at their backs. Gotrek forged ahead with an impatient stride while the young swordsman, Rudi, kept close to Felix's back. Tracking the Beast was not proving difficult. It had left a trail of shattered undergrowth the width of a carriage right up into the hills. They ran with weapons drawn, eyes and ears alert for any sign of the monster or its servants.

'How could a place so small need more than one grave-yard?' Felix managed between breaths.

Rudi would not meet his eye, kept his gaze to the trail and to the hilltop that it led to. 'We don't talk about it.'

'Could you perhaps give us a clue?' Felix snapped back. The pain on the younger man's face made him instantly guilty. Rudi had just lost a father after all.

'You're not from here,' Rudi mumbled, a harrowed look on his face. 'You couldn't understand. This is a cursed land. Nothing grows that a man can eat. It's Sigmar's punishment.'

'Punishment for what, exactly?'

'There was once a city on the moors, a holy place until it fell into sin. Sigmar smote it down with His hammer from the heavens. No one knows where it lies, nor its true name, nor how it came to fall.'

'Typically forgetful humans,' barked Gotrek from up ahead. 'When'll you learn to write things down? This is why your kind are doomed to suffer such things over and over.'

Felix mumbled something as he scanned the darkness. He had just about had his fill of the dark myths of the moors. Just because one happened to be true, it did not mean he was about to start believing all of them.

'Fascinating as that may be, what has any of it to do with our graveyard?'

'According to the legends, it's where the mutants that fled the city were buried once the witch-finders hunted them down.'

'Unsanctified ground?' asked Felix.

Rudi nodded, eyes downcast. 'They still bury folk there sometimes; stillborns and mutants, witches.'

'Reassuring,' Felix mumbled. 'But promising, don't you think Gotrek?'

'A fair bet, manling, a fair bet.'

Rudi's fingers tapped at a spot over the collar of his leather chest piece, casting nervous glances towards their destination.

'You needn't accompany us,' Felix offered. 'Let Gotrek and I go ahead.'

'No, I have to. If Thomas is…' Rudi's voice caught. 'If Thomas is alive, then that's where he'll be.'

'Why?'

Rudi clamped his lips shut, shook his head and looked

away. Felix decided to let him be.

They had more important things to worry about.

The eerie quiet of the hilltop burial site was enough to tell Felix that things were not all as they had been expected to be. Without any barriers to tame it, the wind blew hard and cold and seemingly from every direction at once. Felix's hair whipped about his face. He restrained his cloak with a firm hand. His other hand he held tight about the grip of his sword. The view below was painful to witness. The village smouldered like a hot coal, snatches of light and grey half-shadows roiling amongst the deepening darkness in the crook of the valley.

There was no sense of magic, no aura of evil contained or of evil set free, just a deep feeling of despoilment and senseless loss. A ring of jagged stones struck from the earth like teeth, encircling a pair of ancient-looking crypts and more than a dozen large, unmarked graves. The stones dripped with a mucky slop, clumps of soil and tenderised vegetation indiscriminately scattered. The graves had been exhumed. It did not look as though anything had been left behind. The door to the nearest crypt, a low-roofed wooden structure with hammer and comet finials partially rotted, had been smashed in and looted. The second crypt was oriented at an angle to the first, its entrance out of sight. Felix did not doubt that he would find it similarly emptied.

Gotrek strode to the ring of stones and ran a thick finger through its pasting of filth. He brought it to his eye, mud oozing between thumb and forefinger. He grumbled in disappointment and rubbed his hands clean on his breeches. He glared over the ruined graveyard, then dropped his axe butt-down into the soil slick and shook his head grimly.

He did not say anything. He did not have to.

Felix stabbed his sword into the soil and squatted. His calves burned. The climb had been hard. Keeping pace with Gotrek had been harder. He gazed over the emptied graves, trying to imagine what would do such a thing and why.

'Does it not seem odd, Gotrek? For a mass grave of the Chaos-touched to be left here like this?'

'Everything your race does strikes me odd, manling. I gave up trying to make sense of your kind about a hundred years before you were born.'

Felix clenched his jaw, but let it slide. This was not the time for that old argument.

Within the ring of stones, Rudi crouched over the body of a boy. It was Thomas. He lay face up in the dirt. His skin was a bloodless white, anaemic eyes unnaturally wide. The woollen smock he wore sagged heavy with blood, a crimson tear gashing through to the bone and opening the boy up from throat to groin. Bite marks lined the bloody trench. It looked like the Beast had ripped the boy open and then drunk him dry. The strength required was abominable.

Rudi rolled the body onto its front. It resembled the funerary rite of the earth mother, Rhya. Or perhaps Rudi simply could not bear to look on that horrific wound in his young brother's chest. Rudi looked up, eyes rimmed with red. One hand remained on his brother's back, as though unwilling to let go. He pointed toward an emptied hole that had once been a grave pit.

'Our mother was there. I knew Thomas would run here.' His head hung, heavy with bitter feeling. 'The fool.'

Felix glanced at the indicated hole. He could not imagine what Rudi was feeling. He did not ask what the woman had done to deserve an unmarked pit in the company of witches, mutants and daemon-touched. In a land like this one, it was easy enough to guess.

'You were hunting the Beast already, yes?' Rudi said, voice stiff with grief.

Felix nodded. He willed the stiffened muscles in his legs to drive himself up from his crouch. He winced, then nodded once more.

'Then you will keep on after it? Even now you have seen it?'

'We'll find it,' said Gotrek. 'Even the corrupted dead deserve better than this, being turfed out of their own graves.' He nodded grimly, nose chain clinking as he spoke, almost to himself. 'Aye, we'll find it.'

Rudi pressed Thomas deeper into the sucking earth, then stood. Felix noticed that he was shaking as he waded back through the muck towards the stone ring.

'Then I'll come with you.'

Felix placed a restraining hand on the young man's shoulder. Rudi flinched but did not throw him off.

'I understand why you think you'd want that, but you don't. Trust me, you don't.'

'What would you know of it?' Rudi's arm gestured towards the shallow valley where the village glowed dull red like the last ember of a fire. 'My home is destroyed. My family and everyone I know dead with it. I've been a soldier. I know how to use a sword.'

Felix sucked in his cheeks and tried to find the words. Felix hazarded that Rudi was eighteen, twenty at most. If he had been in Baron von Kuber's militia long enough to experience more than being issued with sword and uniform before the Beast wiped out his detachment then Felix would be astonished.

More than enough for any man, in Felix's opinion.

'I'll take you to the place we'd tracked it,' said Rudi. 'And then I'll help you kill it.' It looked as though Rudi intended to say more, but then bit his lip. His hand moved to his chest, to some charm worn beneath his leather breastplate. He glanced back to his brother. His eyes darted from the body to the broken trail of the Beast and back again. 'Do we have time to bury them?'

Gotrek stood unmoving, still presiding over the desecrated graves with such a brooding intensity that he rightly quivered with the effort of containing it. 'The creature's faster than us, and has too great a head start.' He turned his gaze on Felix. 'Find yourself a shovel, manling. There'll be no rest tonight.'

The sun rose over the moors much as it had done ever since Felix had first been dragged into Ostermark.

Bitterly.

The rain continued to baffle, coming and going like a god's favour. Felix squinted into the sleeting wind, trying to pick out the smear of grey on slate that heralded the dawn. In such an environment, Felix was actually rather glad to have Gotrek alongside. The Slayer walked stolidly, without comment or complaint. Indeed, without much of anything at all bar the occasional swipe of his axe whenever a particularly dense bramble thicket intruded onto their path. Had it not been for the dwarf's bright orange crest and beard, Felix might have feared his eyes no longer capable of viewing any shade brighter than the iron clouds, or that he had, through his disturbed dreaming, been banished to some drab purgatory of endless hills and featureless skies.

Felix rubbed at his temples and sought to banish the spectre of those dreams. He had not had long to sleep, but what moments he had grabbed had been haunted by anguished cries, white-clad ladies with bloody palms, visions of fire-blackened cities hidden behind a pall of fog. Had he not suffered similar nightmares almost every night for weeks he might have put such imagery down to the onerous duties of the previous night. He shivered from the memory.

Felix's career as Gotrek's rememberer had been varied and seldom dull. He had been coerced into some dreadful jobs in his time, but he could recall nothing that compared to the pulling of roasted corpses from their still-smouldering homes for burial. Some were so badly burned that their bones had crumbled in his hands. His cloak still smelled of wood smoke and burned hair. Flecks of ash were lodged beneath his fingernails.

He could not help but imagine where, and from whom, each black flake had come.

Felix caught himself scratching under his nails. All he had achieved was to compress the black rims deeper beyond his finger. The skin around his nails was growing red and increasingly tender, the pain his efforts caused a reminder of their futility. The flesh around his left eye was rising beautifully too. He dabbed at the five triangular punctures around his eye socket with a strip of rain-dampened cloth and prayed that the foul creature he had wrestled the night before had carried no infection on its claws.

Felix sulked at the rear as the party of three trudged over the moors.

It might have helped had there been something, anything, to take his mind off it all, but the Ostermark Moors were as empty as his purse and made just as grim viewing. The wind howled under iron clouds, carving depressions through the miserable brown grasses that spiked from the hills. Occasionally, something small and furtive made rustling waves in that dreary sea. Scrawny, black-feathered birds circled high above, as if waiting for them to die, shrill calls echoing through the emptiness without answer.

After a time, even the obvious trail of human blood and broken plant life abruptly disappeared. Felix wondered if the Beast had left them a deliberate false trail. If it was capable of moving without leaving a mark would it not have done so from the outset?

Gotrek considered the possibility but Rudi was adamant.

'The Totenwald is this way.' He pointed across the moor's unending rolls of torturous grey and drab life. 'That is where the Beast lairs.'

'How much of this must we trek through?' Felix asked. The moors sapped his voice of all strength, made it seem childish and small.

'Do you not like my country?' Rudi replied. He had likely meant it as a joke but his dead eyes betrayed him. He gave a dry snort and shook his head. 'Not far now. The Totenwald and the ford across the Stir into Sylvania should be less than a day on foot.' Rudi pointed ahead, south and west. A pale mist clung to the hilltops in that direction, cloaking whatever it was that Rudi alluded to. The knowledge that there was almost certainly nothing there to be seen did not measurably improve Felix's mood. The white pall was some way distant, but Felix already felt a chill creep into his bones just looking at it.

'Do you think the Beast has his lair in that province?'

'Maybe,' said Rudi, trudging on as if through some harrowing dream, the nearby forest incumbent with primal fears and painful memories. This, after all, was the sight of Rudi's first terrifying encounter with the Beast of the Ostermark Moors. 'Hard to say. In the trees, in the dark.'

'I'd wager that it does, manling,' said Gotrek, hacking through a purplish clot of waist-high heather. 'Where better to unearth the fiend that drinks the blood of men, then steals the corpses from their graves.'

'You think it a vampire?' Felix asked, hoping to Sigmar that it was not.

A blood-drinker of conventional proportions had proven quite enough of a challenge, and that had been alongside the wizard, Max Schreiber, and Gotrek's even more insane friend and fellow Slayer, Snorri Nosebiter. Not to mention a company of Kislevite lancers for good measure. He gave Rudi an appraising once-over. No offence to him, but there was no comparison to be drawn there. Felix did not share an ounce of Gotrek's joy at the three of them hunting down an immortal horror the size of an ogre. He lifted his hand the full reach of his arm, uncertain whether even that could faithfully recount the monster's scale.

'It seemed, I don't know, larger. Like some kind of mutant animal. Sylvania is cursed with more than just the walking dead.'

'It's a ghoul lord,' Gotrek replied with a laugh like gravel. 'I'd stake my eye on it. The biggest and ugliest of the bloodsucker breeds. I've never faced one, but I've heard the tales of those who have. Now there would be a mighty doom.'

'Assuming you're right,' said Felix. '*Assuming*. What does it want with old bones?'

Gotrek shrugged. 'What does anyone want with other people's bones?'

Felix puffed out his cheeks and returned his eyes to the 'road'. He had no idea, and he suspected that neither did Gotrek. Nothing good, that went without saying, and the Beast, whatever it was, had proven itself both willing and wholly capable of mass slaughter in the pursuit of its aims. He wanted to ask Rudi for more details of his encounter in the Totenwald, but the man had retreated deeper into himself as the morning had dragged on. Felix wondered if Rudi regretted the pledge, made in the heat of emotion, to join them on their quest and now, in the cold light of day, was too afraid to back out. Felix shook his head and sighed with feeling

That was a fate with which he could not help but empathise.

Rudi walked under his own dark cloud.

Ever since childhood, Father Gramm had lectured him on the wickedness in his blood. It was impossible to believe that the monster was not somehow drawn to him. How else to explain surviving two encounters with the Beast, when a whole company of Baron von Kuber's militia swords, and now his entire village, could not. He discarded Felix's nonsense of grave robbers. The fault lay with him, with his own daemons.

Memories of his burning village disturbed others he had hoped buried. His mother's screams as she had confessed her sins on the fire, Gramm heeding every word and praising them as the pain of the daemon torn from her mortal soul. In his rasping voice, he had denounced Rudi as the get of Chaos. He could still feel the bite of the old priest's lash, recall the taste of his own tears, as the corruption shared by blood was purged from his sinning flesh. 'Trust to Sigmar,' Gramm had incanted with each blow.

But his god had abandoned him. Perhaps Gramm had been lax in his beatings. Perhaps the taint of Chaos still lingered.

He pressed his palm to his breast, feeling out the bulge in his leathers from the hammer talisman beneath. With a start he realised he had begun to weep and pinched the tears away. Felix and the dwarf were already doubtful of him. It would not help if they saw him crying like a child.

He focused on the solid presence of the dwarf in front of him. Gotrek hacked one-handed at the bracken. His axe was so massive Rudi doubted whether he and Felix would have been able to raise it between them.

He did not doubt they would find the Beast, and that both Gotrek and Felix would die. He envied Felix's courage. The man had no reason to remain, and yet he did. To Rudi's surprise he did not feel afraid, guilty perhaps, but not afraid. Let others talk of vampires and heroism. He did not care. Twice now he had been spared. The third time he would be ready. Somehow, he would see the brute slain. He studied Gotrek's broad shoulders, his fingers closing around the leather grip of his dagger.

Then, he could consign his own black soul for Sigmar's judgement.

The hills slid by, unchanging, as the day wore down. Felix imagined he could discern the subtlest changes in hue amongst the whispering grasses; here an island of tan, there bistre, all of it rustling with uncanny communion. Every change in pitch of the ground beneath his feet was noted as though it was trumpeted from the heavens, every mottling pattern of white light on grey cloud was scrutinised for meaning. The air had grown colder, bleaker, the mist that had earlier seemed distant now rolling in from the hilltops to immure the three of them within its folds.

The damp passed through armour, wool, flesh and bone with a chill indifference.

Feeling his empty stomach growl, Felix forced his limbs to work harder. He could not risk lagging behind. If he lost sight of Gotrek and Rudi then, chances were, he would never see another soul again.

'We have to take care now,' said Rudi, voice lost partly to the fog. 'The baron's outriders patrol these hills. If they find us then the Beast'll not be our worry.'

'If they too hunt the Beast, then why should they stop us?'

Rudi shook his head. 'There are boundary stones across the moors. They mark forbidden territory where the outriders will shoot on sight.' Rudi glanced nervously about. 'We should have reached the markers by now. We might have missed them in the fog.'

'Wonderful,' said Felix, as Gotrek chuckled darkly.

'I wonder then if it's simple coincidence that draws the monster here,' said Gotrek. 'What does the country lordling protect here?'

'Too big a coincidence, I think,' Felix agreed, turning to Rudi. 'Might it be connected to something that was hidden in your village?'

'I don't know,' Rudi whispered. Just speaking on it seemed to be making him nervous. 'The baron's muster is to the north, in Kielsel, away from here on the Kadrin road. When we crossed the line after the Beast, the priests had us blindfolded before letting us on. Whatever's there was long gone before they let us remove them.'

Gotrek nodded slightly. 'Something hidden from a lord's own sworn swords must be very valuable – or very dangerous – indeed.' He gave a jagged grin. 'Here's hoping for the second, eh manling?'

Felix smiled ruefully. His brow creased with a sudden thought. 'Wait, the *priests* had you blindfolded?'

'Baron von Kuber allows no man to disobey a man of the temple. It's a flogging for those who do.'

'This baron sounds more of a joy the more I hear,' said Gotrek.

Felix wrapped his cloak tightly about himself as a peal of thunder rumbled through the thick fog that pressed over the moors. As Felix shivered, Gotrek grimly raised his axe, his one eye staring purposefully into the fog. The diffuse rumble continued without break, growing louder. Felix felt a trembling through the worn soles of his boots.

'What is it?' Felix hissed, drawing his sword and stepping around Rudi to tuck in close behind the Slayer's back.

'Riders, manling.'

Felix followed Gotrek's stare. He could see nothing, perhaps a grey outline somewhere in the distance. From behind him came the twinned scrape of Rudi unsheathing sword and dagger. Felix lowered himself to the sharp, sodden ground and mimed Rudi to do likewise. Gotrek held firm, axe ready, its rune aglow in the wet and gloom.

'Get down, Gotrek,' Felix hissed. 'They surely can't see a thing in this mist. We let them pass, then sneak around behind and make for the Totenwald.'

Rudi agreed with a vigorous nod.

'No, manling. They're coming straight for us.'

Felix bit down a curse. 'Are you certain?'

'Always, manling.' Gotrek's axe cut through the fog. Its runes hummed dimly. 'Sounds carry. It's like being underground.'

Grimly, Felix stood and held his sword ready. As he watched, the smudge of grey he had seen shimmered out into three distinct forms, then five, then seven, then ten, each acquiring definition of their own as the thunder of galloping hooves became all encompassing.

'Shoot on sight, you say?' Felix asked.

Rudi did not answer. Back turned, Felix could only imagine Gotrek's mad grin.

'Best make it quick then, hadn't we?'

Grey flanked and black-maned, sodden with dew, the horses burst from the fog like ghosts granted form, the grey of their riders' cloaks snapping at their tails. The horsemen themselves were no more auspicious, garbed in a chimeric blend of darkened mail and leather. Terror exploded in Felix's chest as they bore down.

They meant to ride right over them!

Gotrek stood his ground and roared down the throat of the cavalry charge, brandishing his enormous axe with a deadly flourish. The lead horse whinnied and reared, Gotrek dodging its flailing hooves and leaping back as it stamped down where he had just been. Its rider screamed curses into his horse's ear, wrapping his wrist into the rein and kicking back into the stirrups. The same was being repeated as the charge fouled behind it, horses fanning out from the rear, shaking at their bridles, a whickering chorus of unnerved steeds and swearing men.

With urgent whistles and clicked tongues, the horsemen directed their steeds around Felix and the others, an overlapping barrier of snorting horseflesh in case any of them should be fool enough to try and run. Their stormy expressions gave the impression that they would actually prefer it if they did, that their being captive had somehow complicated things that they would rather have been simple. Rudi pressed his back to

Felix's, weapons drawn. Felix could not see his face, but he could feel the sweat where their necks touched. He could feel the riders' pistols trained on his back. It would only take one itchy finger for this all to become frightfully simple again.

Felix released his sword with care, trying to avoid any swift movements.

The lead cavalryman, still battling his own stubborn mount, coolly unholstered a stub-nosed pistol and levelled it at Gotrek. It was some kind of hand-blunderbuss. It swayed level as the horse beneath it fought. The horseman regarded the three of them fiercely. Long black hair strayed from the confines of a peaked leather cavalry helm. A thick, horseshoe moustache sagged with accumulated sweat. He twisted in his saddle, gun unwavering.

'Luthor!'

'Captain.' The return came almost at once. A younger rider in similar garb spurred his horse around.

'Make for the township. Tell Father Gramm we've apprehended,' he paused, double checked, the mist making precision difficult, 'two men and a dwarf. Exactly where he divined the boundary line breached.' Felix saw the man sneer. 'Offer my compliments.'

Luthor snapped a salute as his horse turned, digging his heels into its flanks and spurring it into a canter that bore both into the mist. The clatter of its hooves persisted, but even that shortly vanished, form and substance both swallowed whole.

The captain returned his attention to Felix, his pistol not straying from the snarling Trollslayer. He looked down from his mount, his sneer, if anything, setting even deeper. 'I offer one chance to make this easy for yourselves. Tell me what I want to hear and we may let you turn around with no more than a flogging.'

'Try me, horseling,' growled Gotrek. 'We'll see who spends longest peeling blood from their fingers thereafter.'

Laughter burst from the barrel chest of one of the circling horsemen. His thick black beard was crossed with scars and his eyes, set deep into his face, were hard to see from Felix's lowly vantage. 'Whoa there, captain! I think he means it!'

Gotrek shot the man a contemptuous glare.

'I'll ask one time only,' the captain bellowed, evidently a man not accustomed to having his authority challenged. 'Where is the baron?'

Gotrek met the man's hot stare. 'I recall that Osterwald had a great many whorehouses. Did you start there?'

The horseman's sneer twisted into a furious snarl. 'Why you insolent–'

'Wait,' said Felix, setting a hand on Gotrek's shoulder. The dwarf growled, but consented to lowering his axe a fraction. The horseman similarly allowed his pistol to drop the thinnest inch. 'You asked after the baron. Are you saying that von Kuber is missing?'

The rider bared his teeth, a bestial show of rage. 'Ambushed by the Beast of the Moors as he escorted a congregation of Sigmarite brothers to their minster in Osterwald. We found their bloodless bodies and the remnants of their wagon not far from here. The bodies were not a half-day old.' Leather creaked as he leant forward in the saddle. 'You see why I question what brings you here.'

Felix took a step back, but Rudi blocked his attempted retreat. The hate in the man's eyes was fierce to the point of inhuman. 'I assure you. We had nothing to do with that attack.'

'So you would claim,' the man sneered. 'Yet here you are on the moors, with winter coming, in lands known forbidden.' He grasped a silver hammer, worn over his armour on a chain about his neck. 'You wear no article of faith.'

'We don't, but–'

'More likely you are agents of the Beast!' The man was

practically spitting. Felix watched his frighteningly controlled pistol with a tense grimace.

'Have you seen the Beast?' said Felix, trying to sound calm, hoping that it might spread. 'Or those creatures it commands? It's not something served by mortal men.'

'I don't expect you to admit your guilt to me here, but we have... *ways*... of making sinners recant.'

'And just who are you then?' said Gotrek, his axe continuing to menace.

The man threw down an ugly look, pulling himself higher in his saddle. 'I am Konrad Seitz, captain of the militia, proctor of Baron Götz von Kuber's holy protectorate of Sigmarshafen. *I* am the one who will be asking questions.' He aimed his pistol meaningfully at Gotrek's nose. Felix suspected that if Konrad decided to fire, then this gun would fire. 'I am a faithful man, but not a patient one. One final time. Where is Baron von Kuber?'

'Let's just finish them here.' A voice barked from the eerie shadows behind Felix's back. 'We could say they resisted, that we had no choice. I want blood for the baron.' There was an angry jeer at that. 'Gramm need never know.'

The black-bearded thug had his pistol trained on Felix's back. Emotion made it shake. 'Blood for blood, captain. It's your word that counts now Götz is gone. Not Gramm's.'

Konrad glared down at Gotrek, considering his bondsman's words.

'It couldn't have been us,' shouted Rudi. 'And it couldn't have been the Beast. The Beast attacked *us*. We all saw it.' He looked to Felix and Gotrek for support. 'It destroyed my entire village. My own father and brother!'

Konrad withdrew his pistol, used its muzzle to brush his moustache from his lips. He smiled and, with a sharp cry that had Felix jumping aside, urged his horse forward. Gotrek swore ripely in the dwarfen tongue as its bulk shoved him back but, to Felix's relief, stayed his axe.

'Well, well, well, Rudolph Hartmann. If you aren't the dumbest little deserter then I pity the poor mother of the man who is.'

'Deserter?' said Gotrek, turning on their companion with an unpleasant look.

'It's Rudolph Hartmann!' Konrad turned his horse a full circle, bellowing the name to each face within the encircling ring. 'Rudolph Hartmann!' Konrad laughed once without humour, his expression reverting almost at once to its settled sneer. 'We thought you dead in the Totenwald, Rudi. But then why would the Beast kill those with whom it is in league?'

'Lies!' Rudi screamed, lunging for Konrad with his sword, only for the cavalryman's horse to trot nimbly back. Konrad barked with laughter, directing his dragoon pistol toward Rudi's face. The young soldier bared his teeth, the thought of going down in a blaze of furious glory evidently crossing his mind.

'Put it down, Rudi,' said Felix, softly.

'But–'

'Put it down.'

The muzzle of Konrad's pistol nodded groundward. Rudi scowled and let his fingers go limp and his sword drop. Then his knife too. Both hit the thorny ground with a dull thud.

'Still the coward, Hartmann,' observed Konrad with a cruel smile and a wink that had his men chuckling

'This is a serious mistake, friend,' said Felix. 'I don't know how the Beast could be in two places at once, but know that we're not your enemy. We too hunt the Beast.'

'We'll see,' said Konrad with a sneer. 'Torsten, Wolfgang, Klaus, your horses. Mount these three and bind them. The dwarf first. We'll send riders for you with remounts the moment we return.'

The three men so named swung from their saddles. The thuggish black beard, Torsten, pulled a second pistol from a holster strapped to his horse's harness and covered the other two as they converged on Gotrek. The dwarf stood firm and readied his axe. His eye carried a mad glint. The men held off, each daring the other to go first.

'It'll be my cold corpse you strap to that animal, manling. Who'll be first to come and try it?'

Felix quickly looked around, trying to gauge their odds of fighting their way out.

It did not take a second look to tell him that their chances were not good.

Even if Gotrek could overpower the three soldiers that faced him – and that, at least, Felix rated quite likely – there remained six mounted men with pistols primed and drawn and he had no intention of dying over a case of mistaken identity.

'Please, Gotrek. Perhaps it would be best to go with them. There must be someone reasonable in von Kuber's company. Maybe even someone who can help us. It'll be easier to claim our innocence and be back about our business if we're not dead.'

One of the men edged forward only for a swift feint from Gotrek's axe to send him dodging back.

'Listen to your friend, dwarf,' spoke Konrad. 'This ends one of two ways, seated on a saddle or your body lashed dead to its hindquarters.'

Gotrek spat on the ground and snarled. 'Horses are for elves.'

'They are headed our way,' Felix offered.

Gotrek eyed the nearest mount warily, as though it might suddenly sprout bat wings and snort fire from its nostrils. One of Konrad's men came running with a length of twine. Gotrek warned him back with a look.

'I'll come, manling. But don't push your luck.'

Gotrek grumbled as a grey-cloaked soldier bound his axe-hand in twine. The man tied it off nervously, occasional glances to

Gotrek's other ham-like fist. The soldier named Klaus, who had been fool enough to come at Gotrek before he was ready, moaned in a heap on the ground trying to staunch the flow from his broken nose.

'I said I'd come,' Gotrek grumbled, glaring at Felix as if he was the one that had dragged them both across the moors.

Konrad guided his mount alongside, minding the dwarf with his pistol as his man handed him his end of the cord. Baring his teeth, he tied it through his mount's bridle and gave it a tug, testing its soundness and jerking Gotrek's arm. 'It's easy to lose yourself on the moors, dwarf, and it's hard country.' Digging his heels into the spurs, Konrad urged the grey mare to sidestep, hauling Gotrek after it. Some of the mounted men laughed, causing Konrad to grin. 'And I want to be sure you can keep up.'

Worried more for Konrad's poor horse than for Gotrek, Felix mounted with considerably less drama. He was by nobody's measure an expert but he did not hold the entire equine species to the same degree of visceral distrust as did Gotrek. His reins were in the hands of a tall, lean man, green eyed and gaunt. The rider's cheeks were stubbled with coarse blond hair and he regarded Felix with a reptilian impassivity. The man offered a smile of neatly missing teeth that travelled no further than his thin lips.

'Caul Schlanger, meinen herr.' The man's accent was an odd mix but, to one as well journeyed as Felix, the sibilant slither of Sylvanian vowels was unmistakable. He looked more like a footpad than a soldier. Felix shifted position in the saddle to satisfy himself that his scabbard remained in easy reach. Caul caught the surreptitious glances and licked his lips, fondling a throwing knife. 'No ideas now.'

Felix looked away, hoping to be able to ignore him.

Rudi had not been granted a mount of his own. The big lunk called Torsten had remounted on Konrad's order and pulled Rudi into the saddle in front of him. Rudi's hands were bound and placed in his lap, arms pinned by Torsten's as the thuggish horseman hugged him to his chest in order to keep a good hold on his horse's reins. Ahead of him, to Felix's right, Konrad was fighting to make his grey walk in a straight line while Gotrek yanked boisterously on the cord, pulling its muzzle back every time it tried to turn away. Gotrek cackled a little louder with Konrad's increasing fury. With a snarl, the captain tried to ignore him and barked final orders to the two men, Wolfgang and Klaus, who would be following on foot.

Caul Schlanger pulled Felix back around with a fierce yank on his reins.

'Caul!'

At Konrad's command, Caul's demeanour shifted from leering bully to weary professional with such seamlessness that Felix thought he might have been knocked out and imagined the entire last minute. 'Captain,' Caul replied with a bare nod in lieu of a salute and guided his horse forward, reining it in once he and Felix stood level with Konrad

'Anselm, Matthaus,' Konrad barked. 'Ride ahead in case any more of the Beast's minions lie in wait for us. No more prisoners. These three will repent soon enough.' The two riders saluted mid-spur and thundered into the encroaching fog without a word. 'Torsten. Two lengths behind. Keep that wretch from my sight. The rest of you...' He smiled, sour as spoiled milk. 'Be ready to blow his brains out should his friends try something heroic.'

Rudi reddened with useless fury as Torsten scratched his bristled chin against his temples and laughed.

Gotrek looked up towards Felix, one massive hand drawn ahead of him by Konrad's horse. 'If anything happens, manling, I'll remember that this was your idea.'

'Ride!' yelled Konrad, spurring his mount into a trot, accelerating slowly into a canter that Gotrek, already breathing as though he meant it, could match. Dwarfs may not have been renowned for their fleetness of foot, but they knew how to cover ground when moved to do so. And Gotrek was as tough as they came.

Felix would not like to wager on whose legs would give out first, the dwarf or the horse.

Caul followed next with Felix's horse in tow, the thunder of hooves following like a curse as the remaining horsemen adopted formation at their rear. Felix's belly lurched at the sudden sensation of speed, powerful groups of muscle shifting against his thighs. Felix had learned the basics of horsemanship as a boy, all part of his father's noble aspirations for his sons, but neither he nor poor bookish Otto had ever been a natural. He clung to the beast's neck as it tore the bracken beneath its hooves, focusing on staying in the saddle. It would have been hard enough at the best of times. Without the illusion of control granted by reins in the hand, it was like fighting a duel with an unfamiliar weapon and one hand behind his back.

The riders said nothing as they rode. All except Rudi. Felix could hear his muttered prayers even over the hooves of half a dozen horses plus one. If Torsten, or anyone else for that matter, was listening at all, they certainly did not care. Periodically, either one of Anselm or Matthaus would hove into view, cry an 'all clear' to Konrad, then turn, keep pace for a few lengths, and pull away at speed to disappear once again into the mist.

With a crawling of flesh, Felix noted that Caul was still staring at him, unblinking, perfectly comfortable guiding both their horses at speed to finger his knife through a suggestive twirl. His regard made Felix uncomfortable. There was something *unhealthy* about the man's interest that Felix could not fathom. He fervently hoped that he was not to be left alone with him when they arrived at their destination

With a wry smile that had Caul frowning in consternation, Felix accepted that he was fretting over the snotling in his pantry as a green horde roared over the hill. He was worrying over one man when, for all he knew, these riders bore him toward a nest of vampires.

And the clutches of a mad baron's witch-finders.

A sensation of falling, of drowning in frozen honey, then the world snapped into plane.

Hurrlk's feet struck solid earth.

The ground was bedded with pine needles, the sun intense through the tangled fingers of the forest. Hurrlk reached out. His claws wrapped fully around the bole of the nearest tree. It trembled, offended by his unnatural feel.

It had not been there before.

'Saved.' The whispered hiss passed through his minions. They clung to the shadows, avoiding the sun like a sickness, but their relief was palpable. Hurrlk felt his thoughts begin to clear, as if the mists he had left behind had been of the mind rather than of the land. There would be no pursuit here. Even if there was it need not be feared. Out there he was weak, confused.

This place belonged to Hurrlk.

Saved.

Hurrlk moved through the trees, their slender bodies bowing for his passage. The trees began to thin, the forest dissolving away from the ribbon of solidity that struck from the ground to claim the land for its own. City walls. They were fractured and loose, bulging outward after some titanic blow from within. But they still stood. He growled and stabbed a claw at the walls.

Climb.

His minions clutched their bulging packs and hugged the tree line, wary of the light. But something beyond those walls called to them. A power. A darkness. Hurrlk issued another terse command, this time with a crack of his whip, driving the smaller creatures into a dash from the tree line.

He loped on after them, doubts gnawing at consciousness.

Were they saved? Or simply damned anew?

CHAPTER 4

The Saved

The mists over the moors continued to condense. Felix could barely discern Caul's gloves at the far end of his own reins. He clung nervously to his horse's neck, its wet mane flapping to the rhythm of its stride. The air around them was so dense a white that he almost failed to notice as they passed under the canopy of the Totenwald at last. Slender pines knotted branches in the shadows, red winterberries hanging like droplets of blood. Felix noted the jarring absence of birdsong. Only the wind disturbed the high branches.

The forest stayed with them for barely half an hour before the body of trees abruptly fell away. The ground ahead was studded with stumps as far into the fog as could be seen, ranked one after another like memorial stones in the garden of Morr. Unimpeded, the wind struck like a knife. Felix bent low to his horse's neck, hair whipping out behind with his cloak. They did not slow, forging deeper into that wasteland, the earth beginning to blanch until it was as pale as the cloud through which they rode. He focused on the ground below the horse's galloping hooves. It was not imagination. The land here was dead. Not merely impoverished as had been the moors with its uniquely mean and stunted flora, but dead. Utterly.

It was barren white, like ash or old bone.

Shapes emerged, the skeletons of wooden giants, like the bare rigs of storm-slain vessels blown through the mists of the Manannspoort Sea. They were watchtowers. Felix could not tell if they were manned. The riders made no call up and no spectral echo challenged down, but grey banners bearing the twin-tailed comet of Sigmar flapped wetly from their bleached pine ramparts. Felix saw spears and small ballistae, but it was possible they served merely as an illusion of strength.

'Captain.' The voice seemed to come from everywhere at once and nowhere close. After a moment, he recognised it as Torsten's. 'We're close. Should we blindfold them?'

'No,' came Konrad's brusque reply, tugging on Gotrek's tether, making the red-faced dwarf scowl a breathless oath. 'I don't want to waste time. And besides, given these three already owe allegiance to the Beast, they've doubtless seen the City of the Damned with their own traitorous eyes.'

The City of the Damned. Perhaps it was the way Konrad had said it, but it made Felix shudder.

'This city; is that what von Kuber protects?'

'The birthright of the von Kuber line,' Konrad stated with pride, forgetful for the moment who it was that asked. 'Bestowed upon his forefathers by the divine Magnus himself, to maintain vigil over its ruins lest evil again arise.'

'The baron sounds a very pious man.'

Konrad snarled, offended by Felix's attempt at a compliment. 'The City of the Damned would have been rubble once Götz was finished. There would not have been one brick left atop another for the Beast to hide under, and all that was left still able to burn would have made the bonfire for its execution.'

'You're certain then. This is where the Beast makes its lair.'

Konrad regarded him hotly. 'And why the Beast struck back.'
With that, Konrad would say no more.

The horsemen rode on. Felix could see nothing, could feel nothing that would suggest some dark power hidden somewhere in the mist. He wondered whether it was the city, wherever it was, that had killed off the land through which they rode. If so, it must be a force of truly terrifying measure. He wished he could confer with Gotrek, the dwarf was ever more attuned to such things, but his companion was too intent on running. He was about to ask Konrad to call a halt, perhaps give Felix another chance to persuade Gotrek to swallow his pride and get on a damned horse, when he heard something. It was a voice, a whisper only half imagined. He twisted in his saddle towards Caul.

'Did you say something?'

Caul acknowledged the question with a cold smile and rode on.

'Please…'

Felix started, staring into the fog. That was where the voice had come from. Not from any man he rode beside. The voice faded the harder he sought to focus on it, others arising from every direction.

'…why…'

'…spare my daughter…'

'…damn you all…'

'…what kind of god?'

Felix would have closed his eyes if he was not afraid he would fall from his horse if he did. The stream of pained consciousness made him dizzy.

'Who… Who is speaking?'

'The Damned.' Caul's dry voice grated. The man leaned over so their eyes could meet through the thickening fog, so his words might be heard above the whispered din. 'The baron's soldiers seek to reclaim the streets, but not every enemy is a beast. Not every monster can be fought. The city judges men's hearts and damns them. It doesn't want to be saved.'

'Quiet,' whispered Konrad, something in the air making even him speak softly. 'We're almost past.'

Konrad upped their pace. Gotrek made a wheezing sound that turned into a determined growl and upped his own to match. Painfully slowly, the fog began to recede, drawing away the whispers of the Damned with it. Felix could still hear them, a haunting note in the dark that he strove to ignore.

A grey phantasm within the fog and the muted thunder of galloping hooves bespoke the return of Anselm. His steed glistened with damp and was blowing hard. Following a fraught exchange, he led Konrad and Caul through a change in course, veering rightward, further from the last vestiges of the whispering voices and ever so gradually uphill. The column slowed, the tenor of hoof beats deepening, as Felix found his horse upon a genuine road of compacted earth, bordered with what looked like rubble. Konrad looked both ways, left to right, thoughtful, and more than a little frightened, before leading them right.

A signing post around the height of a mounted man resolved from the fog to one side of the road. It was cut from Totenwald pine, its weatherproofing layer of pitch peeling away under wraithlike fingers of fog. Konrad called a halt. From the post's head, arrows pointed in two directions. Ahead, what Felix reckoned to be north-east, the arrow had been inscribed with a curling, antiquated script. The word '*Sigmarshafen*' was only just legible beneath the decay. The arrow indicating the opposite route had been thoroughly defaced with some bladed implement, hammer runes daubed over the top in black paint. Felix leaned nearer in his saddle and strained, perhaps making out a stylised capital 'M'.

Felix felt a shiver pass through him as he turned his attention south-west.

Like a spectre arisen from his own nightmares, the shadow of walls and towers reared from the fog. His heart thudded a dirgeful beat as he looked upon it. Every detail, from the walls themselves to this blasted wasteland upon which it lingered were precisely as he had pictured them in his dreams. What fell influence did this city exert that it could project its likeness into his dreams? And more than its likeness. He felt the same horror, the same translated torment that he had suffered through his nights. He prayed that it was nothing more than wind that conjured eddies in the mist, made it resemble men with halberds and pikes that patrolled those ruined battlements. He prayed for it, but he knew it was not so. He heard the whispers that the wind carried, closed his heart to their anguish and turned away. He wished his ears could be shuttered as easily as his eyes.

'Don't want to go that way, meinen herr,' Caul hissed. 'Some say that at night, the Damned leave their city, cross the wasteland, and march on Sigmarshafen to entreat the living.'

'What do they want?' Felix asked.

'I doubt even they know.'

'Do we wait for Matthaus?' shouted Torsten, as if brazenness might mask his fear. In his lap, Rudi looked determinedly to the ground. With bound hands, he groped for some charm or other that he wore under his leathers around his neck. Torsten gave him a rough shake to stop him fidgeting.

'Maybe he has ridden ahead,' said Anselm.

'No,' said Torsten. 'He knows to meet here. He wouldn't–'

'He has ridden ahead,' said Konrad, firm.

'But, captain–'

'Silence, Torsten,' said Konrad. He turned in his saddle to peer onto those forsaken ramparts. Felix wondered what voices the militia captain heard. Konrad's face set and he looked away, spurring his horse on towards Sigmarshafen. 'We'll pray for him when we arrive.'

Torsten looked as though he would protest, but tightened his lip. Anselm fell to the back of the line as the other riders swept by. Felix saw him draw both pistols, directing his horse forward solely with his knees, riding with body twisted and tense as a screw as he stared back to the damned city.

Onward, they rode, the laments of the Damned slowly diminishing from hearing if not from memory. In the far distance, the dark bulk of the Totenwald grew thick, the mists thinning somewhat as though drawn by some deep inhalation of the forest. Its rustling life haunted the mist, tempting, almost near enough to convince that the dead land they traversed must eventually end. But only almost. The dirt road beneath their hooves was hard as stone and dry as a burned match, split like salt flats into columnar breakages, not even weeds able to take root in the cracks.

The road wound ahead into a steep rise, ascending a grey-earthed knoll, the highest ground in the area and studded with bare tree stumps. A bleak palisade ringed its summit like a dog bite. The road met the palisade at a gate flanked by guard towers from which grey pennants snapped in the stiff breeze. Solid figures in dark grey livery stood sentry on the elevated platforms, crossbows sweeping the mounted column that approached through the fog.

Konrad raised a hand, waving until he received an answering signal from the leftward guard tower. There was a brief flurry of activity, signals whistled between the two towers and hidden men on the ground and, with a sound like trees being tortuously felled, the gates drew outward. Mist spilled from the opening portal, as water dammed. Felix felt its chill touch as it washed through him.

'Sigmarshafen,' Konrad declared, spurring his horse ahead, and drawing Gotrek with it. The Slayer looked ill, throat pulsing as though he might vomit. Konrad did not notice. 'One time home of Magnus the Pious himself. The final bastion of the true faith. Sigmar's haven in the darkness.'

'Wood,' Gotrek wheezed, eyeing the palisade blearily. 'What fool would build a castle out of wood?'

The cavalcade rumbled through the open gate and through the shadow of its flanking towers. Their frames had been erected so tightly that they doubled as chattel pens. Humanoid shapes clotted the tangled interiors, offending every sense that Felix possessed. Their bodies were misshapen, their stench vile, the moans that issued from their mouths as they butted dumbly against their cage a claw-hammer to the spirit. Face contorted with disgust, as much at himself for judging these objects so harshly as at the inmates themselves, Felix looked away.

On clearing the gatehouse, fresh odours arose to impinge on his senses. The township carried a scent of pine, of bitter cold, accentuated by a curious spice that recalled the weekly visit to the temple he had been forced to endure as a boy. The streets were bare earth and filthy, visible only when a passing figure disturbed the ankle-deep skin of settled mist. Hastily assembled wooden huts with shingled roofs and no windows fought for each scrap of ground. They pressed in, as if they were caught in some glacially slow stampede for the gate and freedom from this frigid quagmire. Men and women gossiped under doorways in lowered tones, or pushed handcarts down alleys too narrow for mounted men on quiet errands of their own. Soldiery with swords and hammers in the grey cloaks of Götz von Kuber patrolled the streets. Peasants fell silent where they marched, signed the hammer, and offered prayers to the passing crusaders. Somewhere within the township, a blacksmith worked his forge. The peal of metal hammering on metal rang out like a call to prayer.

On a street corner, a wild-eyed man sang of the end of days from an upturned box. The street preacher wore a sackcloth kilt, his bare and starving torso boasting more tattoos even than Gotrek. The ink was old and faded, hidden by burns, scars, and seeping wounds. His right arm was a messy stump of shoulder, but with his left he scourged his own back with a leathern thong, not even pausing between strokes in his portending of the End Times.

'…the End Times will bring trial. Women will be wilful and without license. Their husbands and brothers will not humble them for they will be lovers of self, of gold, and of Chaos. They will be proud, arrogant, debauched, disobedient, ungrateful, unholy, brutal – enemies of right and of righteousness, treacherous, feckless, fat with conceit, slaves to pleasure, feigning of godliness. This sinning Empire is degenerate. Sorcerers flourish in houses of so-called learning. Churches fail. The End Times are come. We, Sigmar's children, will fight the last war, will burn in its fire and be recast holy. The End Times come…'

His catechistic ravings captivated an audience of several dozen. At the foot of his appropriated pedestal, children in rags fought with wooden hammers and with fluted innocence decried each other as heretics.

Konrad took a heady lungful. 'What you see is the vision of holy men. This is a place of sanctuary and of pilgrimage. The people you see here are warriors, crusaders in Magnus's own example.'

Felix shook his head and allowed Caul Schlanger to lead him on.

A main thoroughfare bore away from the gate and through the scrum of housing. The narrowness of the street coupled to the volume of human traffic compressed the column into single file. Peasants hurried from their path, tugging on caps and signing the hammer across their chests. The clop of iron shoes echoed eerily loud over the hush. The wooden tenements pressed them close, upper storeys leaning inwards, defying the zealots in their shadow to command them back.

Sigmarshafen was quite unlike any town Felix had ever occasioned.

There were no hawking merchantmen, no gaudily painted shop fronts to attract custom. Hushed peasants in plainly coloured smocks and woollen hats and gloves conducted their business and did not tarry. As Felix watched, a broad man, head gleaming like a polished skull, emerged from the doorway of some kind of shrine. His white tabard was stained with dirt about the hem – and with blood most everywhere else – and worn over several layers of mail. The twin-tailed comet, herald of Sigmar, was emblazoned over a steel pectoral. The warrior priest glared fixedly as they passed. A gaggle of initiates hung in the doorway behind him, boys from Rudi's age to as young as six or seven.

They each watched Gotrek in fearful temperance. They all wore scars.

Despite his ignominious appearance, red as raw knuckles and leashed to a horse, Gotrek was drawing looks of awe from more than just the priests. More than once, Felix saw women point and men choke back tears. By their acts of valour alongside the man-god, Sigmar Heldenhammer, dwarfs were themselves practically deified by followers of his creed. Felix looked around. And those here were clearly fanatics, probably unwelcome even in the most extremist of temples in the Empire's cities. The Slayer merely grunted, fixing his one eye to the lathered grey hindquarters of the horse in front of him.

'Captain!' A blond-haired youth in von Kuber's grey pushed through the crowded street towards them. Felix recognised Luthor, whom Konrad had dispatched to send advance word of their coming. The man was out of breath and reeked of sweat, clearly arriving not long before they had. 'Gramm is waiting. He commands these three be presented at once.'

'Does he now?' Konrad chuckled. Luthor spun on his heel to depart. 'And Luthor?'

'Yes, captain?'

'We lost Matthaus in the mist. Report to the gate. See that outriders are dispatched to look for him.'

'To what end? He wouldn't be the first…'

'Do as you are told!' Konrad spat with venom. 'Matthaus has served der Kreuzfahrer since he was young. He would not heed the dreams of the Damned.'

Luthor looked dubious, but was not about to argue. He saluted, held it until Konrad and the other horsemen were well past.

Ahead, the dirt road forced the encroaching buildings back far enough to form a square, flanked on three sides by drab market stalls and on the fourth, the north-west, by a half-stone cathedral. The locals had made an effort. It had tall windows of stained glass and a wooden belfry that craned skyward from its limestone body, but it was a lacklustre affair by comparison with its like in Altdorf or Nuln. Even the penniless clergy of Osterwald would have turned their noses at a secondment to a temple like this. Only the most disfavoured, or the most fanatical, would devote their life to Sigmarshafen by choice.

Skeletons, charred black by fire, swayed from a gibbet erected before the cathedral's pale wooden doorway, such that each congregant might see and be thankful. Fog wreathed the corpses with a sallow touch, setting ropes to creaking, the wind echoing from their hollow skulls like the moans of the unquiet dead. Not all were in possession of the usual apportionment of arms or heads. A crowd had gathered to gawp, peasants and pilgrims come to hawk phlegm onto charcoaled feet, hooves, claws, and jeer. Rising above the hush, from a crenellated pulpit that hung suspended from the belfry, a preacher sang of the End Times, his tune a stark complement to the hush below; the creaking nooses of the saved.

On the fire-blackened earth in the square's centre, none walked. Folk avoided it like a dark omen, clustering instead to its edges where stallholders pegged their wares with quiet pleas and suggestive glances. Young, keen-looking men in pristine mail bright with holy iconography, squires to templar knights, tramped through the filth as beggars and hawkers pawed at their linen sleeves with furtive promises of arcane wards against Chaos, protective relics, and forbidden vices. Men in variegated mercenary colours watched the whole tableau from under darkened awnings, sipping at non-descript potations, dicing, one eye on the swaying corpses, mindful of the righteous.

The column clattered to a halt.

Gotrek took a great huff of the chill air and gripped his thighs, staring hard at the ground, delighted to find it so proximate to his face.

'This is dourer than Karak Kadrin,' he wheezed. 'Where does a dwarf find a drink in this place?'

'This is a place of temperance,' Konrad returned, untying the dwarf's leash from his horse's bridle and tossing his end down onto the heaving dwarf. 'The Empire is slothful and indolent. This is why Baron von Kuber expanded Sigmarshafen to accommodate the truly faithful. When the End Times come, this is where Sigmar's hammer-brothers will make their stand.'

'Is it now?'

'It is.'

Gotrek straightened, hands on hips, and glared across the square. 'You think Sigmar would have liked all this? Manling, I could tell you tales of Sigmar that'd make your whiskers curl.'

'I'd sooner sever both ears than hear his name from your lips.'

'Do you know how much ale was downed after Black Fire Pass?' Gotrek pressed with malicious relish. 'If ever there was a man to match a dwarf pint for pint, it would have been Sigmar. Not that he could, mind. He was only human, after all.'

'Enough!' Konrad yelled, quivering with a rage that Gotrek greeted with a snort of derision. He cast a look to the plain walls and stained glass of the temple of Sigmar, yawing back in his saddle to rip his pistol from its holster. 'Wolfgang was right. We should have gunned you down on the moors and left you for the crows.'

'That would have been most prideful, Konrad. You are familiar by now with the proper penances, I am sure.'

Konrad scowled, rehousing his weapon and swinging down from the saddle as an elderly man in crimson robes emerged from the throng surrounding the gibbet and its grisly display of Sigmar's justice. The man's face was lined and blotched, white hair falling away in straggly clumps, his eyes a damp, dispirited blue. A young page in albus robes fussed over him like an attentive shadow.

'I am indeed, arch-lector,' said Konrad. 'It would seem that they do not work.'

Watching the old priest's approach, Felix suddenly realised he was the last man still mounted. He dismounted, embarrassingly saddle-sore given the briefness of their ride.

The priest paused before Gotrek, looked the dwarf up and down. The page dropped to hands and knees to brush grit from his master's robes. 'Did I not describe the Beast to you?' the old priest rasped, as though his breath bore claws to defy expulsion. 'Does this look anything like the monster?'

'Not all creatures of the dark wear their claws in public, father.' Konrad's horse whinnied, empathising with her master's anger. Konrad gripped the bridle, hard enough to make the leather creak in anguish.

'You are an indiscriminate fool. As bad as der Kreuzfahrer ever was. Sigmar's name, this is one of the elder folk you harass now!'

'You in charge here?' Gotrek asked gruffly, pulling himself upright.

Konrad scoffed, a few of the men muttered under the breaths. The priest ignored them. 'Gramm. Hans-Jorgen Gramm. Arch-Lector of the province of Ostermark.'

'Open your eyes,' Konrad hissed. 'They crossed the border line near the site of the attack. Exactly where the wards signalled an incursion. Exactly where *you* said they would be.'

'Perhaps you'd best leave your thinking to that horse of yours,' Gotrek observed. 'We were after the Beast ourselves. Of course we trod the same path. Or did you think the monster would sit on its plunder and wait to be caught?' Gotrek gave the men present an appraising look, then snorted and turned back to the old priest. 'Not unless it craved more killing. I doubt there's anything your lot could have done to stop it.'

Konrad stepped forward, drawing his horse in his wake, and jabbed the old priest in the collar with a gloved finger. Felix heard a collective gasp from those stood nearby, brave enough to watch.

'The Beast would have been robbed of its hiding place long ago if the temple had given Götz the backing he deserved. That boundary line should have been tightened to a noose about the city's neck. We should each have begged for one tenth of Götz's courage, and prayed for the worthiness to spill our blood in his name, to take the place apart stone by stone and let it drown in a river of its own blood!'

'Konrad, you will be silent!' Gramm's raised voice summoned a hush to the already fearful square. Across the square Felix saw money change hands amongst a group of bored-looking mercenaries; probably wagering on how long it would take for somebody to be thrown onto a bonfire. 'Magnus bade us watch. To contain. He knew better than any that true evil is not so easily purged. It must remain, a monument, an insurance that we never forget.'

'That may be so. But does not Sigmar Himself charge us to oppose evil in all its forms, wherever…' Konrad's eyes glittered dangerously, fixed upon the hunched priest as he spoke, '…and in whomever, it be found.'

Gramm's expression soured, but he offered no riposte,

turning instead to Gotrek with the utterance of a harsh syllable that sounded as though the old man was gargling on gravel. Gotrek's one eye widened, then he growled back a string of hard-edged consonants, shaping his hands through the illustration of some point or other. Gramm nodded along, listening intently. They conversed in Khazalid, Felix realised, the dwarfish tongue. He listened out for any words he recognised, but it was akin to seeking sense in the collision of rocks. He felt a flash of annoyance that, despite all of their travels, Gotrek had never offered to teach him a phrase or two. He had learned more Dark Tongue from the throats of dying beastmen than he had ever gleaned from the language of arguably his closest, if not only, friend.

The dwarfs valued their secrecy, he knew, but did their friendship count for so little?

Gramm was growing progressively more disturbed as Gotrek continued to speak. Felix looked to Konrad, feeling an unexpected kinship. Konrad's face flushed a bloody purple, imagination conjuring its own abridged translation of the dwarf's words.

'Right then,' said Gotrek, clapping his fists and turning back to Felix, slipping smoothly into Reikspiel. 'That's that sorted out.'

'What were you talking about?'

'War stories,' said Gotrek. 'The priest here was the sole survivor when the Beast made off with the baron.'

'One survivor,' said Felix, thoughtful. Something niggled at the back of his mind.

'Your account is troubling,' breathed Gramm.

'Which part, exactly?' asked Felix, irritated by his exclusion and not at all worried about letting it show.

'The timing of the attacks, for one. It must be very swift, or possessed of some *uncanny* means of transportation, to mount attacks on both you and on our congregation on the same night.'

'Was it definitely the same monster?'

Gramm frowned, studying Gotrek. It was as if Felix did not exist to him.

'Aye, manling,' said Gotrek, filling in. 'It was.'

Felix felt the concept of a monster that could be in two places at once rough over every fibre of logic in his body. Even as his mind rushed to rubbish it, he recalled the paths of the Old Ones into which he and Gotrek had stumbled by accident, through a gate not far from here. Was it possible there were more such gates hidden in this haunted province?

'The Beast might then prove impossible to find,' he said, voicing his fears.

'It'll taste my axe, manling, if it takes a hundred years.'

'That may be all right for you, Gotrek, but not if you wish it to be me who records it. It could be *anywhere*.'

'It's in the city,' said Gramm, raspish voice smothering the brewing argument. 'Evil begets evil. We have all heard the voices in the night and in our dreams, calling to our darker natures.'

'Some of us have,' murmured Konrad.

'Then you know more than we do. Do you also know what it seeks in the graves of the moors?'

Gramm pursed his lips, his eyes taking on a troubled glaze. It looked as though he framed an answer, only for Konrad to cut him off with a snarl.

'The Beast's intent is not a fit subject for those who profess to Sigmar's love,' said Konrad. 'The wish to understand the mind of Chaos is a sin. There is no order to it beyond that which we hope to give it. It is Chaos. It exists only to destroy or to be destroyed. And that is exactly what I plan to do!'

Gramm took a deep breath. 'The baron is lost—'

'Then I will see out the last promise he asked of me. And the City of the Damned will die with him.'

Gramm retreated before the soldier's zeal. 'We must consider the succession.'

'Götz has no children.'

'But he has an heir. His late wife's sister has borne sons by March Boyar Kraislav Ulanov of the Eastern Oblast.'

Konrad sneered. 'A warrior by *marriage*.' He spoke the last word as though he bit through a live animal. The men around him seemed to share his distaste. Only Caul remained apart. 'Is that all the legacy of the von Kuber's means to you, old man? This land changes you. It gets into your skin. Has this Kislevite child lived every hour with death on his doorstep, with a shadow over his very dreams? Can he call on the courage of seven generations of heroes who have defied the city's damnation? I say no. Yet this is the boy you would call to lead us into the End Times.' Konrad spat on the ground by the priest's feet. 'I say no.'

Gramm met Konrad's stare, lasting barely a moment before looking away. He nodded slowly. Something in Konrad's expression made Felix want to reach for his sword.

Felix cleared his throat nervously. 'It's clear you have important matters to talk about here.' He turned to Gotrek to avoid meeting Konrad's glare. 'With your permission, we should probably be on our way.'

'Or without your permission,' said Gotrek, with a hopeful leer. 'If you'd rather.'

'Nonsense,' said Konrad. 'The Beast is in the city already. You are tired and in any case it is early still. Only the flagellants brave the city by daylight. I insist you remain here, journey tomorrow. My men can accommodate your needs.'

Felix turned briefly, looking beyond the road they had just climbed and into the fog that cloaked the lifeless downs and the damned city beyond. Right then, both seemed safer than a night spent at Konrad Seitz's pleasure.

'It's a kind offer, but Gotrek and I will find some place to stay until morning. We wouldn't want to inconvenience your men from their search for the baron.'

Konrad stifled a growl at Felix's mention of von Kuber. 'This is not some den of decadence like Marienburg,' he snarled. 'You'll find few inns or brothels in Sigmarshafen.'

Gramm raised his hands for peace. 'The dwarf-friend has spoken and those who glory Sigmar will respect his wishes.'

Konrad scowled. Gramm's lips twitched, satisfied with his Pyrrhic victory. A faint look of confusion crossed his face. 'Three,' he rasped, examining Gotrek, and then Felix in turn. 'Three prisoners, you said. Do you hide something from me, captain?'

Konrad offered a bow, just shallow enough to be disrespectful. 'Torsten!' he yelled, eyes still fixed on Gramm. 'Bring Rudi Hartmann here.'

'Hartmann?' Gramm wheezed. 'There's a name I know well.' Gramm moved closer to where Rudi stood, quiet and shivering, Torsten's brawny hands pinning his arms to his sides. The priest took Rudi's chin in his hand, jerking it that he might examine his throat for stigmata. 'Chaos runs in your line, boy. Had it not been your father himself who exposed Margarethe's mutation to me, I would have had him, and you two boys, staked by your mother's side.'

Rudi's eyes were wide with fright. He mumbled something that Felix could not hear.

'The boy was there in the Totenwald ambush,' Konrad added in a suggestive whisper, eyes fixed on Gramm as securely as the priest's were on Rudi.

'Evil begets evil,' Gramm murmured like a protective cant.

'Only broken and bloodless bodies were left behind,' Konrad went on. 'They hung from the trees for miles. Why was this daemon's get permitted to flee? And why did he then hide and not return?'

'Have you something to confess, boy?' Rudi gasped as the priest's grip tightened. 'Have we stake and oil to spare, Brother Seitz?'

A ready smile crept across Konrad's face. 'Always, arch-lector.'

Gramm shoved back Rudi's face, wiping his hand on his robes as though to rid his skin of filth.

'Lock him away. Tomorrow he'll burn with the others.'

CHAPTER 5

Dreams of the Dishonoured

'Burn?' Felix yelled, barely able to hear his own voice over Rudi's disbelieving protests. 'You can't be serious.'

Gramm was unrepentant. 'It is common knowledge that a daemon haunts this country, an evil that even the Pious could not purge.' He waved his hands through the fog, giving Rudi a pitying look. 'It rides upon the mist, preys on the weak and the unrighteous. The body must be exorcised in flame to free the soul of flesh's taint.'

'That's the most inane nonsense I've heard anywhere on these blasted moors.'

'Cowardice is a curse, friend,' said Konrad. He smiled cruelly. Felix wanted very much to wipe away that smirk with his fist. He would have too, had Gotrek not held him back. Felix tried to throw himself on Konrad, but being restrained by Gotrek was like being chained to a wall.

'He's an oathbreaker, manling. This is their law.'

'That's right,' said Konrad. 'And he'll thank us when he's

granted entry into Sigmar's kingdom.'

Gramm nodded agreement. Torsten and Anselm were already dragging Rudi away. The youth howled and gnashed his teeth, struggling against the heavier men's hold. The townspeople parted before them and hissed.

With a laugh, Konrad leapt into his stirrup and swung his trailing leg into the saddle. The remaining soldiers took that as a cue to mount, all except Caul, stood with his hands beneath his grey cloak, watching like an adder with a strange lopsided smile. Konrad indicated the burned ground within the square. 'There are many accidents that may befall a man on his way to the pyre. Bring me what I want to learn before sunrise and your friend may yet find a swifter end.'

With an inchoate snarl, Felix lunged for the mounted man again, but Gotrek held him firm. Konrad merely laughed as he wheeled his horse away. Under the awnings across the square, money moved swiftly as debtors paid up on Rudi or, eying Felix like buzzards, gambled double or quits on a second burning.

'Come away, manling,' said Gotrek, insistent. 'Not out here.'

Men and women in humble garb crowded onto the road before the pale gates of Sigmarshafen. They came with children, occasional squawks of noise ill-temperedly silenced. The bleating of goats and the hymning of priests drifted over the attentive listeners like the fog that coiled about their shoulders.

Such intrusions were few. Word had spread fast and far and at least half of the township had packed into the strip of dirt road between the pine hovels of Sigmarshafen and the palisade. It was but once in a wandering star that those in inhabited places could hear the words of the blessed Brüder Nikolaus.

It was said that he had been the worst of sinners, reformed

by the intercession of Sigmar. It was said that he dwelt alone within the City of the Damned, preaching the divine word to the lost, to the air and to the stones beneath his bare feet. It was said that he had cleaved his own arm from his body to spite the attentions of Chaos that such communion invited.

It was said he was a living saint.

So it was with great consternation that the rearmost onlookers turned away to face the commotion coming their way down the main street from the Kirchplatz. Those first ripples of discontent spread, building into a wave of revulsion, a rush of hot blood that broke upon pious hearts.

Through a gauntlet of hissing men and showering rubbish, a dark-haired youth struggled between the grip of two of Captain Seitz's militiamen. The man's legs sawed through the hardened muck of the road, flailing for purchase and finding none. He looked normal; perhaps deceptively so, for there were none as adept as Captain Seitz at ensnaring those corrupt in spirit. With a grudging acquiescence, an acceptance that the torment awaiting this spawn of Chaos would reward their patience, the crowd drew back to form a travelling pocket of acrimony and bile surrounding the three men. The grey-cloaked militiamen bawled at the crowd to stay back, but that did not stop the occasional hot-blood breaking ranks to drive a fist or a boot into the condemned man's back. His cries of pain incited the mob all the more.

Atop the upturned box that sufficed so humble a man for a pulpit, Brüder Nikolaus lifted his one hand to the heavens. It was thick with green tattoos. They were faded, blotched with bruises and burns, a constant reminder of the lost soul he had once been. He praised Sigmar for the pain those memories wrought.

'Repent, poor sinner,' he cried, as the man was dragged through his congregation toward the gate towers. With tacit permission to do so, all now turned to watch. 'Like a feeble blade, your soul returns to the great fires of Sigmar's forge. Repent, poor sinner, and be recast pure!'

The preacher's words only made the man thrash harder, as though his holiness inflamed the daemon within. The crowd perceived it as such and began to wail. A woman fainted, caught and clutched close by her husband who signed the hammer on her forehead and roared with his fellows.

'Repent!' Nikolaus screamed. The people echoed him. The whole township rang with it, the word peeling over and over from a hundred mouths as the soldiers tried to strip the recalcitrant sinner of his gear and force him into the pen with the other foul horrors that came unwilling to Sigmar's mercy.

Nikolaus cleared his throat to shout again when he noticed another man forcing his way through the crowd. The man was one of his own flock and garbed similarly in sackcloth. His face was hideously burned, head bound in a bloodied tourniquet, the necessary scarifications of weak flesh. What remained of his face looked troubled.

'What ails you, Brüder Friedrich?'

'A mercenary has been brought to us. It is serious. She needs your ministry.'

Nikolaus nodded understanding and jumped down.

A lament went up from those gathered as he made his way between them, following the path that Friedrich forced open for him. None moved to stop him, but there were scuffles amongst those seeking to position themselves near enough to touch his sackcloth kilt or even his tattooed legs as he passed. They followed at a reverential remove as the two hermits made down one of the many alleys that branched from the gates of Sigmarshafen.

The alley was tight, large enough for two abreast but just barely. The doors to either side were small, narrowed and mean. Water ran from slanted roofs of pitched pine and rusted iron, a relentless trickle of worldly misery. The sun, such as it existed at all in Ostermark, never touched Sigmar's earth. Human filth had frozen into the ruts left by carts and human feet. Nikolaus bore the pain in his bare soles with a grateful heart, each breath summoning its own small torture, needles of bitter cold prickling down his throat with each draw of icy mist.

At one of the doors, Friedrich held and knocked twice. The building was identical to the others, but for a smearing of bloody prints over the latch and the heap of frozen offal that had been left out for the dogs and strays.

For Sigmar was a beneficent god.

The door opened to frame another man, bald, one eyed, face similarly burned and criss-crossed with partially melted scars. There was a tension in the way he gripped the door, but he relaxed at the sight of Nikolaus. He peered out into the dreary street and the long train of rabble that had followed them from the gate. They held back, silent as any such gathering of men ever could be.

The man behind the door grunted and pulled his head back inside. 'It's good you came. The daemon is strong in her.' He stepped aside, inviting Nikolaus in. Friedrich remained in the cold, closing the door quietly behind him. A part of Nikolaus wished he too could have remained without. His breath misted before his face, a frost sent spidery fingers through the joins in the door, but out of the wind, out of the fog, there was a warmth that smacked of vice.

Hocks of goat meat hung from metal pegs, fat glistening white in the cold. The butcher's larder was illuminated by a single candle in the hands of another of Nikolaus's brothers-in-penitence, Brüder Arnulf. The fug of roasted goat spat from the dribbling tallow was thick enough to chew, only partially clouding the stink of corruption.

The two sackclothed men positioned themselves either side of a blood-spattered wooden table. Arnulf set his burden upon a wooden shelf that ran along the rear wall. Its light caught off an array of bladed implements pegged to that wall, from knives and skewers, to huge serrated bone saws.

Nikolaus moved to the table. A woman lay upon it. She had been stripped bare, pale flesh dimpled, breath steaming in short sharpened bursts as she writhed on her bloody pallet.

'Hold her.'

The men did so, each taking an arm. A shudder passed through her body. Every part of her shook. Watching her, Nikolaus felt a knot tighten in his throat. Even now, his own body would seek to tempt him. But then flesh would ever be desirous of flesh. That flesh would be opened this night. Sin would run in rivers.

'She is fresh returned from the City of the Damned,' said Arnulf. One side of his face was gone; burned muscle, bone and crumbling tissue all that remained. It was that face he presented as he spoke, rightly proud in the purity of his disfigurement. 'Those who brought her attest she stepped on something. A shard of the wyrdstone, they say.'

Nikolaus reached out his one hand. His fingers hovered over her belly, pure white, prickled with goose bumps and yet moistened by fever. Even without touching, her skin flexed from the nearness of his hand. He worked his dry mouth and forced his hand down to the woman's foot. It was black, cracks parting the cold hard skin to reveal pink tissue that shed no blood. With blunt fingers, he prodded the dead flesh, tracing upward to where the blight extended its roots into the living leg. The woman gasped, but failed otherwise to react, as his thumbnail scored a mark above her knee.

Stepping around the table, Nikolaus selected the bone saw from the row of implements and then returned, candlelight tinting the serrated blade red. He looked down on the poor creature, the pity he felt all the greater for the lust she so sinfully induced in his own heart.

'Your leg offends you, schwester. With Sigmar's blessing, may the Dark Gods keep it.'

Felix subjected Gotrek to an angry glare as the dwarf stamped down two steins of flat, insipid moonshine onto the table between them.

'I'm not about to sit here and drink with Rudi due to be burned alive in the morning.'

'Do you know how hard it was to find this, manling? What kind of holy war do these men hope to wage without proper ale?'

Felix sniffed at the contents of the pewter stein. It was pungently acidic and looked to be stripping the lead from the inside of the vessel. 'I hope you didn't pay too much.'

Gotrek planted himself onto the stool opposite and took up his own mug in one meaty fist. He gulped down a mouthful, winced, then took another before setting it back down. 'After convincing our host that I wasn't set on turning him in for peddling drunkenness, I may have gone on to suggest that a dwarfish patron might be good for his custom. He may also have been brought round to the idea that it'd be handy if those from that pansy timber deathtrap they call a cathedral should drop by.' He patted his axe where it rested against the side of their table and leered. 'We can only hope.'

'So you took advantage of a man's faith to get a free drink?'

Gotrek chuckled and rapped his stein off Felix's. 'Two drinks, manling.'

Felix snorted and sat back, leaving his drink untouched. 'You know what, I don't care. I've read the Unfinished Book, you know. The temple at Altdorf University had a copy made of that which was lost in the great fire that destroyed Nuln Cathedral. I hate to imagine what Sigmar would make of what these people are doing in his name.'

'They're all of them fools if you ask me,' said Gotrek, wiping sop from his beard on the back of his hand. 'Sigmar was a great man, aye, well deserving of godhood off the back of his deeds. But do you see any dwarf falling over themselves to appease men on account of one man's valour?'

Felix scowled and pushed his drink away and, ignoring the glug of Gotrek noisily disposing of his, looked around the dank cellar of the mercenary flophouse that Gotrek had dragged them too. Grey light wormed in through narrow slit windows just below the rafters with the rumble of handcarts and hymns. Through the greasy panes, he could see the feet of the mercenaries who favoured fresh air on their faces to questionable ale in their bellies. Felix considered the preference eminently the more sensible.

The illicit drinking hall, for such it clearly was however much the wooden hammer set above the bar tried to make it appear to be the landlord's private shrine, bustled with a subdued murmur. A dozen tightly packed tables played host to sodden mercenaries. There was tension in the drinkers' faces, hands playing restive over unsheathed weapons. There was no relaxation to be found in Sigmarshafen, not for men who flouted the commandments of Konrad's *moralpolizei*.

Felix watched as the house's proprietor, a grey bear of a man called Theis, wound between the tables towards them. He was as tall as Felix and far better endowed in poundage, both in muscle and in fat. He stooped under the ceiling beams and hovered by their table, wringing his brawny fists, hammer and comet talismans jangling about his thick neck.

'Is all to your liking, masters?'

Gotrek grunted and made a grab for Felix's unwanted drink. 'Barely, barkeep. Barely. We're scarce three days march from the last dwarf post on the Kadrin road. Is there no dwarf ale to be found in this sorry place?'

'Forgive us, master dwarf, but there's little as gets by Konrad's men.' He gestured at the sullen patrons with a wave of one hairy hand. 'You get used to it when there's naught else to be had.'

'More ale then, barkeep. The sooner I'm too drunk to taste this swill the better.'

Theis bowed and turned to Felix. 'I'll bring over some honey for that eye, my lord.'

Felix crossed his arms, his expression sour, and waited for Theis to leave. As soon as he was gone, he lifted his fingers to his black eye and winced.

'Stop poking at it, manling. You'll only make it worse.'

Felix considered keeping his mouth shut but when it came to feats of sullenness Gotrek was unrivalled. 'Don't talk to me about my eye, Gotrek. I still can't believe you let them take Rudi without a fight. They're going to burn him alive, for pity's sake.'

'You're always lecturing me on tact, manling. Did you want me to kill them all? The priest too, maybe? What of every other man and child in that square?'

'Gramm was hanging on your every word. He would have let Rudi go if you'd asked it.'

Gotrek shook his head grimly. 'I'm no expert, but that horse-loving fanatic is clearly the one taking the decisions now that the baron's from the picture and minds like his aren't for swaying. And you forget the most important point, manling. The beardling did betray his oath of fealty.'

'And what of the oath he swore to us?' said Felix, thumping his fist into the table. 'He vowed to help us track the Beast.'

'And he's fulfilled that part of his bargain ably.' Gotrek pointed to the south wall of the cellar, beyond which, over fog-haunted downs, the City of the Damned lay in wait. 'We know now where it lurks. And even had he not, his oath to his lord was made first.'

Felix pinched his temples and slumped back into his chair. He could forget sometimes how alien Gotrek was. The Slayer looked like a man, but he was not one. There could be no sympathy for oathbreakers.

'It our fault he's here at all. And in any case, this isn't Karaz-a-Karak or wherever. This is the Empire.' He stared glumly toward a particularly joyless group of pale-faced men with the appearance of Middenlanders. 'Nobody *chooses* to serve in their lord's militia.'

'I've said it before, manling and I'll say it again. Yours are an odd folk.'

'I'm getting him out, Gotrek. With your help or without.' Slowly and with feeling, he ground his fist into his open palm. 'And if I have to go through that swine, Seitz, then so much the better.'

'That's unlike you, manling.'

'Maybe it's something in the ale.'

'The way you sniff at it? Hah!' Gotrek chuckled gruffly, myriad piercings jangling. 'More likely some honest dwarfen stubbornness has rubbed off on you at last. Well fine. If he agrees to join us and find himself an honourable end in the damned city, then I'll help you.'

'Thank you, Gotrek.' He wanted to say more, but could not think of the words to use that Gotrek would not consider sentimental or... human. So he said nothing.

'Eat something first, why don't you. And get some rest. You've hardly slept since the day before yesterday. Some admirable dwarfishness may have rubbed off onto you, but I doubt you've yet acquired the stamina to carry on like that.'

Felix felt a tide of weariness rise to the Slayer's words. Had it really been so long?

As Felix's thoughts returned to the problem of his bedevilled sleep, the door to the upstairs apartments opened behind him. Cold plucked at his hackles. He heard people enter, mail rustling, boots creaking over the floorboards. He rolled the chill from his shoulders, pulled himself from his crouch, and tried to ignore them. He tapped the rim of Gotrek's stein. 'I think I will have one of those now.'

'A fine idea, meinen herr. Allow me to purchase this round.'

Felix noticed that every eye in the hall had turned his way, the air adopting a frost that had little to do with an open door. He shifted in his chair to find Caul Schlanger lounging against the plaster wall by the doorway. Like a lizard on a rock. Felix had noted previously the man's dearth of teeth, but for the first time he was struck by the perverse *order* to it. It looked as though every tooth had been deliberately pulled to leave four sets of four. As the man stood there, regarding Felix with those calculating green eyes, two more soldiers entered. They wore grey cloaks over darkened mail and quilted brigandine, their padded biceps bound with the black band of the moralpolizei. The last through closed the door behind him. Both men took position beside it, hands on hips, nonchalant enough to be unthreatening, near enough to the blades swinging from their belts to stress otherwise.

'Ale for these two.' Caul motioned to Theis, then stabbed a digit at Gotrek and Felix. 'And one for myself.' He pulled up the chair next to Felix's, twisted it back to front and slouched forward in a posture of calculated insouciance. Felix felt the skin of his right side try to pull away from his bones. He dragged his own chair to the left to make space between them.

It helped, but not much.

Theis was sweating, eyes flicking from man to man to dwarf, convinced he was being fed into a trap and desperate to figure out exactly what kind. Konrad may have been hated with a passion. But Caul Schlanger was a name to wring knots into the guts of the most hardened. 'And for your... erm... men?'

'I'd advise not,' said Caul, scratching his coarse chin as he surveyed the room with a knowing smirk. 'They are pious men. It is uncharacteristically lax of them to allow this den of iniquity to persist on their watch. I assure you I will see them thoroughly scourged later.'

'What do you want?' said Felix, his fingers reaching for the reassuring touch of his sword's dragonhead hilt. 'We know nothing about what happened to Baron von Kuber. We've already said as much to your sadistic master.'

Caul gaped in mock astonishment. 'Mein kapitän?' He cast his gaze over the warily observant crowd, their drinks left untouched in favour of weapons. 'I thought that all of Sigmarshafen appreciated the benevolent zeal of dear Konrad?' There was a low grumble of assent from the seated mercenaries. Not one of them dared look up from their tables to meet Caul's eye. Caul broke into a cackle with an ironic shake of the head. 'So cruel a world. That the virtuous Konrad should make liars of an entire town.'

Felix ground his teeth. There was something about these sanctimonious prigs that he just wanted to throttle some common human decency into. 'If you have a point to make, Herr Schlanger, I would suggest you make it. My companion and I have little patience for barroom bullies.'

Caul's green eyes glittered with malice, all pretence at friendship bleeding back into his angular face.

'Steady now, Herr Jaeger. Let's not say something we might later regret.'

Felix froze. He was, technically, still a wanted man in Altdorf for his role in the Window Tax Riots, but at no point had he mentioned his, or Gotrek's, name. He found it hard to believe that word of his petty infamy could have made it out to the provinces and to men who, quite plainly, had larger problems to contend with. Caul's smile was etched in copper, Felix holding his gaze through a charged silence as Theis arrived to deposit three overflowing steins before making a hasty retreat. Caul dipped his finger in his drink and sucked it dry without any apparent distaste.

At last Felix could bear no more.

'How do you know my name?'

Caul proffered a practiced, self-deprecating shrug. 'Der Kreuzfahrer tasks to me such things as would sully the hands of one so noble. It would be remiss of me not to recognise the infamous Jaeger and Gurnisson.'

Felix leaned into the table and hissed. 'Does Konrad know?'

'Konrad does not care, so Konrad does not ask.'

'And you do?'

Caul spread his hands, all beatific innocence. 'I'm a carer.'

'Not too many of those about,' Gotrek grunted, knocking back a casual slug of ale.

Felix was still trying to hold Caul's stare but the man's regard was so unwavering that Felix began to doubt whether his eyes had lids. He hoped that he sounded less nervous than he felt as he cleared his throat. 'I'll ask again, Herr Schlanger. What do you want?'

'What is it that you want, Felix?'

'How about a straight answer?'

Caul cracked his unnervingly ordered smile.

'Just spit it out, you tiresome lizard,' said Gotrek. 'This may be the only tavern in this damnable town and I don't care to share it with you and yours.' His hand slid meaningfully for the handle of his axe that rested butt-down against the table.

'Threats are unnecessary, Herr Gurnisson. Trust me that had I wanted you harmed, I have people for that.' His eyes drifted over the subdued drinkers. 'You'd not have seen it coming.'

'Trust you?' Gotrek snorted. 'Aye, about as far as I can ram you down the necks of one of your half-starved ponies.'

Caul took a sip of his ale, eyes glittering over Gotrek's huge torso from behind his simply patterned stein. 'And how far do you think that might be? I'm almost curious to see for myself.' With a fluid smile and a reptilian intensity to his regard, Caul tugged the fingers from his left-hand riding glove one by one and set the glove down. His body flowed over the reversed back of his chair like a snake over a tree stump, his elbow striking into the tabletop. He flexed his four fingers, the middle clipped through just below the knuckle, and grinned a broken alligator smile.

'Shall we see just how strong you are, Herr Gurnisson?'

Gotrek shook with laughter. And rightly so. Caul was wiry and lean. Something in his demeanour hinted at a devilish strength, but Gotrek was... well... Gotrek.

Caul would be lucky to escape with a broken hand and a dislocated shoulder.

'I'm familiar with your escapades, Herr Gurnisson, and it's quite the tally.' Caul lifted his still begloved right hand, fingers splayed. Felix noted how the glove's middle finger there too stood flaccid and unfilled. 'Let me see. There was a daemon, a dragon, a vampire...' He lowered his fingers one by one as he reeled off a list of Gotrek's unsuccessful attempts at atonement. Felix felt bewilderment grow. How had this man come to learn so much?

'Have I missed any?'

'Aye, a bothersome manling or two.'

Amusement gleamed from the man's fiendishly arranged teeth. 'And you think that this prepares you for the City of the Damned? Come Slayer, show me what you have, or do you fear that I'll embarrass you in front of your *dwarf-friend*?'

Gotrek gave Caul a cursory once over, sitting back and crossing his arms behind his neck, tensing his biceps and pulling his enormous tattooed chest wide. The mountain of sheer physical power should have had a sane man quailing. Caul was obviously not that. His arm see-sawed like a cobra, eyes set unblinking onto Gotrek's one as the Slayer slowly unfolded his arms. He held them over the table before him, each massive as a prize stallion's stifle.

'Which one do you want?'

Caul laughed, the mirth as hollow as everything about him. 'You favour right. I favour left. Would left not seem fair, considering?'

Gotrek smoothed the smirk from his lips with his right hand, planting his left onto the table opposing Caul's. A tremor passed through the tabletop, ripples lapping the edges of Felix's stein. Man and dwarf clasped, Gotrek's giant ham enveloping Caul's hand entirely. Caul winced as Gotrek squeezed, a flash of pain too genuine to be smothered at once.

Felix dragged his chair back from the contest and smiled.

Was Caul Schlanger really about to try and best Gotrek in an arm-wrestle? A subdued ripple of excitement passed through the room with a scraping of stools being turned in Felix's direction. The mercenaries sensed a humiliation in the offing and were even more intent on savouring it than Felix.

Gotrek grinned, tightened his grip a little further. 'Just scream when you want to yield. You'll not be the first reptile squashed in this hand.'

'There's a question that's always bothered me,' Caul hissed, suppressing the obvious pain like a true penitent. 'With all the horrors you've faced, the monsters you've slain…' A smile slithered from his lips and he leaned in close enough for each to share the other's breath. 'How did it feel losing your eye to a goblin?'

Felix tensed, fingers gripped to the tabletop in case Gotrek should snatch it from under him. The dwarf's expression was set rigid but, as Felix watched, the tendons running his forearm pulled taut like cables. The clasped hands trembled ever so slightly under the pressure.

'When I win, you'll sod off and not bother me again.'

'Agreed,' Caul hissed, taking it like a martyr. 'And if I win, you'll listen to my offer.'

'I'd demand something more grand, were I you. All the gold

of the Everpeak, perhaps? Or the heart of a daemon prince?'

Caul snarled and threw his strength against Gotrek's fist. It did not budge. Caul groaned, hunching underneath to put his weight into it.

'Started yet?'

'Don't mock me, dwarf.' Caul jerked on his seat, the table rattling as something struck it from beneath and between Gotrek's legs.

Felix started back, hands up off the table. 'You cheated!'

'Sturdy,' Caul observed with a wink. Gotrek had not flinched.

'The one thing you should know about a dwarf's stones,' said Gotrek, forcing Caul's hand to within a whisker of the tabletop, 'is that they're like stones.'

A spontaneous cheer swelled from the gathered mercenaries as, with a casual flick, Gotrek slammed Caul's hand into the tabletop. Gotrek shoved the man off the table and sat back with a grunt of disappointment. 'Leave your ale as you go. Fair recompense for such a pointless challenge.'

Caul reclaimed his hand stiffly. He massaged colour back into his fingers, then smiled coldly, as though pain were the preserve of others. 'A powerful arm you have there, Herr Gurnisson. You're as strong as I'd heard.'

Gotrek was already pulling over Caul's stein and draining its contents into his own.

'I'm in need of strong hands. The fewer the better, and I feel that you two are worth more than one man apiece. I want you two to come with me, to help rescue Baron von Kuber from the City of the Damned.

'I couldn't give a grobi turd for your lord,' said Gotrek without looking up. 'It's the Beast my axe thirsts after.'

'I know a thing or two about *need*, Slayer. I understand compulsion. That void in your belly that can't ever be filled. The daggers in your mind that keep you awake at night and make food taste bitter.'

Gotrek glanced up. He raised the stein of discoloured ale. 'Your food was already bitter.'

'Let me tell you a tale…' Caul's four fingers grated his pale stubble. 'Of a board-hewer's son from the woodsman's vorstadt of Talabheim. An old widow lived on the outskirts there; a hideous hag, blind, cruel to the ways of small boys, scraping a living selling idolatrous little effigies of Taal and Rhya that she made from feathers and dead twigs. One night, when this child was nine, he awakens to the dead of night. Outside it is dark, but in his heart there is a fire. He hears a voice.' Caul directed a finger like a pistol to his temple. 'In here. Sigmar had chosen him, chosen him for something great. He told him to rise from his bed, to take his father's lantern, to douse the woman's home in oil – and watch the old hag burn.'

Felix shook his head in disgust.

'Does faith shock you?' said Caul

'No. Faith doesn't.'

'Götz lives. We all feel it. And Sigmar wants his champion returned.'

Gotrek snorted into his purloined stein. 'Well Sigmar can't have him.'

A collective gasp went up from the mercenaries. Caul glanced up, on some indiscernible level approving.

'Forgive my companion,' said Felix. 'I believe what he is trying to say is that we would both feel safer without your blade at our backs.'

'Aye, sod off.'

'That's as maybe,' said Caul. 'But Konrad is not about to just let you leave. He remains convinced of your collusion with the Beast.'

With a shrug, Gotrek stuck a thumb under his eye patch and proceeded to scratch around the hollow socket beneath. It was a habit that could, and knowing Gotrek likely was, have been contrived to disturb.

'He's welcome to try and stop me.'

'*Kinderkreuzfahrer*, they call him,' said Caul, a narrow smile of some cruel reminiscence. 'He hates that, but it's meant as the highest compliment. Konrad is the mirror of von Kuber in so many ways. There's few can best either man with a sword, perhaps only Reiksmarshal Helborg himself.'

'All the better then,' Gotrek replied, reaffixing his eye patch with a chuckle.

'Meritorious men with a powerful vision and a point to prove are ever the most dangerous. Konrad dreams of holy war, shedding the blood of the impious to nurture the soil of a commonwealth of faith.'

'And what do you dream, Herr Schlanger?' asked Felix.

Caul fell silent. He regarded Felix strangely. 'My dreams are of black walls and ruin, of a white lady marshalling a host of the unquiet damned. I dream of a lord of shadow, a dark master behind the blasted gates.'

Felix felt a creeping unease, as though a wraith had passed through him. He had posed the question largely out of pique; he had not expected an honest answer. And certainly not *that* answer.

Caul Schlanger described his own recurring nightmare.

The moment was lost on Caul. His head cocked as he turned to Gotrek. 'And what passes through the minds of dishonoured dwarfs when they close their eyes?' Gotrek growled, but Caul ignored the threat. 'They say you can't die in dreams. Does that trouble you, Slayer? That there is to be no end to your disgrace, in waking or in sleep?'

Bestial fury raged from the Slayer's throat. He rose, snatching up both his sturdy wooden chair and his axe in one moment of fearsome wrath that brought a frightened murmur to the mercenaries sat watching. 'I'd advise you leave while you still have legs to run,' Gotrek spat, cheeks reddening with fury.

Felix spilled from his chair, Karaghul ripping free of its sheath as he circled the table to put its bulk between him and Schlanger's men.

Ignoring Felix and the mercenaries who muttered threateningly but made no move, Caul climbed slowly from his seat, leaning over the table to meet Gotrek eye to eye. 'Come with me, Slayer. I'll promise you a doom beyond imagining.'

Axe and chair both gripped above his orange crest, Gotrek looked thoughtful. Felix could tell that part of him was sorely tempted, only for stubbornness and a murderous dislike to hijack his tongue. He lowered his weapons. 'It could be the mightiest of ends since Grimnir's, but being led to it by a snake like you would render it worthless. A bet's a bet, now be off, lest I break both legs and toss you out.'

For a moment Caul remained motionless, then eased back from the table. 'Come and find me when you change your mind.'

'Don't hold your breath.'

Caul sketched an empty smile, then turned to his waiting men with a nod. The door that closed behind their departing backs was met with roars of triumph, the seated mercenaries surging from their tables to slap Gotrek's shoulders and demand the honour of his next drink. Theis beamed from the corner, already summing the night's takings. Gotrek accepted the adulation with a stony-faced stoicism, ignoring the buffeting as he set about downing Caul's stein.

Felix rubbed his eyes wearily. All he wanted now was to sleep. It was probably time to raise the issue of lodgings with Theis. He could not help but stare after the closed door, nor fail to notice the knot of Middenlanders looking the same way, their severe expressions worn amidst the revelry like swords to a Shallyan festival. It disturbed him how much the man had known about Gotrek and himself. And it worried him what he had said about having people that would kill on his behalf.

Suddenly, a bunk in the common dormitories no longer appealed.

'The infamous Jaeger and Gurnisson. That was what he said. Have you ever heard the like?'

'I'd think not, manling. That poem of yours'll be titled Gurnisson and Jaeger.' Gotrek set down his tankard and summoned more, glaring at Felix across the emptied cup. 'If you know what's best for you.'

Mannslieb gleamed like a silver coin in the night sky. Tendrils of darkness shredded past it as fog, a wash of whispering disquiet was drawn from the City of the Damned like a tide.

With a dreadful, patient menace it inched over the unliving wastes, inhuman will driving it implacably onto the hills and the walls of Sigmarshafen. The old timbers groaned under the pressure of insubstantial bodies, men crying out from the guard towers as fires were suddenly extinguished. The mist swelled higher, the palisade creaking like old bones on a winter's night as the fog neared its summit.

And then, silently, its capitulation always inevitable, the barrier yielded. Fog spilled over and into the deserted streets.

Or near deserted.

Stripped to his woollen undershirt and breeches, Rudi shivered, cold, terrified, as mist, frozen and yet somehow still vaporous, streamed through the bars of the wooden pen. Moans rang empty through the fog that threatened to bury the township alive, a war cry for this hollow incursion. The voices came from nothing living; devoid of hate, of anger, of anything but pain and the tenebrous need to see that pain shared. Rudi held his breath for as long as he could, maddened by the thought of what spectral horror might be intaken on a lungful of that fog. Crawling backward over the bodies of his fellow prisoners, he pressed his back to the palisade. A scratching, as of many sets of fingernails, came from the other side. He tried to convince himself that it was just the timbers breathing, being rattled with pebbles from the wind.

But he was a man of Ostermark, and he knew better.

The fog was beginning to pool around his ankles, vapour colder than ice trickling over the waistline of his breeches and into his underclothes. He held himself tighter. Trapped in here, with what the gaolers dismissed as the brain-dead, or the mindless, it was easy to expect the worst.

His fellow condemned muttered and moaned, tugging absently at their hair, gazing into nothing as they cupped their hands into the mist to hear its somnolent whispers before it streamed through their fingers. Rudi's skin crawled from the nearness of them.

The brain-dead.

The mindless.

There were horned heads, bloated bodies, flanged necks and forked tongues. Every foul deformity the human body could suffer and still loosely be called human was here, and yet somehow nothing to compare with the blank eyes that stared through the back of his skull with a vestigial, wholly forgotten, hate. Mercenaries often chanced upon these listless mutants, weapons dragged clattering over the cobbles to stumble into their captors' arms. They were a prize more valuable than a mercenary's wage, more valuable even than the occasional unearthed artefact or sliver of wyrdstone. The clergy of Sigmarshafen paid well for the execution of Sigmar's will. And those who dispensed justice in their god's name knew only one punishment

The fire.

The thought of what waited for him tomorrow was a cold weight in his belly. He wanted to be sick, but his stomach was empty, and his chest ached from retching. Part of him wanted to believe that this could not happen, that Felix would not let it, but the world did not work that way. He had been forced to watch as his mother burned, had smelled it, had heard her screams. Out of nothing, his body was wracked with sobs. He brought them under control with a shuddering of his sore ribs.

Rudi tried not to dwell on it, but he could not resist the groundswell of bitterness that briefly threatened to pollute his terror. Whatever corruption was at work on the mindless had set its claws too upon the men of Sigmarshafen. His pen had remained locked for barely an hour at a time, Rudi watching on in disgust as girls of various levels of deviancy were dragged, mumbling and insensible, from the enclosure and into the straw bales of the nearby stable.

Mutation, it seemed, was never far from the surface.

Somehow the rumour had spread that bedding a mutant could lessen its symptoms. The gaolers – attending a steady stream of mercenaries and soldiers confessing to rashes, sores, suspicious lumps and agues that they dared not bring before a priest – had fast become wealthier and more reviled even than the black bands of the moralpolizei.

The mutants' madness still seemed like bliss to Rudi.

Trembling, he peered between the bars of his cage. He could just make out the street, the wooden houses across the road were huddled close, sagging roofs making them hunched. The streets were empty. Even the grasping gaolers had abandoned the night-time streets to the Damned.

The thought of escape never occurred.

Even if he could shatter the tough pine of his cage with his bare hands, it would only put him out there, with whatever undying horrors it was that haunted the streets of Sigmarshafen. And that was a fate more terrifying than all but the most sadistic of witch-finders could devise.

On the pyre at least, his suffering would end.

Felix lay awake, eyes wide, staring at the ceiling of the attic room that Gotrek had won for them in an ill-advised drinking bout with, it had seemed, half the mercenaries of Sigmar-shafen. Rhythmic snores arose from the next bunk, the entire pallet bent like a hammock under Gotrek's squat mass. Felix fought the urge to get up, stumble again around the dark little table to the square of pallid light, and confirm *again* that nothing was there. It was fortunate that the dwarf had stumbled into the bed nearest to the window. Had he been lying closer, he doubted he could have resisted the compulsion.

It was bad enough that the creeping unease that crawled like spiders under his skin meant that he now sought sleep in a pinching night vest of ringed steel. The bed groaned as he shifted, the weight of his mail causing the mattress to close around him. The slant of the ceiling brought it to the wall above Felix's pallet close enough for him to taste the pine. The whorls in the wood made faces in the silver light that penetrated the fog, disturbing grotesques of nightmare and pain. It was disconcertingly like being interred within his own coffin.

The window rattled.

Moans of anguish ghosted past the sill, dark spirits circling the inn, seeking him out, drawn close by his warm and beating heart.

Directly under the beam of sombre light from the window, the white linen tablecloth rippled gently. The breeze kissed Felix's cheek with cold dead lips. He drew his sheets close, wrapped himself in his cloak, and shivered. It was nothing, he commanded himself. Just an over-tired imagination filled to bursting with black tales of the haunted moors. A draught seeped through the join around the window pane. If the wind could get though then perhaps the ghosts on the fog could too! Cold air whined through the cracked fitting. It brought voices, pleas whispered in his ears. They wanted him to help them, to save them.

They wanted him to join them.

'Don't be a fool, Felix,' he murmured, desperately in need of hearing his own voice spoken aloud, but the entreaties would not stop.

Maybe he was asleep after all.

The voices, the mist; it was all so like the nightmares he had suffered since venturing onto the Ostermark Moors that he could well believe it. Only the bone-ache weighing him into his mattress offered the clue that this was real.

A floorboard creaked from the landing. His head rolled over his pillow to face the door, shadows shifting over the sole plate, a groaning pressure against the door frame. Lying still, he fumbled under his bunk for Karaghul.

He could not find it.

Felix's blood ran cold.

They were inside.

CHAPTER 6

Change

Felix fell out of bed, still groping after his sword as the door crashed inward and man-like shapes piled through. Naked swords and mail vests rippled silver in Mannslieb's diffracted glow.

A sword swept down for where Felix lay prone and, without pause for thought, Felix grabbed the nearest thing to a weapon that he had to hand. His pillow met the blade's arc with an eruption of gossamer-white down. He rolled clear as the blade bit deep into the boards where he had just been. His very human attacker released his sword to hack up a lungful of feathers. Felix reversed his roll, knocking his choking foe's sword beneath his body. He kicked up into the feather snow, burying his boot in the man's groin and crashing him into the wall where he folded with a whimper.

Rolling from the captured blade, Felix claimed it with two welcoming hands and came up into a crouch. A large man, black beard stark against the drifting down, came bellowing through the door. There was not time to stand. He slashed upward just in time to batter aside the sword thrust for his neck. Vibrations rang through his sword and into his shoulder. Loosening his buzzing fingers, he stamped his heel into the man's toes, forcing him back with a curse. A third man was already charging, sword held high. Trapped on hands and knees, Felix scrambled back, gasping in pain as the back of his head cracked off the underside of the dark wood table. He yelped, yanked his foot clear just as the swordsman skewered the floor with a good six inches of quivering steel.

Confused screams sounded from the bunkroom below. How Felix suddenly wished he had been down there now.

Felix kicked at the swordsman's hand, but his foot rebounded off a steel guard. The man twisted away from the blow but held his grip on his stuck blade, violently levering it through the floorboards. Felix aimed another kick, only to spot two more men fanning out from the doorway to join the two he already had to contend with.

'Gotrek!' he yelled. 'Wake up and help me!'

The dwarf still slumbered, his drunken snores still louder than the shouts beginning to diffuse through the thin walls of the flophouse.

The swordsman finally got the better of his weapon, wrenching the sword free in a spray of pale splinters. He drove in with a snarl. Felix saw the moonlight strike off the cold edge, felt it cut the air between his legs as he reached back beneath the underside of the table and hauled himself under. On burning fingertips, Felix pulled himself out the other side, up onto his feet, then planted a solid kick through the table's side to send it crashing over. The four men stumbled back, empty plates, steins, and gnawed chicken bones clattering over the wooden floor.

Gotrek shook his head blearily, still half-asleep. 'Again, manling? The pisspot's by the window.'

The big black beard, the leader of the group, vaulted the

upturned table with a wild slash. Felix dodged, footwork instinctual, parrying the man's follow up with a *durchlauffen* that a tragically misspent youth had ingrained so deeply into his muscles that he was scarcely conscious of his own actions. He just did it, edged the oncoming sword aside on the flat of his own, and then felled the man. An elbow crunched through his attacker's nose, an instant of violent impact that owed little to any fencing master of Altdorf.

Two others advanced around the table's near side, warily and together. The last edged towards Gotrek's bunk.

'Gotrek!'

The dwarf snapped awake, looking about in confusion. His one eye opened wide as a long blade stabbed for his chest and, with a speed of reflex of which Felix could only dream, Gotrek threw an arm into its path. An instant too soon and Gotrek would have lost a hand, a fraction too late and he would have been impaled through the heart, but his timing was perfect. The sword struck the muscular inside of his forearm, batting it clear over his body. The blade struck the ceiling, the sharp angle driving its tip up and its unfortunate wielder down. The luckless thug slammed face first into Gotrek's chest.

Gotrek took the man's head between both hands and gave a violent twist, vertebrae coming apart with an unforgiving snap. Gotrek threw the limp corpse to the floor, spilling a tirade of slurred oaths with a ham-fisted struggle at escaping the grip of his sunken pallet.

Felix swore, parrying a fierce effort that left his knuckles ringing and spun from the inexpert follow-through that grazed the mail beneath his cloak. He came about on the second and final swordsman, the man's attention straying as Gotrek finally staggered from his bed. Felix took full advantage, running him through from back to belly. The man coughed blood as Felix withdrew his sword from his guts, tottering for a moment until Gotrek finished the job. The Slayer smashed a chair over his head, driving him to the ground under a rough cairn of bloody kindling.

Felix angled his sword into a guard, but the last man standing had lost his stomach for the fight. He backed away, then turned to flee, another man soon hobbling after, bruised manhood cupped in one hand and leaving a trail of blood-spattered feathers. Felix let them go. He was too tired to even contemplate giving chase just now.

'Can a dwarf not even get an honest night's kip in this town, manling?'

Gotrek stomped around the table. The black beard lay amongst the detritus of the evening's meal, draped between a pair of jutting pine legs. Blood splatted his broken nose and struck through his thick beard. He groaned at the sight of Gotrek bearing down and tried to squirm away. He pulled up with a gasp. The fall had broken something more than just his nose. Gotrek prodded the injured man in the ribs, swaying only slightly.

'What's the idea, eh? Looking to off a Slayer in his sleep?'

When the man offered no answer, Gotrek poked him again, harder this time, then thumped him in the ribs when that too failed to illicit a response. The man choked on his scream. Gotrek raised his fist for another blow.

'Wait,' Felix blurted. He did not blame Gotrek his anger. To be killed without a fight was the gravest end for a Slayer else Gotrek would by his own hand have erased his shame long ago, but answers would probably be easier to extract if the one man that had them was not first beaten to a pulp.

'Give me one good reason?' Gotrek returned.

'I'd like to know who sent him.'

'It was that wretch of a captain, or I'm an elf,' Gotrek growled, immediately slapping his hand to his forehead and covering his eye. He groaned.

Shifting nervously, Felix kept his sword on the beaten

soldier, splitting his attention between him and the hungover Slayer. 'Are you all right?'

'What's that barkeep brewing down there?' There was an uncharacteristic quaver in his voice. He slid his eye patch across his pug nose to cover the bloodshot eye. He grinned as he slumped back onto the bed. 'Much better. Bit of air, manling. That's all this dwarf needs. Finish the man already and let's be off.'

Felix coughed. This probably was not how the baron's witch-finders did it. 'Er…' He nudged the man with his boot. 'Well then? Did Konrad send you?'

The man bent his grimace into a smirk. 'Sigmar guides me.'

Gotrek snorted and almost fell off the bed. 'You heard him, manling. It was Sigmar. Where should we start looking?'

Felix ignored his companion's sarcasm and crouched beside the wounded man. It was difficult to be certain in the grim light, but he looked familiar. 'Torsten,' he breathed as recollection struck. 'Konrad's man.'

Torsten tried to pull himself up, but could not, collapsing further against the underside of the table. 'We should have killed you both out on the moors. No one would have known any better.'

Felix gave a rueful smile. 'Nor cared, I would imagine.'

The man snarled. He probably thought Felix mocked him deliberately. 'Gramm would never have tried you for what you did. Ha! Much less punish you. Not his precious *dwarf-friend*. He forgets that Sigmar was a warrior.'

'Shallya's mercy, how many times must I say we had nothing to do with what happened to von Kuber.'

'Hide behind your feeble goddess, pagan. She'll not raise a hammer to defend the lands of men.'

Felix rose, pressing his fingers to his temple. 'Spare me these lunatics.'

'We'll get nothing from him, manling,' said Gotrek,

somehow willowing upright and scraping his axe from its night berth beneath his bunk. He nodded in the direction of the door. It sounded as though the whole tavern had woken. Only the half-felt horrors that possessed the streets outside kept doors locked and windows barred. 'I give this backstabber a half-hour to bleed out. Let's leave these droppings to Gazul and be off. We can be at this damned city of theirs before sunrise.'

'But Gotrek, you've heard what they say about that place. Should we not at least wait for morning? And what of Konrad? I want to give that man something to think about!'

'Bah! To hell with him. If he wants to be king of this scrap of filth then good riddance, but there's a monster I long to bleed and I'll not have that bloody-minded wazzock keep me from a worthy doom.'

Felix turned to the window. The glass was etched with frost despite the earliness of the season. As he watched, the window suddenly turned to black; a transient blur of shadow, then gone. Felix started back, heart yammering. His stare held but nothing returned. He blinked hard, afraid to keep his eyes closed a moment longer than he had to.

Nothing.

'Are you sure that's wise?' Felix didn't turn from the frosted pane.

'Ha! Don't tell me you're afraid of a puff of wind? Come. Let's find your pet wastrel and be on our way.'

The street was empty, the whole township interred in mist.

Felix tightened his grip on his sword and edged along the pine wall. The wooden tenement across the street seemed to have grown in the gloom, inflated by the shadows gathered under its eaves and its doubly barred doorways. There was not a flicker of candlelight to betray a living soul. He listened out for any hint of a nightwatchman, but there was nothing,

nothing but the wind that whispered through his ears like the laments of the damned.

'A fine night to off somebody on the quiet,' grumbled Gotrek. 'So much for honour.'

Felix nodded silent agreement. Even with the racket that he and Gotrek had made and with two, maybe now three, dead bodies bleeding through to the bunkroom on the floor below, nobody had dared unlock their doors to investigate.

'There must be somebody manning the guard towers,' said Felix.

'A firkin of Bugman's says they're safe abed, cowering under a fleece like lambs.'

Felix eyed the tumultuous shapes ripped into the fog by the wind. By day it had been possible to dismiss his imaginings as no more than that. But by night? He saw faces contorted into screams, men consumed by flames, shapeless figures fleeing from who knew what, clashing together into clear bursts of black sky and stygian moans. He recalled Caul's warnings; of how restless shades marched on Sigmarshafen each night.

The knowledge only added a deeper shade to his fears. For nobody had yet been able to tell him what, exactly, dwelt within the City of the Damned.

Gotrek ran down the lane, axe gripped tight between eager hands. Felix wondered what Gotrek intended to strike with it. Could the *things* that haunted the fog even be slain? The vivid crest, flattened where Gotrek had been lying on it and moonlight-bleached an eerie grey, disappeared into the fog-drenched street. Felix took a deep breath, planted a kiss and a prayer onto his own blade, and raced off in pursuit.

The street led downhill, a short run to the Kirchplatz. The cathedral loomed like a giant, murkily haloed under a clouded moon. The market stalls were empty, carcasses of picked wooden bones and drab skin, a pile of wood massed between them in the middle of the square.

Something within it moved.

Felix cried out with a sudden terror. Faceless black shades hung from stakes of cindered wood. Flames consumed them, flickering at the edge of sight, burning silver and black. The wraiths' mouths hung open but the screams, when they came, sounded from all around. Confined forever within the square, the fog shivered with undying agony. Felix bit his tongue, tasting blood.

The cries came from the fog itself. What tortured souls were these?

His heart struck once, hard enough to break ribs.

The figures were gone. Nothing but mist coiled around blackened stakes.

He wanted to ask if Gotrek had seen them too, but the dwarf had not paused and Felix hurried after him. They fled the Kirchplatz at a run, a deathless tremor echoing between Felix's ears. The street stretched down into pitiless fog, the tenements to either side just dark suggestions in the murk.

'Come, manling,' Gotrek hissed, clutching his axe like grim death, staring anxiously into the whiteout. It disturbed Felix to see him so rattled. Maybe it was too much ale, but nothing sickened a dwarf like undeath. Gotrek shrugged his massive shoulders and lumbered through the tendrils of mist. 'Not far to the gate.'

The buildings slipped silently by on both sides. Faces appeared in windows that turned out to be boarded shut. Cries for mercy rang out over shingled rooftops. Gotrek barrelled under the awning of a potter's workshop and into the jumbled plaza before the gate. Bits of pottery crunched underfoot. The fog was thicker here, denser in this pit of low ground between earth and palisade. Felix could not even see the wall, though it could be no more than fifty feet away. Even the guard towers were passive shades, barely one distinct from the other although it was all too easy to orient by the excremental reek that drifted from the chattel pens beneath them. That was where they would find Rudi.

Felix froze at the sound of voices.

They were coming from the towers. Real voices.

Felix waved Gotrek to silence. He strained to listen, but it was just one more voice amongst a sussarant swell. He held still a moment longer, but it did not seem as though anybody was about to venture down from their posts. He let out a deep breath, feeling oddly reassured by the presence of soldiers nearby. It did not matter that they would probably kill him if they found him. They were something that he understood, something that his mind could deal with.

'Right,' said Felix, looking first to one tower, then to the next. 'Which do you think Rudi is in?'

'Let's not hurt ourselves thinking, manling. You take the right, I'll check the left.'

Felix nodded, but Gotrek was already disappearing into the fog. 'Right,' he murmured to himself, clutching his sword two-handed as though it might engineer its own escape. Silently he cursed Gotrek and his great hurry to die. It would hardly have added much time to their search to check the pens one after the other. He was tempted to follow after Gotrek anyway, claim he had gotten turned around in the fog, but he did not think he could take the look on the dwarf's face

Instead, he turned his back and edged toward the rightward tower. Passing feet creaked over the platform above his head, the dull murmur of frightened men believing themselves quiet. He set his hands against the pine bars and pushed. They did not give. The pen's solidity did little to calm his nerves. He tried to look inside. The slats were set too tightly to tell whether Rudi was inside or not. He moved along, palms running the smooth wooden frame until he came to a right angle and followed the turn to a gate. It was of the same pale pine as the towers and walls, but with the addition of a sturdy iron lock.

There were shapes moving about inside but it was still too dark and crowded to discern Rudi from the confusion of bodies within. Some pervasive terror kept him from calling out. Nervously, he glanced behind his back. The sense of being watched, called to even, by the wronged dead was almost too much to bear. The memory of the spirits, eternally burning each night before the cathedral, returned to him in a flash of dread. It did not matter who was inside. He would not wish that fate on any man.

He sized up the door. Karaghul would probably manage, but it was not exactly the task for which the noble blade had been intended. It would take time. Assuming his fingers did not go numb first. He cast about for something heavy with which to break the gate down.

Behind the towers, a stub of alley sank under the murmurings of the unquiet fog. Right under the shadow of the palisade, it ran from the township gate toward a stable, the pine structure ringed with a picket of sharpened stakes. The whole assembly shifted within its grey cloud, its aspect ethereal. Felix took another quick look around and, finding nothing better, ran for it, vaulting the picket and skidding to a standstill in a tiny paddock.

The stalls were dark. The horses within, chained and blinkered to keep them from bolting, whinnied in fright at what their simple minds knew to fear as well as any man. Trying to ignore the animals' terror, Felix quickly scoured the yard. There were a few lengths of chain lying loose, horseshoes, nails, and an iron drum filled with dried oats. So far so unhelpful. A passing wind made him shiver and pine for the daemon-haunted north. He was ready to give up and set to work with his sword after all when he found what he was looking for.

Propped up against the side wall of one of the stalls was a long-handled cavalry mace. Its flanged head was crusted with rust from too many misty nights and too little care, but he suspected that it could still do a job. He slammed his sword back into its sheath and hefted the mace, whistling softly in surprise at its weight, then tossed it over the picket. It impacted into the dirt alley with a flat thunk and he leapt after it, swept it up on the run and raced back into the fog.

At the tower, there was still no sign of Gotrek.

Felix studied the gate, judged the distance in his mind and aimed a phantom swing at the iron box of the lock. He drew back, glanced up to the guard platform, and prayed that no one would be committed enough to come down.

He swung.

Intended for bludgeoning armoured knights, the flanged head clove through the lock as if it were painted vellum. The gate snapped inward, chewed out strings of wood pulp spraying from where the lock had been. Felix threw down the mace, kicking in the door as it snapped at its hinges and swung back at him. He followed it through, blocking its return swing with his own body.

The first thing that struck him was the stench.

Felix had ventured through ghoul warrens and ogre butchers' tents and never encountered an odour more repellent. From outside he had received a taste, but it was only from within that he could truly appreciate it. It took a uniquely human kind of monster to inflict such inhumanity on one of his own. Breathing through his mouth and the tattered hem of his cloak, he took another step into the pen. His foot struck a body hidden under a mess of rags. He pulled it back. He could not see a damned thing.

'Rudi?' he hissed into the wool of his cloak

Something shifted in the dark. 'Felix? Felix is that you? Sigmar, I knew you'd come!'

'Yes,' Felix whispered, the single word riding a rush of relief. 'Come on, let's get you out.'

He prodded the body he had almost trodden on, but got no

reaction. It continued to mutter. The word '*Master*' cropped up once or twice but otherwise it was gibberish. For its part – its gender was impossible to discern – neither Felix nor his boot were of any interest at all.

'They can't hear,' said Rudi, still just a dark shape in the fog as he made a path through his insensate cellmates.

Anxious to be free, Rudi tried to leap the last two bodies that lay between him and the gate. He landed on a leg that turned under his foot and spilled him into Felix's arms. Felix held him until his wild breathing calmed, then helped him upright. Stripped of his padded armour, Rudi shivered terribly. Felix unclasped his cloak and draped it over the young man's shoulders. Rudi nodded his thanks, cold fingers fumbling with the clasp.

'Just until we find you something warmer,' said Felix, suddenly feeling the chill redoubled himself. 'That cloak and I have been through an awful lot together.'

Rudi's hand shook as it explored the stained and oft-darned red wool. 'H-how much?'

'More than you'd believe. And most of it really was awful.'

A sense of motion from behind made Felix spin. A shadow resolved from the fog, solidifying into a horribly familiar form.

Gotrek.

His fingers unclawed from his sword. He offered up thanks that he had looked before he had swung.

'You found him then. Good. Now close the door, manling.'

'What about these others?'

'Have you seen them? Up close?'

'They're f-from the c-city,' stammered Rudi. 'There are m-mutants on the moors, but not like these. It's like something has s-stolen their minds.'

Felix looked again. The warm-bodied creatures muttered and twitched, carelessly soiling themselves as they wandered unseeing through the whispering murk, or else simply lay where they had been put. It turned Felix's insides cold. What power could do this to a man? Strip a body of its mind? Without another word, he closed the gate, fixing his mace like a wedge between latch and broken lock to keep the wind from springing it open. Whatever fate awaited them come morning, it could hardly be worse.

Gotrek gave an ugly grin, running his thumb around the blade of his axe. 'At last! We'll find the Beast in that ruined city, I can feel it in my bladder.'

'The city?' said Rudi, his grip on sanity so loosened already by horror that he almost laughed. Or perhaps it was merely the cold that summoned a burst of fog from his chapped blue lips. 'Haven't you seen enough of what the city can do to a man?'

'Too bad,' growled Gotrek. 'You're about to see it a whole lot more. You can thank us later, although your own vengeance will have to wait its turn until after the monster has killed me.' Rudi's mouth dropped open and Gotrek filled the void with a harsh chuckle. 'If it can.'

Again, the mad laugh threatened. Rudi peeled open his cloak to reveal a hard woollen smock and breeches. 'My armour, my weapons. What in Sigmar's name do you expect me to do?'

Gotrek planted his free hand on his hip and rounded on Felix. 'This is why you never see a human Slayer. It is beyond a man to seek a doom worthy of his dishonour.'

As Gotrek spoke over him, something in Rudi's character hardened. A little of the mania settled, his dark brown eyes seeming to shade a little blacker. 'Is that why you fight to d-die, herr dwarf? Did you do s-something t-terrible too?'

Gotrek shot Rudi a poisonous glare, then stomped grumbling into the fog. Felix stared after him, struck by a sudden dread that the dwarf had left him alone.

'Did I say something wrong?' said Rudi.

'Yes,' Felix mumbled, still watching the shifting dark, not caring to try and explain.

'I'll come,' said Rudi, soft enough that Felix in his distraction did not fully catch it and the man repeated himself. 'I'll c-come,' he said, louder. 'I'll go with you to the City of the Damned, f-find my own penance there.'

'Forget penance, Rudi. Get away the first chance you get. I'll not stop you.'

'I don't see you running away.'

Felix gave a wan smile, feeling very much the tragic hero. 'I have Gotrek with me. I doubt I'd be nearly so heroic if I had any choice about it.'

Shivering, Rudi offered a blank shrug. 'Well now n-neither of us has a choice.'

More than a little taken aback by Rudi's fatalism, Felix simply nodded. There was something in this cursed night, this crying fog that buried them like earth over their own graves. It bred a defeatist streak. He just hoped that it did not afflict him too.

Three such misanthropes would be a crowd.

For once, he found himself solidly in agreement with Gotrek. The sooner they were gone from this benighted township the better.

The gates were barred and he doubted the guards would be kind enough to open them for him. He recalled from their entrance the day before that the mechanism to open them needed to be operated simultaneously from both towers as well as requiring a man on the ground to unfasten the locking bar. He tried to remember how many militiamen he had seen posted up there when he had ridden through, then cursed himself for failing to pick up that detail. He did not doubt that Gotrek could clear one on his own, but tasking himself and an unarmed waif against an indeterminate number of foes was not a proposition that appealed.

A crash of splintered wood trembled through the fog.

For an instant of horror Felix's heart refused to beat.

Was it possible that the vaporous legions of the Damned had found a way to breach the township gate? The sound of dying wood came again. And then again. Felix drew his sword, steel sweating under the pallid glow of Mannslieb. Alarmed cries filtered from the militiamen above although none looked to forsake their perch to investigate. Not that the blades of the living were prominent among Felix's concerns just now.

Felix stepped in front of Rudi, angling his sword into a guard. For all the good that a physical weapon might do.

'Get a move on, manling.' Gotrek's voice ground through the fog. The tension eased somewhat from Felix's shoulders and he lowered his blade.

'I've found a hole.'

Tormented souls swept the wastelands, their piteous wails making a mockery of the inviolate union by which each was ensnared to countless thousands of others.

Misery shared.

Misery magnified.

Nothing living or dead could be so connected, or feel so alone.

Seen from above, Sigmarshafen was the roiling eye of a storm, a vortex of grey shadow heaving against its flimsy walls. An unseen eye probed deeper into that convulsing cloud, a payload of nightmares birthed in cold screams from the shuttered houses that passed beneath. The fog parted, like recognising like, the township gates emerging from the turbulent white. All was as it had been. So long. So unchanging. And yet…

And yet here was something new.

A fluttering heart, the sensation coming just seconds after a rush of excitement. A strange disconnect between body and spirit. Something powerful was in play, an artefact of ancient might as obvious to eyes born of the dark winds as the full face of Morrslieb in a clear sky. Visions of towers and palisades fell aside. The focus of the spirit-sight narrowed. There were shallow impressions, hollow outlines of human form. Shadows in darkness. There was a fear, a steal of intent, but they were not the source of that power. Something tremendous walked amongst them. A destiny.

Mind quested out after the seeing eye, spectral fingers outstretched to touch.

There was contact, then a roar of power, an instant of delirium, of flaring ecstasy that swiftly became pain. Red rune-light burned the inner eye to blindness. The pain grew acute. The physical suffered, the soul's conviction faltering as a wave of repulsion from an artefact of ancient power drove it and its scrying magicks back into the discorporate masses of the Damned. The mists closed. The white blinded. Further back through writhing white until, as though a barrier had been crossed, the fog was gone. The clear air shimmered with magical distortions, a haze of glittering green madness that eddied and flowed on a hot wind.

The spirit-sight rose to its body's summons.

The wall of fog receded, clinging to the broken black city walls, closing over half of the city as far west as the river that cut it north to south. The water reflected the coloured fires of Chaos like a ribbon of change. Tiny smacks bobbed on the surface. They burned in the fires of damnation. Ruined streets swept beneath, their walls tarred with weird glyphs, swarming with men and things that had once been like them. They fought and toiled and loudly beseeched the blessings of the Dark Master. Torches blazed from every corner. Reddish fire and an aura of brimstone set a garish light, shadows flickered large and uncanny over a honeycomb of sunken rooftops and crumbling towers.

This was the City of the Damned.

Further back and higher still the spirit-sight soared, the maelstrom of change swallowed whole as if by a gaping maw.

A giant amphitheatre had spread through the human streets, a bastardised crucible of rubble and bent steel where the exhortations of a thousand underwent its conversion into a cacophonous roar of hellish power.

The strength of devotion lifted the soul, like an updraft beneath a daemon's wing. Higher, higher, an acropolis rising from the tainted ruin, pure, yet indelibly the begetter of the city's fall. At its foot, the howls of daemon-engines and mutant beasts vied for dominance over the cries of the arena. Crowning the acropolis itself, partially buried under charred and blackened rock, a temple to Sigmar stood transcendent. Its roof of iridescent blue slate was chequered with soot, marble cornices throwing the ash of its host's destruction clear of the elaborate entablature and great columnar walls that remained starkly pristine.

A single tooth, perfect white in a rotten mouth.

'Morzanna!'

She resurfaced with an ecstatic shiver, gasping in enfeebling euphoria as body and soul again enmeshed. Her whole body shook with rediscovered sensation. A fading recollection carved between her shoaling thoughts. An orange-crested destroyer. An axe of iridescent power

'What is it, Morzanna? What is coming?'

Her eyes snapped open. She was smiling.

'Change.'

CHAPTER 7

Into the Mists

Her back to the defiled temple, Morzanna blinked to banish the after-visions that sailed the changing waters of her glassine eyes. A swell of disorientation made her heart flounder, carried away on the ecstatic currents of the new. Let others fret themselves to madness.

Chaos was its own reward.

Colours shifting like oil on stained glass, her eyes flickered over the tumult. The amphitheatre opened before her, gaping jaws like some hellish kraken of black earth and fired stone. Even by the harsh measures of the City of the Damned, it was an abomination of form and scale, every blackened slab and spar pillaged from the burghal graveyard that had given it life. The stands that ringed its vast interior like rowed teeth heaved to the fervour of two thousand screaming bodies. The very air that Morzanna breathed tasted warm in her mouth, heated by the vibration of so many inhuman voices. The warrior that battled halfway down that throat of oblivion was warped by distance and Chaos, tangled within a confusion of tentacled stingers and barbs. The versicoloured spawn to which the majority of those flailing appendages belonged shrieked in insanity and pain, the cries of the worshippers sinking and cresting back in time.

The entire spectacle was a symphony of devotion, conducted at the point of a blade at the behest of the Dark Master.

'Morzanna!' hissed a low, sultry voice from behind her. 'It is one thing for Golkhan to make us stand here and witness his apish prowess. It is another to play *your* games.' The speaker languished within an illusory pool of shadow, her voice describing a condescending sneer. A sorceress of little aptitude, the gods had seen fit to favour Nosta with a familiar of rare abilities, its gifts swallowing her in a thicket of darkness. Power unearned bred arrogance and Nosta was a warning from the gods on the perils of hubris.

A further six figures, eight sorcerers all, had gathered before the temple at their champion's decree. They were cloaked in black or in fabrics so choked with soot as to have had blackness foisted upon them. The shadows the daemon-glare braziers of the amphitheatre threw were long and twisted, astral beasts clawing at a starless sky, the acropolis snarling like a cornered savage before the roar of the stadium. The ashen surfaces gave off periodic flares of black lightning as the knotted weaves of warding magicks from eight untrusting sorcerers earthed into the realm of the material.

In spite of the din and her own gift for obfuscation, Nosta's impatience was as palpable as the others.

Morzanna closed her eyes, conjured the feeling of power. The sense of danger, of fear even, was as clear as if the dwarf that she had perceived were here beside her. 'An artefact of ancient power comes. The bane of the Master's kind. It is unlikely to be mere chance that brings such a weapon here, now. I sense a great destiny at play.' The tip of her tongue pricked against her barbed teeth, spiking the arresting taste of change with blood.

'It is impossible to know what it might mean.'

A bestial creature that had once been a man panted with the effort of convoking words into speech. His shovel-like paws were heavy and clodded with grime, a grubby scrap of cloak cinched painfully tight around his bloated neck. Ubek had once been a magister of the Amber College, but power and a hunger for yet more was the fullness of the man that this twisted aspect retained. Partially swamped by lank brown hair, a third eye glinted from his forehead like a rare flower. With the fickleness of Chaos, it was bone-white and blind. Patiently, Morzanna waited for him to remember how to speak. The arrogant could be ignored, trusted to engineer the conditions for their own destruction. It was the quiet that needed to be watched. Those for whom caution was the mask of calculation.

'What would the… Dark Master have… us do?'

'This changes nothing.' It was an effort not to smile, to dance for sheer, unpredictable joy. *This changes everything.* 'Preparations for the ritual are under way. The excavation of the temple nears completion. The Dark Master will rise.'

'He will rise,' the cabal murmured in unison, Ubek only a second behind.

'I have unearthed… every last hole… in our dominion,' said Ubek, flexing his begrimed paws. 'We have found… every last relic… that there is.'

'Then it is time to reach out beyond the river, and find what the Sigmarites would hide from us behind the mists.'

Of one mind, the sorcerers looked across the sprawl of devastation toward the chromatic dance of the river. A great stone viaduct, the river's sole crossing, vanished into dense fog barely halfway across. Spectrally underlit by reflected fires, shadows duelled with crumbling gargoyles, daemons of fantasy and nightmare perched amongst ruined towers. Hiding in its shadow was the last quarter of the city where the lights of Chaos did not touch. To cross the river was to court death, and only those seeking flight from the Dark Master's growing dominion braved even its banks. Morzanna traced the bank northward from the bridge to a ramshackle redoubt of corrugated rust and slime-crusted driftwood. Set against the ever-changing ruination that enclosed it, it was a veritable bastion of solidity. Her gaze lingered. Too long. By some intuitive contempt, she became aware of Ubek's knowing sneer.

Mortal memories.

Mortal weakness.

'It is im… possible.'

'Not impossible,' Morzanna whispered, consigning the settlement by the river to the past where it belonged.

'He is mad,' said Nosta, a dreamlike mockery. 'Perhaps that is why he is mad.'

'Nor is he truly… one of us.'

There was a moment's silence while Ubek recovered, invaded by an eruption of adulation from the amphitheatre. The spawn heaved, all rippling flesh and flailing tentacles, tenebrous ichor gouting from a hundred cuts. The lacerations were shallow, each one cruelly precise. An onyx claymore wielded in two mailed hands deftly severed a clutch of tentacles. They flopped to the blood-soaked ash of the arena, gyrating like headless worms only to be crushed to paste with a callous deliberateness by a black sabaton. The spawn shrieked from a dozen mouths as the champion of Chaos buried his blade into a pulsating eye-sack, spraying his ornate silver and black plate with gore.

The stands erupted.

'Golkhan!' they roared, vitreous fluids streaming over their champion's spiked vambrace. 'Golkhan!' they wept, in the throes of devotion as he flung his arms wide and thrust his gore-slickened blade into the air.

The champion turned a circle, pausing to exult before the watching mages. The hollow laughter of the dark knight extracted a grudging ripple of applause.

'Another!' The cry came resonant from the daemonic mask of his hell-steel helm. Balefire blazed across the midnight curves of his armour, leaving shadows to linger within the strange, shallow grooves that ran through the plates. They served no purpose that Morzanna could describe. But when had Chaos ever been about purpose?

'Golkhan the Anointed,' Nosta hissed. 'I hope the next one eats him alive.'

The other sorcerers silently joined her in wishing ill to the Dark Master's chosen. The so-called Anointed had risen through their tangled knot of schemes and into the Master's favour with all the indifferent prowess with which he handled a blade. Morzanna would have offered her soul to know who it was beneath that daemon mask.

Had it still been hers to give.

Ubek swallowed heavily, neck quivering with focus. 'After the ritual. What then? When the Master is… risen, and his champion… gloried, what then? Gods are fickle, as you… well know.'

Unconsciously, Morzanna's hand moved to the vestigial horns that erupted from beneath her platinum hair. She could barely now recall the slender mortal she had once been. Her skin was darkening, her hair adopting a lustrous shine. She revelled in the frenetic pace of change.

'We have all made our choices. We knew the enemies we made when we pledged ourselves to the Dark Master.'

The cabal fell into thoughtful silence as they considered that. Their souls were forfeit and, like Morzanna, they had no further to fall.

'What then of the Sigmarites?' said Nosta, tone thick and sulky. 'It is only a matter of time before they brave the mists themselves.'

'Time, indeed,' Morzanna smiled. 'All have their role to serve in the Master's rise. Already, they are caught in the rutted tracks of fate. Their destiny belongs to the Master now.'

It appeared as though Nosta would press for more when a mighty roar boomed from the hollow ring of the amphitheatre. A fat, slug-like beast snapped at its handlers, showering the arena with glowing drool as it was goaded towards Golkhan's restive blade.

Morzanna surprised herself with a laugh. It was a quite forgotten sensation, as alien as fear, lilting from her pale throat with a songbird sweetness. Nosta and the others looked to her in shock. She ignored them, the vision of the Anointed running afoul of the flame-crested dwarf and his axe staying with her like a guilty conscience.

Now there was a bout that she would gladly watch.

With a sigh, she steepled her fingers before her lips and consigned herself to watch. Golkhan's blade hummed, an overture to the coming bloodletting.

'Go, all of you. Prepare yourselves for the ritual. It is me that Golkhan seeks to impress.'

A titter of laughter dappled the shadows. 'Impress is not the word I would choose.'

Fingers dropping, Morzanna turned, her altered mouth a smile of devil teeth.

Nosta fell silent, the cabal peeling slowly away toward the scorched marble stair that lead down from the acropolis. Ubek was the last to leave. He stood panting on the top step, hunchbacked by the weight of his massive paws.

'Some things never… change, Morzanna. Some people…'

With that he left, tramping heavily around the curve of the causeway to leave Morzanna alone. Dagger teeth sparkled with amusement. Not quite alone.

And they called themselves sorcerers. Perhaps she had overestimated even Ubek.

A shadow settled over her shoulder. There was a bass growl,

a heavy tread on the old temple's marble forecourt. The creature had not come up by the steps, nor had it been lurking behind the engraved colonnades when Morzanna had arrived. She considered the rugged scarp of the acropolis, its treacherous stratum of ash.

The brute's agility never ceased to amaze.

He came no closer, repelled as much by the roar of the stadium, as Golkhan meticulously vitiated another unfeeling horror, as he was by the torches. They blazed with a light outside of colour, burning with the intensity of a hundred pliant souls. The creature's scopophobia was strangely amusing. Any one of the aspiring champions just departed would have bled the souls of thousands for a half of the mutations that corrupted its monstrous body and once brilliant mind. It would have been construed as a sign of the Dark Master's favour.

But then, as she was well reminded, Hurrlk was not truly one of them.

'You remembered? I am glad.'

It was impossible to be certain from day to day. Dealing with a creature too far gone in mind to even recognise cause and effect presented, to place it mildly, *unique* challenges. She turned, only for Hurrlk to recoil with a snarl, torn between the compulsion to retreat under the temple's shadows and to rip open the slight, platinum-haired woman that looked upon him.

For a brief moment, Morzanna feared the two were not exclusive.

Hurrlk flexed his claws and slid back, head lowered, arms spread. There was no threat that she could impose on a creature that did not fear to die, no bribe high enough for one already indentured to the Dark Master.

Ubek had been right: the gods were fickle.

Her own most of all.

'We are kindred spirits, you and I,' said Morzanna, eyeing

the bulging sack slung over Hurrlk's shoulder. 'Ubek, Nosta…' She laughed again, as if their names alone were a black joke, caught in a convenient smile as, below, Golkhan turned her way with a bleeding flourish of his dark blade. 'They've not seen the world outside. Not as it truly is, as we have. Would it shock them, do you think? Would it drive them mad?'

Hurrlk shrugged, bone-plated shoulders yielding a rich lode of confusion, of madness.

Abandoning the conversation as pointless, Morzanna gently stretched a hand toward the sack over the monster's shoulder. Hurrlk flinched, then growled. Morzanna smiled sweetly. Despite their timeless association, she did not know whether Hurrlk was unable to speak, or simply opted not to after so many unchanging years of this purgatory. But there was an amusement that rumbled from its hooded throat that belittled in a way that mere words could never muster. To him, Morzanna was nothing. Golkhan was nothing. In his solipsistic view, there *was* nothing. Still growling, Hurrlk unslung the sack and let it fall, spilling its trove of disinterred treasures at Morzanna's feet.

'The Master thanks you.'

Still Hurrlk came no closer. He agitated, shuffling back and forth as though in the grip of some terrible indecision. With a partial shake of the head, Morzanna extended an open palm. The winds of magic blew fast and hard here, the sky perverted into a cracked reflection of a smothered rainbow by the strength of the dark wind, nobler colours blackened to shaded likeness of itself, focused by the prism of the occult that was the City of the Damned.

That was this temple.

That was *under* this temple.

Hurrlk lowered his head and shuffled back, sniffing the air that began to crackle and spark between the sorceress's fingers. Deep within his hood, a scabrous tongue licked hungrily at cracked lips. The motes of green that glittered on eddies of madness began to accrete into a crystalline shard, glowing with an unnatural, internal, evil an inch above her palm. Judging the nugget's weight, Morzanna let the dark magic fold back into the aethyr. The egg-sized lump of warpstone dropped into her hand as, smiling, her fingers closed around it. Fell light seeped through her grip, like a jellyfish through a net.

She held it out, inviting Hurrlk to take it, which he eventually did, snuffling at the dark rock and issuing a low growl of pleasure. Watching him, Morzanna felt the spread of an almost affectionate glow. It was almost enough to suppress the sigh as she turned back to the open sack of soiled bones. There was a power there, a terrible latency lurking amongst unworthy kin. That the Dark Master desired the reassembly of someone, some mighty champion, seemed a reasonable deduction.

But who, and to what ultimate end, remained mysteries too deep.

'Can you feel it?' she breathed. 'Do you remember this feeling, of standing beneath the flowing sand, time moving again at last? Possibilities change even as we watch.' She returned to Hurrlk. The giant beast looked down his snout, as a rabid wolf might observe the impassioned rhetoric of a sophist. 'There comes one who will try and stop you.'

The beast shook, deep cowl echoing to the huffing sound that Morzanna had come to associate with laughter. Morzanna looked to the bridge and the fog into which it vanished. This day had been one of many pleasant surprises.

'I said he would try.'

Gotrek's axe flared a grubby red in the dark, the starmetal blade carving tormented shades from the windblown mists that harried the three over the ash-white no-man's-land. Felix followed in the runes' red afterglow. The fog was so thick, the sky so dark and void of stars, that the ruddy glow, and the bloody mien it cast onto the Slayer's torso, was Felix's only point of reference other than up or down. And even that was not nearly as certain as he would have expected. Trying to ignore the cold, the discorporate screams, Felix focused on the axe. Its light was inconstant. When the wind gentled it would dim, roaring back to a furnace brightness with its return. Other times, the fog circling like feral beasts, the axe spat, fading and flaring like a fire dying beneath a downpour.

And all the while, the dark still circled, just beyond the reach of the light.

With numb fingers, Felix crushed ice from the brow of his black eye. He twisted his neck, the crippling stiffness a punishment for walking so long with shoulders tensed against the otherworldly chill. The dead wastes of Sigmarshafen were the province of some other world, as though he walked on the silvered face of Mannslieb itself. The argent light from the greater moon shimmered across the plain of dried out pine stumps and ashen soil, alighting without touching. The emptiness was oppressive, the stillness total. Dead, brittle ground crunched underfoot. It could rain for a month and a day and not begin to quench its thirst. It was a land that had turned its back on life as Felix understood it. And this was only a taste of what was to come.

He tried not to think too much about where they were going. He cursed himself, but it was too late. No other thought dared share his mind.

They were headed to the City of the Damned.

The signing post that they had ridden by earlier that day corporealised from the clouded shadows. The city walls had been visible from here. He strained his eyes on the dark, but could not see it. It was out there somewhere. Hidden. With a tingle of dread, he convinced himself that the walls would have shifted in the night. In this fog they could be fifty paces away, lurking, waiting, hidden out there in the dark. Taking charge of his breathing, he forced himself to calm down. His lungs ached. They felt stiff, as though caked in ice. The signing post had not moved. Its solidity in the changing sweep of fog and shadow was somehow unsettling. Looking at it left him with an uneasy feeling, the curling 'M' partly overwritten with hammer carvings and sodden with condensed mist. Like there was something obvious that he was not seeing, the hidden script endeavouring to crawl into his eyes and be read.

With a shiver, he glanced back to where Rudi took up the rear, wrapped in the red cloak of Sudenland wool that Felix dearly wished he could retake for himself. The two men shared a look, teeth chattering too hard to share any more. A few paces ahead of the two men, Gotrek strode ahead. Despite his bare body, his silence was not due to the cold. The dwarf had always delighted in physical adversity, the elements a challenge no less worthy than a ghoul lord or a dragon. His aspect was one of excitement, his one eye fixed to the road ahead. It did not seem to concern Gotrek in the slightest that they walked towards a cursed ruin straight from the legends of Old Night, the lair of a monster about which they knew nothing.

Felix had faced more than his due portion of horrors. At Gotrek's side he had journeyed to the Chaos Wastes, fought a dragon, scaled the clouds aboard an iron ship and overwintered in haunted Sylvania. But there had always been a reason. Felix had never, nor would he ever, consider himself a hero, but nor had he ever shirked the call of what was right or forsaken his oath to Gotrek. Even when it seemed his life depended on it. Even when Gotrek had hinted in his stubborn dwarfish way that he could.

But this was different.

As far as Felix was aware, the Empire would not fall if they failed to track down the Beast of the Ostermark Moors. Indeed, it seemed that Konrad Seitz and the rest of the baron's fanatics were frothing at the mouth to be after it themselves. Come the first day of Kaldezeit there would probably no longer *be* a City of the Damned. But Gotrek was not to be denied a doom and, much as it pained him, Felix would follow.

Felix just wished he could be more optimistic about it. The fog leeched the spirit from his bones as, perhaps, it had from the very ground beneath his feet. An image of the mindless mutants locked in their cages back in Sigmarshafen ebbed into his mind on a cold tide. The thought of ending up that way terrified him more than anything he had faced before. More than death. Not for the first time, he wondered what madness it was that drove Gotrek after such dangers.

And did he honestly expect Felix to survive whatever it was that he found there?

Every step bringing him nearer to finding out, muscles frozen both inside and out, Felix almost surrendered to the whispers of the wind.

The City of the Damned would be Gotrek's grave.

Even if that were so, and by some miracle Felix made it back alive, how was a poet voided of mind or soul to immortalise a single line of it in verse? With a shudder of frozen shoulders, he shook off the macabre musings. It was something in the air. It had to be.

Where was this place, this long-forgotten 'M'? What had it been like? What smells had drifted from the chimneys on an autumn night such as this? What manner of people had called it home? He wondered how the City of the Damned had come to its parlous state. Was it possible that something similar could happen again? Could this one day be the fate of Altdorf, or of Middenheim or Nuln? The questions refused to stop there. He wondered if they were even still in Ostermark, or whether they had finally crossed into haunted Sylvania?

From the distance, a haze of black began slowly to condense around a jagged length of shadow. Its claws sunk into Felix's soul, a carrion crow perched over the rim of the next world.

From his back came Rudi's murmured prayer and he repeated it. It was the city wall. A chill whispered down his spine.

They had arrived.

Shapes walked the sepulchral ramparts. They were merely spirits, he told himself, like those he had seen in Sigmarshafen. Theirs was the power to terrify, but not to harm. He repeated the insistence as the shades converged over the gate towers that loomed from the clutching darkness like a titan. A thin sound, like tide bells on a foggy night drifted through the swirling white. Someone, somewhere, was singing a hymn to Sigmar. Felix shuddered.

'Keep close, manling. At least until we know whether that sword of yours can hurt them.'

Felix nodded, watching through several separations of dread as a hand that appeared his own drew his sword. A sensation of warmth spread across his back as Rudi, unarmed, pressed close and shielded him from the wind.

Caught in a glacial collapse, the gate towers sank into the dead earth. Holes riddled their black walls, plain grey banners devoid of heraldic symbols fluttering silently against the fog from their turrets. Felix wondered whose lordship they declared. They seemed incongruous as an icon of the dead. The gates themselves hung open, like the dark mouth of death, as though granting admittance to the kingdom of Morr itself.

A crushing chill pressed down on his shoulders as he passed through the barbican. The ancient wood was black as though burned. One gate hung off its hinges and was buried deep into the road. The other groaned softly as it backed and forthed in the grip of the wind. Fog sighed through murder holes in the walls and ceiling. Expecting at any moment some ethereal arrow between the shoulders, Felix hugged his sword and pressed on. The oppressive dread lifted slightly as the barbican opened out into a courtyard.

But only slightly.

He felt rounded cobbles beneath his boots, but, of the court-yard, he could see only ash. The city was not black at all. It had been entombed in ash. Felix shivered, trying to pierce the fog to the buildings that wavered on all sides. There were hints of rooftops, of a road, but all he could see for certain was ash. In places it was mounded like barrows, but it was still just ash.

Gotrek's tattoos smeared purple in the glow of his rune-axe, the dwarf edging forwards as he stared into the fog.

'Hear that?' he growled.

Felix slid forward, angling his own gently luminous blade to guard Gotrek's left side.

Rudi pressed in between them. 'It's a hymn,' he whispered with a shiver, arms wrapped beneath his cloak as he eyed the surrounding shadow. 'We sing it on Sigmar's Day.'

Felix's breath hissed as a human silhouette emerged from the fog. There was something not wholly natural in the way that it walked. It shambled over the broken ground, arms loose, head slack. The appearance of another caught the corner of his eye, then another, approaching from a second alley. The same dirge rose disjoint from three throats and more, soul-less voices collected in praise. Or in lament.

Red rune-light gleamed from Gotrek's grin as more of the figures came into view.

'I told you that you would come seeking me when you changed your mind.'

Felix swallowed, tearing his gaze from the shambolic march as the cold voice echoed through the courtyard.

He knew that voice.

CHAPTER 8

They are the Damned

'Schlanger,' Felix hissed, raising his sword to guard Gotrek's left side as the faltering shapes stepped fully into the radiance of Gotrek's axe. They were human, more or less. They were dressed in sackcloth robes cinched about the waist with rope. Amulets and talismans of hollowed wood and painted stones rattled like dusty pfennigs in a beggar's bowl. They bore scars beyond counting, the marks of claws and knives as well as bruises, rashes and burns. Their throats were swollen with dark buboes, some so large as to pitch their heads to disturbing angles. All lacked one appendage or other, whether it was an eye, an ear, a clutch of fingers or, in the case of one poor woman, an entire leg. Blood welled around fresh scabs at the stump as she dragged herself behind the others on a tall staff, her eyes bloodshot and utterly mad.

Felix's first thought ran to leprosy. There were widely believed rumours of a leper colony in the ruins of Vanhaldenschloss, which could not be far from this place but closer inspection revealed a truth that was, as was so often the case in Felix's experience, even more terrible.

They had inflicted these wounds upon themselves.

Cruel scars bore the self-inflicted marks of whips, knives and saws, while the messy ridges of white tissue that swept from flat stumps told of amputations crudely sealed with pitch.

These were the self-flagellating fanatics of the cult of Sigmar. Convinced of the coming End Times, they proved their readiness through pointless acts of self-mutilation. What had brought them here, and what they were doing with Caul Schlanger, were other questions entirely.

'I should have suspected you were in league with the Beast,' he shouted, with his left arm shoving Rudi behind him, before thrusting his blade warningly towards a flagellant's chest. The warning went unheeded, the man welcoming the cut of Felix's steel across his collar as a sinning man would receive his lord's forgiveness: with a tear in his eye and a prayer on his lips. 'Schlanger!' Felix yelled, the mass of men slowly pushing them back to the gate.

Gotrek gritted his teeth in disgust as, still murmuring their direful lament, they reached for him, only to withhold at the last; fear of divine forbearance, rather than of his axe, preventing them from laying a hand upon him. With a growl, Gotrek stayed his axe. But Felix knew he would only remain patient for so long. Felix's own sword had cut a shallow gash into the lead flagellant's chest but still the man did nothing but offer him praise. Blood was streaming down the channels of his blade, and he feared that even if he did nothing at all then someone was going to get killed. He drew a breath to call out Caul Schlanger once more when another sombre voice lifted out of the dirge.

'And Sigmar spoke unto the Unberogen: these are the dwarfs, my brothers. Let no man see them unto harm as would speak himself brother of mine.'

Without a moment's cessation in their lament, the flagellants parted to admit the passage of a tall, skeletally thin man as underfed and mistreated as any of his brethren.

It was not Caul.

His legs were wrapped with sackcloth in the form of a kilt. Bare from the waist up, deep cuts took the heads from faded green sea dragons and mermaids, dried blood and florid bruises painting his flesh as colourfully as old ink. But despite the every appearance of frailty, everything from the confident stamp of his stride, the swagger that led with his single arm, to the intensity of the stare with which he fixed the Slayer bespoke a warrior. And Felix recognised him. This was the man he had seen preaching of the End Times from a street corner of Sigmarshafen.

Brüder Nikolaus Straum.

Gotrek snorted, grudgingly allowing his axe to drop. 'I think I've heard that line somewhere.'

The man regarded Gotrek with a crazed intensity. His entire body was dimpled with goose bumps and turning a pellucid blue in the cold. Every inch of the man shivered, but his voice was steady. 'The lessons of Leodan, from the Unfinished Book.'

Gotrek nodded, respectfully. Like any dwarf, he respected a proper appreciation for the written word.

With a dramatic sweep of his one arm, the prophet of doom presented his brethren and the clouded ruin that all the funereal hymns known to man or dwarf could not make rest in peace. 'My home, hammer-brother,' the flagellant proclaimed. 'Our temple, our battleground. The first front of the final war.'

Gotrek regarded the battered assemblage of men. Murmuring softly, they looked back. Those more lucid and with limbs enough for the task, marked the hammer across their chests. 'Your home has seen better days, and perhaps your warriors should spare a limb or two between them for the enemy.'

'Gird your hearts, my brethren,' Nikolaus bellowed without turning away, a momentary flash of mischief alighting on his lips. 'Sigmar surely tests us cruelly this day, sending such harsh untruths from the mouth of this trusted one.'

Gotrek glared into each of the rapt faces of the flagellants, muttering a coarse oath when not a single one flinched. 'My patience is being tested, right enough.'

'Your time will come, Trollslayer, as surely will the time of all. Even the dwarfs will not endure the scourging of the End Times.'

Chuckling grimly, Gotrek lowered his axe completely. 'Aye. And don't we know it.'

Felix studied the pair, suffering an unexpected twinge of jealousy at the lunatic's instant rapport with his last and only friend. Birds of a feather, he supposed, as the old Hochland saying went.

Nikolaus's expression abruptly turned grim. 'I do my best Brüder Dwarf, but all is not well in my ministry.'

Gotrek rubbed his still-pounding head and made a show of examining his surroundings. He sucked in his cheeks. 'You don't say?'

Nikolaus nodded, faith the shield upon which sarcasm was ever doomed to break. 'Sigmar delivers us a saviour, a crusader of visionary zeal and we rejoice.' He paused as a shambolic murmur of exaltation arose from the flagellants. 'But always has it been his way to present the steepest paths to those he most loves.' Mutterings of pained celebration. Nikolaus turned his face to the sky, shaking a clenched fist. 'Ours is not to question. Only to see that Götz von Kuber's abduction is a certain sign, a herald of the impending End Times, and we will be there.' His voice had built in pitch and strength, his followers clawing at what remained of their hair as they joined him in a cacophonous outpouring of joyous grief. 'We will fight beside him in these final days. We offer our worthless lives to Sigmar's glory!' The flagellants cried out, stamped their feet, rattled rosary beads, wept, the din almost smothering the stark rejoinder of a single pair of slowly clapping hands.

Caul's green eyes emerged from the fog behind the flagel-lants, followed closely by the man himself. 'Inspiring, is he not?' With a long-bladed knife plaited between the four fin-gers of his hand, he rapped the tinted mail above his heart. 'Makes you feel it right here.'

'If I thought there was anything warm beneath that metal, I might even believe you,' Felix snapped back, angling his sword to this new threat. Ordinarily, he would not have considered a flagellant a threat to a dwarf and his allies, but he noted the way that Nikolaus and his brethren deferred to Caul Sch-langer. There was no telling what hold a man like that could have over men so far lost to reason.

Shaking his head as he insinuated himself between the peni-tent's ranks, Caul made a tutting sound. 'That silver tongue of yours is a little tarnished, Herr Jaeger. Little wonder that nei-ther merchantry nor poetry truly became you.'

Felix scowled, refusing to lower his sword.

As the man spoke, the shadows behind him deepened, forming into the shapes of men. The darkness rendered their motley garb drab, the cold dampening the coloured scarves tied over their faces with condensed mist. Despite the caution that gripped every footstep and weighted glance, they moved with a muted clatter, each of the six men burdened with nets, steel traps, tools, and weapons for every occasion bar the End Times themselves. The last to appear was cloaked in an ancient-looking white wolf pelt. He cradled a storm lantern, enveloping the entire party in dark streamers of whispering fog. Wary of the shadows that gusted chilly through the derelict street, the mercenaries formed up behind Caul. The man at their lead took one more step to bring him in front of his smirking paymaster. He was desperately pale and gaunt, a northerner worn down by hard years. The red linen scarf covering the mercenary's face shifted as the man chewed on something pungent like decomposing lavender. Moonlight glinted from the iron tip of the crossbow he held pointed at Gotrek's chest. The night wind ruffled his long grey ponytail.

'A schilling per bolt on top, we agreed.' He nodded towards Gotrek, nothing on his face but grim professionalism. 'The dwarf looks like he might take more than one.'

'You think right,' Gotrek growled, squaring his shoulders as if to invite a shot. 'How fast do you think you can reload?'

Caul spared the dwarf a sideways glance. 'You look a little worse for wear, Slayer, Can't handle Sigmarshafen's ale?'

'What do you want, Caul?' said Felix hurriedly as two more men lifted their crossbows to cover the scowling dwarf. At a range of barely ten feet, more than enough to send even Gotrek back to Sigmarshafen with a few unwelcome additions between his ribs.

'Order to my world, Herr Jaeger, what more could any man want? But since your companion is on the wrong end of the finest shot in the Fauschlag, why not answer a question of mine?'

'Shoot a dwarf?' said Felix, indicating with his eyes the flagellants who observed the display with a dour passivity. 'I don't think they would.'

'These *paid* men are Middenlanders, Herr Jaeger, and come late to Sigmar's truth.' Caul shook his head sadly, a companionable clap on the mercenary's shoulder. The man did not move, continuing to chew. 'They will surely pay for their heathen ways in the next life, but I am nothing if not accommodating of difference.'

'Did you say you had a question?'

'The same as I had for you in Sigmarshafen,' said Caul, features turning ghoulish under the pulsing red glow from Gotrek's axe as he turned from Felix to the dwarf. 'But since you had the wrong answer for me then, I felt I should put it to you again some place more... *intimate.*'

'Ask away,' Gotrek growled, running a thumb along the blade of his axe until a bead of blood welled. 'A quiet street works well enough for me as well.'

Caul smiled without humour, arching a thin brow as he slowly raised his hands and stepped back amidst his men. 'We are here for the same reasons, Herr Gurnisson. We both want the Beast.'

'Is that right?' said Gotrek, angling the shoulder of his axe to indicate the gathered mercenaries. The angry gesture made them jump. Their gear clanked as fingers trembled against triggers. Gotrek seemed unconcerned. 'Do you plan to eat it?'

'We mean to track it to its lair,' said Caul reasonably, as though explaining to a child why the sky was dark at night. 'Or, failing that,' he indicated the mercenaries with a nod, 'to capture it and *extract* the location of the baron from it. Between myself, Straum, and Captain Armbruster here,' the crossbowman acknowledged his name with a grimace, 'no one knows the city better. But the Beast we hunt is dangerous, and some added muscle would be no hindrance.'

'We're here to k-kill it,' Rudi stammered trying to control his chattering teeth as a cold sigh drove through the ruined courtyard. Abruptly, Armbruster swept his crossbow around towards the source of the wind. Darkness pressed in from every side.

'Did you hear that?' the mercenary hissed.

'The Damned cry out,' said Nikolaus, beating a fist softly against his heart.

'Quite,' agreed Caul, watching Rudi with a faint smile, as though he were a hound that had just mastered a scandalous trick. He turned back to Gotrek, angling his body, grey cloak draping from an arm outstretched towards the unquiet city. 'This city has never been shy about the provision of doom.'

Gotrek glanced up at Felix, who swallowed nervously and then shrugged. With a scowl, he stuck his bloodied thumb between his lips and sucked it dry.

'Fine then, you can all come. The racket you lot are making, you'll doubtless bring the Beast on our heads and spare me the boot leather.'

Fog closed over the road ahead, spilling from the burned and broken teeth of the tenements that ranged on either side. They were burned out, left to rot until each looked much like another, sagging under their own forgotten weight and the restless memory of the shades that still lingered. Rudi shivered and tried not to look, tried not to listen, following the row of black that plumbed as deep into the fog as the mercenaries' lantern could reveal.

The lantern flame had been reduced as low as it could be. By unspoken consent, it was agreed that the dark was a lesser worry than whatever might hide within it and be drawn to the light. Footfalls echoed from the blackened shells. It sounded like too many. Even Gotrek seemed on edge, the flagellants restricting themselves to an occasional prayer muttered under the breath. The ruined streets might have stretched on for an eternity. The world might equally have ended at the limits of the lantern's feeble glow. Rudi had no way to be sure. With every step, the damned city grew darker, until all that remained to convince oneself that up was up and down, down, was the feel of stone beneath one's boots.

Without weapons, or much idea of what madness had brought him here in such a state, Rudi followed the others. That was all he was really good for. The contempt of Caul and the others haunted him, returning in faceless whispers from the derelicts they passed. They were burned out, condemned, left to rot; partially buried under their own forgotten weight. He hunched deeper into his borrowed cloak, trying to close his ears to the voices on the wind.

'…left us to die…'

'…the impious flee…'

Scrunching his eyes, he followed Felix by ear.

The city was quiet but for those imagined whispers. This deathly murmur, the spectral dark. Had he not been able to recall the walk through the gates he would have thought this the Grey Vaults; the quiet realm between death and life that Sigmar had once escaped to live again. It was not an encouraging thought.

'You are troubled, Brüder Rudolph,' said Nikolaus. The prophet appeared from the fog beside him, approaching from behind. The skin between his many tattoos was blue with cold, but if the man suffered there was no evidence of it. His severe expression was anything but calming, but at least he was a flesh and blood man. 'The flesh fails to leave the soul to stand strong. Gird your heart in the steel of faith, and trust that Sigmar turns only from those who turn first from him.' He looked away, into the formless dark. 'Even here, he watches.'

Rudi nodded to show that he understood and signed the hammer; twice, as his shaking hands made a mess of the first. He spoke, his own voice a whisper, unable to tear his eyes from the shadows that stalked through the ruined tenements after the light. 'How does He see this and do nothing?'

'Who says He does nothing?' Nikolaus turned his face from the darkness, answering his own rhetorical question with a nod. 'We are here, are we not? Sigmar is a leader of men, not our saviour.'

Tucking his hands into his armpits, Rudi stared into the fog, unsure whether he understood the hermit's meaning. The certainty that had brought him this far felt impossibly distant now. 'He could have done better than me.'

Nikolaus pursed his lips, as though contemplating a fine piece of rhetoric. 'Sigmar elects his champions, men like von Kuber, and it is not to us to judge them good or ill. The End Times come, and then we will all be judged.'

Rudi felt his cold heart stir in response to the prophet's

words. No one had ever described him as a champion before, nor suggested that Sigmar Himself had chosen him for anything more than clutching a spear in a crusading lord's rear ranks. The thaw in his soul exposed old, hidden doubts, a blackness he felt a sudden urge to confess.

'But–'

'I know you are a sinning man, Brüder Rudolph.' A stern look greeted the surprise on Rudi's face. 'My eyes have not failed yet, and nor am I old enough to be senile. I do not begrudge the second chance that Sigmar offers you. As he once did me.'

Rudi felt his spirit swell, as if Nikolaus had opened him up and filled his body with something warm.

'May I now confess something to you?'

Astonished, it took Rudi a moment to find an answer. 'Even in my village, we'd heard of you, Brüder Nikolaus. What could a man like you have to confess to me?'

'Sigmar can change a man, but He cannot change his past. I have done terrible things, and I have…' Nikolaus's expression turned pained and he grunted as his nails dug into a recent cut across his midriff, 'terrible thoughts.' he fell silent a moment. The wind whistled its own voice into the emptiness. 'I came here when I first heard the rumours of von Kuber, and in this city found the most apt punishment for my sins. Men say I stay here to purge its streets of wickedness but that is not the reason.'

'Then why?'

'I have the most terrible dreams within these walls. A woman comes to me each night. She is small, almost like a child. She says nothing to me, perhaps I deserve no words, but I feel her anguish. I have wronged many women in my life, Brüder Rudolph, and it does not surprise me that one should wish me damned for it.' For a moment, Nikolaus's face adopted a smile. 'I suffer my penance gladly, but my reasons are selfish ones. I believe that is why Sigmar continues to send me these dreams.'

Unsure what was expected of him, Rudi said nothing at all. Nikolaus nodded seemingly satisfied and the two men joined the others in silence.

The darkness swept through and, hungrily, the shadows closed.

Felix pressed his back to a blackened brick wall, reassured by the solidity of its touch. Blackened and blasted ruins pressed in from left and right. They drowned in murk, shingles rotting over a ruined street. Some had collapsed entirely, spilling rubble into the street that the grim party was forced to climb around, but most remained, hollow brick shells with their door frames, windows, roofs all burned away. Fog padded down the narrow street, probing at entrances long ago consumed by fire, as if scenting warm blood but not able to determine quite where. Feeling foolish for doing so, Felix held his breath, waiting for the next gust of cold wind to carry the fog past.

It was plain that nothing had lived here for a hundred years, yet there was a sense of occupancy, of presence that set Felix's teeth on edge.

Across the street, made ethereal by mist and moonlight, a flagellant smeared red paint onto the charred frontage of a blistered old hovel. Colour dribbled down the long-handled brush, speckling the man's fingers red as he applied rough upward strokes. On the completion of a long vertical line, he applied a cross at its summit and then, to finish, a pair of curt strokes to close the left and right hand openings of the cross. Despite the crudity of the job, Felix could see the hammer sigil that had been the painter's intent. Mirroring the painted hammer with his brush-hand across his chest, the flagellant stepped back, dropping to his knees before the doorway and mouthing a prayer. His task done, he dunked his brush into the pot on the cobbles beside him and, with a creaking that wracked his entire body, rose to shuffle to another wall and begin the process anew.

Felix leaned out, looking back down the street to ensure they had not managed to misplace any stragglers. There was just one flagellant left behind. The man muttered under his breath, words lost to the shrill wind. Every few paces, he pushed his hand into a pouch that hung from the belt above his groin, pulling out a handful of salt which he then tossed over his head and onto the road.

'Alms for the damned.'

Felix jumped from the unexpected voice beside him, but it was just Caul, as unwelcome as any restless spirit. Heart beating almost loud enough for the other man to hear, Felix shuffled along the wall away from him. 'This place is lost. He's mad even to try.'

'A shining faith might, to some, seem madness. Götz used to say that Brüder Nikolaus was an example to us all; braving the worst depravations of Chaos, all within sight of Sigmarshafen's walls.'

'And those who follow him?'

'Men will always follow one who is stronger, wiser, more holy.'

Felix regarded the flagellants, struggling through the rubble-strewn lane in defiance of cuts, burns, sores, and missing limbs. 'Human nature is not always a good thing.'

Caul uttered a soft grunt of agreement. 'I warned Götz that too many were coming to Sigmarshafen. The City of the Damned was always meant to be forgotten. Instead, thanks to the Beast and the likes of Brüder Nikolaus, its infamy spreads further each day. The baron welcomed newcomers with open arms and promises of holy war. His grandfather would have ridden them down before they were a day out of Osterwald.' The look on Caul's face left Felix in no doubt as to whose methods he preferred. 'This is the result.'

'What happened to these men?'

'No one believes that Chaos will afflict them. How could it? Are they not strong of will and of heart? Does Sigmar not love them?' He pointed out the man who shuffled behind the others with his bag of salt. He had no ears, the stumps bound with bloodied sackcloth. 'Friedrich was a pious man, a sergeant of the moralpolizei and one of Konrad's lieutenants. Until one recent morning when he found that his ears had grown spines. He gave himself to Nikolaus's ministry and now he is here. As are they all. They will die for Sigmar long before they can fail Him again.'

Felix watched the broken man trudge past, a fistful of glittering crystals periodically cast to the roadside in his wake. Fingers doused with cold sweat drummed around the grip of his sword.

'Perhaps you should have let Konrad destroy this place after all. Gotrek may have complained, but I'd surely not.'

'Götz wanted nothing more than to destroy this city but he would not. He had a name, a family, and knew what acting against the judgement of the temple could mean. Konrad has none of those things. He will burn this place to the ground and do it with a song. But he must not. An army must never enter the City of the Damned. This much we have always known.'

'But why? What will happen if Konrad were to come searching for von Kuber?'

Caul's expression was as static as a serpent. He had not so much as twitched a hair in the devilled wind, but there was something forced in his dispassion. 'There are no legends of the City of the Damned, Herr Jaeger. You fancy yourself a poet; in Ostermark, every hill hides a barrow, every ford was the site of a tragedy immortalised in song. Yet this place was forgotten.' He spat on the ground and, off his elbows, pushed himself from the wall. 'And good riddance to it.'

'Damn it,' Felix hissed, grabbing the man by the shoulder

and pulling him back around to face him. Caul glowered dangerously, but Felix did not back down. 'Somehow you know Gotrek and me, and that's fine. But I don't like people keeping secrets where my life is concerned.'

'Not just your life, Jaeger, but your soul. *All* our souls.' As Felix absorbed that, Caul shrugged his shoulder from his grip, then slammed Felix back against the wall. Ash rained from the eaves over both their heads. For a moment, Caul pinned him, hands around his biceps like steel bands. Then he let go, glaring balefully as he stepped back and snarled, 'Don't touch me again.'

Felix drew up against the wall, rubbing the back of his head as he watched Caul turn and walk away. The fog swallowed him, and poor Brüder Friedrich shortly thereafter. He would have despised the man even had he not been keeping his precious secrets. What had befallen this city that had to remain so well hidden that, even now he was within its walls, Felix could not be trusted with it?

The dead, the burning, the desiccated wastes that surrounded the walls for leagues. This had not been the doing of the Ruinous Powers. Men had done this. If not Magnus the Pious himself, then men like von Kuber's ancestor who had followed him. They had burned it down, poisoned the earth upon which the ashes rested and then, almost as inconceivable in its own way, consigned their descendants to watch, generation after generation, to ensure that what they left stayed dead. What terror could still dwell within these ruins to justify such a commitment?

He recalled Arch-Lector Gramm and his talk of an evil that even the fire could not destroy. The Beast was fearsome, but Felix had seen it close at hand and reckoned it a creature that would bleed readily enough. If not for him, then certainly for Gotrek. There was something more at work here, something dark in the earth and in the shadows. Felix could feel it, this

'Master' that was spoken of by the mindless and in his own dreams. He dreaded the thought of a confrontation with whatever manner of being could hold an entire city under such thrall.

As he was thinking that, a dull moan passed overhead. Felix ducked, looking up. A drift of instinctual dread streamed from rooftop to rooftop between the clouds of fog, fading but never quite dispersing. Like everything else in this city. With an effort of will, he turned his back on the anguished shade and hurried after the departed men. He pressed a hand to his chest. If only his heart was so easily commanded.

There was nothing to be found here.

Wherever he was, he hoped Gotrek was having better luck.

The young man flailed and splashed through the shallow water. He did not cry out; not a scream, not a challenge, not a plea for mercy. It was as if he were nothing but an exhalation of the mist. A low moan escaped his throat as he flopped under. An iron bolt jutted from his shattered collarbone. The dark water ran ruddy as it flowed over him.

'Hit it again, manling. They're a stubborn lot.'

Lying flat, crossbow rested on the grey stone of the river wall, the mercenary so addressed bit down on the warm mulch between his teeth and sighted down his stock. The wounded man lurched out of the water and stumbled forward. Water streamed from his corrupted body, making the wound in his neck run from pink to clear. The wound had barely given the mutant pause. The mindless could almost be mistaken for the reanimated dead, if not for the ease with which they bled and died.

Taking his time, Bernhardt Armbruster allowed the mutant to splash closer. Ten feet away. Up to his belly in dark water. Just near enough to distinguish its features from the wisps of fog and shadow. The man's head was just slightly too large for its body and its arms obscenely mismatched, one no more than a hideous polyp of grasping fingers while the other dragged through the water in a crooked trail of wrists and elbows.

Joints stiff and muscles sore, he took aim, drawing measured breaths through the red linen scarf that was wrapped tightly around nose and mouth. His lavender-scented breath made the coloured fabric clammy against his face. But there had been too many wasting illnesses, too many seeping rashes and crippling pains amongst those who sought their fortune in the City of the Damned. And Captain Bernhardt Armbruster was taking no chances.

Clearly at least half aware of its surroundings, the mutant reached its lengthily articulated limb for the rungs of a mooring ladder. Rusted and covered in a rough brown mould, its half a dozen rungs counted down to the water from where Bernhardt lay. The mutant looked up at him and moaned. Bernhardt fired.

The crossbow's recoil thumped into the specially thickened wool mesh padding of his right shoulder and flung an iron bolt in the opposite direction. The bolt struck through the roof of the mutant's skull, piercing its foul brain and crushing its vertebrae as its tip lodged halfway down its throat. Without a sound, the mutant slapped back into the water. The outrush from one of the many outlets for the city's sewers forced the body back out into the current, bearing it and its dirty blood cloud downriver.

Bernhardt set down his crossbow, turning his head to offer a scant nod of congratulation to his second, Nils, who lay beside him. The man grinned back, had not even bothered to crank back his whipcord and reload after that initial shot.

'Easier than shooting at targets,' said Nils, his smile almost bright enough to compensate for the clouded moon. Like Bernhardt, he wore a face-scarf of scarlet linen, but the younger man had allowed it to slip beneath his jaw like a neckerchief.

'Targets don't come closer to give you another shot.'

'As you say,' said Bernhardt. He coughed hard, then pulled his knees under his body so that he was kneeling. Calmly slinging his crossbow over his shoulder, he rubbed gum from his bloodshot eyes. The City of the Damned changed a man. He could feel it in his water, in his belly, whispering cold nothings in his ears. He coughed again, clearing the crackling from his lungs.

As empathetic as a plague cart, the dwarf trundled between the two men, stamping his axe loudly down onto the river wall. He tilted up onto tiptoes to peer down. 'Dwarf sewer?'

'Yeah, probably.' Bernhardt thumped his chest until his lungs felt clearer. 'Never been down there. I hear they're haunted. Even worse than up here.'

Sweeping his fiercely crested head back and forth along the wall, the dwarf at last gave a grunt and scraped his axe back across the stone. 'Zombies and ghosts; is this all the damned city has for me?'

'That was no zombie,' said Bernhardt, masked face nodding toward the far shore. A cutting wind struck across the water, carving temporary, uncertain shapes into its black surface. Moonlight and a fraught imagination imbued the water's whisperings with a conscious menace. The mist that occluded that far bank however, remained eerily unmoved, as if it were the emanation of some other plane, a body upon which even the wind dare not impose. 'They come from the other side.'

'What's over there then?'

'Praise Ulric that I never find out. And if that's where the baron is, then I say good luck to him.'

The dwarf grunted something stonily monosyllabic and turned away. 'Things are bloody useless anyway…'

Watching the dwarf stomp back across the derelict wharf, Bernhardt pressed the flaps of his face-scarf to his cheeks, drawing deep on the trapped aroma of lavender wort and

Arianka root. The quayside tenements groaned as if the sky itself pressed the fog down upon it. A cold sweat shone from his brow as he unslung his crossbow and, sighting down it, swept the row of crumbling roofs. It was unloaded, but that hardly mattered.

There was nothing there.

'Caul should have made the Retterplatz crossroads by now.' He slung his crossbow, casting a last look to the still empty rooftop, chewing harder on his herbs as he suppressed a shudder. He cursed the day he had ever brought his men here.

'Let's go.'

Troubled by a growing sense of disquiet, Felix followed the last of the flagellants from the road and onto a large, open square. The flagellants had already disappeared to search the ruins for signs of the Beast. Too impatient, or more likely too terrified, to remain behind, Rudi had gone with them. Felix tried to pick the men out but they were gone. The fog was thick here, enough to consume men whole. The buildings on the sides of the square were naught but shades. Of the far side, he could see nothing, as if it barely belonged to this world at all. The way the fog leapt between the ruins cast a distracting resemblance to dancing flames. Felix could almost hear the crackle of wood.

Retterplatz, Caul had called it. The Place of the Saviour, and a more unlikely name Felix could not conceive. A statue marked the centre of the square, banked within a ring of burned stones. At least it had once been a statue. Now it resembled nothing much more than a stalagmite. The once white rock was pitted and scorched and it was without arms, face, indeed without any human feature at all. Yet it drew his attention.

'Is that…?'

'Sigmar?' Caul finished, the man never far away.

'Yes,' Felix breathed. Something in the aspect of formless rock made his hairs prickle.

'What makes you ask?'

'I don't know. I... I feel it.'

'Then why do you doubt?'

The fog seemed to draw in, the statue growing larger and ever more wreathed in darkness. 'I haven't seen a statue of him like this one before.'

'Sigmar did not forbid the creation of his likeness.'

'I know...'

Sigmar was a warrior; a leader not a saviour. He encouraged men to stand up for themselves; with faith, courage and steel to oppose the enemies of man. As he watched the statue began to blur and he blinked, rubbing carefully under his eyes. His fingers came away sticky. Curious, he opened his eyes and studied them. His vision was still blurred and a little red. It took a moment for the realisation to hit him. His fingers were covered in blood. His eyes were bleeding!

Clenching a fistful of his breaches in his bloodied hand, he looked to see the statue similarly drenched in blood. Red fluid pumped thickly from the pits in its shapeless body. Stifling a scream of horror, Felix spun around. Caul smiled coldly, still as a statue himself. Blood streamed from the corners of his mouth as well as from his nose, his ears, his eyes. Fingers across his mouth, Felix stumbled back, this time giving in to the scream when it came.

The cry echoed, shared and shared again. The wind laughed darkly through his hair, tangling it before his bleeding eyes as he spun a full circle, sweeping the unruly strands from his brow, unwilling to believe his eyes.

Caul was gone. Nothing where he had been but mist. The road behind him was empty.

He was alone.

The wind picked up. It whispered something, something

Felix was too slow to comprehend and, for a moment, the fog cleared. In its place, a darkness bled from the starless sky. As it struck upon the ashes of the city it hissed; spreading outwards, solidifying, redrawing crumbled walls with diaphanous black lines. Felix gaped. The city shimmered, whole but at the same time not, like a picture that showed a different image depending upon how it was viewed.

A prickling sixth sense told Felix that he was being watched.

Spectral outlines, human in suggestion, stood at windows, crowded onto flickering balconies. Everywhere there was space, shimmering bodies were coming into being, boulevards and balconies filled by such an overlay of wavering figures that Felix abandoned the hope of distinguishing one from another. And they kept on coming. He saw them in the street behind him, and across the square. His heart screamed. They stood faceless, their bodies lit by the silver glow of the grave.

And they were not looking at Felix at all.

Unable to control his actions, as if this were nothing but a terrible dream, Felix turned to face Sigmar, the supposed saviour of these tormented souls.

The statue was whole again, but it was no longer Sigmar. Recast in shadow, white had become black. From its fingers there now sprang talons. Beating monstrous wings of inky black, it reached for him. A likeness shivered across its form, recognisably human yet hideously vague. There were horns, a crown.

The Master will rise.

Felix twisted away with a scream, screwed his eyes shut and thrashed his hand through the apparition's claws. He felt nothing. He had expected an icy chill, a spasm of dark energy, a prickling of pins and needles at the least. He tensed and, when still nothing happened, he unpeeled one eyelid. His vision was clear. He dabbed at his face, winced, his black eye still throbbing bitterly.

'I've said it before manling and I'll say it again. Yours are an odd lot.'

Gotrek stood over him, both ham-like fists bunched about the haft of his axe.

Heart slowing by painful degree, Felix swayed upright. A black whirl of dizziness reminded him of the need to breathe. He gave the Slayer an experimental poke and was rewarded with a scowl.

'Praise Sigmar,' he breathed.

'We were already on our way here when we heard yelling,' said Gotrek, jerking a thumb back to the two mercenaries that stood with loaded crossbows and tense expressions at his back. 'Just found you two rolling about like pigs in muck.'

'It was… it was…' Felix found Caul, just where the man had been.

Shaken, and clearly irritated that it showed, Caul dusted down his cloak. 'The Damned,' he finished, breathlessly. 'Every man, every woman, every child.' With a snarl that was borne as much in anger as it was in fear, Caul pointed back the way they had come. 'Forget everything that the priests of Morr or Sigmar have said to you out there. Within these walls, there is no salvation. This is what it means to be truly damned.'

As fiercely as he endeavoured not too, Felix recalled the rank upon rank of faceless shades that he had seen, so numerous that their outlines intermingled with others, and with others, and with others. Like trying to squeeze too many letters onto a page until what was left was illegible and could hardly any longer be called words. Was that why they had no faces, he wondered? Were they simply too numerous, too forsaken, to be remembered? The world may have forgotten them, but they remembered the world. They remembered how to hate. Felix could still feel the heat of it in his chest. And the statue.

He felt the need to check again. It was as it had been.

Pitted.

Scorched.

But there was something else beneath that broken facade. Like a caged beast, something tense and full of rage snarled beneath the surface. It calmed as Felix's heart slowed. But it was still there. Still angry.

'It will only get worse as dawn approaches,' said Caul, pulling Felix's attention from the still-simmering statue. What calamity could be so catastrophic as to deny its victims even the succour of the afterlife? And, more to the point, what would be the fate of Felix's own soul should he too fall here?

It was one thing to pledge his life in Gotrek's service; it was quite another to forsake his very soul.

'And just how could it be any worse?' said Felix.

'The dead march on Sigmarshafen by night. Those left behind are the weak, the less angry, but even so…' He reached under his grey cloak, tugging a knife from his baldric as he studied the ruins with a glazed eye. 'They say that every man sees the city differently. Whatever speaks to his deepermost fears.'

'I'll tell you what I see,' Gotrek rumbled, subjecting the fractured ruin to a harsh glare. 'I see an empty ruin, and two manlings shrieking over naught but a puff of wind. If the brainless living and the restless dead are all this city can afford me, then so be it. My axe will greet them all the same.'

'And what then, Slayer?' Caul hissed. 'Maybe your axe *can* harm them, but have you not been listening? They are damned. There is nowhere for them to go.'

'Did I mention how sincerely I dislike this place?' Felix muttered.

'Then I suggest we make a start,' said Caul. 'Or come the dawn this city will be the grave of us all.'

Felix picked up at that, giving Caul his undivided attention. 'What did you say?'

'I said get moving.'

'No, no,' Felix murmured, a smile spreading across his face

like creeping dawn. 'Graves, you said. Graves! That's where the Beast will go.'

'Solid thinking, manling,' Gotrek chuckled. 'Except for one thing. If a village of a dozen dirt-grubbers and a goat had two of them, then how much ground do you think it'll take to house the dead of this damned place?'

Felix frowned. Gotrek had a point. He had just witnessed with his own eyes how the passing centuries could accrue the dead. How many people had lived and died before he, Felix Jaeger, had been born? It was a tragedy worthy of Detlef Sierck that none now remembered their names, nor even of the city that marked their lives like a tombstone. The thought of the foul ends to which the limitless hordes of the Damned might be turned made him shudder. Uncertain why, he found himself looking again at the statue. What was it that it had said?

'The Master will rise,' he whispered.

'What was that?' said Caul.

'Nothing,' said Felix, discomfited by the sudden intensity in Caul's regard. 'Just thinking. There must be a Temple of Morr. That would be where most of the dead would lie, yes?'

Caul was still studying him carefully, like a chirurgeon debating whether a limb could stay or go. 'This city has a long and... *gloried* past. The House of Morr was desecrated centuries ago.

'I know something better.'

Felix turned at the approach of a familiar voice. Bare skin robed in dark fog, Nikolaus bore a chilling likeness to the black thing that had possessed Sigmar's statue in his vision. Felix shivered and tried, without much success to banish the association. Rudi was with him, stuck close to his back. The young man's hands were black from searching through the ruins.

Nikolaus greeted every man present with a nod, saving the deepest and the longest for Gotrek, who acknowledged it with a grunt. 'If the monster craves the dead then it will find them in the home of the heathen sisterhood.'

'Heathen sisterhood?' Felix asked, uncertain whether he really wanted to know.

'Pacifists,' said Nikolaus, 'Worshippers of a pagan woman-god.'

'Sounds no better than the mindless and the dead, to me,' Gotrek grumbled.

'Brüder Nikolaus speaks of the Shallyan sanatorium.' Caul explained. 'In life they raised no hand in their own defence.' The man looked eastwards into the mist. The bridge hung squat and solid within the thick, drifting fog. An ominous cluster of high-walled buildings stood near it. That was what Caul was looking too. And he looked afraid.

'But damnation changes you.'

CHAPTER 9

Sisters of Mercy

Surrounded by rubble and the crumbling blocks of labourers' housing, the charred brickwork of the Shallyan sanatorium resembled nothing much. Fire had transformed the entire district to something more akin to the inner walls of a kiln, the wind that was a near constant presence streaking the ash like claws with red. The sanatorium itself was of the same red brick construction as the street; a two-storey house abutting a walled cloister where four rounded towers had once stood at the corner walls. Three still did. The fourth, the north, had collapsed inward as though demolished by a giant's club, burying the cloister under a mass of rubble six feet deep. The house itself was partially interred under the avalanche of brickwork set off by the collapse of the neighbouring build-ings. The result of that destruction was that the road Felix and the others now walked was the only route to the house of healing still open.

The hairs on the back of Felix's neck shivered like grasses on the cold hills of the moors. The surrounding rooftops sagged, patient in the pace of their decay. Felix would never have believed his heart could beat so hard for so long. His chest ached with it, drawing breath starting to feel like squeezing into the armour of a dead man half his size. They had left the Retterplatz an hour ago.

Why did he still feel he was being watched?

Rudi tucked in close, sharp breaths haunting the air with clouds of mist. Like Felix, his eyes dodged from rooftop to rooftop. And just like Felix, finding nothing offered no assurance.

'Have you ever been somewhere like this?'

Felix did not answer, did not club the man silent and scream 'No!' as part of him so sorely wished. The young man seemed to regard him as some kind of unlikely hero, as though Felix had it in his power to spare him the world's horrors. Felix wished that Nikolaus could have taken him ahead and spared him the questions.

The flagellant and his brethren were still just about visible through the fog. Staves and peg legs announced their passage over the rubble, the undying echo making Felix wince and eye the shadows with redoubled fear. Beyond the flagellants, their gear making spider-like ghosts in the fog, walked Bernhardt and his men. Caul had ordered the mercenaries to scout ahead, but the 'ahead' part of that instruction had become lost somewhere in the darkened streets between here and the Retterplatz. The three groups had pulled closer and closer, the party bunching tighter like a herd of beasts scenting the approach of a predator. It was instinctual, pre-human, forest savages huddling around the fire until night passed. Ahead, the crimson shadow of the sanatorium brooded over the street. It swelled and shrank in the uncertain dark, illuminated by the mercenaries' lantern only in flashes.

'Before the end,' Caul whispered, 'a plague of madness swept the city. The Shallyans converted this building into a hospice for the afflicted, but the burghers condemned their efforts as witchcraft. They believed the madness to be Sigmar's will, to weed out the weak-minded from the strong. The sisters did not defend themselves.'

'Another glorious chapter for the Unfinished Book,' Felix breathed.

Caul shrugged. 'Look around you. Sigmar passed his judgement on what went on here. The dead were just bones and three deep when Magnus came. It made a natural place for his armies to leave their own fallen.'

Bernhardt's voice called back from the fog. Its meaning was lost by the time it reached Felix's ears, but it was followed by the hollow scrape of steel underneath brick. The sound echoed all around. Felix flinched.

'Clear the way,' came the cry again, this time clear enough to make out. 'Shovels front. Put your shoulders in.'

'Do you think we'll find the Beast inside,' asked Rudi. His face was pale, his fingers playing nervously at the belt where his swords should have been.

Caul breathed a heavy sigh and flung his cloak over his left shoulder to unveil a leather baldric worn over his darkly tinted mail. Knives stuck from the black leather like teeth. Selecting one with every appearance of great care, Caul pulled it free and presented it blade first to Rudi. Rudi examined it fearfully for a moment before reaching out. At the last moment, Caul yanked it away. 'You know which end to use, yes?'

Snarling, but saying nothing, Rudi kept his hand where it was.

'The metal end,' said Caul pressing the knife into the man's palm and then, with a smile, 'But there's no wrong place to stick it.'

The young man flipped it into his other hand, took an experimental swipe at the mist, and immediately looked a little happier. At the same time, Caul proceeded to tug three more knives from their strapping. He let them drop the moment they were free, counting under his breath as the four fingers of his free hand stroked up the baldric, playing the remaining blades like the strings of a lute. He caught Felix's look.

'Where order fails, Herr Jaeger, what then is left but Chaos?'

Felix suppressed a shiver. The man was mad. He was trapped in a city with its long-forgotten dead and men too far gone even for Sigmarshafen.

'Manling!' came a cry from up ahead. Consciously or otherwise, even Gotrek's usual growl had had its edges smoothed. The slip and snarl of busy shovels continued unabated from that direction. 'There's a way in.'

Felix sighed. Madmen *and* a Trollslayer.

Wondering what that must make him, he pinned his scabbard to his thigh with one hand and broke into a jog. The fog slapped at his face, ruined buildings drifting by through the dark. Heavy breaths and the crunch of loose brick from behind told him that Rudi had decided to follow. The flagellants said nothing as he passed them, too busy tossing salt and painting the walls with hammers.

Standing before a steep mound of rubbled brick that was packed against the wall of the sanatorium, Bernhardt Armbruster greeted him with a nod. His crossbow covered the street. Behind him, a pair of mercenaries stood ankle deep in brick, bent double into their shovels to clear the way. They had stripped off their leather jerkins and sweated despite the unholy chill. The path into the cloister of the sanatorium was under a red brick archway. The brickwork was scarred, the work of an axe or a sword. The keystone was about two feet above his head and carved into the form of a dove, Shallya's aspect as bringer of peace. The dove's wings had been charred almost beyond recognition, its beak broken to a stub of pale stone in a blackened face.

'There are no doors,' Felix observed. At first glance, he had assumed them burned away or crushed under the rubble, but there were no hinges either.

'Shallya always welcomes,' said Bernhardt, momentarily removing his eyes from the street.

'Credulous wench,' muttered one of the shovellers, raising a laugh that did not last.

Felix frowned and turned to follow Bernhardt's look. Two blond-haired men, Nils and another whose name Felix had known he would not remember, moved purposefully between the milling flagellants. They trailed a length of steel wire between them, counting out measures as they went, pausing occasionally to peg distance markers into the rubble before continuing.

'What are they doing?'

For the first time, Felix thought he caught the hint of a smile beneath the mercenary's face-scarf. 'Caul wants the Beast captured alive. I would like to retire to Middenland one day. Somehow those two must marry.'

Felix watched the two men set their traps for a moment, then nodded, suddenly glad for this small example of sanity.

There was no sign of Gotrek and two of Bernhardt's men were absent too. Sensing his thoughts, Bernhardt jerked his head back toward the arch. Felix saw that the way had been partially cleared, enough to clamber through if a man did not treasure the skin of his hands and knees. Gesturing for Rudi to follow, Felix twisted his scabbard from his legs and commenced to climb. At the summit, he ducked under the dove keystone, then slid down into the cloister.

The first thing that struck him was the quiet.

Shielded from the wind by walls of scorched brick, there was nothing to disturb the mist that trickled through rents in the walls to pool within the courtyard. It was eerie, like he had disturbed a sacred pool. Already, the scrape of shovels sounded distant. In the silence, Felix could almost feel the cold disk of Mannslieb hum from behind the clouds. Its silver light fell upon an undulating field of broken brick. Immersed in fog, the rubble sloped away from the archway, neglecting the grey-stoned columns that fronted Shallya's house to Felix's right, before climbing unevenly towards the north corner and its stump of tower.

He felt a flash of horror.

An image passed before his eyes as he faced the north tower. A lingering impression of terrified, white-robed women, the sound of screams, the touch of fire.

Breathing hard, he held his gaze. But there was nothing there. The air was funereal, his rigid hackles tingling with the sense of desecration. From somewhere under the rubble, perhaps within the blackened crust that adhered to the walls, a trace odour of burned meat still persisted. How long had it been, Felix wondered? It was impossible to say. No one would tell him anything.

Rudi shuffled past him, sliding down the rubble to the cloister wall. The fog seemed to constrict about his ankles as he walked. His hand traced the damaged wall. 'It looks like a battle was fought here,' he whispered, fingers sinking into a vertical gouge in the brick that looked to have been chipped out by an axe. The walls bore the scars of what could only have been a massacre.

Feeling an itch on the nape of his neck, as if something shared this cloister with them, Felix bent to pick something from the ground. Muddy white against the immuring black. He blew ash from it. It was a piece of skull. With a curse he let it drop.

'There are more.' Rudi walked a short way towards the house, its columned front rising through the fog. Rubble slipped beneath his feet as he toed aside a brick to reveal a tangle of bones powdered with red dust.

It was then that Felix caught sight of Gotrek.

The shadows slunk from the baleful glare of his axe, streaming, sepulchral forms, that screamed in silence and were gone.

The dwarf paid them no heed. He crunched around the columns of the main house, fingers probing every cracked piece of wall. Finding nothing, he moved toward the main building with an impatient oath. The dwarf's moods were never the easiest to discern, but if Felix did not know better he would have guessed that his companion was rattled.

Felix chose to take that as a very bad sign.

'Brüder Gurnisson, this way. Let me show you to the vault.'

Nikolaus's voice set a hollow charge through the burned out atrium. Felix cringed from every grim repeat of the word *'vault'* that echoed between broken columns and out from the main hall. Already crooked where its supports had crumbled away, a second floor gallery creaked. Felix held his breath, half expecting the whole structure to come crashing down on his head.

Sweeping his axe through the fog, Gotrek moved across the hall to where the flagellant waited by the entrance to a stairwell. With exaggerated caution, Felix followed suit. Shards of bone and coloured glass crunched underfoot. Large oval windows, no doubt a blessing to those convalescing under the sisters' care, now admitted nothing but a ghastly mist that pooled around Felix's ankles. Human skeletons of varying degrees of completeness were heaped against the walls. More were doubtless buried under the fog and rubble that veiled the wide floor space.

'I don't like this, manling. I don't like this at all.'

Felix was not inclined to disagree. He shot a glance back the way he had come, just as Caul, Rudi and one of the Drakwalder mercenaries passed over the threshold, weapons drawn. Caul bade the sell-sword to guard the door, and then, abandoning Rudi to his own devices, picked his way through the field of bones. The way his eyes flicked from one to another, it was clear he was looking for something.

'Do you expect to find something here, Herr Schlanger?'

The man's smile tightened. He did not look up. 'I attended a Shallyan seminary once. Briefly.'

'Was that before or after you burned an innocent woman alive?'

Caul met his eyes across the drifting fog, then tightened his cloak against the chill. 'Let's not quibble over definitions of *innocence*. But if forgiveness were solely for the just, then the sisters of mercy would have few supplicants at their doors.'

'Then why did you leave?'

Caul's grin spread slowly; hideously arranged teeth, ordered four by four. 'It… wasn't for me.'

From the stairwell, Nikolaus spoke again. 'The vaults, Brüder Gurnisson. Would you care to see?'

Gotrek exhaled, long and slow, giving the desolate hall one last look over. 'More of the same, is it? Bones and the like?'

'Yes, only a great many more.'

'Then don't bother. I've seen as much as I care to.'

'So now we wait?' Felix asked softly.

'For the Beast to come,' Caul concluded. 'Somewhere out of sight. And don't forget.' He singled out Gotrek. 'We're here to capture it and find its lair, not kill it.

'For how long?' said Gotrek, eyeing the groaning walls with a poorly hidden unease.

'As long as it takes.'

Gotrek shuffled his heavy boots through the thin carpet of bones and debris. 'I'll not sit on my hands in this mausoleum for Grimnir knows how long.' And then to Felix, 'Hold the fort, manling. I'm taking a look around.'

'Wait,' said Felix, suddenly terrified that Gotrek would leave, struck positively numb by the fear that he would expect Felix to go with him. 'The Beast's coming for the bones. It'll be coming here.'

'It wants bones, does it?' Gotrek growled, his axe's glow bequeathing his eye a malicious tint. He bent down, shovelling a mass of the bony shards into a ham-like fist, then clenching it before Felix's nose.

'Then it can pry them from my cold dead grip.'

Hands struggling in the cold, Nils pulled down the jaws of a foothold trap until they locked with a faint click. He rose, stamped his feet for warmth, then dragged a boot through the ash to conceal his handiwork. With nothing left exposed but a few steel teeth that would easily be dismissed as just more debris, Nils unslung his crossbow for one last sweep of the surrounding rooftops. Breath misted into a cloud before his face. His eyes narrowed. The fog treated sounds and objects strangely. For a moment, he would have sworn he had seen something move.

The crunch of gravel from behind made him spin, dropping into a crouch as he sighted down the crossbow track and into the mist that spilled from the archway.

'Put it down, hireling. Unless you mean to use it. I'm going for a walk.'

With a scowl that served well to mask his relief, Nil lowered his weapon and stood.

'Next time you sneak up on me, I'll shoot you.' For reasons he did not care to understand, the proposition gave the dwarf cause to grin. Teeth broken, tattoos shifting red in the harsh glare of his axe, it was the most ferocious display Nils had ever seen. 'Just… shout next time,' he finished, tamely. The dwarf stomped past. He noticed the pale gleam of human bone down the back of the dwarf's breeches. Flummoxed, his voice temporarily caught. 'Wait,' he hissed, 'Wait, where are you going?'

'About,' the dwarf snapped, without turning.

With a slow resurgence of his earlier irritation, Nils realised that the dwarf's path had taken him neatly between every one of his traps. He stepped back, studying the rubble to assure himself they were well hidden, then shrugged. The dwarf must have gotten lucky. He turned, squinting in the general direction of the south tower. A muted gleam of metal in a window was all the fog revealed of Bernhardt. He was about to turn away when the appearance of something on the roof made him look again.

The fog cleared to reveal a weather vane. It creaked back and forth in the wind, charred arms dangling, like a burned corpse swinging from a gibbet. Breathing out slowly, he allowed himself a chuckle. Turning back to the street, he sought out his comrade.

Marten's wolf-pelt cloak whispered against the rubble, shivering white in the cold moonlight. The man was crouched with his back turned, half an eye on the departed dwarf. With the crank from his crossbow, he tightened a trip wire attached to a bell at one end. His efforts caused it to trill softly. The man crunched around.

A nod, wolf pendant pawing his mailed coif. Job done.

Nils threw a thumbs up to that cold glimmer. And hoped that Bernhardt saw.

Bernhardt returned the thumbs up and pulled himself back from the ruined window. He thumped his mitts for warmth and sat down, shrugging himself under a fleece. The hole left in the brick by the broken window was uneven, serrated almost in parts. It bore an unnerving resemblance to a bloody mouth filled with gleaming teeth. Bernhardt stared down its throat, shivering in the bleak mist that froze its outward breath. Throwing a second fleece over his shoulders, he tried to calm his thoughts. Experience made it impossible.

This was the City of the Damned. There could be no preparing for what the dawn would bring.

Fog tickled the back of his throat and he coughed. Lungs crackling, he hawked it up, pulled down his face-scarf, and spat it out onto the street. Holding his breath, he repositioned the scarf, breathing deeply once it was back covering his nose and mouth. He had done everything that a diligent man could. He said the proper prayers three times each day. He had purchased all the right herbs to repel corrupting humours and then, with what little coin the priests and the herbalist left him, he had paid his visit to the chattel pens. The herbs tasted sour in his mouth. His skin still recoiled from the remembered touch of scales. The girl had been the most human he could afford, but then his mother had always told him that the vilest remedies were the most effective. Fingers to his throat he gave an experimental cough, feeling the flesh rise and recede.

He grimaced. 'A whole lot of misery for a scrap of coin.'

He turned to the man watching the window to his left. Bernhardt dimly recalled Kurt as a large man, but the City of the Damned got under a man's skin. It drained the meat from his bones and laid the soul bare. It was even rumoured amongst mercenary circles that, after six generations on this land, that same corruption had prevented Baron von Kuber from fathering an heir. Bernhardt wondered whether it was worth it. Now Kurt was lean as a coursing hound, with hair of the same thin grey. The man glanced up at Bernhardt's words, fiddling with the bronze clasp of his cloak.

'You say something?'

'Just thinking aloud,' said Bernhardt, feeling his throat and collar for lumps.

Silently, Kurt carried on fiddling.

Click, click, click.

'Ulric's shaggy knackers, will you give it a rest.'

'It was a gift,' Kurt answered, eyes hooded, trying to hold the thing shut. It sprang open as soon as he let go.

Bernhardt swore, then coughed again. Finally, the thing snapped closed. The grey-haired mercenary puffed into his fastened cloak, then set his crossbow by the window and stiffly stood.

'I'm hungry,' he said, partly to Bernhardt, partly to himself.

'Nothing for me,' Bernhardt muttered well after the man had crept off into the dark to rummage through their gear for the strips of dried jerky stashed there. Bernhardt's stomach turned, and not with hunger. He stared out of the window, mumbling to himself as he watched phantoms form and split through the murk. 'There's something rotten here. It's in the meat, in us.' He balled his fist into his belly, staring miserably into the creeping fog. 'And I've always hated goat.'

Disturbed by something in that shifting view he could not place, he leaned his head through the window and craned his neck to look up. It was dark, nothing but fog sweeping down off the eaves. Wary of glass shards, he pulled himself back and sat down. He massaged his throat, looking up to the ceiling beams.

Strange how the absence of light made shadows seem denser.

Then he heard something. A faint scratching noise stitched between the rafters. As if something were moving along the roofing tiles. It stopped. As if it knew that he listened.

'Kurt,' he whispered, breath fogging. 'You hear that?'

There was no answer.

He picked up his crossbow, blowing warm mist to melt the frost that was beginning to crawl along the brass track. He clutched the weapon to his breast. To spare the lathe it had been left unloaded and he fumbled through his fleeces for the quiver. He withdrew an iron bolt and set it to the track and then, one foot in the cocking stirrup and his hand to the crank, he paused. He did not breathe. The scratching noise had come again.

'Don't sulk,' he hissed into the unlit chamber behind him. 'I think there's something up there.'

Still nothing.

'Kurt?'

He swore, feeling braver for it, and stood, turning his back to the window.

A shadow passed before his eyes.

A blade passed through his chest.

His mouth stretched wide only for a gnarled, bird-like paw to smother his cry. He screamed into that ghoulish flesh, lungs working now like mighty pistons to draw air through the creature's grip. Jerking against its sharp embrace, Bernhardt felt his struggles grow wearied, his breathing slow. Gently, the creature eased him down and then, as though he were already forgotten, climbed over him and out through the window. Lying flat on his side, unable to move, Bernhardt gasped as though he drowned. There was a fleeting glimpse of bony, lumpen feet and a blotched, egg-shell tail before the creature was gone.

Blood ran slowly under his cheek. It felt warm, oddly welcoming.

With failing, blood-filled eyes, he gazed into the closing dark. A gaunt, grey-haired body lay amidst the stowed gear. Above it, a faceless shade shimmered silver in the dark. It was looking at him. It was angry.

And it was damned.

Bernhardt's failing heart froze. A last breath fled his stiffening lips.

'Kurt…'

The shadow crawled out into open air. The sensation of cold was instant, like a blow to the ribs. It hissed, shrinking deeper into its all-covering cloak and hood. Its claw-hold in the brickwork was good and it swung out, reaching up for another, sinking its claws deep into the aged mortar. Grey paste crumbled away like grave dust.

It was easy to forget just *how* aged.

It climbed a way and then, with a preternatural flurry, threw itself back from the wall to latch claws onto the overhanging eaves. It swung a moment over nothingness. The fog coiled about its legs and tail. There was a disturbing sense of pressure, of hands that sought to close about its ankles and tear it down if only they could. But they could not.

Not yet.

The creature hauled itself up, scrabbling over the tiles until it could look down onto the street. Its eyes were dim, adapted for the night, but it had no difficulty detecting the others of its kind. On the rooftops, lurking within windows, dropping silently into the courtyard behind it. A harsh cry, like a vulture's death song, sounded somewhere close.

The creature tittered, twisted claws scratching the tiles in its excitement.

Soon. Soon this would all be done.

Lifting its hood to the sinking moon, it called.

'Tell me again of how you slew a dragon.' said Rudi, eyes bright in the cold like tiny stars. Felix sighed, cursing whatever malicious muse had allowed him to think that sharing some of the other horrors that he and Gotrek had lived through might ease the young man's fears. It had, but a little too well for Felix's tastes.

'I think that story was my favourite.'

The pair of them were scrunched uncomfortably close, fetched up against a brick-pile that marked the truncated end of the corridor, just off the main hall. The crack of bone echoed from the hall as Caul Schlanger sought out whatever secret thing he seemed to think rested here. Felix was trying desperately hard to be disinterested. The man was not sharing and Felix was not about to go begging for answers. If Caul wanted to spend the day rooting through bones, then that was fine by Felix.

Irritated despite his best efforts to convince himself otherwise, Felix shifted against the brick wall. Bits of brick lumped into his back. Tiny red splinters pricked the bare skin between his gloves and the end of his sleeves every time he tried to move. And his black eye still hurt.

With another sigh, he gave up the attempt at comfort and turned his attention to the crumpled pages of his journal that lay open across his knees. He dipped his quill into its vial of iron gall ink and held it a moment to dry, hoping that Rudi would find something else to distract him. No such luck.

'I'm not some Tarradaschian hero,' Felix muttered, inked quill hovering over the page as he tried to back calculate to today's date. Lips moving silently, he shrugged, simply scratching '*Brauzeit*' below his last entry. All the way back in Osterwald. 'I've seen people die. Honest, good, innocent people. I almost died myself that day. It's not actually something I care to recall.'

Rudi leaned nearer to peer over Felix's arm at the page slowly filling with tidy black lettering. 'Then why do you?'

'It's my journal,' he answered without looking up, his tone one that he hoped betrayed annoyance. 'I promised to compose an epic poem of Gotrek's doom. It's been a long time now and I'd hate to forget the details.'

'So you're a warrior and a scholar too? Your father must be very proud.'

With a wry chuckle, Felix rolled his eyes before returning to his page. 'You'd think so, wouldn't you?'

Rudi sniffed distractedly at the oft-patched Sudenland wool of his borrowed cloak. 'Do you think my father would be proud of what I'm doing now?'

The tension Felix had been carrying dissipated into the freezing mist. He stoppered his ink vial and closed his journal for another time. 'Only you can answer that. But I believe he would be.'

'Last time I saw him, we fought.'

Felix smiled gently. 'In a way I envy you. All my life I've longed to tell my father what I really think.'

Looking miserable, Rudi shaped an answer, just as a thin cry carried down the mist-cloaked corridor from the hall. A hollow bone clacked as it dropped. Caul had heard it too. Felix sat a little higher, freeing the dragonhead hilt of his sword. It had sounded like a bird.

Felix and Rudi shared a look. As one they stood.

They had heard that cry before. They knew what it foreshadowed.

There came another bellow, this time distant; a deeply pitched rumble that Felix remembered all too well.

The Beast was coming.

CHAPTER 10

Ambush

The wall of fog that lay across the bridge broke for the passage of something vast. White threads coiled around its rags, snapping one by one like the strands of some ethereal cobweb as the monster pulled its bulk clear. At once, its posture shifted. It slumped into a hunchbacked shuffle, sniffing the air in confusion. Mad red eyes gleamed from the hooded depths of its cowl. Images ghosted across his troubled eyes. Scents were there then gone.

Where am I? Am I still?

One moment the air was ripe with the dry stench of roasted bone, the next it was naught but ash on a cold wind. The quay was packed with intangible, smoky figures. Bunting shimmered between the balconies. Boats tangled pennons as they jostled for the shallows. It was all of it a lie. They awaited the second coming of a god, but not the one they expected. And his gifts were madness and death. Their debauchery revelled through the wind like a lure, like a dancer. He could smell the colour. Synaesthesia rendered their inevitable deaths to a cold coppery confection, dead blood clinging to the walls of his throat.

He licked his lips and snarled, confused.

Why am I? Why is this?

Buildings clustered to the riverside like sheep to a water trough, blurring together in the fog. The phantom bleat of river bells sank into the wind. It blew cold and callous across the water. His nose twitched in the supernatural chill. Periodically, a memory emerged from the blackness, but his thoughts were clumsy and slow, and grasping for it only pushed it deeper under.

He lumbered forward, nearing the ungainly skeletons of the bridge towers. The piled bodies of the Damned turned their shapeless features to him, then recoiled. He was one of them, but not.

Dead, but not.

Damned, but not.

A frustrated snarl rose from his ruined throat. With claws like butchers' knives he ripped at the rags about his face, shredding the soiled cloth to ribbons that fluttered free like ash rain. Blisters burst, smearing his claws with blood. He stared at them in horror.

He remembered the ash rain.

Who is this? When was I?

He squinted skyward, into beclouded black, then moved to the edge of the bridge, claws encircling the damp stone as he peered down. The water was dark, roiling with the lost souls of the burning and the drowned. It cast no reflection. Blackened and bloody claws dug into the stonework. Lips peeled over monstrous yellow fangs.

'Huurrrrlk…'

A call like a vulture's rang amongst the shifting ruins and, at once, he pulled up. He sniffed the air. The call sounded again and he turned towards it. His memories were elusive.

A revelation came and then went, passing in a moment of understanding. They had not happened yet. He broke into a run as the call came again.

He would make them happen again.

For the last time.

Sword in hand, Felix burst into the cloister just in time to witness the surrounding walls and rooftops erupt into deadly life, harsh calls firing across the street like the hunting shrieks of birds of prey. Felix saw their dark shapes flocking the rooftops, clustering over the ridges to loose death into the street before dispersing in shrill bursts of shadow.

The three Middenlanders that had still been working in the cloister scrambled into cover around the archway as missiles whistled over the wall.

Felix spotted a scrap of sackcloth in the fog-clouded street beyond the archway, but no sooner had he wondered what the flagellants were doing outside than, as if Felix had laid a doom upon the man's shoulders, he was struck in the side of the head by a slingshot. He did not scream. His death was too sudden for that. The man beside him did howl, and righteously so, anointed with his brother's blood and then losing his leg to the swollen knee joint in the jaws of an iron trap. Their fellows flowed around them, belting their pious cries into the mist. The trapped man bellowed the name of Sigmar before a bullet punched through the back of his skull and his body fell beside his silent brother. Perhaps it was just the ripples that the charging flagellants had left in the fog, but Felix could see silvery silhouettes rising from their corpses.

A cry shrieked from somewhere near at hand. A dark body scuttled over the roof of the nearest tower.

Felix was thinking just quickly enough to shove Rudi back inside the house and hit the ground himself before a bullet tore a chunk of brick from the column where his head had been. He bounced swiftly back to his feet, holding Rudi down and threw a sharp look back to the tower. Mist moved across the conical roof, but nothing else. Felix swore, trying to find where the creature had gotten too and finding nothing.

Rudi's face was pale with fright. Felix waved a 'come' gesture, trying with just the two eyes to mind the myriad angles of attack that the cloister afforded, and made a crabwise run for the south wall. He flung himself against it with a relieved gasp. Rudi was a second behind.

Two mercenaries were pressed under the flanking curves of the archway, loaded crossbows tight to their chests. One poked his weapon under the arch only to snap back from a storm of fire. The second man whistled under his breath and did not move as bullets ripped up the rubble between them. The third Middenlander, recognisable in his heavy white wolf cloak, stood back from the wall, crunching slowly back over the sloping rubble towards the north tower. His eyes were dark as though infused with smoke, lips moving without sound as he stroked the shrivelled wolf paw at his collar. He was pale even by northern standards.

'Is he all right?' Felix shouted, and then to the man himself when no one answered, 'What's your name?'

'Kurt,' the man murmured as though to himself, shivering with some private chill.

'Marten!'

The shout made Felix flinch on instinct, turning to see Nils fleeing the house. A missile shot from the roof and missed the man by inches, cracking the bricks between his feet. The man impulsively dropped low, swivelling about to catch a burst of chittering laughter before the shadow dispersed back into the fog. The mercenary snarled, unslinging his crossbow and trying to ram a stiff bolt into the track as he ran towards Felix and the others. The first thing he did was slap the wolf paw from Marten's hand.

'Put that damned thing away and put a weapon in your hand.' The man looked dazed and Nils shoved him against the wall with the others. 'And take cover, you dolt.'

Startled, the man came around, his face undergoing the subtle shift from incomprehension to confusion. He let go of the paw of his wolf cloak, as if it burned. Deliberately, as though acting out a dream, he unslung his crossbow.

Felix wondered if he was the only one to notice that he was not loading it.

'Sorry captain,' said the mercenary. 'It was…' his eyes glazed, turned shadowy, and then cleared, 'it was a gift.'

'Gift,' Nils snorted, abandoning the crossbow to hang by its strap from his shoulder and unhitching a hand-axe instead. 'Straight from the back pocket of Morr.' He turned to Felix, something almost pleading in his manner, as though desperate for someone to bring order to this chaos. 'I was down in the vaults with Schlanger, just looking, when I heard…' He waved a hand over the cloister, flinched from another banshee shriek and shrank into the cloister wall. 'Ulric's teeth, is this the plan? Is this what we planned?'

Felix shushed the man with a wave and edged nearer to the arch. The men had done a good job clearing it, the earlier blockage now just a hump of brick. He could make out Nikolaus's voice above the twisted birdsong and the crack of slingshots but, judging by the corpse trail that disappeared into the fog, the flagellant could have precious few of his followers left with him.

This was probably the worst ambush that Felix had ever been party to.

'What possessed them to go out there?' Felix hissed.

'Something about helping the dwarf,' one of the crossbowmen answered with a nervous shrug.

'As if Gotrek is the one needing help,' Felix muttered, but no one was listening.

'Back inside,' Nils snarled, sweeping his axe back to the house. A bullet whistled overhead to crack against the gable. 'There are doors in the vaults. We'll get Caul, we'll find Bernhardt and the others, we'll bar the doors and wait them out.'

Felix backed away and looked to the house. It did sound tempting, but something stopped him.

'Nikolaus said there were more bones down there,' he said, feeling something grim clench his guts into knots. 'Lots of them, I think he said.'

He swallowed, stumbling further back over the rubble as a faint but shrill whisper from the murk behind the wall grew steadily louder, bringing with it the first inkling of just how misguided the mercenary's plan was.

Shadows were sprinting across the rooftops, converging on the sanatorium, bypassing entirely the road and Nils's carefully lain traps. Like grapnels, the first wave of bloodthirsty shrieks were cast over the walls and the creatures leapt after them. Black cloaks bit into the wind, their dark arc bearing them the dozen feet from the final roof and well across the accidental glacis of crumbled brick that surrounded the sanatorium walls.

'Run!' Felix screamed, finding his voice and spinning away.

Just as the first murder of cawing shadows sank claws into the parapet at his back.

The whine of whipcord was loud enough to drown out Nikolaus's prayers. A ferocious volley from the fog ahead mowed down three men, driving the survivors onto a side street. Brüder Henke was the last through. A missile thumped under his armpit and burst out from his back. The wall behind him flourished with the blood of the holy and the man himself then slumped against it. Bullets continued to chew the corner wall to dust as Brüders Friedrich and Arnulf hauled him clear.

Nikolaus knelt beside him. The man moaned as Nikolaus stuck his fingers into the bloody puncture under his arm. Fingers slick with blood, he traced Ghal-maraz over the man's sackcloth robe. The man ground his teeth, staring at Nikolaus with wide, grateful eyes.

'Scream, brother, if you would scream. Let Sigmar know you come to his gates.'

And Henke screamed. He howled with the lungs of two men.

'I say we take them,' growled Brüder Arnulf, flayed jaw set contemptuously, twin hammers crossed over his chest.

'With pride comes disgrace, with humility vision. Our lives are inconsequential, and with that understanding comes glory.'

Arnulf lowered his hammers and bowed his head for forgiveness of his pride.

An animal bellow ripped through the confines of the alley. The surviving penitents turned towards it. Even Brüder Friedrich, earless and largely deaf as he was, hefted his mace and prayed for a swift death. It was close, from the far end of the alley.

'The Beast, brothers,' Nikolaus roared, drawing the leathern thong that was his one and only weapon before thrashing it across his own back. His followers mumbled their approval. Missile-fire continued sporadically from the street behind them. Nikolaus's killing days were far behind him, and most of the blood he had shed had been spilled over the open waves, but that did not mean he did not recognise a trap when he saw one. The smaller creatures were feeding them to their master. Nikolaus simply did not care. 'As Sigmar did throw down the Great Necromancer at the Battle of the Reik, so too will we face this evil unafraid.'

The flagellants signed the hammer and charged. Nikolaus lashed his back once more and followed, turning once to note the shadows probing at the alley mouth to cut off their retreat. With a smile, Nikolaus grasped his bloodied thong and charged after his brethren.

There could be no retreat from the End Times.

Black shadows boiled over the front wall of the cloister, descending on the courtyard with a hissing fury. Curved talons tore through the bony screw, shovelling anything that even remotely resembled a bone into black cloth sacks. A shriek came from the roof of the house. More of the creatures were descending from the eaves and streaming inside. The whole scene put Felix in mind of a sinking ship, dark water spilling in from every side until all aboard were drowned.

It was only the fact that the invaders clearly had no interest in the men between them and their treasure that meant Felix and his companions were still alive.

Only the north wall and the brick slope of its fallen tower were currently free of the black-cloaked scavengers. Shadow-creatures flitting past them, Felix and the others ran towards it. There was an unquiet presence around it, a resentment of this intrusion, but the immediacy of their peril forced any misgivings aside. The creatures might be content to ignore them for now, but he did not expect it to stay that way.

One of the mercenaries turned and drew up his crossbow. He did not even bother to aim, just pointed it into the seething crowd, firing from the hip.

'No!' Felix threw out an arm to knock the weapon aside, but too late.

The iron bolt burst through a full sack and into the back of the creature that carried it, throwing both a foot forward and skewering them together to the brick wall. Squirming in its death throes, the creature dissolved. Bones spilled in a foot-long trail from the point of impact to the ruptured sack. A keening wail went up around the cloister and discoloured eyes, glowing with madness and hate, swept up from their bones to regard the living. There was a moment's peace as each side regarded the other, then a hiss sounded from all around and the shadows surged. The mercenary heaved his crossbow into the charge and bolted for the tower.

'Run,' Felix yelled, seeing some of the other men standing stunned. 'Run now!'

Another mercenary loosed, the bolt pitching a sprinting creature from its feet. Half a second into the process of reloading, he dropped the cumbersome weapon and ran. Felix gave him a foot head start and then followed.

Inhumanly swift, the shadows closed on the fleeing men like the jaws of death. Felix spun, directing a feint across the front rank of the charge. The shadow-creatures stumbled back with a chorus of squawks. Rudi and the others were already halfway, scrambling on all fours up the slope of loose brick, towards the north tower. Death at his back, Felix sprinted after them.

The flat of his blade smacked against the pile. Angular chunks tumbled through his fingers and sank around his boots. It was like trying to run up a sand dune, if sand were rust red and bone hard. The creatures were climbing fast, barely slowed by the loose footing and already nipping at his heels.

Feeling a tug on his boots, Felix rolled onto his back and smacked his boot through a creature's long snout. It emitted a bark and flapped wildly, unable to prevent itself from pitching backwards and tumbling down the slope. Channelling his terror, Felix ploughed his heel through the brick pile and kicked out. Bricks, as well as small scraps of bone, went tumbling downhill. The creatures below squealed and covered their hooded heads in their hands. With a snarl, Felix kicked off another small avalanche onto their heads. If they were protecting their faces, then they were not climbing. Shovelling brick beneath both boots, he hauled himself backwards. A brick flung from the cloister sailed towards him. Felix saw it with time enough to gasp as it cracked just beside his ear. He ducked, the next striking even closer. The impact peppered his hair in red dust.

The drizzle of missiles suddenly became a storm. One struck him in the shoulder, summoning a retaliatory surge of pins and needles all the way down to his fingers. Fighting the urge to curl into a ball, he shuffled back onto hands and knees and climbed. Below him, the creatures shrieked their triumph and pursued.

At the top of the slope there was a crest of ruined brickwork where the remnants of the north wall and a few feet of the tower's interior floor still stood and adjoined the rubble. The others had already claimed it. Felix could almost reach out and touch the scuffed leather of their boots. Rudi had his knife in one hand and was hurling bricks with the other. Nils was fumbling again with his crossbow and backing away until the twelve foot drop behind him changed his mind. The remaining three mercenaries readied blades and axes, bawling into the black tide as much to bolster their own courage as to dent the enemy's. One of the men, Felix was too preoccupied to notice who, hooked his arm in theirs and hauled him up. Felix wasted no time getting back to his feet. The men pressed in tight.

From the roof of the house, to their left, a shadow-creature dropped onto the wall. Nils's crossbow cracked the air, the bolt punching through the creature's chest, throwing it against the hanging eaves and off into the fog that cloaked the courtyard. More were pouring down from the roof and dashing along the narrow wall with the assuredness of riggers between masts. Nils unhitched his axe, shuffling from the tower stump towards the top of the wall before it widened enough to admit more than one creature at a time. Exhausted, Felix shook dust from his ears and sank into a ready stance. Rudi stood ready beside him.

He felt strangely jilted that the majority of the creatures had still not even bothered with them at all. More were coming in all the time, leaping over the walls to rifle through the house and cloister, filling their sacks before departing as expeditiously as they had arrived. That still left more than enough. Twenty or more of the creatures were scrambling up the slope.

And not a loaded crossbow left between them.

Now was the time for sword and axe.

Felix sliced through a pallid wrist as it emerged. The severed limb started dissolving the second his blade exited. Swallowing his disgust at the foul stench of burned fur, Felix kicked the screaming creature back. Another sprang up to replace it, forcing Felix to parry a swift lunge for his belly. The notched blade screeched the length of his sword. With his greater strength he shoved the blade aside, but the creature rolled his counter, dodged his sluggish riposte, and was immediately raking its rusted blade across his mailed vest in an astonishing display of speed. Hastily he backpedalled. An instinctive lurch of vertigo told him his back was to a precipice. His attacker tittered mercilessly as it came on. More followed onto the bridgehead.

Rudi committed his knife-arm into a diagonal slash. The creature's spine twisted into a most unnatural contortion and the blade swept over. Seeing its weight rooted, a fighter's instinct kicked in and Rudi booted it hard in the shin. Bone splintered with a hollow crack. The creature's howl echoed through the cloister as Rudi jerked its longer blade from its bandaged grip, then sloppily beheaded it in a frothing shower of ichor. The mercenaries cheered to see it fall and Felix nodded his thanks. But it was just one amongst many. The creatures were agile and seemed to possess no fear.

'We have to jump!' Felix shouted.

'It's too far,' Nils returned. His axe blurred with a frenzied zeal. His attackers tittered and danced. Blood spotted his neckerchief. It was all his own.

'Not down, across. To the next roof over.'

'It's still too damned far.'

'Are you suggesting we stay?'

Nils punched his blade through a flap of cape, barely avoiding a disembowelling as the creature ducked the lunge and lashed out with a blow of its own. He stepped back, only the presence of Felix behind him keeping him from stepping right off the edge.

'Do it then,' he snapped, swinging an axe that was dodged with ease.

'What about Caul? And Bernhardt and the others?' Rudi's voice was tense enough to snap. With both newfound blades, one low and one high, he thrust forwards only to see both smoothly dodged. 'Shouldn't we… go back for them?'

Nils laughed once in Rudi's direction, then finally managed to fell one of his attackers, smashing the haft of his axe through its face. 'Just for making me laugh, you get to go first. Go on, boy.' He jerked his head back to indicate the rooftop across the street behind them. 'Jump.'

'Go on,' said Felix, forcing his own body between Rudi and the closing shadows, pressing the man ever nearer to the edge. 'We'll follow.'

Not daring to turn his back, Rudi eyed the gulf from the corner of his eyes. The jump was almost ten feet and the roof only about a foot lower than their own position. From a standing start, it looked more like twenty.

'I'll be lucky to get halfway.'

'Don't worry about it,' Nils replied, inexpertly smashing aside an incoming thrust. 'The fall's not big enough to kill you.'

'Lying with two broken legs in the City of the Damned? If that doesn't kill you—'

'Just jump!' Felix screamed, fending off both his and Rudi's assailant at once. He hissed a small triumph when his parry cut a strip from his attacker's arm.

'Sigmar spare me,' Rudi muttered.

He spun to face the gap and flung his weapons across. The two blades scattered on the rooftop shingles. They slid noisily, coming to a rest about halfway down the harsh surface. He dropped into a crouch and then sprang. The wind struck him side-on with a sudden blast of black hair, red cloak rippling, arms swinging like oars. And then he hit, smacking the roof like a drunk's fist into a tavern wall. The steep slope turned his ankle, pitching him shoulder-down onto the shingles and into a roll. He spread his arms and legs, ripping his clothes to rags but halting his slide to the edge with a foot to spare. Felix did not catch exactly what he screamed.

'Who's next?' said Felix, fencing against four whirring blades. The remaining men exchanged fraught looks.

Without a word or a glance, the one Nils had called Marten lined himself up. His fur cloak looked too heavy, but the mercenary jumped, sailing the gap without fanfare. Rudi screamed for help, but the man offered none, wrapping himself in his furs and kissing the wolf paw at his collar. The shadows clung to him a little too closely, but a snarl and a flash of grubby steel kept Felix from attending too closely. One after the other, the final two mercenaries leapt. The first slid down the shingles to help Rudi up. His comrade landed in a breathless heap behind him.

Felix and Nils fought back to back. The Middenlander hissed in through his teeth as a blade opened a red track the length of his forearm. He lunged for the creature only to see it flow away and another take its place.

'All yours,' he breathed as he spun, then flung himself from the wall.

Inches too short in his leap, Nils slapped into the gable, his axe spinning down into the clutching fog with a crash. He scrabbled at the ruined brickwork, screaming as it crumbled to ash in his fingers. Slowly he began to fall, only for the swift arm of one of his men to catch him and haul him up.

Felix's blade entangled with another. He could have exploited his strength to bring the creature down but he had not the space or the time. He was alone and with nowhere left to run. Felix looked into the snarling faces of his attackers. He snarled back, body and blade flowing to hammer aside a speculative thrust and then, with a berserker cry of which Gotrek would have been proud, spun his longer weapon through a chest-high sweep that sent his assailants scrambling clear. It was just for a moment, but a moment was all he needed. He took two steps forward, close enough to hear his foes' shrill notes of surprise, then drove the outside of his boots into the broken tower and spun.

He ran for the edge, sword gripped as though he fled with the power of flight from the gods. His toes dipped into emptiness and he cast off, body flung into open air. The sudden blast of wind struck him like a hammer. Time seemed to slow and he hung there, limbs dangling as though he really did hang. Abruptly time accelerated, the ruined shingles welcoming him like an elf to a dwarfen ale hall. A single punch knocked the air from his ribcage. Groaning agony, he dragged himself over the roof ridge and, straddling it, looked back.

The shadow-creatures clustered over the courtyard wall, eyeing the jump and then eyeing him. Their hissing speech became a snicker and, one by one, they peeled away to rejoin their industrious kin below. Felix watched in bemusement. He was not too dazed to recall his first encounter with these creatures. He knew full well that the distance between them would be almost less than nothing if they cared to attack.

But clearly they did not care.

With a long breath that was as much relief at still tasting air – however foul – as it was about the numbing weariness in his chest, Felix sheathed his sword. Flexing his fingers, he edged down the slope of the roof to get a look at where he was.

His body just wanted to lie down, but Felix had been through enough battles to know that if he did then he would never get back up. He reached the bottom and planted his feet into the slight upward curvature of the eaves. He held for a moment, caught his breath, and surveyed the City of the Damned by the light of the coming dawn.

The rooftops were shrouded and indistinct in the fog, but he could discern the barbican to the north and, to the east, the high towers of the bridge and a slender structure that looked like a bell tower. The city extended in all directions, further than he could see, a dusty black sheet of steepled shapes. Beyond the river in the east, a finger of red light teased the edges of that cover, awaiting the fullness of its strength that it might rip it back and reveal what lay forgotten beneath the dark. Felix knew that the darkness hid more than mere bricks and mortar, something older and more wrathful than anything the city had yet shown him. He tried to remember what the seamen in his father's employ had used to say about a red dawn.

Knowing sailors it was probably nothing good.

Carefully, Felix leaned forwards, looking into the fog for the least precipitous route down. The need to find Gotrek had become a compulsion almost as great as the dwarf's own need for an honourable death. He just knew he had to find his companion before sunrise.

'I have to find Gotrek,' he said quietly, just loud enough for Nils and the others on the ridge to hear.

'Good luck with that,' Nils scoffed and then, when Felix did not laugh, 'Mane of Ulric, you're serious.' He pointed east, his voice a frightened snarl. 'Bernhardt knew better than to spend the day in this place. Everyone does.'

'There must be some way. Caul wouldn't have risked his own life otherwise.'

'Schlanger was a nut and not one that'll be missed. I'll bet he gave no thought to how we'd make it out of here alive.' The man gripped the shingles between his thighs in a nervous grip and rocked. 'Best I can think of, find somewhere good and quiet to hunker down and sweat it out. And…'

'And?' Felix asked

Nils shrugged, gazing eastwards. 'Pray.'

Felix looked into the stirring cityscape. 'I don't think Sigmar has looked this way for a long time. Or any god that I care to name for that matter,' he added with a nod to the Middenlanders.

'Today, I'd take any that'd have me.'

'Mind what you say,' Rudi snapped. The man was scratched head to toe and shivered. Whether through pain, cold or simple zeal was unclear. His fingers shivered to the hammer talisman at his breast. 'Men of Sigmar, blood of Magnus…'

The mercenaries sneered.

'Stay with these men, Rudi,' said Felix.

'I swore an oath too,' Rudi cried. 'To slay the Beast or die trying. Either way, this is Sigmar's land, and he'll see it done.'

'Sigmar doesn't care about you!' Felix shouted back.

As soon as the words left his mouth he regretted them, but he did not try to soften them. Perhaps it was for the best that he had never had children of his own. Two days with Rudi and already he had turned into his father.

Rudi's face was red enough to ignite. He said nothing, but if looks had the power to ignite the souls of the impious then Felix would be naught but ash smouldering within his chainmail.

Spotting a window ledge that looked like it would support his weight, Felix shuffled until he was directly above it. He turned onto his belly and looked back. Still Rudi would not speak, but nor did he try and follow, so perhaps a harsh parting was for the best.

'If you don't see me again, you can keep the cloak.'

* * *

Hurrlk pounded down the ruined streets, brick and stone beaten to powder beneath his tread. All around, black shapes fluttered and flew, as though a swarm of moths had trailed him all the way from the river. From the dim confusion ahead there rose a sprawl, an ashen ruin rising from its sickbed for one last valedictory glimmer of life before its corpse was burned and buried again.

And again.

Hurrlk could feel the heat on his eyes, smell the ash on his tongue. Black cloaks fluttered over it, flags of surrender that burned, and burned, and burned…

A piercing shriek jarred the fragments of his mind into alignment. From the conical roof of one of the towers, fighting the wind for its drapery of black cloth, his minion lifted its hooded snout to the fog again and called. He snuffled in confusion, hesitating at the sound of another cry behind him. It was not one of his own. It was deeper and in a language he did not know.

Did not yet know.

Had long forgotten.

And yet it was familiar. The memory of a memory trickled like salt water through his wounded brain.

Yes.

There could be no surcease. Not for one of the Damned. But someone had thought this creature could stop him. Or at least that it would try.

Even half-remembered, it was too tempting to ignore.

Ignoring the frantic screams and waving paws of his lessers, Hurrlk ground a circle into the rubble until he faced the sounds of battle. A brick wall stood before him. A breathy laugh huffed from his chest.

And he charged.

'Hold still, you squirmy beggar.'

Grabbing for an insipid flash of tail, Gotrek blundered after the hooded creature. It darted deeper into the flame-gutted hovel. The creature reared its head from behind a half-buried table. Gotrek kicked it apart, making the creature squeal, and then, with a brusque feint, drove the creature into a corner.

'Ha! Got you now!'

With a wittering of breathless laughter it ducked Gotrek's swing, wriggling under a beam as the starmetal blade clove through the sagging joist that had been behind it. The creature dived out through the window just as the ceiling began to groan. Glaring contemptuously up into the trickle of dust, Gotrek gripped his axe and the whole thing came crashing down.

A mocking laugh drifted through the ash haze from the other side of the window. Gotrek snarled and shook himself free. The ceiling boards had been of the thinnest pine to begin with and after two centuries of rot and fire, there was little left to them but ash. Employing a combination of axe and shoulder, he hacked his way free and charged through the open door.

The creature was gone.

In its place was Nikolaus Straum and a lepers' handful of his followers.

'It fled that way, Brüder Dwarf,' Nikolaus pointed down the road.

The street was empty but for rubble and wisps of cloud. The blackened husks that flanked it shivered only slightly to the animal shrieks that riddled the wind. A bullet pinged off Gotrek's axe blade from a second storey casement on the opposite face of the street. Gotrek bared his broken teeth at it. 'Come face me you rotten-skinned, ork-breathed cowards! You'll take me to the Beast if I have to run every last one of you to exhaustion to do it.'

A loose smattering of fire answered him from both sides of the street. Nikolaus and his faithful retreated under the eaves of the hovel that the Slayer had just exited. Gotrek roared as a ricochet bloodied him across one massive shoulder. The bullet glanced off his thick skin, leaving an ugly red bruise. The brick wall did not get off nearly so lightly.

Gotrek hefted his axe, gave an ululating war cry, and charged. With their own motley cast of oaths and cries, the flagellants staggered after him.

Black-cloaked figures sprang from every mortis-jawed ruin they passed. They scrambled through cracks in their ruined frontages, crawling for vantages too slender for any man from which to unleash a salvo and then ran, sprinting from roof to roof in eager pursuit. The creatures that lingered on the road scattered before Gotrek's charge. Some made expeditious work of the walls, shooting up as though zipped on hidden wires, while a handful scampered down a side alley. Ignoring those that mocked him from the eaves, Gotrek roared into the alley.

Heaving for breath, Nikolaus stumbled after. The dwarf's stride was short but he ran like a steam engine. And Nikolaus would not be found wanting.

The lane angled downhill to a fog-shrouded denouement where water lapped against stone. The fog smelled of rotting algae. The ground shifted underfoot. The mess of fallen masonry became tighter as they ran. Gotrek barged through it but, taller and frailer, Nikolaus was forced to duck hanging beams, jagged brick shards knifing his bruised frame. Something behind him gave with a soft moan of surrender and collapsed. There was a rush of red dust and a chorus of coughs.

Gotrek cackled, his axe making swift work of a pile of broken lumber.

The scrape of agile claws permeated the fog, closing from ahead and behind. They were trapped.

'To our deaths, my brethren,' Nikolaus cried. 'Give praise that we are spared the horrors of the End Times.'

Nikolaus placed his hand against the wall. At once, he pulled back.

The wall trembled.

The whole alley was shaking. Charred, horribly organic grit drizzled from above, beaten loose by some percussive force. Nikolaus dodged a falling tile. It smashed where it fell, the broken fragments twitching with each rhythmic pulse. With nervous squeals, their pursuers withdrew. Something was coming.

Something big.

Gotrek slowed, a gap-toothed grin splitting his hard face. He turned his axe toward the closing thunder. It seemed to be approaching from behind a row of houses. The loose bricks visibly rattled.

'Here we go. This is what my axe has thirsted for. I'll–'

A titanic crash resounded through the wall and it spat mortar as though it had just been hit by a cannon. Gotrek gawped, red dust plastering his face as the whole edifice began to tilt. Gotrek's head craned back to follow the tipping wall. A brick slipped loose and cracked across his forehead, snapping him out of his shock. He growled an oath against all human handicraft as another brick struck his knee. Gotrek ran for it. The wall shed bricks like buckshot from a gun barrel as it fell, colliding with the other side of the alley with an unflinching crunch. Gotrek looked up and flung himself to the ground.

As if mortar had suddenly become water, the whole wall simply came apart.

Burying Gotrek Gurnisson under a mountain of brick.

CHAPTER 11

Sunrise

Nikolaus hacked bloody phlegm into the dust cloud. Just breathing was a torture, like swallowing gravel. He coughed again onto the back of his one hand, painting his faded tattoos with blood. Even that was flecked with brick shards

'Gurnisson,' he rasped.

Those three syllables ravaged his throat, each a greater penance than the last.

An impression of broad shoulders wavered within the gloom, a dark spectre where the dust did not linger. It was huge. Too massive to be the Slayer, too large even for fierce Brüder Arnulf. It could only be the Beast, scourge of Ostermark, the captor of der Kreuzfahrer. The dust settled, the veil of blood-red destruction cruelly withdrawn from the titanic bulk of the Beast. Ten feet tall and almost as broad at the shoulders, it slunk within the brick haze as though inhabited by the mind of a creature a third its size. Its snout was long and distended, raked as if by its own claws, and buried a pallid face between those mountainous shoulders. Red eyes gleamed with a ravenous insanity, an intelligence that could scarcely be considered animal.

'Sigmar!'

With an appeal for vengeance, Brüder Arnulf flew past, launching himself over the mounded brick, swinging his hammer mid-air for the head of the Beast

He was dead before he hit the ground.

Like a bear batting at a leaping salmon, the Beast flung a monstrously bandaged fist into the man's path. His body snapped, torso caving around the brute's fist, and then was slapped aside. The soulless meat that had once been Brüder Arnulf punched through the weakened alley wall in a scarlet spray, coming to a final stop against an interior wall with force enough to flense his organs between the bars of his own ribcage. Blood smeared the wall as he slid limply into the wreckage. Dead.

But not wholly still. A shadowy nimbus flickered silver across his form.

The Beast's shoulders heaved with mirth, a rush of mephitic breath fleeing its jaws. It cast its mad eyes down, examining the ruins beneath its feet. It shuffled back, bricks bursting to crimson showers beneath its weight. It gave the shattered brickwork a cautious sniff and then, with the absent pattern of a child with one hand in the water, drew its claws through the broken pile.

It sought the dwarf, Nikolaus reasoned. But why?

Not caring to wait and see, Nikolaus ensured his final words would be ones of penitence, and charged. He had no true weapon – the End Times would not be averted by axe or spear – and the Beast did not even look up as his scourge whipped across its snout. Brüder Friedrich piled in a breath behind. His mace smacked uselessly off the thick bone that knotted under the Beast's rags like armour. With a shrug of one shoulder, the Beast hurled them back. Nikolaus howled as his feet were parted from the ground. His head struck brick and his vision swirled with colour, as though the gulls of Chaos circled for a feast of sinning flesh. He saw Schwester Karolina stumble. Her stave caught in the rubble, pitching her from her single remaining leg before she was within six feet of the Beast.

The Beast ignored them utterly. They were nothing and it knew it. Instead, the monster lowered its snout to sniff at the body it had unearthed.

The Slayer was still, dusted red like a cinnamon loaf, orange crest flattened under a jumble of loose brick.

Bent onto all fours like some cadaverous hound, the Beast's wet snout snuffled over the dwarf's body. It lingered on the dwarf's breeches, drawing deep. The Beast gave a snort of pleasure, a dull light gleaming within its mad eyes. With an urgency it had not previously betrayed it exhumed the body, then swiftly rolled it onto its front and pressed the dwarf's face into the rubble with force enough to crush a man to marrow. The monster turned to the shadows and gave an angry hiss. A nervous chirrup arose in answer and a pair of black-cloaked figures scurried from hiding.

They crouched beside the dwarf's body and the Beast stepped back to let them work. They snatched the bones that had been stuffed into the dwarf's breeches and stashed them in their own black wool sacks. One of the creatures then pounced onto the dwarf's back. It bore a length of cord between two bandaged hands and set to work binding the dwarf's wrists and ankles. Satisfied, the Beast uncoiled a whip from its right arm. With its twin tails it reminded Nikolaus of the herald of Sigmar, and he smiled.

There was a crack and Nikolaus gasped in pain. Blood streamed from two bite marks in his chest. A poisonous fire raced through his veins, swiftly quenched by a cool numbness that promised oblivion. He flopped back. The sky was turning red. It was oddly warm.

And he could smell burning.

A figure approached bearing twine, but it was fading. It was Brüder Arnulf. At least it looked like him, but his face was wreathed in smoke. The apparition wavered, anger as raw as the rising sun.

Nikolaus tried to reach out but found his hands tied.

'Forgive me, brother,' he mumbled, tongue fat, 'we have sinned.'

Felix dropped from the rooftop and into a crouch. The reddening sky was awash with harsh cries, but they, surprisingly, were actually the least of his concerns.

Something was stirring within the City of the Damned.

He looked back to the rooftop. Fog drifted across the shingles, cloaking Rudi and the others well. He shivered but, oddly, he did not feel at all cold. The new day promised to be a warm one, if a shred of sunlight could warm the mists of this benighted burgh so thoroughly. Cautiously, he crossed the alley until he came again to the main street.

It was as he recognised it from his earlier approach, but now the way was littered with sackclothed corpses and the fog carried a coppery trace of fresh blood. Pressing himself against the wall, he peered out, ducking back as four yapping shadows leapt between the roofs above his head and sprinted past. Each clutched a black sack as if it hid gromril or gold. Felix shifted from the alley to follow their progress. They were fleeing east. Towards the river.

Felix took a last look back to the sanatorium while he waited for the shadow-creatures to pass out of sight. It was as quiet as a graveyard, barring the occasional shriek like a startled crow.

A distant roar sounded, rebounding through the fog-shrouded ruin like a challenge.

It was difficult to be certain through the fog, but it sounded like that had come from the east as well. And, much as he tried, Felix could conceive no surer way of finding Gotrek than by tracking the Beast.

Fast as he dared, Felix left the alley behind and made after the departed scavengers. The ground was treacherous, a bed of rubble studded with corpses and weapons both ancient and new and, every so often, a fresh pack of shadows would come sprinting overhead to force him into a doorway or behind a pile of debris. Felix tried to be thankful for them, for they at least meant he would not get lost in the city's maze of ruined streets, but he was beset by a creeping dizziness. Each breath was coming harder than the last.

The air had ash in it; hands, boots, mail, and even his sword were similarly begrimed. It was as if the city had remade him as one of the Damned, an elemental of divine vengeance. The air was close against his skin. It carried a heat that he would have sworn had not been there just moments ago. Ashen fingers pulled out the mail collar of his shirt. He was sweating, and the metal was hot. He could almost hear the crackle of wood. The red glow on the horizon suddenly struck him as something quite different than sunrise.

Fire.

Silver-black, it flickered across the barren rooftops. By some witchery, the dead city burned.

Fog banked the street ahead. Except it was no longer just fog. The dry ruin offered nothing for mortal flame to consume, yet wherever dawn's rays fell it burned and vented a choking black smoke. Pushing his mouth into his sleeve, Felix ran into the smoke. He spluttered before the sudden surge of heat, coughed and looked around, eyes filled with tears.

Flames licked at buildings long since burned. The fires were transparent. Felix could see the damaged brickwork beneath. Reason insisted this could not be real, but the blistering of his face urged otherwise. Smoky effigies of men shimmered, caged behind bars of flame. From many hidden mouths there came a scream, obscured by time and darkness, conjoined into a single everlasting plea. With both hands, Felix tried to cover both face and ears and run. Stripped of emotion, of self, the unending cry was as hollow as the vaporous forms of the Damned.

Making a sideways dart across the street, Felix flung himself into the relative calm of an alley. It was a little cooler and the smoke was thinner, and he was able to take his sleeve from his face. He coughed and tried to get his bearings. Smoke and fog made it impossible to see, leaving only his own flawed mental map with which to work. He was as certain as he could be that he was still heading east. With a frown, he looked down at his boots.

And found himself gazing into the face of a corpse.

Felix swallowed the cry before it was halfway to his lips. It was another flagellant. The man sat upright against the alley wall. One side of his body was mangled and bloodied, a messy puncture beneath the arm. Fresh blood sprinkled the ground and the corner wall at his back was riddled with holes, like it had been gnawed on by rats. Felix could not look away. It was only that his eyes had never left the man that he was able to convince himself that he had *not* just seen the head roll around to face him. Ash trickled from its hair. Its eyes were blank and yet somehow accusing.

No.

It was simply the way the body was positioned. It had always been facing Felix's way.

Heart stamping into the roof of his stomach, he left the body and continued on. More red droplets led deeper into the alley. And the ash looked scuffed. The flagellants had come this way.

Coughing into his sleeve, Felix followed the trail of blood.

Stricken still with horror, Rudi watched from the small garret window as the entire city crackled into flame. The fire was silver-tinged black and partially transparent, exposing the ruined piles over which they raged.

'This can't be real,' he whispered under his breath, clutching the arms beneath his borrowed red cloak and staring blankly into the fire.

He could feel the heat closing in, the wind hot and laden with ash. The skin of his face drew back to the bone before the rising heat. And it was real enough to the thousands of voices that screamed from every quarter as one. Rudi wondered if one of those interwoven cries belonged to Felix, or to Nikolaus.

In terror, he watched the flames, so reminiscent of those he saw every night in his dreams since he had been small. His anger at being left behind faded, but rather than relief it was guilt that knotted his guts around his heart.

Again, his cowardice spared him over better men.

'Get inside.'

The wolf-cloaked mercenary set a hand on his shoulder. Rudi had been so mesmerised that he had not noticed the Middenlander's approach. The man's eyes were shaded, more so than simple darkness could account for. And something in his touch made Rudi shiver.

Rudi nodded all the same. 'Nothing but evil out here.'

Smoke stung Felix's eyes, burned the hairs inside his nose and brought blisters to the roof of his tongue. Crouching beneath the layer of smog, Felix gave the corpse he had found a shake. It was a futile gesture. The big flagellant looked as if he had been crushed by a giant and *then* tossed at the wall. The alley outside was a mess of brick, silvery flames sparkling from the rubble like weeds. The destruction was recent and Felix could see fresh blood on the bricks. There had been a fight here, but this flagellant was the only body. He gave the corpse another hopeful shake, but it gave no answer. He shuddered.

He should probably be grateful for that fact.

He returned to the alley, trying to get some sense of where

the other flagellants might have gone. Smoke and ruin made a difficult task harder. It was possible they had triumphed and moved on, but somehow Felix doubted it. There were no abandoned rags, no alchemical burns on the bricks. If Gotrek and the others had been here when this flagellant fell then it must have all been over quickly. An ambush, perhaps? With no better options, and with the soles of his boots baking over the hot bricks, Felix headed towards the muggy red glow in the sky that he recalled as east.

The wall he passed through looked like it had been demolished by a blast of dragonfire. To left and right, through broken partitions, the tenement crawled with flames. Shimmering simulacra wavered through the smoke, screaming with an inhuman unity of purpose and pain. They saw him. Their regard made his flesh hot and his eyes dry and, forging through the heat, Felix burst coughing onto a wide street on the other side.

Would this happen every day until the end of days, he wondered? Were these damned souls condemned to burn for eternity? How did the gods allow it?

Felix drew in a ragged breath and stayed flat.

Down the street to his left, black cloaks almost invisible in the smoke, a pack of shadow-creatures clustered over a rooftop. The building on which they roosted had been spared the flames, shaded from the rising sun in the lee of the nearby bell tower. The creatures gabbled nervously, twitching back from the fires that licked the edges of their sanctuary. Felix looked past them. Smoke made even the bell tower ethereal, but he could see what looked like a market, squared by high-sided buildings of bruised stone.

And beyond that, the bridge.

He saw figures running through the murk towards it, thought he heard avian shrieks above the undying cries of the Damned. That was where the Beast was headed.

Where he would find Gotrek.

The monster had stationed the creatures on this rooftop as a rearguard. Felix lay still, weighing his options and finding them all heavier than he cared for. The abilities of these creatures were inhuman in almost every way that Felix had yet had cause to judge. He doubted he could sneak by them undetected. He questioned even more his chances in a straight fight.

As Felix considered, the sun slid infinitesimally through the thick sky, alighting on the corner of the creatures' rooftop. The tiling burst into sudden flame as though doused in pitch and lit. The creatures shrieked and scuttled back. Something had them terrified more than mere flame, for there was a human figure staked within the blaze. Felix covered his mouth to stifle a moan, cold dread dousing the hot blisters in his palms. The form was that of a woman, but indistinct, wavering with a silvery halo within the smoke. Hands tied behind her back, her sepulchral gown twisted as she writhed. Her silken hair blazed like tapers, crowned by a crackling laurel of mistletoe. The woman turned her smoky, faceless gaze up the slope of the roof. The creatures clutched each other and screamed, packing themselves into the shadow of the bell tower.

The rope binding the apparition to the stake burned through and she fell forward.

Out of the fire.

The bone-white brooch of a dove upon the woman's robes was scratched and dark. Felix's belly filled with ice. A sister from the sanatorium.

She had followed him.

'Shallya have mercy…'

Nils's footfalls brought a nervous creak from the floorboards. They were merely old. There was no sign of the fire damage that ruined most of the city. Rudi turned from the window and slid down the plaster wall. Hopefully that meant the ghost-fire would spare them too.

The four Middenlanders – Nils and the cloaked man, Marten, included – that had survived the attack on the sanatorium sat around or, in the case of Nils, paced. The garret was just barely sufficient to accommodate them all. There was one narrow window just within arm's reach of a now burning rooftop below, one door onto a broken staircase. In other words, no clear way out. The ceiling was low and sloped down towards the window. The walls leaned in close to the musk of surrender. The men watched him, and they watched each other. And they watched the walls. Shadows trickled down the plaster, crack to peeling crack.

Rudi gave a start as Marten swept out his cloak and sat down beside him. The man did not say anything. With the dreamlike motions of a sleepwalker he picked up his crossbow, inserted a bolt into the track, and slowly started to wind it. The rhythmic crank then strain sounded loudly above the whispered prayers.

'Put it down,' Nils snarled. If Marten heard, he ignored him. Nils just kept on pacing.

'Now what do we do?' one of the mercenaries whispered through clenched teeth. He was sweating in the heat. It was as if they sat above a stove.

'We're damned,' Marten murmured, all his attention on his crossbow.

'Shut up, Marten,' Nils growled. 'And I told you to put that thing down. Think you're going to shoot the dead?'

'What else?' said Marten without looking up.

With a click like a Bretonnian guillotine, Marten's crossbow cranked to its limit. A shadow flickered across his eyes, a faint silver halo playing through the hairs of his white-wolf cloak.

'Captain.'

Nils exploded, rounding on the seated man. 'I said shut u–'

Point blank, the bolt opened Nils's ribs like a crowbar

through a wooden chest, smacking his body back and skewering it to the wall. He was dead in a second. The mercenary's body slumped forward against the iron bolt. Too numb to do anything but watch, Rudi watched the man's eyes go cloudy. As if the smoke had taken his face.

'Ulric's teeth!' roared one of the mercenaries, ripping his sword from its scabbard as he rose.

The garret was too tight to swing a punch, much less a sword, and the blade lashed across the face of his still-seated comrade. Flesh and muscle split from nose to ear tip and the man fell, screaming, blood gushing from his jaw to pool with that spreading from Nils's feet.

'It was a gift, captain,' Marten murmured in a voice that was clearly not his own. 'You brought me here to be damned.'

The swordsman fell on him with a howl, hacking into his haunted friend as if the man were just meat. Marten made no effort to defend himself, the hewing longsword scattering blood to the walls like holy water. He did not scream. It was as if he were mindless.

It was as if he was already dead.

The final Middenlander was still yowling, pawing at the bloody flap hanging across his jaw as he ran stooped across the garret, chasing his errant blade across the floorboards before coming up to tackle the swordsman from behind. The two men slammed into the wall by the window in a shower of plaster, then slapped into the ruin of Marten's remains and rolled. Bloody as newborn babes they grappled for the sword. More voices than just their own screamed for murder.

Rudi screamed, drawing his weapons, and retreated into a corner. Whispers in his mind urged him to join in, to finish them both and flee, to escape this city with his soul. Beneath the window beside him, a shadowy figure was beginning to pull itself from Marten's body. A wolf cloak billowed like smoke. Unconscious of the mewling sound that escaped his lips, Rudi pressed himself into the wall and away from the window. It brought him closer to the door.

His hands tightened around his weapons as he stared at the wrestling Middenlanders. And he relented to the voices' urgings.

The Damned could take them.

They would not have him.

Cinders sparkled black and not at all as they tacked to the wind, like burning cutters sailing from the city and across the river's black calm into the shiftless fog. In places the motes swirled, like cannibal fireflies circling the weakest of their own. Occasionally one fell, plummeting like a stone to sizzle in the water or to burn, lost, alone and undying upon the algal weave that matted the river wall. Hurrlk sniffed at the changing air, heat gnawing through his strata of bandages and grime. Somewhere on the water, a bell tolled, its voice muffled by fog. Hurrlk shuffled, lips drawing muscle by uncertain muscle into a mad grin.

Bells for the dead.

In the street behind him, two-score of his scavengers cowered from the veiled glare of sunrise. They buried their heads in the hoods, hunching their shoulders beneath the grisly weight of plunder. The scent of panic they exuded excited something he had long forgotten. It was a thrill of danger, the knowledge that even the Damned could be afraid. He rounded on his minions, whip licking the air with a doubled *crack* to give voice to his command.

Move.

Those to the fore flinched, then broke cover. The rest were sharp on their tail. Hurrlk offered another lash to encourage them towards the bridge. The dead were rising, and even he would not choose to linger.

There were fates worse than death, and countless degrees of damnation.

The last from the alley herded a coffle of sinewy mortals onto the quay ahead of them. They were bound together through wrists and ankles by a single, oily length of cord. Some were mindless, others drugged, and they stumbled witlessly regardless of the desperation with which their herders applied the rod. Hurrlk was tempted to leave them behind, but the commandments of the Dark Master were clear.

He would have fresh souls. And somehow, that struck Hurrlk as good.

One of the captives was beginning to stir. Its axe, bolted to its bracer by a length of chain, trailed noisily over the flagstones. A herder lay into the muscular animal with a smooth-headed mace until it subsided. Reeling in his whip, Hurrlk stuck out his tongue for a taste of its barbed end. His accursed physiognomy was as resilient as a corpse, but he recalled the taste of poison, and the effect those flavours induced in softer flesh. His taste buds sang out the sapor of burned caster and lemon peel. He growled. The flame-fur was a fragile mortal, but he had the metabolism of a river troll.

The voices had been wrong. He could not be stopped.

The bells he had thought imagined grew louder as he pounded the circuit of the river wall towards the bridge. Their mournful song carried across the water. Slowly accreting a critical mass of interest, Hurrlk diverted his attention to the river. An outline of claws, spines and ridges rippled in shadow. It was growing larger and more defined as it cleared the fog and, as he watched, a low-sided river smack clove through the hanging cloud, yawing sprits trailing mist as it came. A single white sail billowed in the burning wind, dragging its course leeward and its starboard hull across his vision. Hurrlk made out the emblem outlined in silver on its prow. A black hand, fingers crowned with silver claws. The ship's bell clanged as the boat rocked. Mutant men, slack-jawed and blank-eyed, packed the decking. Occasionally, one would slip over the rails and plummet, nothing but the resistance of thin air inducing limbs to flail before they punched the river surface in a great spume of dark water.

The craft veered inexorably towards the bridge. It was not slowing down. It was crewed by the mindless. With a tremendous howl of splintering wood, it crashed into the bridge's wing wall, the aft piling over its stricken stern as though a daemonic hand drove it to its destruction. The shell crumpled, showering the quay with wedges of planking, scraps of white flax and bloodied, twisted bodies.

Not all of the bodies were still.

A low moan drifted up from the wreckage. A blubbery hand, unguided by conscious will, emerged from beneath a pile of wood. With a groan the mutant began to dig itself free. Others followed, mindless as the living damned.

Hurrlk regarded the train of captives, then hammered his whip-bound fist towards the wreckage in their path.

Take them.

Stowing blades and slings in favour of cudgels, his minions gave an angry squeal and charged forward to obey. The mindless were not dead, but misplaced. The Master would have the bones of his gloried champion and the Damned, living or dead, would heed his will. The Master would rise.

And then Hurrlk could finally be at peace.

The guttering along the rooftop rippled with flame, the fires eating inch by inch into the tiling as the sun's gaze burned through fog and shadow. Silvery gown haloed in fire, the dread sister stepped free of the flames and into the shadows. The tiles cracked beneath her charred feet. She extended a hand as if to tender mercy. Black smoke leeched from her sleeve.

Shrieking terror, the huddling scavengers scattered, biting at each other's arms in their haste to flee. Cloaks flapping in the fiery updraft, they leapt for the street. One took an elbow to the jaw and staggered back. Only its wavering tail and preternatural balance kept it from falling. The apparition stepped in behind it and wrapped both arms about its chest. The creature screamed as though branded, wriggling around to gnash its fangs through the smoky gauze of the woman's face. Smoke billowed through its jaws, achieving nothing. It howled, the shade offering a soothing whisper as both bodies ignited into silver-black flame.

Felix found his hand across his mouth, fearful that he was going to be sick. The scavenger's wail of torment persisted even as the fire took on a greenish tinge and the body dispersed to smoke in the phantom's arms. The dread sister met his eyes, smoke twisting across her face into the grim semblance of a smile. And then she was gone. Only the greenish plume of smoke rising above the flames suggested that his mind had not conjured the whole episode. Another shriek sounded from deeper down the street. There was a flash of silver within the smoke that burned down to green, a scattering of screams that swiftly grew distant. Felix could not believe his luck – if that was what he dared to call it.

The shade had just cleared his path to the bridge.

Without stopping to think why, or if the spirit had simply been drawn to the scavengers greater numbers, Felix firmed his grip on his sword, pressed the sleeve of his left hand to his face, and ran.

The street opened onto the market square and he paused for a frantic look around. The bell tower that cast its shade to the west was part of a square block of stone buildings. They were stout, angular affairs that aped a dwarfish style which had not been fashionable for centuries. But dwarfish style did not imply dwarfish make and columned frontages had crumbled amidst the rubble of roofs they had singularly failed to support. The flagstones burned sporadically, smoke rising from the cracks as though some hubristic baron had paved a caldera. On all sides, creatures screamed and scrambled for the rooftops. Others simply bolted across the burning square as fast their inhuman grace could take them.

It was not fast enough.

A silver form crackled into being within the fleeing pack. With both hands, she took the ragged scruffs of two necks. There was a scream and a spark of fire, and a heartbeat later a pair of immolated cloaks were cast to the wind. The creatures wailed, nimbly swerved around her, but did not alter their course. They were headed for the river. Felix could see it through the smoke. The black water was eerily calm despite the shrill calls of the shadows that drove along it left to right and, muted by the fog, the unmistakable clangour of battle.

Felix moved towards it, but this time, the apparition did not depart.

The black-cloaked multitudes teemed along the quay at her back but she did not move. Her gaze was for Felix and Felix alone. She held out a hand, palm front to command him to stop. Numb with dread, he did so. The shade's slender wrist was prickled with splinters, as if from a wooden stake, and bound in bloodied cord that fizzed like a lit taper.

'*Back, Sigmarite.*'

Felix gaped, heart thumping, desperate to flee yet terrified to do so lest the apparition come for him in the time it took to blink. Her voice was cold, flat, brimming with hate. Scavengers streamed around her in blind terror. She ignored them. Before Felix even realised it he was running, hurdling a flickering pyre of rocks and sprinting for the colonnaded verandah of the large stone house on the near side of the square.

The building looked like it had been the office of a merchant. Felix could not have cared if it was the gartenhaus of the Imperial Arch-chancellor. Shoulder first, he charged up the stone steps of the verandah and straight through the front door. The oak had been sturdy enough to withstand the fire but this was an act of violence too far. The wood splintered down the middle and spilled Felix into the heaped debris scattered across the antechamber. Still moving forward, he scrambled upright and hastily snatched his bearings.

A staircase curved inside the left-hand wall toward the wreckage of a first floor gallery. Beyond it were ceiling beams and, through gaps in the roof, smoke. In the time he watched, a dozen black shadows flapped across the broken roof for the riverside beyond. The shrieks of their kin were muted, if only slightly, by the thin limestone walls. And Felix doubted that such a barrier would prove any impediment to the passage of the dead.

Several doors led off from the antechamber and Felix bolted for the one in the opposite wall. He was not thinking clearly, he knew, fleeing from the shades of the Damned towards the sounds of battle. But his racing thoughts brought him continuously to thoughts of Gotrek. He never thought his mind would equate the Slayer with safety, but right now he would have preferred his companion to all the gold in Marienburg and then some.

And where there was battle, he would surely find Gotrek, so he pulled open the door and dove through.

It led into a warehouse. The cavernous room was unbearably hot, thick black smoke belching onto the river front from the shattered door in the far wall. Through the opening came snatches of figures, dull moans, fraught screams, the slap of wood and iron against pliant flesh. Teary eyed and choking, Felix gauzed his mouth with his sleeve and forced a path through the heat.

The only light was from the fires that licked darkly at the river-facing windows. They were set into a thin strip above a creaking iron gantry, accessible by a set of wooden steps to

Felix's right. They were charred black. It was a miracle they had survived at all. Beneath the gantry, warped tracks of iron shelving ran the length of the walls. Heat had buckled them, ripping them from their corbels and splaying them across the ground. They had been melted into odd shapes, like claws. Felix took pains to avoid them. Thinking clearly enough to be wary, he angled his sword and pressed deeper.

Breathing was becoming painful. He coughed on acrid fumes, could almost feel the ash lining his lungs. The smoke churned, random eddies drawing imagined terrors into the murk. The ceiling gave an ominous creak and he glanced up. The instant he did so, he sensed movement in front of him.

She was here.

Felix stumbled back with a cry and, remembering his sword, swept the ensorcelled blade through the shade's wrist. There was no resistance to his blow, the blade passing ineffectually through her arm and spinning him round, feet tangling and spilling him to the ground. His heart beat surrender, but a fighter's instinct turned the fall into a roll, and he found his feet to hasten back. His back hit the ladder to the gantry. It gave an iron moan.

The shade had not followed. Smoke drifted through her as easily as had his sword, her hair gusting like sizzling motes towards the doorway. The same doorway that her presence barred.

'Why do you haunt me?' Felix screamed, throat hoarse from inhaling too much smoke.

The apparition merely extended its hand once again, reaching for Felix's black eye. There was a tenderness there that bitterness could not fully expunge, but rampant heat boiled from her hand. It was not that of a warm body. It was more akin to a hot coal. Or a roasted corpse. Felix beat his hand through the shade's arm, feeling nothing but hot smoke and then, with a strangled roar, spun and raced up the ladder to collapse onto the gantry. It shook hollowly as it took his weight, an ominous groan spreading along its length as each corbel in turn announced the imminence of its demise. He gasped and scrambled to his feet.

The iron gantry was white hot. A fiery welt pulsed across the back of his neck where he had lain on it. His mail was beginning to sizzle, his boot leather to melt, and the smell of his own singed hair pursued him as he stumbled to the windows.

Each one had been shattered inwards, as though some mighty spell had been detonated on the other side of the river. The central casement opened onto a triangular platform, ash-coated limestone projecting above the quay. The iron parts of a large derrick lay tangled, twisting under Felix's boots as he staggered out into a scream of cold air.

An instinctual dread made him turn and stumble on the debris.

The faceless shade was at the window. Smoke wreathed her, gouting through the blasted windows. Coughing on the fumes, Felix backed off. Without making any kind of gesture, the spirit beckoned. She wanted him to join her. She wanted him to save her.

'*Back, Sigmarite.*'

Was that all she could say? Continuing to back away, Felix's foot slipped into emptiness. He kicked up into smoke, his mailed body drawing him the opposite way like a dead weight. The smoke-filled apparition suddenly surged forward, rearing large in his vision, only to then recede in what terror made slow.

He was falling.

His back hit something massive and hard.

He bit his tongue, then bounced, slamming side-on onto stone flags. He groaned. Something kicked him in the shoulder and he opened his eyes. Agile figures were vaulting over him to engage in a battle that sounded suddenly close. Taking a fevered grip on the sword still in his hand he prepared to push himself up, giving a startled yelp as a set of monstrous claws sliced beneath the underside of his collar and yanked him into the air. Felix gasped in pain. Hot blood trickled down his spine where those claws dug in. He dangled two feet from the ground at the end of a mummified trunk of an arm.

And before him snarled the Beast.

It was unhooded and for the first time Felix got a good look. Its snout was long and grey, with ebon fur peeling from eyes that glowed fierce and mad. Its black cloak was buckled with bone at its throat, swept back across its ogrish shoulders. A thick, wart-encrusted tongue licked its broken teeth as the Beast examined him with a strangely absent gaze. Its pallid tail flicked through the smog as though itself confused.

The Beast was the most debased and disfigured specimen of that already foul race that Felix had ever encountered, but he was in no doubt. The Beast was neither ghoul lord nor daemon.

The Beast was a ratman.

CHAPTER 12

The Claws of the Beast

With a disinterested growl, the Beast flung Felix from its claws. He sailed through smoke-filled air, then hit the ground with a metallic clank. He rolled over the broken flags like a felled log, cloaked skaven hurdling his body as he rolled, finally fetching up against what felt like an array of legs. There was a rusted jangling of chain. For a moment he lay still, appreciating the full depth and favour of his pain.

Burned, bloodied, dizzy, he sat up.

Between the low limestone barrier of the river wall and the buttressed stone of the riverside warehouses, the dense fog seethed with cloaked rats. Felix watched as one of them smacked a steel bludgeon into the skull of a mindless, bone-plated abomination. The dark exoskeleton splintered under the blow, but the mutant expressed no pain, no shock. It came on, its bulk bearing itself and its attacker both to the flag-stones. The skaven savaged the mutant's throat, then shrieked as the thing fumbled over its face and, with a hideous absence of mind, gouged its eyes from their sockets.

Ignoring their kin-rat's wails, more of the cloaked scavengers were tearing into the fray to lay into the dead-eyed shells of misshapen men with cudgels and nets.

The mutants advanced through the smog from the direction of the bridge, relentless in their indifference. And more were coming. Dripping wet, cloaked in rust-coloured algae, hair and clothing struck with splinters, they flopped over the lip of the river wall and fell ashore. They acted like zombies but for the breaths that made their chests rise and fall, and the way that they so freely bled and died. Dozens lay dead but twice as many more lay trussed and bound.

Wading into the fray, the Beast unspooled a whip, testing its bite with a doubled *whip-crack*. It was doubly barbed with bone, what looked like the incisors of some monstrous rat, and glistened with a black lacquer that made Felix think immediately of poison. The great whip snapped over the shrieking ranks of his minions, drawing strips of flesh from the misshapen multitudes that pressed them. Where the whip drew blood, mutants spasmed, went slack and fell.

Something stuck a toe in his kidney.

'Wake up, manling. Get up and give me a hand.'

Felix coughed, thinking smoke must have gotten into his ears, and looked over his shoulder. Hurriedly, he stood. The Beast had thrown him deliberately to where two abject files of almost-humans had been lashed together, bundled against the river wall, and abandoned. They moaned to themselves, pulling limply in all directions. And in the middle of the foremost file, as belligerent amongst them as the strains of a Nordland drinking ballad in an Estalian cantata, orange crest quivering with fury, was Gotrek. The Slayer glared at the mutants that flanked him, their conflicting efforts dragging him from side to side. He spat onto the back of the gelid-fleshed abomination to his left.

'Don't just stand there and gawp. I refuse to meet my doom

lashed to some daemon-spawned wretch and without an axe in my hand.'

Gotrek looked as though he had taken every bit as much punishment as Felix had and then some. His axe, still bolted to his bracer, dangled from its chain between his bound wrists. His face and beard were dusted red. It looked as though the dwarf had fallen under a wall.

'Seems you were right,' Gotrek grunted, grudgingly presenting his bound wrists to Felix's blade. His one good eye was bloodshot. It glared beyond Felix's shoulder to where the Beast battled. 'The brute was after the bones. Caught me by surprise and took what I had.'

Felix carefully inserted his blade between Gotrek's wrists and began to saw. 'It drove us from the sanatorium too. They're all gone. Caul, Bernhardt...' He paused, freezing mid-stroke. 'Damn, maybe even Rudi.'

'You left him?' Gotrek's brick-dusted eyebrow arched. 'After all you insisted the little oathbreaker come along.'

'I thought it was for the best,' Felix hissed. 'I didn't realise the city was about to sink into some fiery abyss!'

Gotrek grunted and pushed his wrists towards Felix's sword. 'Less with the talk, manling, and more with the blade. Or must I talk you through it?'

Felix scowled, sawing through enough of the rope's slippery outer coating for Gotrek to rip off the rest with a triumphant roar. Felix flinched and looked around, but the skaven were far too busy to notice what was happening behind them.

'What happened? Felix asked as Gotrek wiped oily residue onto his torn breeches, then gripped his axe in a pugnacious, two-fisted embrace. 'Why didn't it just kill you?'

Gotrek gave a crooked leer, running his thumb around the rim of his axe blade until it bled. He jerked his bloodied thumb over his shoulder to the Beast. 'I'll tell you what I'll do. I'm going to march over there, rip off its troll-ugly head, and bring it back here. You can ask it questions until you both turn blue. How does that strike you?'

Felix smiled wearily. 'Like a Mootland summer.'

'Ha!' Gotrek roared, no doubt in the hope that something would take note. He started into the fray, then paused and looked back. 'One thing, manling…'

'Yes?'

A look of embarrassment coloured Gotrek's brutal face as he hid his oil-smeared left wrist behind his back. 'When you pen that final verse you have my permission to haze over certain details.'

'If I survive to see the inside of a book again, I'll write whatever you like.'

'There's the spirit,' Gotrek replied, giving a brothers-in-arms slap that near dislocated Felix's shoulder. It was times like these when Felix doubted whether the Slayer actually heeded a word he said. 'Stand back, manling. My axe thirsts from chasing shadows, and only the blood of every last one of these vermin will sate it.'

Gotrek issued an ululating cry and, axe held high, charged for the skaven's backs.

It was oddly reassuring to note that even such twisted specimens as these were still paranoid back-stabbers at their cores. The ears of the nearest twitched the second that cry left the Slayer's lips. It turned its head just as Gotrek's axe swept it from its shoulders. More of the skaven hissed and broke off from the mindless to face him. Gotrek laughed at their approach, ripping his axe through a brutal figure-of-eight that sent limbs, heads, as well as the suckered feelers from the manifold limbs of a mindless, spinning asunder in a grisly shower.

'…he is my courage. I will trust and be not afraid. The Lord Sigmar is my strength and my song…'

Felix looked down, away from the Slayer as the familiar, broken voice rasped at his back. The flagellant's eyes were glassine and half lidded, as dead as those of the mindless. His lips were flecked with spittle and moved slowly, unconscious vessels for their master's message. He was sandwiched between two of his acolytes, the last two, and bent against the river wall within the second file of the chain gang.

Felix collected his sword and began to saw.

'Hold on, Brüder Nikolaus,' he murmured, painfully aware of Gotrek's joyous howls. 'I'll get you out of there.'

Hurrlk thumped down a gasping, waxen-fleshed fusion of man and monster, then grasped it by the tentacles burgeoning from its clavicle and tossed it back for his minions to bind. The mindless swarmed the quay. They were clumsy, they were slow, but they were relentless. And they were numerous, like mayflies on a marsh. He had never seen so many.

Did not.

Would never.

He snarled and lashed his whip, another pair spitting froth and jerking as though ravaged by warp-lightning. It was then he noticed the waxen one was rising. It rubbed its head and moaned. Anger flared within his breast like a star thought dead. Why had it not been bound?

'Oi, ugly!'

With a low growl, Hurrlk turned. His minions were dead or in flight. The cretinous fools; as if death held terror for one of the Damned. Surrounded by singed rags and bits of meat, the flame-fur gestured with his axe. The peeling grey flesh of Hurrlk's lips pulled back over his pale, translucent teeth, his throat rattling like the bars of a daemon's cage. He drew back his whip.

'Aye, come on then. Come give this dwarf a mighty doom.'

Gotrek ducked the stroke of the monster's whip, gritting his teeth as it parted a layer of his skin and a clutch of hair from his scalp. It did not draw blood. He rose again, glancing over his shoulder as a skaven fumbled at the tear in its chest, coughed liquid foam into its cowl and fell limp. A soft-shelled mutant stumbled over its body and groped mindlessly for Gotrek's throat. He cackled grimly and shattered its face with an elbow.

'The lash might cow these vermin, but they've not a dwarfish constitution.'

The Beast swung its head furiously from side to side, as if muddled by a train of events too swift for it to follow. Unchecked, a pack of mindless pressed into its back. With a scything sweep of its tail it threw them down, a pair sent flailing over the river wall with a distant splash. Snorting and snarling, it focused its mad eyes on the dwarf.

'That's right, Beast, I'm going nowhere. Come to me or I come to you.' Gotrek's lips twisted into an expectant leer. 'My axe thirsts.'

The Beast threw back its head and barked, a shrill burst of sound that tore the smoky gauze to scattered shreds. It stamped, dropped its shoulders, spread its monstrous arms wide enough to encompass the entire quay with their span, and then charged.

Gotrek twitched in readiness as it thundered over the broken flags. The skaven shrilled and skipped from its path, but the mindless were not nearly so cogent of their peril. A ram-horned mutant went down under a massive foot, silvery blood splattering the monster's bandaged calf. The Beast sprung off the mutant's ruin, a paw like a knife-studded shovel shearing towards Gotrek's face. The dwarf stepped clear, deflecting the blow off the flat of his axe, then spun to deliver a counter that clove deep into the monster's belly.

The Beast hollered, but did not stop, its charge bearing it right through the swing and slamming Gotrek to the ground. Gotrek wheezed as the Beast fell on top of him.

There was no skill at play; neither the instinct nor even the desire for its own survival.

Pinning the Slayer under one great paw, the Beast drew back the other for a finishing blow. Gotrek had the strength of a pack of oxen. Felix had seen him fight hand-to-hand with a giant, but even he could not wrest himself from the grip of the Beast. Like a rock from the sky, the fist plummeted down. Gotrek threw everything into one last shove, shifting the pinning arm just enough to throw his shoulders from the path of the blow. The flagstones shattered, the Beast's arm disappearing past the wrist. Arm buried in the ground, the monster roared in Gotrek's face. Gotrek spat in its open mouth, making it choke in surprise.

With a stony oath of his own, Gotrek crooked his left arm around the Beast's buried paw, locked its wrist into his elbow, and then hewed his axe one-handed into its triceps. The Beast howled in pain and tried to pull away, but Gotrek gripped it tight, its struggles only causing the starmetal blade to sink deeper into the muscle. The treacly dribble of blood caused both their arms to darken.

'Not so tough without a wall between us,' Gotrek growled, wiggling his axe, causing blood to spurt across his face.

The Beast grunted, thrashing against Gotrek's hold, dragging the Slayer's back across the flagstones but failing to break his grip. Gotrek winced as the Beast lifted him and smashed him back into the ground. The mutated creature pressed down, as if to crush the life from him. The stones beneath him cracked, their make as nothing to dwarfen bones. A grin of animal cunning pulled back its rotten lips and, with a bellow of raw power, it slammed its free hand into the ground and threw itself upright. Rubble raining from his clothes, Gotrek came up with it. He swung from its wrist.

Panting heavily with laughter, the Beast spread its claws to strike.

* * *

Felix swore and redoubled his efforts to sever Nikolaus's bonds. Across the quay, skaven fell upon the mindless that their master's charge had felled. They clubbed them into submission, bound them with a practiced efficiency and, Felix could not fail to notice, slit a few throats now their master was not watching. And more than a few of those glittering, versicoloured stares were now turning towards him. One advanced with short sword and club. Another came bearing a cord in its wake.

'Perfect,' Felix muttered, sawing for all he was worth before abandoning the job half done, swinging his sword around to guard and backing into the moaning coffle. Nikolaus continued to mutter, dumb to Felix's efforts. The two flagellants beside him seemed incapable even of that. 'Absolutely perfect.'

The skaven's short sword flashed before him, appearing in a downward arc with the speed of a murderous thought. It was instinct more than any application of skill that angled his blade and sent the notched length skirling down the length of his own sword. There was barely time to draw breath before a second sword-rat rounded the first. It clutched the neck of a bulging sack to its collar with one paw and stabbed a serrated blade for Felix's throat with the other.

Felix spun back, stamped the sword from the first ratman's paw, using its body for cover as he rolled around it then lashed back across the throat of the second. The skaven fell with wasted breath whistling through its claws. The forgotten sack dropped, disgorging its contents onto the quay. The rope-rat squealed alarm, dropped its length of cord and snatched up the sack, sweeping the spilled bones back inside. It glared at Felix before bolting for the bridge. Felix did not have time to worry about it.

He swept aside as the steel-capped bludgeon of the first sword-rat whisked for his skull. The heavy club caved in the face of the bound mutant at Felix's back. The mutant gave a final moan but, lashed to the flagellants and its fellow mutants, the corpse leaned and did not fall. The skaven withdrew its bludgeon, shook it clear of pink matter, and hissed annoyance. Felix gave ground, circling the coffle until his foot struck the stone of the river wall. He teetered backwards, only just deflecting the gut-thrust that sought to take advantage. The vibrations shook his shoulder like the jaws of a wolf. His body was burned out, it was ready to drop. The arrival of a second ratman, this one dragging a weighted net, told him he was done.

Felix leapt back and onto the wall just as the net snared the air where he had just been. His boots skidded on the slimy stone and, for a moment, he teetered on the brink of falling into the haunted water. Then his left foot struck a mooring ring and checked its slide. The club-rat hissed and swung for his trailing leg but, with the mooring ring for support, Felix dragged it in and the club whacked the algal mat so hard that it sprung free of the creature's paw. The rat yelped as its bludgeon hummed to the foggy water. It looked stunned. Felix made sure it stayed that way, driving a kick across its snout that sent it sprawling into its captives.

The wall was about a foot across and pasted with slime. The sword-rat was picking itself up, the net-rat egging it on. Spreading his arms for balance, Felix hastened along its top, heart lurching with every slippery step and doing flips every time the bound hand of a mindless groped for his ankles. More skaven were becoming aware of his presence, struggling to shift the uncooperative train in a bid to get at him. But the wall ahead was still clear. A sibilant hiss told him the sword-rat had joined him.

He risked a look back.

Quicker and more agile by far, it was closing the distance fast. Felix dared himself to accelerate, clearing the train of mindless and the snarling vermin that fought to make them move, but he knew he was not about to outrun a skaven. He considered diving into the river, using some of the floating wreckage to swim to the opposite shore, but the Middenlanders had called the water haunted and even now, with the choice between a rusted blade and that whispering dark, he knew which he favoured.

And he could not abandon Gotrek.

The dwarf's arm was still locked around the Beast's wrist as Gotrek drove a two-footed kick into its belly. The monster doubled over with a startled wheeze and let the dwarf fall. Gotrek's axe was swinging before he hit the ground. Winded, taken aback by its foe's ferocity, its claws flashed to deflect the torrent of blows and, inexorably, it was driven back. The mindless were barged aside or else stood there to be crushed. Gotrek ignored them, intent on the Beast. Felix saw them both fade into the bridge's fog, nothing visible but the red blur of his companion's rune-axe.

Felix looked away to parry a sword thrust. His feet slipped under him, causing the ratman's punch to swipe an inch past his nose. He swayed, too intent on not falling and cracking his skull to retaliate. His sure-footed foe showed no such qualms, fiercely pressing its advantage. Felix did not know how his own sword kept pace, but somehow it did. He could beat this rat, but not here, not with his footing constantly sliding out from under him. From the corner of his eye, he saw another pair of skaven get up from the wriggling body of a bound mutant to come his way. He had no choice.

Mouthing a prayer, Felix turned his back and ran.

A swift thrust stabbed between his shoulder blades. Felix grunted, feeling the bone bruise, but the mail took the brunt and he accelerated away. The sword-rat was hot on his heels.

The river wall ended a few paces ahead. There was a gap of a couple of feet where it adjoined the angled slope of the wing wall. Felix braced his nerves, upped his pace, and leapt.

He landed on the wing wall and swayed for balance, already

slipping down its slickened slope. The sword-rat followed a second later. Felix half-spun to meet it, half-skidded on slime, swinging a kick that poleaxed the creature mid-leap. It screamed as its fall parted layers of mist and then smacked into the water with a dark spume. The tug of a weary smile announced his triumph, only for his feet to then slip and pitch him from the wall and down onto the flagstones with a ringing elbow and a curse. Rising painfully, ratmen already shrilling after him, Felix sprinted for the bridge.

It was a mighty ruin, riding twenty feet above the river astride limestone columns each twice the girth of a man. Fog clutched its wreck possessively, making it its own, the battling forms of Gotrek and the Beast rendered ethereal in its embrace. The Beast bellowed, thinned by fog but still enough to break a splinter of dread to worry at Felix's spine.

The monster's claws scraped blue sparks from the flat of Gotrek's axe. Felix tried to run to his companion's side but Gotrek had already pressed his foe deep into the mist. Felix could feel the fog slow him down. It was like running through freezing water, like fleeing from a nightmare. It was doubt-less a trick of the shifting murk, but the Beast appeared to be standing taller the further into the darkness it was forced, its animal snarls adopting the vaguest spark of sentience.

Gotrek roared, swinging two-handed for the Beast's midriff. The Beast slapped the axe aside, then pulled up with a pained growl, the action causing its split triceps to spurt. Gotrek pressed his attack, raining down blows that would have been too swift for Felix to follow even had they not been seques-tered by fog. The Beast howled in pain. Blood painted the mist red. It retreated further, enough for breathing room. It poked at its bloodied hide and panted with what looked like surprise.

It was beaten.

Gotrek cackled and swung his axe high above his head. The Beast issued a mighty roar and threw itself into the weapon's path, the starmetal blade crunching through its plate-like pectoral bone.

The Beast shuddered and, clutching the weapon to its breast, staggered back. The embedded axe yanked at its chain and jerked Gotrek's arm after it. The chain groaned, but held, and dragged the dwarf cursing over the rubble after the retreating Beast. Blood thumped between its claws, but the Beast held the buried axe firm. On reaching the bridge's wall, it leapt onto it, the taut chain flipping Gotrek from his feet and slamming him face down into the stone flags. It backed to the ledge, dragging Gotrek another inch along on his chest.

'Kill us both,' Gotrek roared. 'That'd be a mighty end!'

The Beast tittered, saliva spooling from its fur as its twisted jaw shaped into a word.

'Huuurrrrlk.'

And then it jumped.

The short length of chain raced over the edge. Gotrek bellowed like a wounded ox as his arm snapped up.

Felix cried out, mustering the strength to burst through the clinging fog, but too late. Gotrek's body slammed into the wall, then was dragged over it. His ham-like left fist closed over the side of the bridge, but its surface had been burned smooth and coated with slime. The dwarf's arm checked his own weight and that of the bone-plated Beast for barely a second.

Felix made the wall a moment later. He heard one distant splash, followed by another. Desperately, he sought out a shock of orange, a glow of red, anything, but he could barely even see the water for the fog. Numb, he ran further along the wall, deeper into the fog, staring down into the water. Part of him expected to see his companion swinging from a stanchion, or dripping wet and climbing one of those mouldering columns. But even Gotrek could not fail to find his doom eventually. And the dwarf's end had come exactly as Felix had always secretly feared.

With him left to the mercy of Gotrek's slayers.

The leaderless skaven flooded the bridge in pursuit. Felix backed away, angled his sword, but it felt so heavy. He tried to come up with a plan that did not involve him joining his companion in the river or being hacked apart by vengeful vermin.

He tried to think, but… just… could not.

The mist coiled about his arms and drew him back, its embrace welcoming and cold. There was more than just solidity to it, but will. It moved with the urgings of a thousand minds, suffering as Felix could not conceive.

'Felix.'

Feeling halfway between wakefulness and sleep, Felix looked back to the warehouse he had just fled. It flickered with spectral fire. The fog darkened his eyes, but he could still discern the silvery halo that glazed the loading platform. It was a woman. Her white robes burned with a distant heat. Cosseted by the fog, his brain pleasantly dim, Felix felt no fear. She wanted something. He did not care.

'Felix.'

The mists closed. So too did his eyes.

And she was gone.

'Felix!'

Panting and out of breath, a fierce pain stitching his sides, Rudi slumped against the ashen stone of the loading platform. His throat was caked in soot, his skin burned dry and peeling black. His sword dropped from his fingers. Flesh and steel were both drenched with human blood. Caul's knife had been lost. He tried to remember exactly where, but his flight across the city had been such a gauntlet of terror that his mind refused to look back and face it.

He crawled to the edge of the platform.

On the quayside below, cloaked creatures herded a hideous pack of mutants towards the bridge. Their chittering voices were low and excited, like warriors returning home from victory. Brüder Nikolaus was amongst their number. Rudi called his name, but the prophet did not turn. He yelled again; no words this time, just a pain in his chest that demanded to be expelled. Nothing noticed.

Rudi considered whether he might already be dead. He would not be surprised that his soul had been consigned to the Grey Vaults. He looked again at his bloodied hands. He had been tested and he had failed. Sigmar did not give third chances.

He looked on as more of the shadow-creatures scurried in their captives' wake. Their claws scratched through the rubble and beneath fresh corpses in search of any tiny fragment of lost bone. Their ecstatic squeals when something was unearthed made Rudi shudder. Unconsciously, he reached for his sword.

He did not think he had ever held his mother's hand as tightly.

Squinting through blood-lashed eyes into smoke and fog, he waved his hand and yelled Felix's name again. The man plainly heard. His face turned Rudi's way. Before Rudi could call again, Felix was gone. It was as if the fog had claimed his body for its own.

Rudi grunted as his eyes were speared by a sudden light.

Dawn was creeping across the city with the false tenderness of a torturer. The ruined husk lightened while, at the same time, somehow darkening, sinking into its own shadows, like a rat to its burrow to wallow in its pain. He raised a hand to his eyes and peered through glowing fingers into the light. Undying screams welcomed it in ungodly chorus. Flames flicked between the tendrils of fog as though the ethereal barrier had itself been ignited by the sun's rays.

For in the east, the sun rose as it always had over Ostermark.

Bestride the burned bodies of the Damned.

* * *

Blearily, Felix shook his head. Everything had become dark, muted. The ground beneath him was strangely yielding, as if he lay on a bed of kelp at the ocean's bottom. He could hear screams but they were passionless. Nearby, or perhaps distant, there came a resounding *crump*. The shocks passed through his body. They reminded him vaguely of the test firings at the Nuln Artillery School. There was an answering rumble, as of a building's collapse. More screams. Quarrels flicked by overhead.

What was happening?

He remembered passing through fog, and the fog had stayed with him. It was a gauze around his eyes, and not just his eyes. He could feel it smothering his mind. Other thoughts, other *minds*, contested the occupancy of his skin. They came with memories he could not recall, scenes and faces he did not know. But they were too many, and unable to make him do more than twitch where he lay. Giving a low moan, he slapped his palms clumsily to his forehead. He could feel the knot behind his eyes. If he could just get his hands to it then he could pull away the veil and think again. His fingers butted cloddishly against his skull. It was with a detached concern that he noticed he felt no touch; not on his forehead nor in his fingers. He thought about rolling his head.

Half a minute later his head rolled.

A wiry creature in a black cloak noticed the movement and crouched beside him. It flinched as a quarrel zipped past, then poked him in the collar with a crooked black claw. The creature tittered, dragging back its hood to reveal a long, hideously disfigured face. Felix tried to speak, but could not. Muddled by conflicting thoughts, he tried to think of what he should be feeling. All he could remember was fire, pain, mutation.

And madness.

'*How does it feel,*' the ratman snickered, '*to be damned?*'

CHAPTER 13

Other Times

Felix stirred with a groan. He felt as though he had matched Gotrek through a head-butting contest before finally going down in the twelfth round.

And then had a drink to celebrate.

He lay with eyes closed on what felt like gravel. The sound of a flowing river passed somewhere nearby, the dapple of water on rock weaving with a wilful breeze to conjure an unsettling melody. His black eye stung as if it had been dabbed with vinegar and the rest of him ached almost as much. The air was warm, unseasonably so, a midsummer mugginess that promised hotter days to come. And yet he felt cold, fog's damp fingers in his clothes. As if the sun was a lie. Felix airily signed the hammer and prayed for death.

But Sigmar, as was his way where Felix was concerned, failed to oblige.

How had he gotten here?

He remembered stepping into the fog, crossing the bridge and coming out... somewhere else.

With one hand he massaged his temple. He recalled feeling other minds in his head but they seemed to have left him. The concoction of water and wind crafted a murmuring akin to voices. Disturbed, he opened his uninjured eye, wincing immediately before the unexpected brightness.

An open blue sky flamed with a pink aurora. The quixotic display continued in mesmeric silence, pinks giving way to blues, which then sublimed to pink in turn. Felix stared into it, wondering what fury could make the sky itself burn. His gaze focused through the flames towards the largest and brightest body in the sky. The sun guttered fitfully in its shadow. Twice the size of its warmth-giving rival, the bloated disk of the Chaos moon, Morrslieb, throbbed a baleful green.

Felix could not believe what he was seeing. He could just about accept that something in the air of this city might make the sky burn with pink fire. But Morrslieb had not passed so near to the world in years, and surely nothing at work here could make it so.

Painfully, he sat up and looked downriver. The river shimmered with reflected light, as though aquatic sprites pulled at the flotsam that flowed from right to left. Upriver, more distant than Felix would have imagined possible, the sullen grey stone of the bridge was a shaded spectre in the fog. For a moment he had the strangest sense that he heard Rudi calling his name. Without warning, he doubled over, his gag reflex finally besting the resistance of his thumping skull, and vomited Sigmarshafen's finest goat stew over his boots. He regarded the mess and grimaced.

'What could possibly make this day worse?'

Something hard and unkind prodded one of many bruises on his back. He shifted around, a blur of pinks, reds and dreary stone-greys swimming into slow focus.

He wished they had not.

The most loathsome mutant Felix had ever seen greeted

his look of disgust with a scowl. He focused on the mutant's hand and on the long metallic object with which it had summoned his attention. It was Felix's sword. He looked up into the mutant's face and smiled ruefully.

'Of course.'

The courtyard that adjoined the eastern side of the bridge was a charred waste, the scar of flame upon all that had not collapsed to ash. The townhouses across the cobbles were black-walled ruins. The tavern overlooking the river was a shell, its former purpose discernible only by the cellar into which the remainder had collapsed. And neither had the bridge itself been spared. The proud grey stone was scabbed black, as though recently savaged by a beast's claws.

It could not have been so recent. And yet…

Flakes of black snow swirled gracefully from the charcoal sky.

Rudi looked up. There was no sensation of cold as they flecked his face. He brushed them off, crumbling the grimy flakes between thumb and forefinger. The black was speckled with green, motes guttering like wicked stars in a night sky. Rudi cleaned his hand on his borrowed red cloak, then hauled it up over his head to shield it from the strange snow. The green was wyrdstone, the Chaos rock, and a man did not live with the legacy of the Pious in his veins without learning its power to corrupt.

It was said that even a touch could drive a man to mutation and madness.

Sheltering hands and face beneath his cloak, Rudi licked his lips warily. The air was furnace dry. Even the river flopped muddily downhill. Rudi's eyes narrowed. From the other side it had been swollen.

Voices whispered between the drifting darkness, memories at once familiar and strange. He sought out the pewter hammer that hung at his breast. He caressed it, murmured a half-remembered canticle and moved deeper into the courtyard.

'Felix!' he hissed.

He flinched as soon as the words left his parched lips. There was something disturbing in this black snow that made him wish to go unnoticed.

But he had seen Felix cross. The man *had* to be here somewhere.

Even as that thought arose, it brought the certainty that this place was not as deserted as it seemed. Holding still, he heard breaths punctuate the murmuring wind. Soft treads caused the ashen ground to whisper. He released his talisman and slid his hand down to the bloodied sword at his belt.

He was not alone. Something had followed him from the mists.

Felix gave what he hoped was a cooperative-sounding grunt as a scruffy hunchback in tarnished plate pushed his face into the shingle and patted his boots and breeches for concealed weapons. Felix tried not to cringe from the mutant's touch. He cursed himself for forgetting about there being warpstone-twisted abominations still at large in the City of the Damned. Felix had had enough first-hand experience of mutant settlements to know that there was more than a grain of truth to rumours of cannibalism and Chaos worship. But his ill-feeling was about more than that, more even than the gelid feel of the man's fingers.

It felt like he was being touched by a wraith.

He risked a look up, blinking grit from his eyes. Two-score bulky mutant warriors watched him from the shingle just upriver. They were garbed in a motley assortment of coloured cloaks and partially corroded armour of copper, bronze, and tin. They were burdened with booty and appeared in good spirits. Each was heavily armed, but none had troubled themselves to bring said weapons to bear on Felix's account.

He could not explain it, but just looking at them was disturbing. Their eyes were shadowed, their voices tinny. As if they were not truly there at all. Felix shivered.

The unease was the same as he had felt in the presence of the Damned.

'Nothing on him.'

The hunchback ground his face into the grit, then stepped back to collect the spear it had left just out of Felix's reach.

'Are you mindlesh, outshider?'

The mutant that bore Felix's sword was a sight to send hardened witch-finders early to bed. It was obscenely side-heavy, the musculature on its right side swollen out of all proportion to its left. No doubt this had something to do with the immense black crab-claw that rested its barbed tip in the shingle. But the final flourish of cruelty, as though quite literally to rub the poor horror's face in the wreck of its human form, was a hairy foot-long spike that erupted from the base of its neck to flatten its face against that swollen right shoulder. The mutant slurped and leaned closer, prodding Felix with the tip of his sword.

'Do you undershtand what I shay, outshider?'

The mutant's face was squashed against its shoulder, like a rotten potato from the bottom of a sack. Feature's converged on the opposite side such that both eyes were stacked upon one side of its nose and white lips ran like scar tissue behind the left ear.

Felix stared dumbly.

'Mindlesh all right. Take him.'

Two more warriors with far too much muscle to be borne of nature downed weapons and split from the watching group. One of them was wearing a black cloak that had an arrow hole through the collar and alchemical burns on the inner lining. The mutant smelled like a pickled rat. Each hooked one of Felix's arms in theirs and hauled him off the sand. Felix groaned. His flesh crawled from where the mutants gripped. His head span from Shallya knew what.

His next thought came to him with such unexpectedness that it made him start. The heavies tightened their grip, fearing he was about to make a fight of it. There had been a battle, he remembered. The skaven had been ambushed as they had crossed the mists.

Did that mean that while their slayers made off with burned rags and rusted knives, their precious bones were lying untended?

Felix struggled against the heavies' grip, but their arms were like beef hocks.

'I have to go back.'

The mutant's vertical slit of a mouth widened with surprise.

'Please,' said Felix, pulling on the mutants' arms. 'It's more important than you can imagine.'

'You are hasty, Ologul. As always.'

The large mutant spared Felix a glare, then ground aside to admit a slender, white-haired man. The heavies did not release their grip, and Felix felt rather like a market fowl as the newcomer looked him over. Felix studied him in kind.

Neither the patchiness of his black Sudenland wool cloak nor the way that brocade splayed from cuffs and collar like straw from a scarecrow's sleeves could hide the richness of his attire. The former province of Sudenland produced the finest droves, and that brocade was pure silver. He looked like one of the down-at-heel noblemen that frequented the quayside taverns of Nuln, but the tarnished brooches and amulets about his neck gave a conflicting impression, like something between a burgher and a witch doctor.

'His wits are his own, I believe.'

'Then he playsh the mindlesh to trick ush. The time hash come, Morschurle.'

Felix could not think of a word to say. Both mutants spoke

in heavily accented Sylvanian, but their diction was archaically clipped. They reminded Felix of the more eccentric players who immersed themselves a little *too* heavily in Detlef Sierck melodramas of misted moors and haunted castles. And both bore a shadow that haunted their brows. Even the squat power of the big brute, Ologul, was chillingly hollow.

'Shpeak then, outshider,' said Ologul. 'When doesh Albrecht von Kuber march?'

Albrecht von Kuber?

Felix's experiences had left him dazed, but he was certain the baron was named Götz. He vaguely recalled the first von Kuber being named Albrecht.

Eyes locked on Felix's, the man named Morschurle opened his palm flat. He held it a moment until Ologul grunted and placed Felix's sword in his master's hand. Morschurle gave an empty smile, and passed the sword across his stare.

'A fine blade,' he conceded, turning it over in his hands. The rune-sharp steel reflected the sky's aurora as though it were doused in pink fire. 'These symbols now.' Morschurle's pale finger traced a series of runes, then nodded to Ologul whose pincer clipped the ground like the beak of a starving bird. 'We are devout men, though He tests us, but have few friends amongst those bearing weapons of the Templar orders.'

Drool snarled from Ologul's lips and down his neck. Felix tried to lift his hands in a gesture of peace, but both arms were still held tight. Sigmar was going to get him killed without even trying.

'Yes, the sword once belonged to a holy order, but I came upon it in the ruins of the Worlds Edge Mountains. I assure you that Sigmar and I are *not* on speaking terms.'

Ologul thumped his pincer to the sand. 'If not to deshtroy ush then why are you here?'

'I came with a friend.' Felix hesitated before choosing to omit the part about the search for von Kuber. He doubted that anyone dubbed *Kreuzfahrer* by the men of Ostermark would find favour with the denizens of the City of the Damned. 'We were hunting a beast. A giant skaven that loots from the dead.'

Some of the mutants exchanged glances. Ologul slurped knowingly.

'Thish monshter, we know. We watched the animal crossh, but it did not return.'

'It… It fell,' Felix mumbled. 'And my friend fell with it.'

There was a murmuring at that.

'The Beasht is a vile animal,' said Ologul. 'We have thought it dead many timesh.'

'Trust me, I saw it fall; an axe through its heart and then sunk to the river's bottom.'

'Trust,' said Morschurle. He handed the sword back to Ologul, and drew one of the muddy-brown talismans from his neck. He pressed it into his palm, binding it loosely into his fist with the cord. 'Darkness consumes our home from within, while the Pious comes from without to burn the taint back. We caught between are short on trust.'

Felix blinked. *The Pious?*

Surely he misheard.

'You say you are not a scout of Sigmarshafen,' Morschurle continued. A dark glow was beginning to seep through the fingers clenched around his talisman. His amethyst eyes did not waver from Felix. 'Tell me something else that is true. Tell me your name, outsider.'

Felix regarded the man with suspicion. He was clearly some manner of sorcerer. It was likely the dark power constrained within those amulets that was the source of Felix's disquiet. Felix scanned the man's robes and the sigils hung from his neck to identify the school of magic to which he belonged. He saw none, which only deepened his apprehension. Since Emperor Magnus established the Colleges of Magic, it had been law for their members to be identifiable, to the laity and to each other.

A firm pressure from the mutant with his left arm came as a ready reminder that he had little choice but to cooperate.

'My name is Felix Jaeger,' he replied and, for reasons he did not understand, except perhaps his oathsworn duty that his companion be remembered, he added. 'And the hero that slew the Beast was named Gotrek Gurnisson.'

'A dwarf?' said Morschurle, eyebrow arching yet higher.

'Alwaysh do right by dwarfsh,' Ologul rumbled.

The mutant warriors nodded pious accord. Felix stared at them in astonishment. He had always been sympathetic to the plight of the cursed degenerates that the witch-finders forced into the shadows. Despite the pronouncements of the priests, mutation struck the pious and the perfidious equally. But he was amazed that, after all they had suffered, these men would still pay heed to the commandments of Sigmar.

Morschurle opened his fist to let the bound talisman spool down. It was slick with blood, rivulets streaming down the cord from his cut palm.

'Dhar always requires sacrifice,' the man explained, eyes rolling to the boiling sky. 'Lies are the get of darkness and the dark wind is powerful here.' The man snatched the hanging pendant from the air and, shaking his head, nodded towards Ologul. 'There are no lies in him. Give him his sword.'

'My lord reeve–'

'He is not our enemy. Return him his weapon.'

Chastened but still grumbling, Ologul angled himself to his slimmer human side to present Felix his weapon. He held it out, blade down. The heavies let go of Felix's arms. He teased some life into his fingers, taking his sword with a nod of thanks. He took pains to sheathe it as unthreateningly as he could, then turned to Morschurle.

'The ratmen took something from the other side,' he said. 'I have to go back for it. I'll not let my companions have fallen for nothing.'

Morschurle grinned broadly, a disturbing gesture that caused shadow to stream from the corners of his eyes to his lips. Felix shuddered as Morschurle looked away, to the knot of warriors upriver.

'You can come out, Mori. It's safe.'

A young girl, no more than ten years old, shyly edged out between the warriors legs. They stuck protectively to her, and she to them. Her skin was inhumanly pale, almost translucent, and he did not think he had ever seen hair that cold a silver, nor eyes so starkly purple. What struck Felix most unsettling was the absence of the smoky second skin these others wore. She shone like a lantern's glow in deep fog.

With a fearful look at Felix, she ran to Morschurle's side, bent backwards against the bulging black sack in her hands. She dropped it at his feet, then hid beneath the man's arm. She watched Felix from hiding. Morschurle ruffled the young girl's hair, smiling as she wriggled free and ran down the shingles to splash into the shallows.

Letting the girl run, confident in the watchful guardianship of two-score warriors, Morschurle crouched beside the sack and untied it. It fell open to reveal hundreds of fragments of human bone. He was not smiling now. His face was long and serious, almost dangerously smooth.

'There were more,' Felix mumbled. 'A lot more.'

'None of consequence. Let the vermin recover them.' His fingertips ran the top layer of fragments. He glanced up to watch the girl play, a fleeting smile, then snapped his fingers for the attention of Ologul. 'Bring the man with us to Die Körnung. Put him with the other.'

Felix's mouth framed a question, only for a shove in the back from the spear-armed hunchback to make him stumble forwards and lose his words.

Other?

Was it possible they had found Gotrek, stricken witless as Felix had been?

Morschurle had not stirred. He stood with open hands before the bone sack, as a winter traveller would extend his palms to a fire.

'The skaven will return for these,' Felix warned. 'I've crossed them more than once now, and they aren't going to give up lightly.'

Morschurle's open hands clenched into fists and, stiffly, he rose, turning to the waterside where the girl, Mori, waded up to her ankles in sparkling pink water. 'Come daughter, the wardens will worry if we are much later.'

The girl kicked her foot through the water as though she had not heard.

'Morzanna!' the man barked. 'Now.'

The toil of daemon engines shook the City of the Damned to its pearlescent heart. Caged by ribs of striated stone, the rumbles passed through solid rock to bring a trickling of dust from the pristine walls of Sigmar's great temple. Morzanna eyed the silver likeness of Ghal-maraz that was suspended from the ceiling. It rattled at its tarnished fittings, like a bloodhound at its chain.

Unlike the rest of the city, permitted to linger on in dejection and decay, the temple had received the care due a royal hostage. The roundel windows had been painstakingly pieced together and reset, the floors swept, the marble altar wiped clean after every bloody sacrilege. Banners bearing the twin-tailed comet hung between the windows. The breeze from the imperfectly restored stained glass ruffled the weighted fabric.

Morzanna advanced down the central aisle, footsteps summoning a forlorn echo, the fluting banners bringing a smirk to her dark lips. Sigmar had not been the first man to ascend the road to godhood. Nor had he been the first to appropriate that most ancient and destructive of portents, the comet, as his herald.

Shaking her head as she rounded the altar, Morzanna opened the darkwood portal to the crypts. Warplight and pink witchfire glowed in the depths of the spiral stair, stalking flighty shadows across the rough stone walls. One hand to the outer curve, she began her descent. The roar and thunder of fevered excavations built to a din as Morzanna emerged from the stair and into the crypts. Sharp hoots and strange growls echoed through the hallways. Dust streamed from the walls.

Deep into the roots of the acropolis, this complex had been sunk. None, living or Damned, knew how deep they plumbed, nor how extensively they spread. And none but a soulless few could say with confidence what ancient devilry remained imprisoned there. But Morzanna was one, and the Dark Master was close enough to freedom for her to taste his power in the air. Pink fire washed across the ceiling, spontaneous and incandescent, burning like lit spirits in a crystal glass. Her platinum hair took on a bluish shine as it absorbed the static charge.

The forces of change were potent here, and only where the physical plane bled so freely into the Realm of Chaos could abominations of the kind she now passed exist.

Hellish fusions of daemon and machine howled, attacking the walls with the immortal fury bound within their iron frames. Dark runes pulsed from their riveted cores. The massive weight of chain slaving them to their workface looked barely sufficient. Effervescent creatures burst cackling into the material, then vanished but for the echo of their laughter, somehow audible over the noise. A ratman overseer lashed his whip across a gang of miserable grotesques. They had been men once. Their bones were stretched by warpstone-sorcery, skin pulled taut. Third, fourth and then fifth arms had been formed from their torsos, grafted to hammers, shovels, picks and to revving drills that glowed dark with warplight and vented a choking smog as they shrieked into the rock face. The overseer spun about with a snarl, chittering curses in its verminous tongue as it felt for some tool that had just disappeared from its belt. Giggling through the folds of the immaterium, the childish horrors scattered, revelling in the entropic rapture of Chaos.

Surrounded by a gaggle of black-garbed supervisors, a squat and grime-cloaked figure turned from a busy section of the rock face. Needle teeth gleamed a sickly yellow as a paw cleared Ubek's three eyes of hair.

'We have… found it, Morzanna. It is… here.' The animalistic sorcerer beat a ponderous paw against the wall and grinned. The ratmen chittered softly. 'Do you hear… that?'

Morzanna scowled. Steam-drills whistled, bound souls raged, countless mutants beat hammered hands against the wall, and she heard nothing.

'It is… hollow. The shadow-paths to the Master's temple are… here.'

One of the ratmen sloped forward. Its eyes were dim, its posture hunched, not out of submission but from sheer apathy. Morzanna sought within its hood for a glimmer of recognition, but there was none.

'We dig-dig all around, great-many tail-lengths,' he murmured blankly, then waved a palsied paw bound in rags, barely fingers enough to grasp his doubly-barbed whip. 'That way, deep-deep.'

'Why the delay? The ritual is almost prepared. The final pieces are being gathered now.'

Ubek sneered. His head rolled around his bloated neck to the ratman who had landed himself the role of mouthpiece. The skaven was neither honoured nor distressed. It was as if breathing was a torture, and speaking no less.

'Wall is hard-rock, lots-many metals and layered. Makes dig-dig hard.'

Morzanna touched the surface where the other sorcerer had. She could feel the power that bled through. It warped the surrounding space, making the daemon-engines strain against their soul-cages and the pink horrors gibber. Ubek's sightless eye shimmered a blinding silver.

'Has it been so long that you have forgotten the meaning of haste? Tear this wall apart!'

The skaven dropped its snout in habitual obeisance. 'Yes-yes, most malignant of white mistresses.'

Ubek was wearing the same clumsy smirk as he pawed muck through his lank thicket of hair. 'This is not... why I... summoned you. Golkhan looks... for you. Your... pet rat was ambushed and... lost his prize.' He chuckled slowly, as if copying a memory as to how. 'Would you still have us... hurry, Morzanna?'

Morzanna glared at him, hatred of the man still warring with disbelief when she spun away.

'You have not asked... who took the bones or... where they were... taken.'

'Because I am not a fool,' she snarled back.

Ubek panted, laughter flecking his grimy chin with spittle. 'You could have destroyed... that place any... time. Do you claim... you can?'

Morzanna rounded on the grimy sorcerer. The ratmen slouched by his side, unmoved by Ubek's announcement of their kin-rat's fate. But then they knew better. Damnation was forever.

'Stay here and dig. That is what you are good for. *I* will bring the Master his prize.'

Rudi heard footsteps draw closer, padded by the falling ash. With a frightened yell, he spun, bringing up his sword for a downward hack at whatever spectre had trailed him from the mists. It was a cloaked figure, tall and lithe, and with a swift lunge caught his wrist as it was high above his head. Rudi gave a startled yelp, then doubled over with a whimper and a mailed knee in his groin. His sword clattered to the ground, fingers suddenly like grass. He scratched pitifully at darkly tinted mail as his legs caved. Ash billowed out where he fell, making him choke. A knife materialised from the fog at his throat.

Lying supine, unable to feel his legs below the agony that was his groin, Rudi focused on the blade and tried not to swallow, followed the wiry arm that held it all the way to a hard face. Its coarse blond stubble was smeared with blood, its green eyes wild.

'I'm unhappy, Herr Hartmann,' hissed Caul Schlanger, forcing the flat of his knife into Rudi's throat. Blood trickled from the younger man's jaw where the blade bit. 'Ask me why.'

Rudi squirmed under the knife. His eyes pleaded.

Caul tutted, leaning down to pin Rudi's forehead with his free hand. 'I said, *ask me why*.'

'Why?' Rudi choked. Speaking made the blade cut deeper. Blood trickled down his neck.

'Why what?' Caul sneered as he leaned closer.

Rudi could smell the gore on his face. Was this Sigmar's punishment for him, to come so close to redemption and be butchered like a swine?

'Why are you unhappy?'

'You're a rare animal, Hartmann. You're a man who does as he is told when he is told to. I like that. It's orderly.' Caul's cruel smile became a snarl. 'Corner the Beast and trap it, I said. Was that too much even for cowards, poets, and damned fools?' Blade suckling thirstily at Rudi's throat, he craned his neck to the strange black snow. 'Now, thanks to all of you, I find myself in a hell reserved for Sigmar's special sinners. Little wonder the world goes to Chaos in a coracle, for Herr Schlanger is its last bastion of order.'

'I can help,' Rudi moaned, forcing himself to lie still yet desperate to cup his groin and still the pain. 'My life is Sigmar's. I never meant to leave this city.'

'Spoken like a martyr.' Caul sneered, withdrawing his knife

and roughing it clean in Rudi's fringe before returning it to his baldric and rising. 'Dear Nikolaus would be so very proud.'

Rudi felt out his bruised groin and groaned, staring dumbly up until Caul kicked him in the side. Rudi snapped alert, blocking the second kick off his elbow and getting stiffly to his feet.

Caul chuckled coldly at the younger man's vengeful glare. 'What happened to the others? Gurnisson, Armbruster, they were all gone when I followed the last of the vermin from the sanatorium.'

Rudi rubbed his side, looking to where his sword lay, remembering a madman's scream as it had pierced his chest.

'Hartmann!'

'Gone,' Rudi managed, 'though I saw Felix cross the bridge before me. It was a matter of minutes, he can't have gotten far.'

'You still have no idea where we are, do you. I thought there was no secret safe from peasant's gossip. I never thought I'd be glad to be proven wrong.' He turned, peering into the black surrounds before, seemingly at random, starting off downriver.

Rudi hastened after him, dodging back as he remembered to collect his sword, then hurrying in his silently filling footprints. 'Aren't you going to tell me where we are?'

'Even if it were a question of *where* we are, then I still would not.'

'At least tell me where we're going.'

Caul pointed through the snow to their left. Jagged tusks of shadow loomed in the middle distance, surrounded by an indeterminate haze of formless black.

'To the first place you look for one as devout as Baron Götz von Kuber – the temple of Sigmar.'

'And what…' Rudi shuddered, eyeing the black drifts that descended over the city. 'What if there are more shades?'

Caul turned back, soulless green eyes like painted lead.

'This is the City of the Damned, boy, be assured there will be.'

CHAPTER 14

A Doom Comes

'Sigmar is with you, through the oceans and the rivers…'

Felix tried to hide his disappointment, felt guilty for it. The *other* of which Morschurle spoke was not Gotrek.

Nikolaus Straum stumbled through the sand between the marching warriors, occasioning a brusque shove to keep him from wandering into the river. The cuts to his wrists testified to Felix's earlier, apparently successful, efforts to cut him loose.

'…and the waters will not overwhelm you, and when you walk through the fire it shall not burn you.'

The flagellant was looking at no one when he spoke, his eyes glazed and wandering. Felix wondered if the man was drugged but it was something more than that. It was tendrils of what looked like smoke that clouded the flagellant's eyes, and his forehead and tattooed chest were lathered by a fever of the mind.

'Nikolaus,' Felix whispered, laying a hand upon the stump of his right shoulder and giving it a shake.

The flagellant's gaze drifted across the water's fog. 'Remain faithful, Brüder Grahl. As we purged the north of Chaos, so we shall this accursed city.'

Felix shuddered. The flagellant's mind was clearly elsewhere, but something in what he said made sense and that was what made Felix's skin crawl. He followed the flagellant's gaze across the water, watched it disturb the mist with its passage like a cold wind beneath a lady's dress. On some level he too felt the presence of Brüder Grahl, shared the dead man's fears.

'He will not shpeak shenshe,' Ologul reminded him. The big warrior marched at the column's rear, deliberately close to Felix and Nikolaus. Morschurle insisted the two men were guests, but Felix was not so sure.

'He ish mindlesh.'

Felix ignored him, seeking a spark of self in Nikolaus's eyes. There was none. But the shadow upon him was different to that which hollowed the mutants. Tendrils leached across eyes, and mouth. As if something was trying to get in.

'There were others with him,' he spoke at last.

'We did shee others, but the ratsh retreated to a ruin, and took their captivesh with them.' The mutant drooled grimly, moistening his neck. 'Morschurle brought it on their headsh with magic. Killed everyone inshide. I should know becaushe I had to take Mori through the rubble to find hish bonesh.'

Felix looked up, tracking the column on its downriver march to where the reeve and his young daughter took point.

'A little dangerous for a child.'

'She ish a sheeresh ash powerful ash her father. It wash her vishion that forecasht the croshing of the Beasht. It ish she that feelsh the power in the bonesh.'

'So there *is* some power to them,' Felix mused. 'I wonder what the skaven want with them.'

Ologul said nothing, nodding in time to his lopsided stride.

Felix fell silent, listening to the tramp of feet and the clatter of bronze. The river whispered softly, drifting past with a pace only slightly swifter than their own. The air was warm, but the wind that gusted across its body cut like a knife of edged darkness.

'Brüder Fritsch, what answers do you seek in the fire? Is it not enough to know only that it burns?'

Ologul gave a soft slurp. He sounded wearied, his claw dragged in the sand as he shoved the flagellant away from the water.

'The ratsh are shlavesh to the Dark Mashter. Shome of our own kind sherve him gladly, but it ish shaid the ratsh do sho in return for wyrdshtone. Hish temple ish to the easht.'

The mutant directed his human left hand that way. Spires and towers were visible in the fog like the spines of some slumbering beast. There was no sign of any temple. But he felt something, an emptiness in his gut, that made him shiver. It was that name.

Dark Master.

It had been muttered by the mindless within their cage in Sigmarshafen. He had heard it from the lips of a statue in the Retterplatz. Now it came in the slobbering rasp of a mutated brute beneath a burning sky and in the presence of... *something* he could only feel and not begin to describe. It had never yet chilled him more. Arch-Lector Gramm had spoken of a daemon in the city. One that fire could not purge. He had not spoken the name *Master*, but it was likely that the two were the same. The understanding was not a reassuring one.

For Felix had no desire to be alone with a madman in a haunted city that was ruled by a daemon even the Pious could not slay.

'Who... what is the Dark Master?'

'A daemon from the dawn of man. We know where he liesh but he ish too powerful and in any cashe hash no body to

263

shlay. All we can do ish wait, maybe one day run, brave the misht ourshelvesh.'

Felix shivered and said no more. He had learned enough to worry him to his core.

A single horn sounded from up ahead and Felix looked up.

Caught in a wide meander the river ahead broadened into a horseshoe-shaped vastness of shimmering pink half a league across. Within that bow of water there was a crescent bar of gritty sand. It crawled with distant figures, as did the sheltered straits between it and the riverbank. The slow-moving water was crowded with nets, lines, flat-bottomed craft and wading men. Beneath the tenacious cawing of gulls, they worked to haul the detritus of the river into a half-flooded district of ruined stone that these mutants called home. It clung to the bend of the river like a scab to a man's elbow.

The mutants called it Die Körnung, the grit, and the name was apt.

The horn had sounded from a tall building that had been fortified and converted into a guard tower. It was part of a square array of such structures, connected by sloping walls of compacted rubble. The fiery sky caught off crossbow bolts and javelin heads across its length. Directly ahead of the returning warriors, abutting the river, there was a gate. It seemed to be the only one

'And Magnus did find a sickness in that place,' Nikolaus murmured. 'He returned to them with faith and with fire and did say to them: *repent, for the kingdom of Sigmar is come to you*.'

'Shut him up,' Ologul slurped gesturing to one of the warriors with his more-human left hand. 'I don't want to hear that name shpoken.'

'Sigmar will wipe away every tear, and with death then death shall be no more. Neither shall there be mourning, nor crying, nor pain. For the End Times come, and all that came before will pass away.'

'What's he saying?' said one of the mutant soldiers.

'Pay him no mind. He'sh mindlesh.'

A vile chant filled the city's streets, following the flickering line of braziers and steel that snaked into the maze of ruins and all the way back to the acropolis. Its length bristled with bill-hooks and pikes like a barbed serpent, armour shimmering as if it was sheathed in mail. To the rear of the host, bunched like a club tail, ratmen were goading huge spawn from Golkhan's amphitheatre. They bristled with twisted strength, confused by the change on the wind, their warped bellows igniting the sky like lightning to the chanting mutants' thunder.

Their voices were raised in discordant praise of the Dark Master. Chaos was his essence and he was revered by many names.

He was the godless; the accursed divine. And he would rise.

Morzanna shifted, uncomfortable in the saddle of the massive sable-coated destrier. It had been offered as a token from one of Golkhan's pathetically devoted subordinates, given with the air of one for whom horsemanship was as natural a part of life as drinking and whoring. The condescension, the ill-tempered lust; it reminded her of the Sigmarites whose dreams she often shared. How she despised them. She could have smote the man's eyes with Tzeentchian flame.

She allowed herself the slenderest smile, patting her mount's powerful neck. Her claws knotted through its mane and she tugged cruelly.

In a multiverse of infinite probabilities, all things were possible.

The horse snorted in fright. Its eyes were wide, alighting in dull, animal horror upon the misshapen monsters that marched alongside.

She had lived here.

Some distance ahead yet, the river reflected the sky's aurora, a ribbon of amethyst and tourmaline that wound between the ruins of home. It was not just the telltale broadening of the water that told her they were close. She remembered these streets, how they had looked and how they had smelled in every one of a hundred times. A storm of mortal memories caught her unawares.

She had lived.

Here.

A dull ache clenched her jaw. Golkhan rode ahead with, at the warrior's demand, Nosta at the rear. Morzanna had risen too far to show weakness to either now. The ruins of Die Körnung had been settled at the Dark Master's subtle behest, its expansion according to a fate he conceived, its survival a consequence only of his desire. Its people had lived the dream of freedom, but were about to waken to learn just how provisory was the benefaction of a god.

For if Morzanna could not destroy her home, then those other champions assuredly would.

The gate of Die Körnung was a hole in the wall, barred by a pile of timber lashed together by a corroded chain. The gate was open now, hoisted by a group of obscenely muscular mutant guards with the aid of a straightforward block and tackle. The column tramped through the gate, the guards reserving a wave for Morschurle and then for Ologul at the party's rear. There was a whistle from the gate tower, there was a zip of cord as the pulley was released and the stack of logs unravelled to come crashing down behind them.

Felix could not shake the feeling that he was being sealed into a tomb.

The place stank like a sewer and likely was. The faecal damp was everywhere; in the rocks that sagged into the soft earth, upon the children that picked over the morass for anything that did not fall apart in their hands. On every wall a brownish crust five feet from the ground marked high tide and under every algae-stuffed crack there lingered a shadow. Felix's gaze swept side to side, Ologul shoving him forward whenever he hesitated.

The settlement's most disturbing aspect was not something he could see, nor even smell.

Shadows thrown by nothing living followed him. Walking these streets, these men around him, made the hairs on the back of his neck tingle with disquiet. It was like looking upon a grave, feeling the dead man's hand upon his shoulder.

Felix wondered what he was doing here. The Beast had been slain and Gotrek had earned a doom worthy of his deeds in the doing of it. He supposed he still had to remind himself that battling daemons was no longer his responsibility. And it was true, that his mind was still not working quite as it should. He would stay for a time, he decided, get some food, get some rest, learn what he could about the Dark Master and, when he figured out how to broach the subject, about the whereabouts of von Kuber. He would take what he learned back to Sigmarshafen and to the ears of the Pio–

He checked himself, then winced, a dull ache like a coming migraine behind his eyes. This place had clearly muddled his thinking.

He would take the information to *Captain Seitz* and to *Arch-Lector Gramm.* Of course, that was what he had meant.

After several minutes squelching through filth, the ruins gave way to a wide gravel shore. The river shimmered beneath the fog, like a shield set above a frosty hearth. Felix could see the mutants toiling on the bar. He paused, watching the boatmen and the dredgers work the straits. Their calls rang hollow through the mists. As if they were not fully there. Circling his gaze to the outer, incurved, face of the bar, Felix saw a gang of dredgers working a net that snaked out into mists beneath an articulated boom. The wooden segments thunked together in the current, muffled by fog, like the falling of axes upon an executioner's block. Ghostly in the murk, a black-hulled smack glided in silence, its single cotton sail trimmed, a silver hand glittering dully on its starboard prow. The boom tied it to the bar like an astral tether. Felix felt a sudden nausea.

The craft looked disturbingly familiar to one he had just seen destroyed.

The mutants bore him onto the shingle and he had little time to dwell on his disquiet. The shingle was littered with driftwood, around which gulls stalked the rock pools for mussels and stranded fish. The birds glowered as Felix crunched past and did not trouble themselves to flee. The odour was repellent, the chilling breath of the river as nothing to the stink of bird droppings, rotten kelp and the thinly disguised bite of corruption.

Morschurle and their escort were heading towards the riverbank and slightly upriver, towards a stub-nose jetty where a bonfire blazed upon the shingle by the decking. The fire burned silver-black and partially transparent. It gave off a smoke that coiled through the fog into strangely human forms and emitted no heat that Felix could feel.

He shuddered, telling himself it was the cold. There was a mugginess to the air, but the fog and the wind that gusted through it had teeth of ice. They brought whispers from the other side and the remembrance of cold. Shivering still, Felix followed Morschurle and the others to the fire.

The mutated river-folk clustered around it. Some sat in wicker chairs, but most were cross-legged on the pebbles. The air popped as the dried kelp packed beneath the fire sizzled and burst. The wind ruffled Felix's long hair into tangles, and was cold enough to convince the mutants around the fire to keep their heads down and their mildewed shawls tight.

But it did not touch the fire at all.

Felix turned deliberately from that uncanny blaze, looking the short slope down to the jetty. A pair of two-man skiffs butted either side. Their hawsers floated in furry coils, long enough so as not to drag the boats under with each rising tide.

Morschurle moved to the fire, untroubled by its strangeness, and warmed his palms. His charms gleamed darkly.

The seated mutants murmured greetings to the reeve, and to the others as they moved to sit amongst them, but Felix felt their eyes linger on him. They counted his two arms and ten fingers, judged the symmetry of his face, the shade of his skin, the simplicity of his form.

He could feel their hatred, their envy.

They wanted to string him from the gate towers. They wanted to be him.

Despite himself, Felix moved nearer to the fire. Still he felt nothing from it. It was an illusion of flame.

One of Ologul's warriors shoved Nikolaus into a chair. The flagellant mumbled through the oiling rag that a mutant had stuffed into his mouth and did not try to rise.

The young girl, Mori, dropped the sack of bones at her father's side, then buried herself under his arm. She stared into the fire, and then at Felix, trying to pretend that she was not. She looked familiar but Felix was too beset by feelings of unease to figure out how.

'Who would have believed it?' Morschurle murmured, apparently for the attention of the fire. 'The bones of Kharduun the Gloried exist after all.'

'The bones belonged to a man?' said Felix, trying to shake off the crawling unease and think. The name struck him as familiar but still he could not quite think. It took longer than he liked to remember. It had been mentioned in one of the forbidden texts belonging to Doktor Drexler, when the Nuln physician had been aiding him in his researches of the skaven. As hard as he forced, he could not recall the context. 'Is Kharduun the Master?'

'He was the Mashter'sh champion,' said Ologul, leaning

stiffly to deposit a blade-rimmed buckler from his back to the ground by the fire. 'In the time after the punishment there were many warbandsh that fought for the city and itsh wyrdshtone, but Kharduun wash bleshed and none could rival him.'

Felix hugged his chest, exhaling a plume of fog. He noticed that mist shrouded no other mouth but his.

'Clearly, someone defeated him,' said Felix, unwrapping a finger to indicate the bone pile.

Morschurle looked up from the fire, finding Ologul's gaze waiting and nodded, turning back to the silver flames.

'It has long been believed by some that Kharduun was not just the Master's champion, but that he *was* the Master.' Morschurle gave a short laugh, and rubbed his daughter's back, releasing her so as to squat down beside the black sack. He untied its neck and gazed inside like an oracle into a see-ing pool. 'So ambitious was the Dark Master, so it is said, that the Ruinous Powers united to strip him of his body, damn-ing him to immortality without form. But Dhar is strong here, enabling him to claim a mortal host, Kharduun, and cheat the gods' curse.'

Felix tilted his face from the chilling blaze, disturbed by the caw of the gulls that circled the clouded shallows.

'It didn't work out, I assume.'

'His power was too great, even for a mighty champion of ruin. The body he took burned to naught but bones. Those bones were found, separated and taken, scattered throughout the city and beyond.' Morschurle smiled, face aglow with a possessive lust, almost as if the bones themselves shone with their own dark power. 'But now a fraction of the daemon's power is mine to wield. Now we can fight back, retake our city and sway its followers back to Sigmar. We can be united when the Pious comes, impress upon him our conviction.'

'You think a shcrap of the Mashter'sh hosht will help against the daemon himshelf?' Ologul turned to Felix, as if seeking the support of a fellow sword. 'They shay he tried to shet himshelf ash a god, to become the fifth great power, and that wash why he wash casht down. And *thish* is the daemon he would have ush fight.'

'Better than fleeing across the water as you would have us do,' Morschurle replied quietly. 'Remind me how many of your scouts have returned from the other side?'

'I would shtill take my chancesh with the Pioush.'

Felix put his hand to his forehead and closed his eyes, fending off the wave of unease.

Something here was *wrong*. The air was warm when Ostermark stole itself against the march of winter. At the same time, he alone shivered with cold. The Chaos moon was full in the sky. The mutants spoke in a cryptic dialect of Sylvanian, and spoke of the Pious as if expecting the revered saviour of the Empire to lead a flotilla upriver at any moment. Either they were ignorant of the passage of time or warpstone in water and soil had addled them in mind as much as in body. Likely, they simply conflated the threat posed by Götz von Kuber with that his ancestor had brought upon theirs. But that did not ring true, even to Felix. The mutants were certain. And something *was* wrong.

'You believe the Pious is coming,' he murmured. 'Emperor Magnus the Pious?'

Morschurle pinched his lips, regarding him through arched brows. 'His elevation by the electors will be a formality, I am sure, but yes. Our last missive said that the Great War was over, and that Magnus's general, our own Baron Albrecht von Kuber, was escorting him here. First to Sigmarshafen to muster, and then...'

He trailed off. Ologul looked grim.

Felix felt a memory jostling for notice amongst the confusion of thoughts. He had read this somewhere, he knew it. It was a forbidden history, and certainly not one he had learned in the libraries of Altdorf University. After achieving victory in Kislev, Magnus had returned through the northern provinces, Ostland or Ostermark had been the scholar's guess, to destroy a city so lost to Chaos as to be beyond salvation. Every brick and every stone had been burned, every record of its existence and hence of its fall expunged. Well, nearly every record. Felix had definitely read of this somewhere.

But if he had read this...

And Emperor Magnus was two centuries dead.

Felix's gaze washed over the mutants around the fire, those that sailed the straits and dredged for flotsam. He recalled the sentry towers, the warding stones, the patrols that swept the moors of Ostermark to this day, the salted earth that Nikolaus had diligently maintained, the insistences of Schlanger and Gramm that this place be forgotten. And he felt that same feeling; that his warm body shared the ground with the dead.

He returned to Morschurle, trying to keep his voice calm.

'What year is this?'

Morschurle gave the question a depth of thought it surely did not deserve. Time enough for Felix's mouth to run dry.

'The year stretches interminably,' he spoke at last, 'yet the season does not change.' He squinted skyward, as though a glimpse of the Chaos moon through the maelstrom could reveal anything that was true. 'Sun and moons cannot lie, and by their measure it remains the month of Nachgeheim, in the two thousand three hundred and third year since the crowning of Sigmar.'

Felix closed his eyes, clutching himself tight.

'No,' he murmured. 'No, no, no, that's not possible.'

Was it possible?

He found himself thinking back to an old philosophy professor who would posit theory after theory to explain how magic today was so much weaker than it must have been in ancient times. The professor had once claimed to have acquired an ancient scroll, which he had proudly shown despite there being none amongst his students able to interpret the writings of the asur, which spoke of a great ritual performed when the world was young. It had been a working of the elves' greatest masters and had drawn the magic from the world, sequestered it at the heart of the elves' island home. As a consequence, he had claimed, those mages were now trapped in time, condemned to re-enact their earth-shaping ritual in perpetuity.

Felix had not been surprised when that professor was quietly relieved of his teaching duties.

But what if it were true. Could something similar have befallen the City of the Damned? Did the power to accomplish such a feat still exist in the world? Or rather, *had* it existed, two centuries past?

Which still left the question of why.

It was clear from the faces of the mutants around him that his question would find no answers from them. As far as they were concerned it *was* the year 2303. It had been for two hundred years, and it would continue to be until the end of days.

Little wonder that crossing the mists had stricken his mind.

Felix attended the gathered mutants more closely. He recognised them. Whatever damage the passage through time inflicted, it seemed to work both ways, for these were the mindless mutants he had seen slaughtered on the other side. And the boat, the sleek black shade that haunted the mist; he recognised that too. He understood now the shadows he saw upon these men and women, and the whispers upon the crackling fire. These people were dead.

They were going to flee this place as Ologul wished, and they were going to die.

Felix's neck tightened. He trawled his thoughts for a more rational explanation but could find none.

A long blast from a horn scattered his attempts at thought like the startled gulls that lifted noisily to wing. Their harsh calls sounded like an evil chant, the rustle of the flight's hundreds of wings beating the air like drums. Noisily they settled, skimming back to the shingle and to the water.

And Felix could still hear drums. He could still hear chanting.

A look of worry circled Ologul's molten features and he turned due east, in the direction of the horn. His pincer snipped out a nervous tattoo.

'It will be Iascu's scouts returning home,' said Morschurle. 'It is one sound for friend, and two for–'

The horn blew a second time. The assembled river-folk fell still.

'Two for the Dark Mashter,' Ologul finished.

'It will be another raid,' Morschurle stated calmly, standing protectively over his precious bones. 'Everyone should return to their homes.'

A handful of the seated mutants had begun to rise when Nikolaus suddenly thrashed in his chair, screaming into his gag. Felix pulled the oily rag from his mouth, almost losing a finger in the flagellant's mindless determination to be heard.

'To every man comes his time,' he blurted, causing his chair to creak as his agitation grew. His withered torso shone with fever sweat. 'Every time has a purpose. A doom approaches, the doom of all, so be courageous.'

The mutants stared as the prophet's fit subsided. The shadows shaped masks of terror.

But Nikolaus was not quite done. He shivered as though, despite his sheen of sweat, the eldritch fire chilled him. He gazed east to where the march of witchfire was just beginning to sear the eastern parapet, showing a brilliant sliver of crimson like a false dawn.

'The End Times come.'

CHAPTER 15

The Gloried

The clash of drums beat upon the walls of Die Körnung. The pound of feet and the harsh chants of the Damned made them tremble. From their ramparts, the horn sounded twice more in succession, the same outcry peeling down the length of the wall, racing from the source of the alarm in terror. Men galloped from barracks and guard towers to attend the walls. Their bronze armour rattled until, one by one, they stiffened and spun, shields fore, locking into a wall of oak and pine with a rolling shudder. Yelling curses and oaths, the defenders stamped their spears upon the battlements. Crossbow bolts whined from guard towers, horns blared from both sides of the wall, monsters bellowed, drums pounded like anxious hearts.

And into that din screamed the families of Die Körnung.

From balconies and revetments, roped ladders were flung, men and women leaping after them before the bottom rungs had hit the ground. Some clutched spears or battered swords, running with the lopsided gait of men buckling armour on the run. They were the selfless few and the majority fled, tiny rivulets running through the alleys to become streams that fed the panic into a surge for the river.

Directly in their path, Felix watched them come with a sinking feeling.

'It ish not a raid,' said Ologul, eyeing the twisting shadows that witchfire bade dance against the high towers of the township. 'The *Hand* ish loaded and ready to shail. We have boatsh enough to get all to the other shide.'

'No one leaves,' said Morschurle, calmly rising to confront his fleeing people. 'We are not defenceless. Get these people armed and get them to the walls.'

'And what of your daughter?' said Ologul, gesturing the girl with his crab-like hand. 'Ish she to die by my shide?'

Morschurle twitched, but did not answer. He squatted down beside his daughter, stroked her hair down her cheek, then held firm her jaw as if fearful of letting go. 'Take the bones and run home. Bar the door and do not open it until I return.'

'I thought not,' Ologul muttered, but hefted his buckler and turned into the coming crowd nonetheless.

Morschurle turned back, looked past his commander of the guard and gesticulated to the boatmen and gangmasters that crowded the shore.

'Cast off. Nobody boards.'

'Are you inshane? We'll have no eshcape.

'The walls, Ologul,' said Morschurle, already hitching up his tattered robes and running up the shore.

Ologul scowled but, seeing no alternative started after him. His warriors, still dressed for battle, were quick to form up. Following their leader's example, a handful of the running mutants fell in behind Ologul's warriors, but most were still fanning across the shore like a swollen estuary, running wild for the open water. And a good number were coming towards Felix.

Just downriver, a mob blundered into the water alongside a laden skiff and dragged its pilot into the water. The craft tipped wildly as a dozen men and women each fought to board. Felix looked over his shoulder, through the transparent bonfire to where the two boats were still tethered to the jetty. Beyond it and the capsized wrecks that littered the boating lanes, the black wraith of the craft Ologul called the *Hand* drifted through the fog.

These people were going to die. He could not let them board that boat.

Leaving the wall to Ologul and the others, Felix retreated to the jetty. The planking creaked beneath his weight. A mutant man barrelled after him through the bonfire in a cascade of sparks. His wet clothes were singed, his hair like dank mould, his brow lathered with terror. And he was not alone. No sooner had Felix registered his appearance than five more charged around the fire and through. He saw Nikolaus thrown from his chair, disappearing under the stampede that followed.

Felix raised his sword high above his head as the mutants closed. Fear widened their eyes as they saw the blade gleam with a pink fire. This was madness. This was *someone else's* madness.

And he would end it here.

The sword came streaking down. The lead mutant screamed as the blade clove through the sodden hawser tethering the first boat. Cursing Sigmar for these poor souls' fate, he drove his boot into the craft's side and shoved it out. The current bore it downriver. The mutants wailed and veered from the jetty, crashing into the water after it. A dozen pairs of hands had the skiff from both sides. The water seethed as more joined the fray.

'You can't leave,' Felix yelled above the splashes and cries. 'You mustn't!'

They were too far gone to hear, and Felix doubted he could have made them heed his words even had he been able to explain.

He could not explain it to himself.

The mutants of Die Körnung stormed the jetty by the dozen. More ploughed directly into the water, driven under by the desperation of those that followed. The planking groaned under so many.

Felix raised his sword to hack through the second hawser, but a mutant tackled him around the waist and slammed him against the groaning boards. The mutant scrambled up and dived for the boat. Dozens more leapt after him, causing the boat to rock, tipping them all screaming into the water.

'Stop!' Felix yelled at their fleeing backs, helpless to do anything but watch as still more stormed into the water. He heard the cry from a hundred mouths, the conjoined torment of the Damned. *The Dark Master has come.* Felix felt weak. He was one man, and there were so many. 'You go to your deaths!'

Fate would not be denied. He had seen it. It had happened. *Would happen.*

As he struggled for an answer, a shriek sounded from the walls. Felix saw a spider-legged creature surmount the distant rampart. Its forelegs waved in challenge, chitinous mouthparts spreading for another hellish wail before a guard smashed the butt of a spear between its eyes and it fell. Watching hell descend upon the walls, Felix imparted a last look to the floating shade of the *Hand*. His fingers flexed around the grip of his sword.

There was nothing he could do here.

He was about to force himself into the flow of bodies and make for the wall himself when his returning gaze alighted on one of the many capsized wrecks that littered the straits between the riverbank and the sandbar. A wide tear in the prow had been partially, almost deliberately, curtained with matt-brown algae. The water around it eddied strangely. It butted into the jetty. Then moved backwards a foot.

Against the current.

Felix was still staring when a black-cloaked figure boiled up from the water between the wading mutants. Knives flashed. Blood and water scattered in equal measure, body parts slipping into the water before any had a chance to scream. Those further back wailed and tried to fall back, only for the press to force them onto the killer's blades.

A second ratman burst from the water's surface with a gasp, then back-flipped onto its craft's back. Its cloak was sodden, its breathing sharp, water wept from a pair of arrow-straight throwing knives. The boat rocked beneath it, pallid tails breaking the surface like sharks' fins as more of the ratkin struck for the shore.

Felix set his feet on the planking and angled his blade into a guard.

Fate would be cheated after all.

There was no way out.

Feral mutants continued to spill from the city's roads, gathering into packs just shy of the missiles zipping down from Die Körnung's walls. Between walls and city there lay a partially demolished strip of grey dust and ruin. It was a minefield of loose rock and treacherous ground that promised broken ankles and worse. But the sight of the walls stoked the invaders' fury. Those walls were little more than rubble piled upon rubble, their foundations slipping through squalid earth, offering handholds aplenty to any whose faith sufficed them to dare. Their fevered chants preceding them, the warriors howled their bloodlust to the sky, assaulting piecemeal under a volley of crossbow fire, then to withdraw and lick their wounds while others succumbed to that same savagery and charged.

Ordered regiments in loose mail and wielding long billhooks advanced into the clearing behind the rabble and mustered out of bowshot under the stewardship of Golkhan's cloaked and black-mailed lieutenants. They were hard-faced and cruel, more human-looking than most and, like the lord they served, hailed from outside the City of the Damned. Each wore matching livery of grey cloaks emblazoned with a silver comet and smaller icons of Chaos, swords drawn and pistols braced at their waists.

The armoured steed of Golkhan the Anointed cantered the length of the battle line. Its gait confounded the eye, sickening the bellies even of the perverse. Each of its six legs were doubly jointed, as dark as fired logs and riven with spines. Eyes like onyx glared with sadistic intent from beneath a silvered champron, the metal harder and heavier than mere steel. The steed's teeth snarled like those of a predator, curved and coloured red by daemonic saliva. Golkhan drew hard on the reins to bring it around for a second pass. The unholy steed of Chaos slowed, snorting at its master's gall.

'The earth will be made to tremble,' the champion bellowed, amplified by his daemonic mask to a crescendo that made the blockish missile towers shiver, as though this was prophecy already fulfilled. 'The mountains will kneel, the rivers will bleed with the blood of men, and the sky will fall. Your souls are sweet wine to the Shadowlord.' Golkhan beat the flat of his massive claymore into his chestplate and bellowed like a shackled beast. 'He is the harbinger; the herald of conquerors, of the Anointed! Spill your veins for he who is godless!'

The hell-beast that bore him stamped its bladed hooves and brayed to be a party to the coming violence and Golkhan swept his claymore high, riding on a wave of acclamation.

'Rivers! Of! Blood!'

With a final snort of ill-tempered bloodlust, the daemon-steed reared. Golkhan's lieutenants marshalled their units and, as one, the host of Chaos marched.

The earth trembled.

And now the rivers would bleed with the blood of men.

Ologul hurled a javelin into the front rank of the host, watched it rip through the heart of a black-scaled fanatic, an eight-pointed star tattooed across its chest like a target.

From the turrets of the guard tower to his left a group of crossbowmen loosed, the rattle of hoary old wood lost amidst the thunder as men charged through the ruins and monsters howled. Weapons were reloaded and men spun, screamed, and fired. A soldier rose above the ramparts and levelled his crossbow to fire. The weapon dropped from his hands. Blood spat from the billhook blade that had torn through the top of his spine. The man pawed feebly at the spike jutting through his throat, living still as the billman yanked him from the wall and into the screaming frenzy below.

The front rank made the walls and, chanting in discordant unison they climbed.

'Rivers of blood! Rivers of blood!'

A final volley of missile-fire rattled across the parapet before men stood back drawing short spears and swords.

'Shtand to repel!' Ologul roared, abandoning the stock of javelins and snatching up his buckler. He anchored his stance, locked shields with his neighbours, and leaned his shoulder into it just as a flayed and faceless horror brained itself upon his boss and died by a comrade's spear.

There were more. Too many to hold. This time the Dark Master meant for nothing but their destruction. That thought did not trouble him.

He had long been plagued by the impression that he was already dead.

Upturned skiff rocking in the disturbed waters, the rat-man hurled its knife with a precision that, under other circumstances, would have been impressive. Felix flinched back and swept his sword across its path, meeting the thrown blade with a resounding clash. The ratman hissed and readied to hurl another. Felix narrowed his body to meet it.

Beside him and beneath, terrified mutants thrashed through the water, those desperate to get out wrestling under those still anxious to get in. They crushed up against the pilings of the jetty and Felix swayed as it groaned beneath him. A skaven clambered from the water and onto the end of the jetty. Dripping wet, it drew a short sword and snarled.

And then the jetty collapsed.

Amidst a splintering of rotten wood, Felix, the ratman, and a dozen mutants were tipped into the water, skidding over the planking and slamming together into the crowded shallows. Felix came up gasping, only to be shoved back under. Claws sank into his scalp, his own blood dispersing to mingle with that of the bodies that scudded across the water's surface. His mouth filled with silt-laden water and he resisted the urge to cry out. The sounds of frantic swimmers rushed through the water. Oars pounded the surface like drums over a chittering undercurrent. Air streaming from his lips, Felix beat at the paw that held him under. His blows were clumsy and slow. Then, remembering his sword, he slid it up through the foul creature's belly. Its hold slackened.

The distant murmur of battle rushed nearer as he resurfaced with a gasp.

Water streamed between the links in Felix's mail. He hungrily sucked in another breath. The water around him was littered with bits of wood, with bodies, its surface slicked with blood. The skaven had pursued the surviving mutants onto the bank. Screams were coming from everywhere. A pink glow was rising from the walls.

A hiss from behind made Felix spin.

The knife-rat leapt from its upturned skiff, its blade an

extension of its own downward arc that stopped only against the angle of Felix's sword. The creature squealed at the pain in its knife-paw, let the weapon fall and swiftly drew another. Water splashed around them as Felix countered, ripping a bloody strip through his foe's black cloak. The creature snarled and dived.

Its tail thrashed once and then it was gone.

Felix circled on the spot, trying to control his breathing, to listen. But the cacophony from the beach and from the walls was too much. A chant carried over the clash of steel and the zip of bow cord.

'Rivers of blood.'

His attacker did not break the gore-slickened surface. With any luck it had fled.

A child's scream banished his thoughts of catching breath.

It had come from close by, from the bonfire that, by virtue of its eldritch nature, continued to burn. The area was littered with bodies, but these had fallen to the stampede rather to an enemy's blade. Felix found his missing knife-rat stalking amongst them. He heard its tittered laughter and the scream came again, long and harrowing and painfully shrill.

Mori, Felix realised, already running.

The girl was still here.

And she had the Dark Master's bones.

The wall heaved with bodies. Across a line no wider than the distance between two shields, mutated warriors on both sides hacked and strove and spat and roared. Nightmares of Chaos-blended flesh stamped over supposed allies to haul themselves onto the parapet to hammer the rank of shields with fists like lead. Claws shattered on shields. Hardened flesh and armour-like scales split before knives and spears. Bodies rolled down the sloping walls like the last fruit of a fire-ravaged tree.

'Your lives mean nothing,' Golkhan roared. 'The Dark Master cares not for your pain.' The champion's daemonic steed stamped madly, dark eyes roving and hungry. 'Morzanna!' This last erupted from his visor as a screech of tormented steel.

'Your will, black lord?' said Morzanna, doing her utmost to ease her own beast's dread

'Bring down those walls or I will flay your hide right here and use your carcass to bard my steed!'

'Even you would not dare.'

'Your patron does not frighten me, witch. He is a means to an end. *The* end. I know his true name and I know he needs me more than I need either of you.' Golkhan leaned forward. His daemonic mask snarled. 'Lest we forget that he is the one in a cage.'

Morzanna bared her teeth, barbed enamel enough for fear and disbelief to share.

'You are an ignorant fool.'

'I am a champion of Be'lakor!' Golkhan roared, loud enough for the defenders on the wall to hear, to clutch their ears and moan in horror. 'He who serves no master.' He swung his claymore to the walls. Warriors flickered through the fogged clearing, plumed helms and feathered crests, a riot of disorder as though the dead plain burned. 'Sunder those walls for your champion. If you cannot, I am sure the shadow-bitch, Nosta, will do it gladly.'

Morzanna's claws sank into the muscle of her horse's neck. It whickered in pain, Morzanna's face turning dark in the gust of shadow that ruffled both their hair.

'Your will, black lord,' she growled, power making her voice husky.

Golkhan's steed edged back, nostrils flaring as its uncanny senses caught the flow of Dhar.

She cast both from her thoughts. Words dribbled from her

lips, honeyed by dark magic. The din of battle sank like rain-water into parched earth, the pink torches turned grey, the sky dark. Through the Wind of Dhar she could feel Nosta, the arrogant waif throwing her witless strength against the gate. But there was another of power at work. She could see him like a cloud in the night sky. She traced the shimmering path of his efforts to a tower where a man knelt. He was in agony. Blood streamed from his hands from his efforts to annul her casting. Men stood around him releasing a hail of quarrels but they were small, dim things. She focused on the tortured mage. With a single word she could break him, paste his brains across the roof of that tower. The word was on her tongue, but a child's sentiment would not let her speak it. No matter.

Skill alone would not suffice against one twice forsaken by the gods.

Terrified beyond restraint, Morzanna's steed reared, fore hooves flailing as it tossed its head from side to side. Morzanna's claws dug deeper into its neck. Blood streamed. Dhar always required sacrifice, even to one – *particularly* to one – as far down the road as she. With a wild snort, the horse smashed its hooves to the ground. The earth beneath them split, cracks spidering outward in chaotic patterns. Morzanna hissed a word and dark energies spiralled from her bloodied claws to tighten around the horse's neck like a noose. It gave a strangled snort, power spreading into its shoulders, its fet-locks, its hooves. It continued to stamp.

The earth gave a calamitous groan.

Morzanna set her sight upon the guard tower. Bolts spat from its turret like wasps disturbed by the flight of a dragon. She was not like the Pious. She was not. Her father was already dead. This was just sweeping away Magnus's mess.

Golkhan watched, holding his breath, expression unreadable behind his mask.

Morzanna cradled the world in aethyric hands. She felt its bones creak.

And she twisted.

A sudden tremor passed through the township and under the gritty floodplain just as the ratman shaped itself to pounce. The quake tossed it from its feet and into the bonfire. It squealed and threw its arms above its head to cushion its fall, rolling clear in a fizz of sparks. A dozen strides too many down the shore, Felix was swept sideways, as though the earth had just been dragged six feet to the left. He landed on his chest, looked up to see the agile ratman rise first. The creature slapped down the little fires that burned through its rags and sniffed for the child. It found her hiding beneath a chair and hissed delight.

Felix snatched up his sword and rose with a roar, pounding up the gravel slope. He was too far away to save the child, he knew that, but perhaps the distraction would grant him the time he needed.

As he had hoped, the skaven turned around at Felix's yell. Its muzzle peeled back to a mocking snarl, then snapped brutally sideways as something struck it from behind. It fell in a slack heap and behind it, beaten purple by the stampede, stood a man.

He lowered his fist and, swaying slightly, looked down on the unconscious creature.

'And Sigmar made unto them a wall of steel...'

A smoky nimbus flickered around Brüder Nikolaus. The words were his but the voice was not, at least not entirely. Felix examined his own fingers, looking for a similar shadowy creep, but there was nothing.

The shaking ground made the flagellant fall to his knees before Mori's hiding place. The blood on his knuckles was bubbling down to green vapour and he wiped the residue on his sackcloth kilt before extending the hand to the girl. She stared at it, flinching further as Felix appeared from behind the fire.

Felix raised his hands and backed off, trying to look unthreatening. Nikolaus whispered something Felix could not hear and pushed his hand forwards. The girl hesitated a moment, then reached forward to take it. Nikolaus reacted with a beatific smile and pulled her free.

Felix took a deep breath, not knowing when he would get another chance, and looked to the walls. They held, but Die Körnung was being shaken to its sodden roots, decades of fortification and repair coming loose in minutes to batter the street with rock, wood, and filth. Even through the fog, Felix could see the cracks that were spreading through the walls.

'Nikolaus,' Felix hissed. 'Can you protect Mori for me?'

'White lady,' Nikolaus murmured, then looked to Felix as if realising for the first time that he was not alone in some dream. 'Sigmar empowers the weak, he inspires the strong.'

'Good,' said Felix. He grasped the man's shoulder and stood, swaying with the shaking earth. 'Take her, take those bones, and get out of here. Take one of those boats; just whatever you do *don't* take her across the water.'

'And how will you serve, Brüder Arnulf?'

Felix shook his head and turned away. It had been too much to hope that the man was lucid. At least he could tell friend from foe.

'I'll be at the wall.'

Magic shrouded Morzanna's eyes in darkness, her body now little more than a conduit for the primeval fury of the Dark Master. She blazed with power, and with a pain commensurate. Blood slicked her hands and lathered her animal's neck. The destrier pounded the earth with every fading ounce of strength.

The rock beneath her wrenched apart, as though gods played tug-of-war for their share. Morzanna lifted one shadow-bound hand, pointed to her father's tower and screamed a word of power. With a shuddering that plunged deep into the earth's heart, one of the disseminating fissures widened, the ground before it falling away. The ruins before her cracked in two, piling rubble and screaming men into the opening abyss like gravel tipped from a spade. The earth continued to tear. It reached the wall.

The wall could not stop it.

The scream of stone blended to that of men, a single outcry of terror as earth became air and together they fell.

Breathing hard, Morzanna watched the wall crumble, destruction reaching out its claws to drag more of the construction into the gaping trench. She had missed the tower.

By accident or unconscious design.

She clung on as her exsanguinated steed shuddered and died, but Morzanna's claws were sunk so deeply into its neck that she could no longer see her knuckles and she remained secure in the saddle.

'Death for the Dark Master,' Golkhan roared. His daemon-steed snorted in fury, bearing the Chaos champion into a charge as his voice boomed over the destruction like thunder. 'Bring me the bones of the Gloried. The first to find them will live to see his rise. Every other one of you will die by my sword!'

Howling like dogs, Golkhan's warriors scrambled over the heaped rubble of the wall. From some ingrained reserve, shell-shocked defenders found wit to raise shields, form a line, and see battle joined. The two hosts came together with a staccato thump of brazen flesh upon bronze, discipline and desperation pitched against rabid ferocity. Men yelled and monsters roared, blood of every colour and thickness spraying across the rictus snarls of all.

A pistol cracked, flooding the gritty air with ash and thunder. A defender fell with a steaming crater in his cuirass. A warrior with flesh like coal and knives for hands threw himself into the gap, tearing two defenders apart before the line could be closed. A tramp of feet sounded above the din, a regiment of mailed billmen marching in ordered file through the smoke. The line faltered. Another pistol round took out a spearman.

At the heart of the line, Ologul thrust his claw into the air like a standard and bellowed for order. For a moment he got it. The defenders roared defiance. The invader's shock troops bellowed bloodlust and charged.

As if it had never departed, the clash of steel was rejoined with a vengeance.

Then came something far worse.

Felix's chest tightened, glimpsing the armoured knight through the clashing billhooks like a wolf spied through swaying grass. Its mount was a creature straight from the realm of nightmare, equine only in the most disturbed way. A horse would have broken a leg on the loose ground, but the six limbs of the daemonic steed took it with ease, driving its master onto the defenders' shields and smashing them down like a battering ram.

Felix squeezed his fingers around the reassurance of his sword, but found it had little to offer. This was not the way he had thought to die although, thinking on it, hearing the screams of the mutants as blood and broken bones turned defiance into rout, one way was surely no worse than another.

The thought was darkly reassuring. For die he was about to.

He faced a Chaos warrior.

Ologul screamed a command, the wavering defenders hastily falling back from their defensive line. With a feral scream, the host of Chaos harried their retreat, snatching shields from unsteady grips and tearing men apart. Ologul issued another bellow. There was a weary clatter as the men reformed into a schiltrom, spears threatening every angle.

The Chaos warrior laughed at the projecting blades, seeing how they shivered, and turned in his saddle to wave his reserves into the township. Ologul slurped defiance in the face of the charging hordes. He dragged his mutated body into the knight's path, lifted his buckler, and snapped his monstrous claw in challenge.

Wailing like a flock of daemons, the invaders swept past the Chaos warrior and the defenders' embattled formation, sprinting well clear of the fallen wall. Black-cloaked vermin took advantage of the chaos, sweeping over undefended walls and onto the highest rooftops. Slingshots whirred and cracked, punching bloody holes through fleeing fighters. Those the ratmen missed were swiftly overtaken by the pursuing host, bringing isolated pockets of mayhem to the streets of Die Körnung.

Felix struggled to tell friend from foe as one muscular abomination struggled to rip the throat from another. Then a pack of bloodstained monsters screamed his way and the distinction became moot.

Felix met their charge with one of his own, his blade impaling a crazed fiend through the chest. His charge bore him into the skewered monster shoulder first, throwing it to the ground as he wrenched his weapon free in a spray of fragmented ribs. From his left, a scaly-faced creature swung at him with a club. Blood rained from Felix's blade as it swept upward, the mutant's belly spitting scales from the touch of steel. The mutant's guts hung open but it came on. Felix spun around its clumsy swing, deftly severing its spine with a backhanded swipe. The creature jerked and fell and he kicked the paralysed mutant onto its face and leapt over it, eyes on the melee at the wall.

Ologul was taking a hammering from the Chaos warrior. His shield was in pieces, his arm bleeding, his warriors buckling before those of the champion. And the knight's black, weirdly grooved armour looked unmarked.

Felix ran forwards, Karaghul flashing across the hand of a swordsman that came too close, sending the blade and a clutch of fingers to the ground. The warrior screamed from its two mouths until Felix punched it in the face and ran on. The ground beneath his feet became rubble and the scale of the tear in the earth that had toppled the wall became clear. The rising scent of sulphur almost made him gag.

Attackers came at him from every side. He no longer held to the hope of survival. His runesword split a billman's mail, sending him shrieking into the abyss. To his surprise he was not much troubled by that. He parried a sword thrust meant for his belly, turned the blade, tripped the wielder, then stabbed down through his armpit. All he felt was determination, a resolve to hold the breach for as long as he could. To grant Mori another few minutes to flee.

To earn a mighty doom on Gotrek's behalf.

Through the never-ending tide of foes, he saw Ologul's claw scissor uselessly across the black hell-steel of the daemon-steed's barding. The Chaos warrior hacked through the arm at the elbow, laughing as the daemon then butted the mutant champion to the ground and stamped his bones into rubble. With his fall, the defenders' resolve crumbled. They broke and ran; the hosts of Chaos at their heels.

The Chaos warrior did not pursue. Some instinct made him hold, turn, and meet Felix's eye across the field of battle. Felix could not see the warrior's eyes through his closed helm, but the look was one Felix had learned to feel through the back of his skull. It was the look of a noble spying a merchant's son.

And sensing sport.

Felix growled, angling his sword into an inch perfect *schrankhut* guard.

The knight chuckled and swung from his mount. Rubble crunched beneath heavy black sabatons. Feral mutants gibbered and fell back as he strode through them. His claymore looked twice the weight of Karaghul and was half as long again. Felix backed off, settling into a ready stance, pebbles scuttling into the creaking abyss as he circled. He tried to position the Chaos warrior between him and it.

It was a slender advantage but he would take what he could find.

'I tire of bleeding beasts and spawn,' said the warrior, in his element amidst the shrieking packs that charged past them, screams and clashing steel sounding continuing defiance from the township. 'But you are wearied. Perhaps I should be chivalrous and fight you with my hand behind my back.'

Felix felt surprisingly calm for a man squaring off with a champion of the Ruinous Powers. His guard was true enough to spear a hangman's noose. 'I assure you, I know how to handle a sword.'

'Before I was anointed with the destiny of Be'lakor…' the warrior returned, stowing one murderously spiked gauntlet behind his gorget. He mirrored Felix's circling steps, onyx claymore in his left hand.

'…men would say similar things about me.'

The straits between the riverbank and the sandbar were littered with corpses and debris. In amongst the floating carnage, swimming creatures drove up from beneath to stuff still-moving bodies with knifes. Nikolaus ploughed into the river belly-first, swallowed a mouthful and swam upright, gagging on blood and slime. He felt feverish, confused, and the water had a sickly warmth, as though he floundered in another man's guts.

Sigmar's judgement had fallen again upon the City of the Damned.

Shaking gore from his body, he waded deeper and grabbed the boat that was still moored to the stricken jetty. There was a corpse in it, a foul thing with no eyes and a nose too large. It was a woman, and disconcertingly appealing in death.

Even here. Even now.

He shuddered, wishing for a punishing pain, and tipped the body into the water. Unhooking the mooring line, he dragged the boat to the bank. His actions were automatic, but they nudged aside a portion of the shadow that veiled his mind.

He had been a seaman once.

The white lady waited on the gravel. She clutched a black sack. She was frightened, but Nikolaus could help. For some reason, that filled him with warmth.

'Get in, my lady.'

The girl glanced back to her home, then took Nikolaus's hand and clambered up onto his shoulders. He took the sack from her and stowed it beneath the aft rowing bench. The girl jumped in and then turned to him, slender hand outstretched.

It was then that Nikolaus noticed he had only one arm. The realisation stunned him.

When? How?

'Quick!' the girl screamed.

She was looking over Nikolaus's shoulder. A pair of cloaked shadows were sprinting down the shingle, a third already slipping through the water like a poisonous eel. Voicing a prayer, Nikolaus rammed his shoulder into the skiff's hull and shoved it off. The girl wailed, but he ignored her.

'Be stout-hearted, you sinner. Step through the fire of battle, and let sins be cleansed.'

He found a leathern thong tied at his kilt and unhitched it.

It felt good.

* * *

Felix's sword moved swifter than his hands could command. Steel blurred before sweat-blinded eyes as survival instinct somehow forced his blade to counter the Chaos warrior's every stroke.

A pity the fiend was barely trying.

The warriors of Chaos were peerless, those select men and women for whom a lifetime was insufficient for the slaughter they craved. They had been the best and the most brutal, even before their Dark Gods elevated them above their mortal foes, gifting them power and strength for the havoc wrought in their names.

An impact rang down Felix's blade. He grimaced, but his arms had numbed long ago. It was a miracle he still held his sword at all. Felix backed off, searching for an opening in the warrior's guard.

There was none.

The knight stabbed for Felix's left side. Had Felix's head been able to keep up, he would have recognised the feint. Instead, instinct parried the blow, inviting the head butt that crashed the bridge of his nose in a burst of hell-steel and gibbering daemon-lights. Felix screamed and fell back, too beaten to do anything more than twist his neck as the blade skewered the rubble by his ear. An armoured boot stamped into his belly. Felix yearned to scream, but had breath enough only for a sharp gasp of pain.

The warrior leaned forward, laying his vambrace across the banded steel of his thigh like a huntsman posing with his kill.

'I am Golkhan the Anointed, destined Everchosen of Chaos, and you were no sport at all.'

'Sorry to disappoint,' Felix managed, blood dribbling from his nose and into his mouth.

'You are tenacious for one so insignificant. What brings a civilised man to the City of the Damned?'

'For the baron.'

The warrior chuckled hollowly. 'A thousand millennia without form has taught Be'lakor to sculpt the fates of men. He wished to bring outsiders to his city and he has.'

Felix pulled at the spiked sabaton that was driving through his mail and into his gut, but the foot within may as well have been cast of lead.

'You're from outside?' Felix wheezed. 'You know when we are?'

'I see all Be'lakor promised me coming to pass. And your von Kuber will be the key to it all!'

Golkhan upended his blade to Felix's heart, lifting it so the comet motif that crossed the hilt drew level with his eye slit.

'I have enjoyed this distraction. But all good things must come to an end.'

'Why?'

'Because otherwise they go on forever.'

Felix swallowed, pain spearing from his gut, crying eyes fixed upon the hanging blade.

He tightened his grip around his own sword and prepared.

CHAPTER 16

A Hero's Return

Bloody water splattered Nikolaus's face as he lashed his scourge across the face of the first of the two cloaked creatures. Its scream became a torrent of bubbles as it went under. The second splashed around its kin. It feinted and jerked back, seeking to circle into deeper water towards the boat, but Nikolaus blocked it. It stabbed again, earning a lash across the knuckles that made it hiss with pain. It was swift, but the water robbed it of that advantage.

There was a scream from the boat. Nikolaus thumped his scourge into his opponent's snout and turned.

The swimmer had pulled itself up onto the prow, causing the skiff to rock. It stood, dripping, rolling with the waves. The white lady stumbled over the black sack as she backed into the stern. The creature snickered and advanced.

The first whose face Nikolaus had bloodied was now swimming in an arc for its stern. Already waist deep in water, Nikolaus waded after it, helpless to do anything but watch as the child raised one hand.

The shadows around the girl condensed, as though a cloak had suddenly been drawn in, and there was a blinding flash. A spear of lightning leapt from her arm, a black nimbus washing out to envelope the entire boat. There was an implosion of sound. Nikolaus's ears popped. And then a scorched ratman shot across the prow and plunged into the river with a spume that was already turning to steam. The girl was flung back the opposite way, screaming as she splashed into deeper water.

Ignoring her, the swimmer pulled itself into the boat and made a grab for the abandoned sack. It did not look back as it tightened the cord, hefted the thing to its shoulders and dived headfirst into the water.

Nikolaus watched it go.

Protect the bones, he had been told.

A plea for help pulled his attention back.

Protect Mori. The girl floundered. *Don't take her across the water*.

Ploughing into the river with a clumsy, one-armed stroke, he let the vermin keep its prize.

Flicking horsemeat from her claws, Morzanna watched without a flicker of emotion as savages plunged through the breach her power had torn from the earth. Men with faces she dimly recalled were cut down and trampled. There could be no mercy for those that crossed the Dark Master.

She was empty inside, but such was the price of dark magic. It was a fair exchange, considering her soul was already the jewel in the crown of Be'lakor, the Dark Master, first of the daemon princes.

Claws to her cold, dark breast, she tracked the ruined wall to the tower she had failed to destroy. She sought within herself for a glimmer of anger, of gratitude. But there was nothing.

No, that was wrong. Not nothing.

She ran her fingers through her hair, claws tapping the

vestigial horns. It was danger she felt. And one she recognised. She had felt it once before.

She glanced across the killing field to the breach where Golkhan prepared to break his mortal toy. A vicious smile played with the corners of her lips.

For this was a bout she would gladly watch.

A sloping bed of rock dug into Felix's back, stiffening the back of his throat with the scent of powdered granite. Screams carried over the shift of rubble, sounding from all around, making his own feeble cries all the more piteous. Through his tunnelling vision, he saw Golkhan the Anointed. The Chaos warrior laughed as he forced his boot into Felix's belly. Blood drained down the slope of his body and into his head. It felt heavy, a thumping presence to contrast the hollow agony in his gut. Fighting against the crushing weight with a howl of defiance, Felix lashed his sword from the ground and up, aiming for the join between plates around the warrior's groin, but his arm was ponderous, his aim wide, and Golkhan merely twisted to deflect the flat blow harmlessly off the steel faulds that skirted his hips.

Golkhan greeted his effort with a hollow chuckle and smashed Felix's sword from his grip. It rattled to the rubble and slid several feet downhill towards the abyss and out of reach. It shimmered pink where dust did not cloak it. Felix grasped for it and the warrior pressed down a fraction harder. Felix whimpered, reduced to pawing at the champion's grieves.

Upside down, through fog and rock dust, with one beaten eye and another that swam with pain, Felix saw mutants run, fight, scream, and die. A piercing shriek rose above the lesser wails and rang through the beclouded ruins. It was familiar. A shadow struck from the township. In its paws it clutched a sodden black sack.

Felix felt the pit in his belly open out to consume him.

Nikolaus and Mori were dead.

The ratman swerved past the pockets of combat, its light step skipping over the stinking morass into which those few armoured men that might have given chase sank. Felix watched a bronze-armoured defender down his foe and heft his short spear like a javelin. His cuirass was struck red with blood, his wide face frantic. A shot rang out, close enough to make Felix's eardrums shiver. Splinters of bloodied bronze erupted from the mutant's chest. The spear dropped from its hand and it fell. The ratman chittered anxiously, speeding towards Felix and the Chaos warrior. Felix felt the pressure on his stomach ease and then release.

Golkhan turned, finding a grey-cloaked soldier stood upon the rubble behind him. Black smoke leached from the muzzle of his pistol. The man offered a crisp salute.

The Chaos warrior returned it. 'Matthaus! See this rat to the temple. And sound the retreat, we have what we came for.'

Felix felt the pressure return, his vision blacking out as Golkhan rolled him onto his front.

He lay on his face, too broken to stand and stared into the fog, distracted from the crunch of hell-steel boots by the distant peel of a bell. The black hull of the *Hand* slipped through the distant murk. It was heading upriver. To the bridge. Fate could not be averted. Nikolaus had been right all along.

The End Times were coming.

The grey cloaks of the Chaos host parted to admit the fleeing ratman and his escort, then smoothed into file, all while beating an ordered march back over the sundered wall, billhooks presented like the gift of an early death. Islands of frenzied bloodlust were left in their wake, howling defiance of the call to retreat before suffering wounds enough to staunch their craving for pain.

Stiffly Felix rose. He had it in his mind to chase after the ratman, but he ached like the end of the world and one look at the bristling wall of billhooks disavowed him of any thoughts of heroics. Mutant soldiers in leather and bronze limped past him, part of a weary counter-charge that was bludgeoning its way over the hold-outs and towards the breach. Felix bent, winced, and recovered his sword, wondering if it had always been this heavy, and joined them.

Blood was a great leveller.

The left side of Felix's face was puffed around his black eye. Gore dyed his blond hair crimson and pasted it to his face. His gait was hunched, exhausted, his sword dragging like a broken limb. He appeared no finer than any within these walls – and in that he counted the dead no less than the living.

The sounds of continuing battle raged from beyond the wall.

Perhaps there was still hope.

With just a score of battered warriors at his side, Felix crested the breach to look out onto the killing field beyond. The cleared ruins and been cloven in two by the fissure that had demolished the walls. The great trench jagged towards a point at the centre of a crater on the far side of the clearing. It had split the Chaos host almost completely in two. It was difficult to see in the fog, but Felix judged anywhere between fifty and two hundred men retreated in a narrow line across the clearing. Their withdrawal was orderly, those still intent on fighting either inside the city already or bleeding into its soft ground.

The battle Felix had heard was being fought to his left, the direction of the riverside gatehouse. The Chaos forces there were being beaten back, confusion spreading as some other force assaulted their flank.

Felix caught a flash of orange hair and a familiar roar as a starmetal axe severed an arm from a mutant's body. His mouth caught itself in a smile. He lifted his sword so the mutants beside him might see and be encouraged.

And then he charged into the killing ground towards an army of Chaos.

Panic was a contrivance of Chaos, if any facet of nature so universal ever could be. It snarled from the helms of billmen, displayed its vigour with bristling billhooks and the virile scent of saltpetre and sweat.

Buffeted by fleeing warriors, Morzanna watched in astonishment – and a little satisfaction – as the host of Golkhan the Anointed dissolved before her eyes.

'It is one dwarf!' Golkhan howled, loud enough to make Morzanna wince and raise her hands to her ears.

The warrior's steed stamped and shook out its mane, until Golkhan finally exhausted his patience and hauled so hard on the reins that the daemon's fore hooves were dragged from the ground. It snorted defiance until Golkhan smashed a gauntlet into its champron. Blood ran from the eye hole, streaming over the dried gore that caked its muzzle. It whinnied. Golkhan raised a fist and it fell silent.

'It is afraid, black lord,' said Morzanna, raising a placating hand that itself dripped with horseflesh.

'Daemons are animals. They understand stronger wills, and pain when that will is defied. And like animals, they cannot fear.'

Morzanna's lip curled before she caught it. The warrior's ignorance was almost as stunning as his pride.

'This dwarf is vision-sent, black lord. A champion of light and not here by chance. The weapon he bears is the bane of daemonkind. Your horse recognises this better than you.'

'This *champion* is small, like a quail's egg, and I will crush him as one.'

Morzanna bowed low. 'It will be glorious, black lord.'

Golkhan caressed the neck of his now docile mount, steel

scraping steel, then turned on Morzanna with a voice colder and no less hard. 'I am new to your schemes, witch, but do not mistake me for a fool.'

Morzanna forced a smile, suddenly conscious of the grey cloaks and tinctured mail that surrounded her and their lord.

'The bearded pest is not the only one with a destiny. I am to be Everchosen of Chaos. The herald of the End Times promises this is so.'

'But, lord–'

'But nothing!' Golkhan roared, slamming his fist into his mount's barding, then singling out one of the men at Morzanna's back. The man stepped forward. His face was blackened with gunpowder smoke. The colour matched the thick curls of his head and the short crust of his beard.

'I am not some mindless berserker to be tempted by a worthy foe, nor a hapless dilettante to be swayed by the forked tongue of a comely witch.' Golkhan spat the last, before dismissing her from sight in favour of his summoned man.

'Send the gladiator spawn to cover our retreat. Let our sorceresses witness the emptiness of their hearts.'

Felix fended a blow, creatures fleeing on all sides in a clattering blur of faces and weaponry. The mutant swordsman grunted and came again, lazily thrusting for the exact same spot on Felix's chest. Felix caught the blade with his, deftly twisted it from the mutant's grip, then kneed the creature in the groin. It doubled over Felix's shoulder, a gasp of vile air washing past his ear and he rammed his pommel stone into its belly. It fell off him, crashing over a rump of rubble.

Felix shook hair from his eyes and, with a wince, tested out his knee joint.

The invaders were in full retreat, and Gotrek seemed determined to butcher his fill. The Slayer roared, axe spinning high above his head, a shining harbinger of blood-wracked ruin. By his side, two warrior-penitents howled like sinners at the stake. Their sackcloth coverings were torn, bloodied, riven with brick dust and ash, but the savageness of their appearance was as nothing to that which gripped their faces. The one-legged sister beat at the mutants with her stave and a ferocity that surpassed that of the abominations that fled before her. Her brother-in-faith lashed wildly with a mace, a trail of mangled fingers left in the Slayer's wake. The three warriors cut a swathe into the Chaos ranks, mutants turning to the sound of bloodshed, only to be dispatched to their Dark Master by axe, mace, or splintered stave. Grey-cloaked lieutenants screamed into the spreading panic. Pistol-fire crackled across the line of retreat, masking the scenes of summary execution under a pall of smoke. The dwarf spotted Felix through the swirling carnage. He smeared blood from his one good eye and winked.

'Good to see that you made it over that bridge in one piece, manling. For a time back there, I was worried.'

Felix sidestepped an axe-blow. The blade struck sparks from a crumbling length of wall. '*You* were worried about *me*? You were the one that fell in the river.'

'Drop of water never killed anyone,' Gotrek roared, slamming his axe so hard through a mutant's skull that he had to strain to rip it out. 'Hah! More's the pity.' A mutant fled past him. A sharp thrust from his axe's shoulder shattered its spine and it spasmed and fell. Gotrek beheaded it before its knees were fully bent. He laughed, looking over its toppling shoulders to the two flagellants that battered gamely, if blindly, through the fleeing host.

'Bit the worse for wear, but they do as they're told if you tell them loud enough.' As if to prove the point, the dwarf wind-milled his axe above his vivid crest and bellowed at the two to rally to him. The woman crashed her stave across the back of a mutant's neck and moaned. Gotrek shrugged. 'Well, sometimes they do anyway.'

Felix parried another opportunistic thrust, actually grateful for the host of Chaos that kept his attention from the two mindless fanatics. A short time ago that had been him. But for the grace of Sigmar that might be him still. Within that anarchic swell, Felix could see the Chaos warrior, Golkhan, high on the saddle of his giant mount, as easily as if he rode a skiff across a bumpy lake. The warrior was surrounded by a cohort of grey cloaks mounted on more mundane steeds. One of them hoisted a slight woman into their saddle. She was garbed in black, hair as white as the chalk cliffs of Nordland, but with tanned skin like a Tilean corsair's. There was something about her that was familiar. And then it struck him.

Nikolaus's white lady. The visitor to his own dreams.

The glimpse came and passed in a moment, seen through the wave of billhooks like a corpse rising from the ocean's depths. The withdrawing horde was sinking into the fog. In the path of their retreat, the fog wavered around a trickery of spidery silhouettes. A foghorn blared.

Felix noticed that those delicate shadows had grown very large.

A hairy limb like an articulated pike stabbed through the mist and crashed into the ground. Rock shattered. Another leg followed, this one multiply jointed and plated to a black mirror shine. On four more weaving, drunken, limbs, the creature's bullet body heaved from the mist. Chitinous mandibles clacked hungrily either side of a clutch of tentacles that felt the air in place of eyes. A second monster emerged in the wake of the first. Its worm-like body was segmented and slimy, borne from the mist on the rustling of thousands of spike-like feet. A collar of spines bristled about a hugely armoured headsection that split on all sides into beaks to emit a redoubled foghorn bellow.

From the walls of Die Körnung, there came a command to

fall back. The beasts of hell bore down. To Felix, the order seemed somewhat superfluous.

Gotrek's one eye lit up, and he started forwards, parting a terrified mutant warrior from his legs with an impatient hack of his axe. He called back. 'Which do you want, manling, the big one or the ugly one?'

In lieu of a forthcoming answer, Felix's mouth simply hung open and waited for one to arrive. The creatures were huge, advancing together, crushing against the sides of the street and drawing screams from the mutants whose retreat bore them through the gauntlet of legs, spines, skewers and clicking mouthparts. He wondered which was the ugly one.

'You decide,' he managed, leaning wearily against a blackened stub of corner wall to catch his breath as Gotrek charged ahead with a roar.

The spider-spawn clicked its mandibles, scuttling about on the spot to meet the dwarf's charge and sending out a maggoty scream of tentacles. Gotrek bellowed a war cry, his axe cleaving through a dozen, spraying himself and the spawn's carapace with oily mucus. The spider-spawn squealed and lashed out with a bladed limb. Gotrek ducked. His axe tore a chip from its black carapace as it whistled by his crest.

The centipede rippled around its embattled cousin, weaving between the scraps of ruin towards Felix. There was a mindless deliberateness to its intent that curdled the contents of Felix's stomach. He gripped his sword tight and retreated behind his stub of corner wall. The spawn paused before the wall, tapped it with one of its many beaks, then reared onto its hindquarters to peer over the top and hiss. Felix stumbled back, sword ready. The giant centipede watched him from the myriad holes in its armoured headsection that may have concealed eyes. It clacked periodically against the intervening wall, as though confounded by its very existence.

Felix gave a relieved laugh.

Big, but not too bright.

A ripple of segmented muscle swept back from the creature's headsection, rearing it back. Felix's grin faded. He had time enough to spin on his heels and run as, with a blistering torrent of bony clicks, the spawn smashed its skull through the wall. Masonry crumbled like soil.

'Oh Sigmar,' Felix panted, his companion's pugnacious roar carrying over the rippling crunch of a thousand peg-like feet.

'Why do you hate me?'

Not daring to look back, Felix just ran, vaulting the rubble that littered his path. The pursuing monster undulated between those same scraps of ruin like an eel. And it was gaining fast. At a particularly solid-looking bit of wall, Felix jumped, gripped the top and hauled himself up. Old masonry crumbled in his fingers, boots scratching uselessly against the brick face as his biceps strained. He cleared the wall, then dropped eight feet in a battered crunch of chainmail. He groaned with feeling, placing a hand to the wall to steady himself as he rose.

He could still hear it coming.

'Felix! Back from the wall.'

Without pausing to think who would be screaming orders, Felix did as he was told. He took one step away from it and dived, the very instant that an armoured head came crashing through. A beak snapped inches shy of his toes, almost exactly where his neck had been the moment before. For the second time in as many seconds, Felix hit the ground with a grunt of pain. The centipede thrashed its head section. The wall crumbled like burned bark.

'Down!'

Dark matter uncoiled like a whip. The taffeta veil of fog seemed to flex.

Felix pushed his face into the ground, gravel pouring the smell of char into his nose as a single black lance seared over his prone body. It was followed a split second afterwards by a thunderous crack and a long, drawn-out squeal. A wash of burned meat found his nostrils and settled there. Felix rolled onto his back. The centipede gave a strangled warble, its beaks scorched black, and pulled its head back through the wall.

Felix battled a wave of dizziness, mouthing a 'thank you' as he tilted his head back to address his saviour.

Leaning fully into the breastplate of one of his soldiers, Morschurle dismissed Felix's gratitude with an exhausted wave. His robes were torn, plastered with ash and dust as well as blood, much of it his own. Both hands and the underside of his chin glittered like stars in clear water. Each pinprick was a shard of glass. The talismans around his neck were no more. He had lost every one contesting the sorcery that had shaken the walls of Die Körnung to their knees.

'No thanks are needed,' the sorcerer wheezed. Peeling himself away from his supporter, he sank down against a stretch of wall with a grateful sigh. He summoned his men with a loose flap of his fingers. 'Go. Finish it off. But be wary. It is still dangerous.' The soldiers saluted, clutched spear and shield, and ran in pursuit of the wounded spawn.

Once they were gone, Morschurle abandoned any pretence of vigour. He dabbed at his lacerated jaw with a piteous whimper. Felix cast an anxious look after the reeve's soldiers. He could still hear Gotrek screaming curses. There was a crunch, as of a starmetal blade hacking through six inches of exoskeleton, followed by a belligerent roar.

'Don't leave me just yet,' said Morschurle. The man panted through his mouth, his nose clotted with blood. His eyes were wide with pain, but there was a determined set to his jaw, as if what he meant now to do was a thing he had long vowed to do before he died. 'I have something to tell you and,' he gave a sickly smile, gesturing to his bloodied robes, 'not long in which to do it.'

Felix began to protest. 'I've seen graver wounds heal.'

'Shut up and listen. I came to tell you about the Dark Master. About Be'lakor.'

Felix stilled his retort and nodded, crouching by his side.

'Go on.'

'I told you before that the daemon is without body, but he is everywhere and he is everything; air, soil and blood.' Morschurle held up a bloodstained and glittering palm, face riven with pain. 'He is the portents of death that I see in my mind.'

'And the bones, the bones of its champion Kharduun, what does it want with them?'

'That I do not know. But what Be'lakor craves even over his vengeance on the gods is freedom.' He swept a bleeding hand across the sky. Pink clouds roiled. There was a chitinous crack like a thunderclap. 'He is trapped here, damned as are we all.'

Felix pinched his lips, waiting for the man to continue.

'Yes, Felix. I am a seer after all. I understand that in a sense I am already dead. That I died long ago. That was why I made my pact with the daemon prince.' He grimaced at the accusing look that passed Felix's face, waved a hand to bid him quiet. 'I am no friend of Be'lakor. I fought him with every tool I could find. But all he wanted was for me to protect my people, to ensure that they did not try to leave and to take in any that crossed from the other side. Like you.'

'If that's all he wanted then why does he kill you now?'

'I do not know that either. Only that his plans go beyond mere escape.' Morschurle slumped back against the wall. He was clearly in great pain, but he looked content. 'I kept my part. The daemon will keep his. It is what daemons do.'

Felix gave an incredulous snort. An arachnoid shriek brought dust trickling over Morschurle's silver hair.

'You may not have noticed in the confusion of your home being ripped open from the ground up, but your honourable daemon has just about killed you all.'

'The deal was not for my life,' said Morschurle, eyes flicking to the violated ruin of Die Körnung. 'And it was not for theirs.'

'For Mori's,' Felix finished for him.

'My daughter in exchange for every life in this city. Dark Gods demand a high price, but they are fair. Look me in the eye, Felix. Tell me that the Pious would have offered even this meagre an exchange. Tell me that and I will tell you I am sorry.'

Unable to say it and mean it, Felix said nothing.

Morschurle lay back and closed his eyes, crossing his arms across his chest in death's repose.

'Then do not judge me.'

Felix shook his head angrily and rose, slapping dust from his breeches.

'The Dark Master's soul is caged beneath the temple of Sigmar,' said Morschurle, eyes fluttering open as Felix turned to leave. 'It is the one constant in this place, the place that all roads lead. I cannot say with certainty what you will find there. Know only that Be'lakor cannot be slain. It is his curse. But maybe you can prevent his escape.'

'How?' said Felix.

Horror painted Morschurle's features.

'The Master is everywhere. He is everything. He knows you are coming. And he is not afraid.'

'How do I stop him?' Felix asked again, dropping to his haunches to give the man a shake, but the man had no answer.

Morschurle was dead.

CHAPTER 17

The Aftermath

The marble steps of the acropolis sang their praises to Golkhan's return, the hooves of his daemon-steed sounding out like bells. The exaltation rang down the escarpment, resounding from the ramshackle bowl of his amphitheatre. From the temple's colonnaded approach, daemonfire crackled from sconces, somehow rendering its flawless colouration black.

Rejoice, went the unspoken cry, *the Dark Master will rise.*

A bent mutant in grey livery lumbered from the temple to take Golkhan's reins. The champion acknowledged him with a nod, then swung his leg over the daemon's rear to dismount. He thumped its hindquarters. Respect, if not affection.

Squashed into the saddle of a flesh and blood stallion with one of the Anointed's lieutenants, Morzanna remained mounted. And not by choice. The horseman's bladed riding gauntlets enclosed her like a cage. She glared at the warriors and worshippers that turned the temple's courtyard into a bazaar. She had been the Master's chosen, her body moulded into his dark likeness. At what point had his eye alighted upon Golkhan? When had she become a canary in another champion's cage?

A black-cloaked figure appeared before Golkhan and pulled back its hood. Its eyes were dry and cold, like machined rubies. When it spoke it was with all the feeling of a reflection.

'Our task is done. Kill-work many creatures, but portal to shadow-paths is found-found. Master's temple-cage is open-free.'

Golkhan raised a fist, turning triumphantly to his men. They cheered him, as though their lord had just returned victorious from a joust.

'And the relics,' Golkhan shouted above his followers' acclaim. 'Are they prepared?'

'As we speak-squeak,' answered the overseer.

Golkhan rounded on Morzanna, arms spread wide, and laughed. Even distorted by hell-steel, it was the truest sound she had ever heard from him. His arms flexed back, armoured fingers scraping beneath his helm's seal. With a grunt of pain, he began to pull.

Morzanna watched in fascination. She knew as well as any that the gods' gifts were not readily returned.

Golkhan the Anointed howled in agony as the helm wrenched from his face in rivulets of blood. The howl became a cathartic roar as he hurled the device from the acropolis, then sank into a cold laugh. He turned to Morzanna and smiled.

The man beneath the helm was gaunt, grey-eyed, older than Morzanna had imagined, but handsome in a severe sort of way. The flesh of his cheeks and forehead were red raw. His raven hair was crushed where the helm had sat. And she recognised him.

'You…' she whispered.

'The End Times come,' said Golkhan, ignoring her. 'The pieces are ready and it is time for the pawns to move.' He gave his mount one last clap, meeting Morzanna's eyes with his for one fierce instant. It was a sight more terrible than any mask ever bound to the souls of daemons.

'See that it is done.'

Water lapped soullessly at the gritty shore. The burned pilings of a jetty were blackened and crisp, the tips sharpened to brittle points. It was not quite real, ephemeral as the spirits that lingered on the breeze. Rudi held his breath, layer upon layer of unease settling upon his shoulders like a weighted shroud. His gaze swept the ruin before him. The evidence of rebuilding was everywhere if a man was careful enough to look for it. Rubble had been cleared from the streets to construct new walls. The buildings themselves had been fortified with layers of rock.

This had been somebody's home long after the calamity was supposed to have cleansed the city of its sins.

Was it possible that Sigmar had selected a handful to live on? Perhaps to earn absolution. Or maybe not all the residents of the damned city had been equal in their impiety. It was a strange and unsettling thought. But then, in this place, most were.

The ruined burgh slumped into the river, surrounded by the remnants of a wall that looked to have been demolished brick by brick. The east wall had taken the heaviest punishment. Lumps of stone carved with gargoyles and delicate engravings lay broken and scattered over the nearby streets. They had no place there, unless hurled from above by catapult and Sigmar's wrath.

The wind whistled through what remained and Rudi shivered. Somewhere within the desolation, a rock cracked against another.

Probably just the wind.

'What was this place?'

'Even Sigmar will miss a few fleas when His mighty hammer crushes rats. That way.' Caul's knife indicated the broken east wall.

The whispers followed them from the river as the two men picked their way through the stricken township. The rubble underfoot was fluffy with ash snow. Fog spilled from rusted embrasures, sweeping doorway to doorway and away down alleys. Rudi took a tense grip on his blade.

At last they arrived at the wall and, at Caul's insistence, Rudi went first, emerging on the other side and taking shelter behind a jumble of masonry. He looked across the clearing to the thin line of houses at the far side. Mist lay upon the field of ruin like a murderous lover. It pressed itself to lumps of limestone, tightening over the arms and necks of breached breastplates. When Rudi squinted, tried to focus on what looked like a spire or a balcony on the other side, it was as though daemons manifested from the shadows until his eyes jerked back and there was nothing but mist. For a long time he stared. His heart thumped as if to remind him he still lived.

'I don't think we're alone,' he hissed.

'The Damned walk here as they always will,' Caul whispered back. His garb gave a leathern creak as he crouched down beside Rudi. 'All who ever lived. All who ever died. Sharing this space in their own time. Aware of us only as we are of them.' He threw his knife into the air and caught it, proceeding to toss it quietly from hand to hand. 'In Nuln, folk still speak of the great fire and that was a thousand years ago; in Aquitaine, they whisper the name of the Red Duke, and then only in daylight.' Caul smiled grimly, eyes unflinching green, blade blinking left to right. 'Scars live on in a city's memories, even as those that suffered the cut die and are replaced. This city has suffered as others dare not dream. Dark magic suffuses it – its sewers, its skies, and even the very souls of its people. Magnus came to destroy and he did. But answer me this, Hartmann.'

Caul caught the knife in his left hand, then placed it flat on the ground between them. 'If you returned to Sigmarshafen to destroy the painted window of its cathedral with only this blade, do you think it could be done?'

Sensing a trick, Rudi thought for a moment, then cautiously shrugged. 'Yes. Easily.'

Caul covered the knife with his four-fingered hand and dragged it back.

'You misunderstand destruction. I speak of the utter annihilation of a thing. Dark magic and violence are a foul mix that Magnus, in his faith and in his blindness, could not begin to comprehend. It was only afterwards that he realised what it was he had done.' Caul gestured across the ruined vista. The scope of destruction hazed even as the two men watched. 'The city, like a window, could be broken, but not destroyed. Shards remain, and we are in but one. Beside us lies another, and another, and another; powerful moments, fractured in time without end or beginning.'

'So, Felix…?'

'Is probably here somewhere, in the next shard or the one after, doing as we are doing.' He picked up his knife and slowly edged from cover. 'If it's not too much trouble for the lesser half of Gurnisson and Jaeger.'

'So… are you saying we might be in a… er… other time?'

'Smart boy,' Caul whispered, recovering his condescending smile. 'I see now why you chose to flee rather than fight the Beast.'

Rudi ground his teeth, making the other man's grin all the broader.

Caul nodded towards the ash snow that was still falling in fits and starts. He drew deeply through his nose, as though causality was something he could smell. 'Knowing my history, I would say it looks like Magnus has just been and gone. Would you not agree?'

Rudi tingled at the thought that his feet might grace the same earth as Magnus the Pious. The scene of spent, but still latent, fury took on a kind of purity, the quiet of a cloister, rather than a crypt.

A distant crack echoed through the flowing fog and this time both men started.

'Come,' said Caul, quietly. 'As we both know, Magnus left something alive here.'

'The Beast,' whispered Rudi, sweating despite the chill of the fog, the creeping shadows more menacing than they had been before.

Caul waved him quiet.

'We don't stop until we reach the temple.'

An evil-looking gull tore its hooked bill through a mutant's belly, gobbling down a lump of flesh before Gotrek startled it into flight with a sweep of his axe. The dwarf set the weapon on a ridge of rock, then planted his backside upon the mutant's breastplate with a grunt of pleasure. If Gotrek was bothered by the blood and filth that marred his impromptu stool, then it clearly troubled him no more than the corpse it contained. Its arms and legs wiggled with morbid anima as the dwarf bent forward and shook off his first boot. He turned it upside down, releasing a trickle of brown water and an odour that belonged nowhere but the foulest marsh. Felix drew back with a scowl, but the stench concerned his companion about as much as the bodies and blood. Gotrek unplugged his second boot. The tough, hobnailed orc-hide came loose with a slurp and he set down both beside his axe. He looked over the battlefield, airing his toes, giving every indication of judging the nearby feet for a matching size.

'Strange company you've been keeping,' Gotrek observed, nodding to the mutants in their battered armour that staggered through the ruins in a daze. Some were already at work stripping the corpses, but most just blinked up at the sky, as if to burn the memory of such destruction from their eyes. He turned back to Felix with a crooked smirk. 'But a decent scrap, nonetheless. I envy you, manling. I wouldn't have minded a crack at that champion myself.'

Felix growled, staring across the field of slaughter towards Die Körnung. These were *people* that lay dead around them. Families. He said nothing because he knew Gotrek would not care. Suppressing his anger made his next question harsher than he had intended.

'Where have you been anyway?'

The brow above Gotrek's one good eye arched. 'If you wish someone to follow *your* every footstep then I suggest you find yourself a rememberer of your own.'

'I suppose I should count myself fortunate you came looking for me at all. With the Beast slain you might have just walked back to Osterwald.'

Gotrek chuckled, making the body beneath him jerk. Sarcasm appealed to the Slayer's bleak sense of humour.

'Actually, I was looking for the creature's body when I found these two.' The dwarf jerked a thumb towards the two flagellants. They strayed amongst the mutants, muttering, clenching and unclenching their fists, regarding their surrounds with a dazed distaste. 'Wandering like chickens and ankle deep in the river, not that they noticed. They were like those mindless we saw on the other side, only not quite, raving on about holy war and some long march from Praag.' Peeling bluish blood off his knuckles under his teeth, Gotrek shuffled around on his breastplate to watch them. 'Shame the witless oafs keep calling me Thangrek.'

'Who's Thangrek?'

'Grimnir's hairy arse if I know. It's not as if they had the sturdiest minds to begin with.'

The earless flagellant that Felix recalled as Friedrich, stood looking up at the pink sky, calling a name over and over, but

Felix could not make it out above the cawing gulls. Felix saw patches of darkness split from the ruins they hid beneath to move within the fog. It could have been the dancing lights of the aurora, but Felix suspected otherwise. He saw one such shadow occupy the same spot as Friedrich, the man's voice momentarily twinned to another's before the darkness passed and the penitent clearly stood alone.

'Do you see any of this?' Felix whispered. 'Tell me it's not just me.'

Gotrek frowned, looking to the burning sky and then back across the corpse-strewn clearing. 'I don't think you're losing your mind if that's what ails you.' He rapped his axe with his bare, hairy toes. The runes glowered a dim red. 'You're soft, man-ling, but you're not mad. There's something foul afoot here.'

Felix let out an overly dramatic sigh. 'Thank you, I suppose.'

'You're welcome,' Gotrek replied with a grin.

Felix's eyes narrowed. The broken walls of Die Körnung wavered even as he watched. It was not fog or settling rubble. It was more than that.

'When I look at something, it's as if I'm seeing it from different eyes, all at once. It's like–' he hesitated, uncertain how to continue. Gotrek regarded him, patient as a cliff face. 'Do you realise where we are? Or when, I should say.'

'Aye,' said Gotrek with a slight nod. 'Two hundred years past, give or take a day or two.'

Felix gaped, stunned that Gotrek could say something so implausible as if commenting on inclement weather.

'A dwarf always knows where he's about, manling. And besides,' Gotrek directed an ugly glare towards the sky. Pink fire ignited and flared back in waves. Suffering in malignant silence, Morrslieb glowered an ugly green. 'Chaos moon's as big as a troll's backside. It's not passed so near since the end of the Great War. Two hundred years past, give or take a day or two.'

'How is it even possible?'

'You recall Karag Dum?' Gotrek flexed his toes, studying him archly. 'Chaos twists time as hard as it does earth and flesh. Trying to understand it is as likely to melt your eyeballs as do anyone any good, so I suggest you just accept it.'

'Accept it?' Felix spluttered. He did not know what he had expected from his companion. Panic? Helpless rage? But Gotrek faced change in the time-honoured tradition of the dwarfs – ignoring it and waiting stubbornly for it to pass. Felix resisted the impulse to try and strangle him.

'Put your boots back on. We're not done yet.'

'Not that I'm complaining, but that's uncharacteristically keen.' Gotrek leaned closer and looked into his eye. 'You've not had one of those…' he waved his meaty fist vaguely, '*things* in you have you?'

'I wish people would stop implying that.'

With a sigh, Felix located an armoured corpse of his own and sat. Metal creaked like his own joints as his weight spread. He kicked aside a length of spider-leg and then, wearily massaging his aching temples, related to Gotrek all he had learned of the Dark Master, Be'lakor, and of the curse that afflicted this city.

The dwarf listened with an eager intent. When Felix had finished, Gotrek wore a grin as wide as the Reik and was hurriedly fastening his boots.

'So there's some truth to that fanciful talk of a daemon that cannot be slain.'

Felix nodded grimly, spreading his arms in not-entirely-mock surrender. 'One whose plan all along has been to lure people to its city. And here we are, like rats to its bait.'

Gotrek gave a sideways leer, pulling his bootlace tight. 'Sometimes rats bite.'

'The two of us against a Chaos warrior, a sorceress, their army and then, in case that's not enough for you, their daemon lord? As plans go, I think that even we've had better.'

'Even Sigmar did not fight the hordes of Chaos alone.'

Gotrek craned his neck to look around Felix's shoulder. Felix swivelled around.

Nikolaus walked across the ruins towards them. He was sopping wet and the discolouration of his bruises was beginning to blend with his tattoos. A gull disturbed from its feast flapped at his head, but he did not notice. His eyes were distant and, though he spoke, he gave no indication that he knew who it was that listened. Mori shuffled quietly behind him, empty-handed and similarly bedraggled. Fright not yet departed made the girl's eyes a vivid, sparkling purple. The depth of colour changed as he watched. It was striking. And somehow familiar.

Boots tied, Gotrek collected his axe, his one eye focusing as he screwed its chain to his bracer and muttered into his beard. 'Sigmar didn't want for a mighty doom.'

Felix lifted his leg and twisted so he rode his corpse side-saddle. He nodded to Nikolaus, but got no response.

'The temple of Sigmar is no place for a child.'

'His grey fortress is for all,' Nikolaus mumbled, picking at the scabs on his chest as he rocked on his heels. 'Young and old and men of all lands. The white lady will forgive me there. Only the sinful will break upon its walls.'

Felix's mouth framed the words.

White lady?

Felix looked at Mori again. He could not believe he had not seen it before.

Time was broken here. She could be young *and* old. She was the sorceress he had seen at Golkhan's side, the visitor to his and other men's dreams. His regard made the girl clutch even more firmly to the back of Nikolaus's thigh. So sweet a child. What horror had driven her to the path she was predestined to take? Her father had been right. Dark Gods demanded a high price. But they were fair.

He wondered if he should do something, but the idea of what he might have to do sickened him. The thought of what

Gotrek, or even Nikolaus in his right mind, would do if he knew offended him even more. As if sensing the course of his thoughts, the girl let go of Nikolaus's leg and ran back for the ruin of her home. Nikolaus wept though he clearly had no idea why and did not turn.

Gotrek grunted, a familiar refrain to the weaknesses of men, and stood, planting his hands behind his hips and bending backwards until his spine clicked. He levered upwards and limbered his axe arm with a sweep through the fog.

'Are we moving then or not? Before even I grow old and the Pious finally decides to show up and burn this place down.'

Felix sighed, checked his sword was secure in its scabbard, and spared a last look to the now-orphaned child. There, at least, was one thing in their favour.

'I doubt that Magnus will be coming.'

Konrad Seitz awoke with a thundering heart. He sat bolt upright, sheets crumpled and strewn over the wide foot of his bed, his linen nightshirt clinging to his chest with sweat. Stiffly, as if the limb that grasped it belonged to another man, he lowered his sword to the bed. He stared at the blade, his body still living the nightmare they had shared.

With a breath of cold morning air, the beat of drums and marching columns that had filled his dreams faded into the drumming of rain against his sill. Through the window, high in the baron's stone manse, Sigmarshafen emerged into a new dawn of fog and misery. Konrad recovered his sword. It shone with a dull lustre in the beclouded sun.

When would it all end?

A clamour of mailed boots rang from the grounds immediately beneath Konrad's window, followed by urgent shouts from the hall. Still unsettled, Konrad swung from his bed and arranged his sheets into an order more befitting a captain just as the first of several fists hammered at his door.

'Yes!' Konrad snarled. 'Bloody Sigmar, come in.'

The door swung inward to disgorge three grey-cloaked militiamen. They were dripping wet, breathless from an uphill sprint from the township to the fort. They must have been freezing, but pride would not let them shiver. Their familiar faces and the black bands at their biceps marked them as Konrad's own feverishly loyal moralpolizei.

'Captain,' said one, cold frosting his wiry beard. 'The pens have been broken, and the gate breached in the night.'

'An attack?' Konrad hissed.

'No, from within,' said another. 'The dwarf and his man are gone. And they have taken Hartmann. Two of our men were found dead in the inn where they were staying.'

'Two of mine? What were they...?'

Konrad shook his head violently, stalking to the window and the blanched offering it beheld. The City of the Damned festered in the distant fog, like a bruise on the earth's dead flesh.

Remnants of the nightmare stirred his blood, imbuing the bone-white sink of misery with glory, terror, all the trappings of a righteous war. He was not even sure that it had truly been a nightmare. It felt so vivid even now, like a vision. Like a memory. He could still taste the blood, feel the warmth in his breast as the hideous get of Chaos were slaughtered like animals, the purging fires raging from horizon to horizon. The acclaim of his peasant army rang in his ears, the humble soldier who would be Emperor. It did not matter that it was not his name the memories sang. He would do just as much and more, and this time he would finish it. In Götz von Kuber's name.

He would burn out the Dark Master.

'Empty the town,' he growled, voice hoarse from a night spent bellowing orders to his dreams, visions of dark lords and their white ladies triumphant in his mind. 'Every child old enough to walk. Every woman strong enough to carry a blade.

'We march on the City of the Damned.'

CHAPTER 18

Twisted

Felix walked stiffly along the deserted highway, sword low, muscles tired. The buildings either side stood tall and thin, shrouded in black like priests at a funeral. They were well back from the roadside, withdrawn behind walled gardens, twisted hedgerows, and weed-choked lanes. Apart, yet some-how close, and with every breath Felix took contriving to edge closer still. It was as if space were being constricted, gaps being closed. The air twinkled with malevolence. The city around grew dark, adopting a strange hyper-solidity as reality upon reality shivered into place, one atop another atop another, until every brick and stone was an amalgam of an infinite number of near identical others. No wonder everything was closing in.

There was not the space in one world to fit it all.

How long had they been walking? It felt like hours.

The road ahead seemed to *twist* as he watched, yawing side to side like a ship at sea. There was a lurch of nausea and he threw his gaze to the weed-choked slabs beneath his feet. He was thankful he had not eaten since Sigmarshafen.

But the worst part was the voices.

They were whispered and indistinct and, like the walls, intertangled with many times a thousand others. It was garbled madness hiding under the illusion of words. And it was slowly driving Felix mad.

'Are you sure this is the path?'

Felix's voice trembled as much as his hands. It was impossible to believe that a force of hundreds had just fled this way.

'Aye,' Gotrek grunted without turning from the narrowing, never-ending path. 'You can see where these weeds have been recently trodden.'

Felix examined the weeds. He could see where they had been crushed under marching feet, where they were thick, where they were burned to brittle crisps. He could see where there were no weeds.

And the temple of Sigmar drew no nearer.

Every so often, Felix caught a clear view of the acropolis through breaks in the ruined buildings. Always ahead although, despite their path remaining straight, sometimes a shade to the right or to the left. Despite his best efforts his eyes were drawn to it. Streams of cloud circled its pinnacle, as if they too were slave to its might. That sky was the reason he had tried so hard to avoid looking at the temple. And it was the continual punishment for his weakness of will. It juddered like a stalled machine, the pink aurora that had troubled him so nothing but a facet of a vast continuum, every instant of which sought its place in the heavens. As well as pink, the sky was alternately and simultaneously blue, and black, and steely grey. Moons of every size and phase filled it. And across it all, blazing in an arc of golden majesty before bleeding to a violent crimson over the western sky, was the sun. Felix tried to make out an individual source of light but could not. A thousand suns shone from a thousand different times.

And still Felix felt cold.

Leaving Gotrek to forge ahead, he glanced back the way they had come.

The road behind them bent in what would have been a sickening contortion had it been performed by a worm, much less by brick and stone. It was endless ruin, a maddening allegory for the city's damnation. The horizon twisted to a point infinitely compressed and indefinably wide. It roiled, inconstant, a degree too high in the sky. It was enough for Felix to question the plausibility of his own existence.

What was any man in a place where time and dimension meant nothing?

The three flagellants taking up the rear seemed of a one with the madness that surrounded them. Their eyes wandered with independent wills, their faces slack and lathered with perspiration, muttering to the voices as they stumbled on. Their words were gibberish, sentences changing halfway through as whatever madness gripped them at that moment passed over their mind to another.

'Sigmar, hammer of man. Sigmar, hammer of man…'

Nikolaus muttered, over and over. The prophet seemed relatively coherent, or at least more constant. Every so often he would pause in his chant, stare into the shadows and rub his face in confusion before beginning afresh.

'Sigmar, hammer of man.'

Felix looked away, hugging his sword arm to his chest for warmth. He heard the voices too, though he struggled to shut them out. The feeling that Rudi walked beside him was so powerful that he was surprised to turn around and see nothing but mist in vaguely human form. He shuddered.

It was like being haunted.

Rudi eyed the ground as he walked. It crunched where he trod. It was a strange sound. Not at all like brick or stone.

And it was uneven, lumpy beneath his thin soles and brittle like chalk.

'I find it hard to believe you are descended from the warrior-pilgrims of the Pious,' came the voice of Caul Schlanger, out of sight but not of hearing a couple of paces ahead.

'I am,' Rudi whispered, angered and yet strangely not.

His body felt too far away to be reached by anger. His ancestors had been peasant warriors, uprooted by the Pious's crusade and settling in Ostermark when it was won. He felt them around him, those forefathers that had fought to cleanse the City of the Damned. There were others too, his mother, his grandparents, folk of the moors, their remains again uprooted and brought here. They welcomed him.

As though he had returned home

'A recent arrival perhaps,' Caul went on. 'A dung-gatherer's son fled the greenskin siege of Osterwald?'

At last, anger smouldered through the fog that separated himself from his body. He looked up, saw Caul's green eyes pass over him as if he were rotten.

'I am of the blood of the Pious.'

'Then act like you feel it. This will only get worse as we get nearer.'

Rudi shivered and looked to the horizon ahead. And gasped.

They stood upon a field of bones.

Rudi turned, shattering a rib to powder. Bones and fog as far as the eye could pierce. A dark wind glittered with a cruel will, making bones creak and the two men's cloaks snap. He heard voices in it. All of a sudden, Rudi began to shake.

'What happened to the road?'

Caul shrugged and continued on his way. Head spinning, Rudi stumbled after, shuddering with the snap and crunch that each step brought.

'I see people I know,' Rudi murmured. 'I think Sigmar meant me to come here. To find them.'

'There are thousands here,' said Caul. The man's calm was jarring, as if it was him, rather than the field of death, that had no place in this world. 'Tens of thousands. They came for warpstone and riches and now they are all damned. It stands to reason you would recognise one or two. That they would recognise you.'

'Can they not be saved?'

Caul shrugged again and walked on.

'You know a lot, Herr Schlanger, can't you tell me that?'

'I know all I could learn. Gotz was not my only master. When I was young I was adopted by a vigilant brotherhood, and placed in his service to watch the City of the Damned.'

'Truthfully?'

Caul did not turn, but Rudi saw a smile shape his jaw. 'Truth is the chain by which fate makes each of us her whore.' A gust of wind took Caul's cloak and he turned into it, calming the snapping wool under one four-fingered hand. 'When men accept that things are as they must be, then Chaos will always thrive. Remember that and that only, and you may yet prove yourself a son of Ostermark.'

Rudi nodded, trying to remember what Nikolaus had said about Sigmar being within every man, whoever that man was and wherever he found himself. It was difficult to imagine that his god could reach him in a place such as this, but he prayed all the same. He prayed for the chance to do his pious ancestors proud, for the strength to find Baron von Kuber, slay the Beast, and free the souls of the Damned. It was a lot to ask, but he was a man of Ostermark and he would see his country cleansed. He prayed that Felix and Nikolaus were alive.

And, almost as an afterthought, he prayed for his own life.

For what seemed like forever, Felix walked, passing one benighted ruin after another until they blended into a continuous smear. Hours passed. The band of sunlight throbbed but never shifted. The sky fluxed with a constant change that told him nothing.

And still the temple drew no nearer.

'Stop dragging your feet,' Gotrek growled.

Even the dwarf had lowered his voice, his scarred face, while not afraid, was nevertheless taut with worry. His axe glowered red, but the ruddy glare did not travel far, lost to the cracks between dimensions long before it could alight upon Gotrek's face. The sight of those ancient runes glowing dully within the confines of their starmetal cells was the single most terrifying sight of all.

'It didn't look this far when we started.'

'We're not lost if that's what you're getting at.' With a scowl, Gotrek glared back at the flagellants who muttered and raved, inconsistent in voice as the wind through the husks of the Damned.

'I thought that you liked them,' said Felix, one hand splayed across his collar. His throat felt like the street looked. It was closing, sinking into his belly.

'They disappoint me as men so often do.'

'It's not their fault,' Felix murmured. 'It's this place.'

'Then why hasn't it affected you?'

Felix swallowed with an effort. The shadows were closing, the voices getting louder. The road ahead stretched out, screwing up to an infinite horizon.

'What makes you think it hasn't?'

Felix unclawed his hand from his throat. Shadows overlay it like a second skin. Without even realising that he fell, he felt Gotrek catch him in one arm. The dwarf smelled earthy and raw, real, his sheer rigidity a barrier behind which a man might shelter. Gotrek held him steady.

'Can you go on?'

Felix found it within him to laugh. Even to him it rang false. 'I don't see Brüder Nikolaus composing that epic.'

'I suppose I can't leave you behind then,' Gotrek reasoned, apparently in all seriousness.

'Trust in Sigmar...' Nikolaus mumbled, lifting his tattooed arm to point at something over Gotrek's shoulder. 'Acknowledge him and see your paths made straight.'

'Helpful,' Gotrek grunted, but turned all the same. For a moment he was silent. 'You seeing this, manling?'

Felix shook his head, keeping his face down. 'Whatever it is I'd rather not see, if it's all the same to you.'

'You're wetter than a wood elf sometimes,' Gotrek growled. 'If I didn't think you'd want to see this, then I wouldn't have wasted my breath.'

Felix looked up, over his companion's shoulder.

Disorientation warred with disbelief, dragging him between them into a miasma of horror. They had been following the road for hours. They had never turned.

This was impossible.

And yet the five them were standing within an enormous amphitheatre. The arena was dusty and flat. There was blood in it, the sand broken by strips of gristle and bone that nodded like flayed rats in the focused howl of the wind. Felix spun around. The street was gone. Instead, stepped terraces of blotched, veined stone rose on three sides into a confusion of wood, as though the upper levels were fused from the workings of a mad bird and a giant spider.

'Aye,' said Gotrek, planting his hands on his hips to glare out across the fog-sated belly of the arena. 'That was about what I was thinking.'

The plain of bone wavered at the edges, as though hazed by a heat Rudi did not feel. Figures drifted through the fog. Their voices reminded him of men he once knew.

Caul stopped walking abruptly, raising a hand in warning. Rudi stumbled into his back and stopped. It was becoming difficult to concentrate. There were too many voices, too many memories. Caul drew a knife into each hand and crunched forwards. After a few paces, he crouched amongst the jutting bones, like a reptile stalking through tall reeds. The shadowy figures were familiar, yet remote, seen through the gauze of a burial shroud. He struggled to understand their voices, moved to quiet tears by the garbled nonsense.

Caul tossed one of his knives into the air, caught it by the blade, and gauged the distance.

A blistering wind loaded with sand and chips of bone pattered against Felix's mail. He felt it scratch his face as he turned on the spot, gaze tracking upwards to the tangled mess of wooden spars that sprouted from the upper tiers of the amphitheatre. It was deserted as only a structure meant for thousands could be. Balefire torches clawed at the wind, sending shadows to run and hide amongst silent stone terraces.

'Did you not say all roads would lead to the temple?' said Gotrek.

The runes of the Slayer's axe glowered balefully in the dust storm swept up from the arena, his stiff crest buffeted this way and that.

Felix nodded dumbly, squinting into the full strength of the wind that drove through the frame of timber and stone that made the amphitheatre's open side. And through it, he saw the acropolis. Like a bitumen shard its jagged edges rose from the ash and fog that clung to its base. Steps cut into the sheer sides followed its climb towards the marble-paved court at its summit. And there, so white amidst the ash and ruin that it glowed like Mannslieb against a black sky, was the temple of Sigmar.

Where all roads lead.

Unbidden, an instant of true faith flared within his breast. It was like nothing he had experienced, like a pure fire burned his heart clean. From those pristine walls there seeped a sickness and, inconstant as his faith was, it disgusted him. Every occasion that he had called to Sigmar for strength, to Shallya for protection, to Ulric for mild winters, he remembered in that moment. He was at once uplifted and appalled.

Be'lakor was a daemon that recognised no god. It was empty. It was godless.

He stared, breath held lest the touch of the divine flee his chest on exhaled wind, the dust blowing across shapes that appeared almost human. Felix's heart fluttered. He spared them a glance but no more, he had seen shades aplenty this day. It was Gotrek that rapped his arm with an open fist, grunted in the spectres' direction and readied his axe. Felix slid behind the Slayer's back with a habitual ease. What devilry did the Dark Master send now?

Man and dwarf watched, hands tight to their weapons as the apparitions drew nearer. They emerged from the dust, close enough to see a face. Felix's eyes widened, sword lowering. Gotrek held his axe firm.

'Schlanger!' Felix laughed, unable to staunch the flood of relief that was making his chest shake as if with mirth. He rammed his sword into its scabbard. 'What are you doing here?'

The man gave a bewildered cough, looking around as though the innards of an arena were the last place he expected to find himself. In his hand was a knife, which he self-consciously slid back into his baldric. He coughed again, shielded his mouth from the dust with a handful of his cloak, offered Felix a terse nod as though passing an acquaintance in the street, hissed 'Jaeger', and turned his back so as to regard the temple.

Laughter fading fast, Felix turned to Gotrek who met his look and shrugged, lowering his axe if only a fraction.

'Some men are born pains in the arse.'

The second shadow, forgotten in Felix's initial surprise, stumbled into view.

It was Rudi. Felix shook his head in disbelief and ran to greet him. At the last moment, he checked his stride. There was something wrong. The man's brow was damp, his eyes unsteady, his face shadowed. It took him a few seconds but he noticed Felix's presence, acknowledging it with an uncertain smile.

'Rudi,' Felix breathed.

'Yes and no,' Caul answered him, turning back around. With the four fingers of his left hand he pointed out Rudi and, muttering softly, the flagellants. 'The pious fall first to the calls of the Damned. I don't know why. Maybe their minds welcome the intrusion of another.'

Rudi muttered something under his breath and started fumbling with the clasp of his cloak. Felix stepped back from him, rubbing his own temples, as though the reminder of the malady was sufficient to bring on its symptoms.

'I always knew you were a fraud, Schlanger. Have you ever been inside a temple?'

'Oh, I feel it. The wheel of time turns but here, at its hub, all things stay the same. The Damned are drawn here as we are. That is why it gets worse.'

'You know a lot,' said Gotrek. 'Considering.'

'I know my history,' Caul answered, offering the grimmest smile, then mocked a courtly bow. 'And in my youth was one apprenticed to a magister of the Gold College.'

Felix groaned, swept up a hand to cut the man off.

'I still recall a cantrip or two,' Caul concluded with a smirk.

'I wish Konrad had just killed me in my sleep,' Felix muttered. 'It would have spared me this.'

'Konrad is a virtuous man,' said Caul.

'Yes, I think I saw his virtue come for me with a knife in the dark.'

'Konrad holds men to nobler standards.' Caul chuckled briefly, then shuddered in a sudden cold that all six men felt.

Gotrek merely stood with arms crossed over his bare chest and glowered. 'It is no discredit to him that *all* men cannot meet them.'

Felix turned his face to the temple. He was cold, he was hungry, he had been beaten half to hell. He vented an exasperated sigh.

'What are you–' He spun back, finger raised to Caul as though it was a knife. 'You! You sent those men to kill us that night in Sigmarshafen.'

The man greeted the accusation with a grin, only for a tattooed ham of a fist to close over his elbow and wipe that smirk from his face.

'Did you put something in my ale?'

'No, I put something in *my* ale.' Caul struggled against the dwarf's grip but abandoned the effort as pointless. 'Maybe this will teach you not to steal.'

'I've a lesson coming for you as well, manling. You think a handful of cut-throats and a mug of tainted grog will fell me?'

'Of course not,' Caul laughed. 'If they could then you were not what I needed and I would not have mourned you. But as it was, I needed you in the City of the Damned before Konrad's… *virtues* bettered him at last.'

Gotrek shoved the man off with a snarl. 'Tell me why I shouldn't kill you.' The dwarf patted the haft of his axe against his meaty palm. The chain jangled against his bracer. 'Maybe I'll consider it.'

Caul spread his palms in peace. His gaunt features betrayed no fear, but Felix suspected there was nothing about the man that was true.

'I am here for von Kuber. And to prevent a daemon's rise. That should be reason enough.'

Gotrek leered, his axe twitching for the man's neck, but pulled back at the last with an angry snort.

'Well come on then. Show me this daemon I've heard so

much about. This city's a haunted bloody deathtrap and even I grow sick of it.'

Felix could not help a wry smile. He flinched at a touch on his neck, jerking around to find Rudi laying his cloak across his shoulders. The Sudenland wool was ragged, singed, and with a few more blood stains even than it had had before. Felix proceeded to fasten the collar ties. He felt a little more himself just for wearing it. He smiled thanks, but Rudi had already turned his back, shuffling through the dust towards the temple.

On second viewing, the temple did not appear nearly so unmarred. Its walls were dusted with dirt and mould, more grey than white, slumped under the weight of ash on its tiled roof like an arch-lector under his robes of investiture. It summoned no fire to Felix's heart.

'Sigmar and those that serve him created this,' he murmured. 'And Sigmar was once a man like us. Does that make him less than powers like Be'lakor?'

Gotrek shoved past Caul Schlanger until he was at Felix's side, hands on his hip before the temple of Sigmar. 'You're speaking to a dwarf, manling. Our gods lived, wed, drank, and aye, they died.' A thick digit like an Averland bockwurst scored the line of blue tattoos from his eye patch, down his cheek, to his dyed and crusted beard. 'Grimnir didn't take these with a mind to a long and happy life.'

Felix stole a deep breath. The temple beckoned but, despite Gotrek's words, the presence of Sigmar was well distant, his aegis unfelt. In his heart, Felix knew.

It had not been the god of men that had spared this place.

Overcome by emptiness and regret, Morzanna's spirit reunited with her body. Nerves fired, expecting cold winds and drizzle, and finding instead the harsh glare of balefire. The temple was oddly quiet and it took her a moment to rationalise the change. The acropolis was empty, the amphitheatre deserted.

It was as if the End Times had passed and left her behind.

The sudden beating of her heart was a ready reminder that she was not too lost to humanity to fear. She knew what it meant to be alone. The power of fire, of death, had taught her well the true face of suffering. Nothing survived forever; not unchanged.

Vividly, she remembered her black world after Magnus had come, when nothing stalked the ash but loneliness. The visions brought by second sight had been as close to contact as she could grasp. She could not remember now how many years had passed before she learned the consequences of her far-seeing; dark magic crystallising from the contrail of her spirit self, raining like pollen to seed the subconscious mind with nightmares. Nor could she recall how, exactly, she had come to master the ability to manipulate how and in what form those seeds would flourish. The ability to share her thoughts through the dreams of another. After so many years alone, it had been glorious.

'Do all follow-come?'

The flat voice startled her, a clawed paw settling upon her shoulder. The skaven overseer regarded her without emotion or recognition. Morzanna covered the ratman's gnarled hand in hers. Even in the darkest days, she had not been truly alone. And even as the disfigured Beast had shunned her, had hidden from all the monster it had become, in its way it had been as lonely as her.

'Then come-quick,' the rat insisted, drawing back on her arm. She gasped as its claws burrowed between her fingers to clasp her hand in its paw.

Morzanna smiled and let it lead her.

'You have served well, Hurrlk. We have all earned our rest.'

CHAPTER 19

The Temple of Sigmar

The arch of sunlight throbbed against the sky like a vein. An intermittent drizzle came and went, dappling the marble steps of the acropolis. But always there was the wind. Felix's hair and cloak thrashed, as if even they wished to climb no higher. He tried to ignore the elements, and it was not hard. His mind was numb from the legions of voices. They grew louder as he scaled the steps of the acropolis.

Halfway up, the amphitheatre spread vast before them like a gaping maw, Rudi cried out, weeping as if seeing a loved one in pain. He started towards them. Felix grabbed him before he could throw himself onto the escarpment.

'They died,' Rudi yelled, fighting against Felix's arm. 'The Beast took them in the Totenwald. I saw them die and I *see* them.'

Felix and Caul shared a glance. They both felt it.

'It's getting worse,' said Caul. 'It will get worse still.'

'Wonderful,' said Felix, shepherding the boy towards Nikolaus who seemed to be a calming influence on the others.

The flagellants stumbled ahead. The wind whipped at their sackcloth, throwing their knotted belts like censers. Felix's calves ached like something Shallya had forgotten. But he could see the top. Growling a hymn to fortify his mind against the voices, he soldiered on. He only recalled the chorus, but there were only a handful more steps.

Gotrek, his dwarfish stamina indefatigable, met them at the summit. He stood upon a courtyard of lustrous white marble. The stone was pigeon-coloured, swept clean but stained with dirt. Ash had sunk into the joins. All manner of rubble had been piled up around the sides of the courtyard, like some mountaintop rockery.

The dwarf's one good eye was bloodshot from the constant buffeting of ash and the glittering warpstone on the wind. His beard pressed to his mouth to strain the air, he turned to Felix. 'Something's shifting beneath us. I can feel it in the stones.'

Felix covered his face with a bundle of cloak and moved to join his companion. Caul was moving towards the temple's colonnaded frontage. His eyes darted above the rumpled grey wool he had pressed to his mouth. Rudi and the flagellants had been herded towards the centre of the courtyard. Too mindless to know better, they choked on ash between their crazed utterances. Their cheeks were stained crimson where their eyes bled.

'What's this?' Gotrek muttered, attention drawn by a rectangular panel of marble entablature recessed beneath the decorative cornices above the columns. The principle motif was of a comet, but it was circumscribed by the angular engravings of a runic script.

'We haven't the time for this,' said Caul, making a futile effort to usher Gotrek from his find.

'Shift your hand or I'll shift it for you,' said Gotrek without removing his eyes from the engraved script.

Wisely, Caul removed his hand.

'For once I agree, Gotrek,' said Felix. 'We should move while we still can.'

Without answering, the dwarf looked around, found a hunk of rock as long as he was broad, and wrapped his arms around it. Baring his teeth, he strained, slowly dragging the stone backwards until, in an astounding feat of strength, he tilted the thing up, letting it teeter until, with a shove in the right direction, it crashed into one of the pillars.

Caul's cloak dropped away from his gaping mouth.

Still not offering an explanation, Gotrek proceeded to clamber up the impromptu ramp towards the cornice. There, he licked his thumb, reached up on tiptoes, and wiped a layer of dust from the marble frieze.

'Is it dwarfish?' Felix asked.

'Aye,' Gotrek nodded, cleaning his thumb under his armpit. He lay his fingers to the frieze, shifting them slowly left to right, left to right, as though by touch reading words upon a page. 'Little wonder this structure endured while the human-built rubbish around it crumbled.'

'Gotrek, Can you please hurry this–'

'Shhh!'

A sudden drizzle spattered against Felix's face. It was the harsh, vivid chill of the Ostermark Moors.

'Gotrek?'

'Here we go.' Gotrek cleared his throat, then read aloud. 'And on the sixth day of the two hundred and thirty-ninth year after the crowning of Sigmar, was this temple completed in his name. This last stone is laid by Hadri Greyback, master stonesmith of Zhufbar. May it endure as long as the mountain from which it was hewn, in honourable service to the dwarf-friends of…'

His finger held over some runic inscription at the frieze's bottom. Felix held his breath. Caul watched with one hand buried beneath his cloak; possibly for warmth, but suspiciously close to his belt of knives.

'Of where?' said Felix, after the silence had become untenable. He glanced warily towards Caul. He needed to know. 'What city is this?'

In silence, Gotrek climbed back down. He looked first to Caul, then back to that last runic mark.

'Mordheim,' said Gotrek. 'This place was called Mordheim.'

The mention of that name gave Felix a shudder. He tried it in his own mouth, uncertain where he had heard it. It was not a name commonly known, even amongst those who made it their business to learn that which was uncommon. And then Felix remembered where he had come across it. The books of Doktor Drexler, in Nuln. At the time he had thought it apocryphal. In its descriptions of comets directed by the hand of Sigmar, of warbands of every race converging to battle for the city's scraps, of the exploitation of its dark power by daemon princes to manifest human form and wreak terror, it had seemed wholly fanciful. The clues had been here for him to see. He should have put them together before now.

'Mordheim,' Caul scowled. 'The City of the Damned. Trust a dwarf to be unable to keep a secret.'

Gotrek bristled at the implication. 'This place was no *secret*. Your people forgot, as you always do.' One meaty fist thumped his chest. The arm was grazed red from dragging the massive stone, but its strength was undiminished. 'We remembered and knew well enough to keep away.'

'Forgotten, indeed, and rightfully so. If we could have purged every record from your books of grudges we would have done that too. Albrecht von Kuber made emissary to King Barundin of Zhufbar to that effect, but was given short shrift.'

To Felix's surprise, Gotrek burst into roaring laughter.

'Aye! I'd wager.'

Caul positioned himself beneath the architrave at the temple's entrance, pulling a long knife from his baldric. 'So now you know. Know also that Albrecht's diaries make it clear that the daemon prince Be'lakor must not be slain, that doing so could free it to return to the Wastes, to enact its purpose as bringer of the End Times.'

'And anyway,' Felix cut in. 'I was told that it can't be killed, that it has no body.'

Gotrek chuckled, clearing his beard from his nose to take a hearty draw of the tainted air, which he promptly spluttered back up. 'Such foulness as I've not tasted since our voyage to the Wastes. A daemon could be solid here if it chose to be.' Gotrek flourished his axe with a manic grin. 'It's freedom it wants, and I've got freedom for it right here.'

'You'd risk the end of the world for your own impish *honour*?' Caul spat the final word as though it tasted bitter.

'Better hope it kills me first then, hadn't you.'

'In Sigmar's name, I'll kill you both!' Felix screamed.

His eyes were trembling, the sky turning cartwheels, and a strange darkness was thundering towards him under the architrave.

There was a snort, the clatter of hooves bearing down, and before Felix could shout a warning, the daemonic mount of Golkhan the Anointed burst from the temple. Felix saw dark eyes flash with hunger within the deep sockets of its champron. Caul was dashed aside, the man's lissom frame thrown from the daemon's hell-steel barding. It threw its mane and, ignoring Felix entirely, snapped its jaw for Gotrek's face.

The Slayer screwed back with a curse, twisting his axe to swat the daemon's muzzle aside, only for the creature to rear, flailing its fore hooves and batting the axe down. Gotrek drew back, switching his axe from right to left and shaking out his ringing hand. Felix charged, Karaghul thrust underarm like a spear for the creature's throat. Six legs rattled like a spider's and the daemon's hindquarters swung around, smacking Felix onto his back and sending his sword skimming across the courtyard.

With an exultant snort, the daemon kicked at Gotrek with its hind legs. The dwarf ducked, spinning underneath to come level with the creature's formidably armoured broadside. He lifted his axe high in both hands, bunched the muscles of his shoulders and gave a mighty roar as he sliced clean through the daemon's neck. The daemon's head thumped to the flagstones. Its torso wavered upright for a fraction of a second before that too yawned backwards, crashed into a marble column and slid down.

Gotrek clapped dark blood theatrically from his palms, then turned on the recumbent form of Caul Schlanger.

'I forget what it was you were saying.'

Caul grimaced, but thought better of picking up the argument where they had left off.

Recollecting his sword, Felix gently stabbed the daemon's unarmoured belly. With daemons, it was impossible to be too careful.

'This was the mount of the daemon's champion. I saw him ride it.'

'A gift from his dark master, no doubt,' said Gotrek.

'If he left it behind then my guess is he went somewhere it couldn't follow?'

Gotrek grinned. 'Below my feet, I tell you.' He started inside, calling over his shoulder as he passed under the architrave. 'Look for a low door. A tight stairwell. Something like that.'

Leaving Caul to recover his dignity and muster the others, Felix followed his companion into the temple of Sigmar.

Morzanna descended the stair to the crypts, following the rhythmic *click* of claws. The darkness was so complete she could no longer see the hand upon the wall beside her face, but she could hear the slither of his tail across the stones, smell the soft, peppery scent of his fur. She did not try to speak. Unless he had something to say, then she knew she would be wasting her time. Warpstone, mutation, and the cruel perversion of immortality the master moulder had thought he craved had broken him. That was how he and the twisted ghosts of his clan-mates could cross the mists while no other could.

They were already mad.

And that was not going to be changed, however many warpstone-spawned monstrosities he created to then 'cure'. The work pits and the arena were littered with the insane monuments to his failure.

The stairwell opened onto eerie quiet, their footfalls echoing through the roughly excavated chamber. Daemons did not scream for release. Men did not gnash their teeth or make futile struggle against the drills and steam-hammers that Hurrlk had grafted to their limbs. She missed the cry of steel and rock, the pressurised whistle of steam. For unchanging centuries those sounds had been with her. They were comforting. Like the sound of her father's prayers when she had been a child. Her heart hardened.

She was not a child anymore.

Columns of limestone marched in sombre procession from the arched entrance through to a bloodstained altars where there hung the tarnished likeness of Ghal-maraz. The benches had been taken to leave standing room for a thousand. The open floor was bathed in shifting colours, alternately gold, crimson, pink, and aquamarine. The creeping display made Felix's guts clench, but he soon realised there was a prosaic force at work. Roundel windows of stained glass were set into both longer walls. They had been broken. Felix could see the creeping tracks of some murky brown adhesive, as though the windows had been traversed by a maddened slug. The walls were panelled with marble. More dwarfish letters ran their length, the script passing unbroken from panel to panel the full circumference of the temple, interspersed only by windows. Even after centuries of neglect, the gold of hammers and the silver of comet's tails glinted with colour when the light struck them just right. Felix held, just for a moment.

Only the great Cathedral of Altdorf represented a grander sight.

'A door over here, manling.'

Gotrek pulled open a darkwood door situated behind and just to the left of the defiled altar. It led to an unlit stair. It spiralled only one way. Down. Taking a sniff of the foetid air, Gotrek positioned his axe so that its steady glare would illuminate his way, and began to descend. Felix paused just long enough to ensure that Caul saw where they were headed, and then followed.

At last, Morzanna saw evidence of Hurrlk's workforce. Bloated, ironclad abominations lay slumped at their stations in chains. Steel had been worn to flesh and then finally to bone, before Hurrlk and his minions had let them be discarded. Morzanna moved through them without pity. Soon the city would be liberated. Time would flow and mortal bodies would perish. They would acclaim her. Had their minds not been destroyed by torment, stimulants and, evidenced by the tangle of nails and copper wire over their craniums, Hurrlk's obsessive 'treatments'.

The passage grew progressively narrower as they entered the more recently excavated regions of the crypts. There was blood on the walls, increasing numbers of damaged constructs evidence to the labour directed here. The presence of bodies did nothing to negate the sense of emptiness. Their breathing was listless, autonomic. They would stop if they could. The walls were rougher, recently gouged, supported by wooden joists scavenged from the ruins without. The City of the Damned held no shortage of lumber, particularly when the same derelict could be exploited over, and over, and over again.

The air this deep was warm, moist and well used. A magical haze distorted rock and air with equal, ambivalent power. With every breath she felt it. It lit a fire like vodka in her belly, the taste lingering inside her throat like a sticky liquor. So much more than she had felt before.

Inconceivably more.

The effect grew more intense the deeper they delved. Her breathing became laboured, fingers tingling, head swimming with dark potentiality. Hurrlk walked through it, appearing to feel nothing and perhaps he did not. With an effort of will, Morzanna followed. And that was when she noticed something amiss.

The daemons were gone.

A measure of the empyreal dread that had driven them out began to creep into her mind and suborn her subconscious. The magic was not merely some exudate from the Realm of Chaos. It was possessed of a dark malice, an evil so ancient, so elemental, that even Morzanna felt tainted.

Vibrations passed through the thick air, will alone enforcing the generation of sound from the fickle particles of the aethyr. The voice of her daemon patron struck her like a crushing blow to the soul, it mocked rather than encouraged, daring her to fail even as it threatened failure's consequence.

Deeper, my daughter. Do not surrender now.

The stairwell under the temple was narrow, wallowing in a dull, even red that slowly faded as Gotrek bore his axe around the turn of the stair. The steps had been smoothed over the centuries and were too narrow for Felix's comfort. He was grateful the walls were close enough for him to lay hand to each side. Gotrek showed no such caution. The slaying of the daemon had only whetted his appetite for killing, and the dwarf took the spiralling descent as one born to stone. The light grew dimmer and Felix, unable to match the dwarf's pace, was swallowed by darkness. Panic threatened. He took a calm breath and buried it. There were only two ways; up and down, and he needed light for neither.

In fact, with the departure of Gotrek's light source, Felix could see an actinic pink picking at the corners of darkness below. It did not look far. Both hands to the walls, Felix counted the steps, ninety-three in all, the pink glow brightening with each one until he emerged into a fierce light. He squinted, eyes adjusting to the illumination and sudden space.

He was in a rough-hewn chamber; walls, ceiling and even the floor gouged by shovel and pick. It extended for about twenty feet before, as if by ill-luck, falling into a corridor. A pair of balefire torches burned in perpetuity from corbels on the wall. The air was warm and thick as mud. His chest ached from breathing it, but he welcomed the pain as a flagellant did the lash. It was a distraction from the voices. Hearing the careful tread of Caul and the others from the stairwell, Felix started down the corridor.

Like the chamber before it, the way was hand-cut. Every dozen paces there was a wooden brace against the ceiling, every three dozen another bracketed torch spewing acrid pink fumes. Coughing into his cloak, he hurried on, emerging into a second, wider, chamber just after Gotrek, and just in time to hear the dwarf's indignant cry.

Slumped against the walls in chains as thick as Gotrek's arms lay abominations which even the Ruinous Powers would have cast from their realms as obscene. Steam-drills hung idle and crusted with blood. Iron-plated chests glowed hot, causing necrotising flesh-grafts to bubble and bleed. Mutated beyond nature's scope, bodies fused with mechanical elements and infected with daemonic taint, the wretched core of each was something inviolably human. Felix signed the hammer, trying to ignore their distant stares.

'Someone should put them from their misery,' said Gotrek, axe twitching, but doing nothing. There were too many to deliver mercy to them all.

The chamber widened further into a cavern as they progressed. Occasionally, a rough gash in the rock face revealed smoothly laid stone or the corner of an engraving. Shafts bore down and off at tangents, sloping shelves of bare rock curled up towards secondary, long abandoned work faces. Felix swore he heard voices ahead. But then he heard voices from all around, and in the cavernous deeps, it could have come from anywhere. These catacombs were not just being excavated, they were being *re*-excavated. Perhaps the first baron, Albrecht von Kuber, knowing what was trapped here, had collapsed the acropolis upon the daemon's head?

With a worried look back, Felix hurried in step with his companion's brisk pace.

He did not need a dwarf to tell him the baron had been less than thorough in his efforts.

Hurrlk awaited her, infinitely patient, hunched before a ragged tear in the rock face. The signs of haste were plain. The edges were jagged, blackened and glassy, and chipped with metallic debris from some explosive device. Cracks extended through the rock and into the ceiling. Rubble had been left where it was blasted out. The opening itself was unsupported.

The skaven had rightly presumed that it need not remain open for long.

Morzanna gazed into the breach. Therein lay the mercurial glow of a portal to the shadow-paths, the ways between worlds. The dark magic it exuded was afflicted with the most mephitic taint. With an irony that must have delighted the Ruinous Powers, it was both the wellspring of Be'lakor's corporeal might and the source of his damnation. Following the purge of the Pious, the daemon's sundered essence should have returned to the Realm of Chaos.

But it had not.

It had come here, to this buried temple, to be trapped liked every other soul.

But soon the great daemon king would be free.

Morzanna hesitated only a moment at the threshold. Power beat at her face like a furnace. It was a garbled distortion of darkness and colour, of energy and form. The shadow-paths belonged to the realm of daemons and gods and other, older, entities stranger and more powerful even than they. A mortal did not simply walk into the lands of the gods.

Not unchanged.

She smiled and stepped forward. It had been too long since she had felt something truly new.

The cavern ended abruptly at a granite face. Gotrek's axe blazed in the magic-soured air, crystalline arteries of zircon and quartz glittering in the glow. The digging here had been fierce. Bits of rock were scattered, seared with alchemical burns that varied in colour from rock to rock. Gotrek gave a disapproving snort.

'Effective job, but hasty. Skaven work if ever I saw it.'

Felix frowned, turning as Caul and the others panted into view. The man breathed as Felix did, slow and deep, face flushed like heated iron. Rudi and the flagellants mouthed unheeded nothings. They wavered on their feet. It looked as though they would collapse at any moment.

Gotrek traced the breach with his fingers, presenting the dust to his good eye and rubbing it in with a low chuckle. Felix saw what had caught the dwarf's attention. Beyond the Slayer's broad shoulders swirled some manner of portal. At first glance it was a silvery-grey, but colours flowed like oil over water. Gotrek lifted his axe towards it. When the blade came within six inches the portal began to crackle like kindling, its cryptic colours bleeding to the edges to reveal a pellucid window of silver light. Gotrek twisted around and grinned.

'You coming?'

Felix gave a sigh, then set his jaw and nodded. As if he had ever had a choice.

The portal spat small arcs of black lightning that raked the flat of the starmetal blade. The air stung with ozone. Gotrek's beard began to turn fluffy and rise. The axe pressed into its surface and the skin of energy flexed, the instinctual flinch of living flesh from a flame. Gotrek continued forwards until first his axe, then his arms, and then finally his entire body had disappeared. The portal continued to writhe, as though physically pained.

Felix had learned well the effect Gotrek's weapon had on daemons and their manifestations, but the malignant will he sensed from the portal had not been dimmed.

Merely redirected.

Felix took a deep breath and climbed in.

Best then to be on the other side before it looked back.

Reality flexed, like the beaten skin of a drum, and Morzanna crossed the threshold of reality into the shadow-paths. There was a sensation of *travel*. Stars diffracted their light all around, vibrating like wasps in a spider's web. They were blurry, milky smears that faded into infinity behind her. The flow of lights gave the impression of incredible speed, and of direction, but she felt nothing, as if her velocity was so great that sense and sound could no longer reach her. And she was not alone. She saw shades, pellucid echoes of the Damned. Like the bizarre streaking lights, they streamed past without so much as a whisper. Faceless. Voiceless. There were hundreds of them. Thousands.

Tens of thousands.

My army, thundered the voice of Be'lakor. As puissant as

before, it came now from everywhere, all the more intense for being the only sound admitted to his pocket reality. *They answer the muster as will all. Service to the Dark Master is timeless and does not expire with death.*

The words of Be'lakor reverberated within Morzanna's skull, pounding on her ears from within. At that moment she would have stepped back if she could, retreated to her own dimension of ash and fire and been content. Dark laughter flexed its fingers beneath her skull, kneading the bruised lobes of her brain.

The gods betrayed you child, as they once betrayed me. Come. We are all damned now.

Sounds surged towards her, like wolves on a wounded deer. There were voices, broken squeals, a blinding palette of noise that breakneck acceleration smeared into a funnel of dark glory. Then suddenly it stopped.

Her feet were on solid ground. Her lungs drew real air that smelled of warpstone and sweat. The chanting voices of mutants and the chittering of ratmen flooded her flesh and bone ears with sound.

The mutants she heard packed the floor of a large, circular chamber. Its high walls were obsidian smooth, carved with archaic glyphs that twisted before the eye and sank unread into the stone. Pillared arches led to other doorways, presumably onto shadow-paths to other dimensions and other times. Bodies rippled and twisted in a warpstone haze as though viewed through a distorting glass. Smoke drifted between them and through them. Morzanna saw human-like shapes but there were so many that it was impossible to distinguish one figure from another. They were silent, waiting. At points around the chamber, arranged into the motif of an eight-pointed Chaos star, galleries sat atop grooved pilasters. Skaven leaned over the rails, lassitude infecting every inch of their bearing. Their shoulders were stooped even beyond their racial hunch, eyes dim, tails drooling from the platforms to lay across the bowed heads of the mutants below.

Morzanna turned her attention to the chamber's centre, the object of the mutants' devotion and the ratmen's dejected stares.

Rendered in glittering warpstone chalk, an eight-pointed star mirrored precisely the orientation of the galleries. At its centre, an altar rose organically from the obsidian flooring. It was the length of a coffin and about half as high again, barbed at both ends with elaborate curving spines. It was black, but of a shade far beyond the mundane darkness of the walls, columns, floor, and the cloaked ranks of degenerate ratmen. Emptiness incarnate, the witchfires and sickly warplight were drawn in to their deaths. Upon its stygian face lay the skeleton of a man. He would have been tall, no less than seven feet, with broad shoulders that bespoke immense strength in life. A pair of mutants, eye-less and with long, ribbony fingers caressed the remaining fragments, mewling mad devotion as they actualised its assembly.

A swelling awe overwhelmed Morzanna's earlier uncertainties.

For the possession of a single knuckle of this skeleton would sorcerers have gone to war. Kharduun the Gloried was the former, mortally flawed, avatar of Be'lakor himself. Even in decay a measure of the Master's potency imbued them, somehow contriving to overshadow even the altar upon which they lay. Morzanna could not shake the fear that, at any moment, the skeleton would rise from its repose. That it had power enough to do so was beyond question.

All it required was the will.

At seven of the eight points encircling the skeleton a darkly robed sorcerer assumed their position. Ubek flexed his mammoth paws. Nosta gave a distorted ripple of unbidden excitement. The others similarly made ready. The air, already suffused with the vitiating power of Chaos, began to warp.

Morzanna felt the accrual of magic as a pressure on her eardrums, painless at first but rising. It swelled against the walls, like a dragon chick against its shell.

Your place, daughter.

As though her limbs were the daemon's to command, she moved to the northern point of the star. The position was the most powerful, and the most perilous. First amongst the eight, she was the channel through which the others would draw the Wind of Dhar from the Polar Warp Gate. She was the one who would suffer the most. Ubek, in the ancillary position to her left, welcomed her with a covetous growl.

She wondered what these petty sorcerers expected to happen next. Each had been plucked from their own time before the coming of the Pious. They had not seen the world that she had seen. And even she did not know what Be'lakor intended for his former champion. The uncertainty should have thrilled her.

It did not.

The walls trembled, flecks of chalk flickering around the corona of the Chaos star.

Bring forth the Anointed, Be'lakor rumbled. *With the death of a champion shall a champion be remade.*

Golkhan strode through the kneeling mutants. They did not attend him, focused on their chant. The smoky haze broke and re-knit as he passed. The channels carved into his armour collected deep shadows, as though the Chaos warrior was being hollowed. His armoured shoulders trembled with anticipation, grey eyes fixated upon the altar and its promise of power. He approached the Chaos star. There was a ripple of energy as his foot crossed the chalked line, the disturbance spreading thin as the rest of his body crossed. Then, with a flash of silver, the wards sealed behind him.

You will be my weapon on this earth. My will again made flesh.

As one, the sorcerers began to chant the words that Be'lakor positioned, syllable by syllable, within their minds. At each point of the star, hands traced their unique sequence of sigils, the magic so dense that they held their shape once formed, oozing like jelly through their fingers.

Golkhan approached the altar.

One of the sightless mutants selected a fragment of ulna, enwrapping it within tendril-like fingers and caressing it with its lips. Golkhan spread his arms as the mutant came and, with great reverence, fixed the fragment to the matching depression in Golkhan's vambrace. There was a *click* as it slotted home. The mutant held its breath.

And then the champion let out a howl of agony, clutching the offending forearm in his other gauntlet.

'It hurts!'

The laughter of Be'lakor reverberated between column and stone.

You desire power the gods themselves shun. Of course it hurts.

The fingers of the second mutant willowed over the array, a gourmand at a feast of power. Golkhan ground his teeth.

A shard of pelvis, perhaps. I would have my champion scream again.

Felix dove through the portal just as the cavern around him began to shudder. There was a wave of repulsion that sought to throw him back, its hatred a physical force against his skin. It was like being bound in wire wool. But its full fury was directed elsewhere. The mercuric skin swelled and broke before him.

Felix could not begin to imagine what Gotrek was suffering.

There was no sign of his companion ahead, or of others behind. Felix tried to take in his surroundings, but he had entered the realm of the ethereal, a world that his mind could only superficially process. There were lights, voices, spectres of men briefly beheld, a sensation of forward speed.

Wavering tentacles stretched through the grey. The black tendrils extended from his direction of travel and, for a moment of panic, he feared they came for him, but they reached past him. The voices were drawn to them, changing in some strange, feral, way as they drew near. With their every twitch, the entire sub-dimension trembled.

With a sudden scream of sensation, Felix felt hot air on his face and his body was expelled back into the world of the physical.

Still struggling to translate his perceptions of that other plane, he saw fading tendrils flickering across his vision. They reached into the portal at his back, and for the numerous portals that ringed the circular chamber in which he found himself. Losing them with the realignment of his senses to the material plane, Felix tracked the tendrils to their source, shielding his eyes from the electric shell of energies that marked an eight-pointed star at the chamber's centre. There was a black-robed sorcerer at each of its eight points, an altar enshrined at its core, an assortment of human bones lying upon it. A powerful figure struggled in the grip of torment between two others. He was difficult to make out in detail. Power shimmered across his armoured body as though it were concealed behind a waterfall.

But, even without the warrior's voice-distorting helm, Felix could not mistake the cries of Golkhan the Anointed.

The energies of Chaos roared through Morzanna's veins like floodwaters through the cities of men. It purged, it renewed, it reminded the forgetful of its power. Retaining a grip on her sanity was challenge enough, her torment on a plane that surpassed anything Golkhan could suffer or conceive. Slaaneshi princes would have spent a year in solitude for a portion of what she felt now. Straining every sinew of her will to each ritual word, she fought to keep her head above the flood.

She was aware of the others' suffering as she was of the pulse in her thigh, the ache in her fingers. They hurt as she hurt, cried as she cried. Through the guileless veil of the firmament they were connected. To her left, Ubek panted with the effort of matching her. Nosta's piteous wails passed through the minds of all as an understanding of true power finally bludgeoned its way into their skulls.

The gates are opened, spoke Be'lakor, words manifesting simultaneously into each sorcerer's mind. *Now you are ready to begin.*

New instructions appeared in Morzanna's mind. In that one moment she knew his intent and, through her, the others learned it too. She felt their horror as if it was her own. It went far beyond the creation of a champion. She struggled to keep up with the Dark Master's bidding. The air was already thick with magicks and it resisted. A force of attraction drew on her temples as though to rip her soul through the roof of her skull.

The world was changing, realities aligning. The ground rumbled beneath her feet and her body overflowed with the warping power of Chaos, spilling from her pores to lance through the eight points of the star.

With one mouth and one mind, the sorcerers screamed.

The black temple rumbled, the columns shaking. The Chaos star rippled and sparked, flaring across Golkhan's armour as the champion widened his stance to keep from falling. The willow-thin mutants that flanked him swayed. The captivated mutants kept up their chant as if the acropolis was not being shaken apart around them. The walls shook again, harder this time and for longer, and Felix crouched behind a column, inexplicably terrified that the rattling of his mail would betray his presence to the keen-eared skaven. He was so intent on what he was seeing, that he failed to notice the arrival of Caul Schlanger at his side. The man's face was impassive, his eyes cutting across the disordered rings of kneeling mutants to the warrior within that sorcerous star.

The gaunt features of Golkhan the Anointed were stained silvery black by the energies that shot around him. And he seemed to have grown. A horned shadow loomed over his shoulder, and his armour was bulkier than Felix remembered. For where once the black plates had been run with hollow channels, now there were bones. They interlocked as smoothly as they would have done when bound in that giant's flesh, as though one champion of Chaos had been subsumed into the living skeleton of another. Arms spread in rapture, Golkhan tilted back his head and knelt. Felix could see his face clearly. He was grey-eyed, with furrows in his forehead and silver in his dark hair. Balefire raced across his ossified armour.

Slowly, Caul slipped a knife from his baldric. Then another.

'Too late,' he hissed.

'I don't think so,' Felix replied, unconsciously adopting the man's whisper.

Gotrek was standing nearby, searching over the mutants' bowed heads for a sign of the daemon prince. Rudi and the flagellants mingled together by the portal. Rudi looked around in confusion, but clearly none of them had a clue where they were or where they had just been.

'It looks like they aren't finished yet.'

As he spoke, the two mutants that shared Golkhan's incandescent cage stepped behind his genuflecting bulk, arms describing an arch with, at its top, a horned and thick-browed skull. Balefire defiled its bleached surface to a densely shadowed silver. The warrior tensed, jaw clenched ready, palms balled into fists. The skull closed over his cheeks, fusing to the vertebral column embedded in his backplate and coif.

The champion's tormented howl sent a shudder through the enveloping magicks and out across the floor, the hellish lights a fitting shrine for this apotheosis of pain.

Golkhan doubled over, then arched back, fingers grasping under the jawbone as if to rip it off. But it was fused more rigidly than his own bones. The chant of the mutants pitched higher. Even the formerly lethargic ratmen leaned from their galleries and chittered excitedly amongst themselves. Still screaming, the champion struggled to stand. He crashed to his side as the floor shook, torment flowing like a libation to the Dark Master. Sheet lightning crackled across the ceiling.

A silver spark leapt from Felix's sword, earthing in his fingers with a sharp crack.

'It's over,' Caul repeated, 'because that...' With his knife, he pointed to the Chaos warrior who was now climbing to his feet, fists clenched in acclamation of their own resurgent strength.

'That is Baron Götz von Kuber.'

CHAPTER 20

Black Horror

Their champion's howls did not signal the end of the sorcerers' work. If anything, it marked its beginning. Power flashed across the eight points of the Chaos star, earthing into the material in fiery tracers of dark energy and a terrific rumbling that shook the deep chamber to its core. Crouched behind a pillar, Felix set his palms to the floor as the whole edifice trembled. It was warm.

'Tricked,' Caul hissed, calm melting down to a terrible wrath. 'Me! The Beast did not capture Götz; it just slaughtered his escort so he could escape.' Caul's voice was rising in pitch and fury. Felix grabbed his shoulder to shake the man quiet but he was having none of it. He shouldered Felix off and flipped a knife into a throwing grip. 'The fire is too good for him. The flames would sooner gutter and die.' With a scream, and before Felix could stop him, Caul flung the knife.

The blade hissed through the charged air, streaking a perfect course for Golkhan's open mouth. It struck the energy field. There was a brilliant flash and tempered steel tore itself asunder in a luminous hail. Caul snarled and drew back his second blade, but this time Felix was ready and grabbed his wrist, slapping down Caul's second hand as the man grasped for the knife. Felix twisted the man's wrist to dislodge his grip but the man held the knife as though double-jointed and wriggled loose, shoved Felix back and shaped to backhand the blade across his unguarded throat.

'I told you to never touch me,' he hissed. But he held his strike, looking over Felix's shoulder.

A sibilant hiss pulled Felix around. A ratman dropped from the nearest gallery. Another followed, scabrous feet meeting the floor with a delicacy incongruous with the hatred in its eyes. The mutants kneeling around the Chaos star continued their chant, too absolved of wit to recognise what was happening at their back, but from galleries all around the chamber ratmen noticed the intrusion. They shrieked outrage and – if Felix was not mistaken – terror.

With a gravelly chuckle, Gotrek limbered his axe arm. He paid the ratmen no mind, his one eye for Golkhan alone. And he would butcher every mutant between them whether they deigned to notice or not. Felix tucked in behind the Slayer, pressed his own back to his and angled his sword against the closing skaven.

He hated this part.

While he might not choose to visit Ostermark of this era again, had he the option of returning to an Altdorf tavern to dissuade a young poet from making the acquaintance of a certain Trollslayer, then he might consider it.

'Ready, manling?'

Felix shook off his thoughts, giving the Slayer an incredulous look. 'Are you?'

Gotrek's grin was infectious. 'I'll take that as a yes.'

* * *

The mutant did not utter a sound as Gotrek's axe clove head from body. A gout of arterial blood drove the severed appendage eight inches from its neck and on an arcing trajectory like a hobgoblin rocket, leaving a haemic contrail until it smacked into the side of another's face. It did not notice. The Slayer jovially severed its spine, then cracked the jaw of the mutant knelt beside it with the haft. The dwarf shoved both bodies aside, and barged through to the next. The chant continued unabated. The mutants acceded to the Slayer's axe with the apathy of martyrs.

Felix retreated over his companion's leavings, stumbling on limbs as he fended off the hissing ratman that was trying desperately to get around him. It feinted, dodged, probed, then like the sudden crack of a whip followed through with its off-hand weapon. Felix swiftly reoriented to counter the mazy knife-work, parrying the blade before it plunged under his mail shirt. Already he was sweating, lungs heaving in the thick air.

By Sigmar, these rats were fast.

Nearer the portal, Caul Schlanger was similarly engaged. His grey cloak flowed between two opponents as though the three of them danced, ribbons of blood cast for the acclamation of the crowd. But his audience was in an unappreciative frame. More ratkin were descending from the nearest gallery and the three flagellants battered into them like sealers from the frozen north. The vermin were swifter and more agile, but the men failed to heed the wounds they took. Flesh split and bones cracked, only to then fall upon their would-be killers and rip them apart with bare hands and a vicious fervour. Rudi fought right alongside them.

The ceiling gave a sudden groan and the temple shuddered.

Felix swayed for balance as the ratman, already spinning into its next attack, stumbled. Its arms swam to keep itself up, but when the ground pitched a second time it was tossed onto its back. Felix ran it through. His sword struck stone and he pulled it back. There was a look of hatred in the creature's eyes, right until the moment its head dissolved into green vapour.

Felix left it and sought out Gotrek. The Slayer was not hard to find.

He had gotten ahead, cutting a corridor of bloody ruin for Felix to follow. Blank, blood-spattered mutants flanked the path. Their empty, mindless chant made his skin crawl. Between every mutant, there wavered a dozen faceless spectres. They attended the ritual, but their mere presence was enough to make Felix's skin flush as if it burned. If Gotrek saw them he did not share Felix's dread. The dwarf's axe glowed, streaming with vaporous tendrils as he barged through. The shades did not regard him, and simply reformed once he was past.

One of the spectres twitched.

Felix rounded on it with a yell, his blade passing through it as smoothly as Gotrek's body.

The apparition began to spasm. It fell to the ground, smoke churning through its body, thickening into what looked almost like claws that gouged into the flagstones. Felix backed away, warding it with the full length of his blade as it writhed upon the ground. Was it possible he had hurt it? Smoke knit together into muscle before his eyes, twitching with each spasmodic pulse of dark magic. Its arms turned black and gnarled, stretching to ape-like proportions. Its head, though vaguely human, sank into its shoulders. Its eyes gleamed a quiet blue, captive shards of the damned soul to which this body now belonged. It bared its teeth, dark lightning spitting across the salivary skein that sheathed its maw.

Felix recalled the dark tendrils he had witnessed emanating from the Chaos star, how the shades had been drawn to them, turned savage, how those tentacles had reached past him for the City of the Damned.

On dumb instinct, Felix readied his guard.

And the first black horror of Be'lakor pounced.

Morzanna screamed the words her patron bade her utter. She could no longer hear the voices of the others, just power, pounding through her skull like the pulse of a god, crackling before her eyes like grey lightning. It was a lot, but she could control it. Just. The world lurched, and Morzanna was one of the few that did not heave with it. She was an anchor, her will sharpened by the *present* as a hook for time itself. Realities that for two centuries she had not even considered separate were reuniting.

And she understood what Be'lakor planned.

A ritual of a power and scope that had not been attempted since the Great Ritual of Nagash. What was such a working to one who had measured his existence in aeons long before ancient Nehekhara felt the tread of the Great Necromancer? Be'lakor would heal the flailing tear in time the Pious had left behind. With minds like hers as glue, he would unite the broken shards and drag the City of the Damned, whole, five centuries into the era of the End Times.

It was terrifying in its audacity.

But Morzanna was one mind. Even she was not powerful enough to draw an entire city from its cell in time. There were others. Morzanna could feel them, connected by a shared experience of time, the Slayer and his human companion, the hermit and his devotees, Golkhan the Anointed. Their spirit auras sharpened to flickering points. Reality compressed around them.

Her tortured awareness expanded, and gladly, distance no boundary to a seeress with body and soul flooded with the stuff of Chaos. Across the damned city of Mordheim, buildings phased in and out of existence, as though the city itself sifted through a billion iterations before settling on that which it would occupy for eternity. Buildings rose and fell, were burned and then remade, then changed.

Across it all shades slipped through the cracks of time, thrashing as their bodies hardened and changed. From those displaced souls would the Dark Master forge an army, a host that Golkhan, invigorated by his patron's might, would lead from their city, march upon the Wastes, and wrest the crown of the Everchosen for himself. Be'lakor would usurp the chosen of the Great Four.

And he would announce his triumph with the ashes of the End Times.

Shuddering in pain, Morzanna's focus spun towards a troop of men, saw them storm across the bridge and, with a mighty horse-drawn wagon at their head, into the narrow streets of the city. Almost at once, the growing legion of black horrors descended upon them. There was screams, a peremptory crackle of musket-fire, the waving of banners and the vainglorious charge of the pious. She saw the wagon itself crash over the first wave and into the ruins of the city's roads.

Though ignorant of the Master's true ambition, Morzanna had cultivated his cat's paw to perfection.

Her spirit-sight grasped upon Konrad Seitz.

The man was exactly as he appeared in his own dreams. He stood tall at the forefront of his wagon as a deluge of black horrors loped from alleys, walls, and sewers. The men rallied to their captain. They would survive long enough to draw the city into their time. In valour, Konrad would assure the Master's rise.

As much as his traitorous liege, von Kuber, ever had in spite.

The chatter of repeater handguns filled Konrad's ears, spitting Grey Mountain lead into the smoke. The heavier *thump* of a Hochland long rifle sounded from the war wagon's rear, pitching a black horror from its perch atop a ruined wall.

Sulphurous black smoke washed across the wagon's open top. The men coughed, but did not for a second dare relax their trigger fingers.

The war wagon of the von Kubers was a scarred veteran of the Great War. Its hoary oak chassis was plated with iron, a curtain wall that surrounded the forecastle of the driver's perch. Rain beat at the grey pennants that rippled from each corner of its ramparts, droplets sliding down slack reins to the disembowelled remnants of the four horse team.

The driver was dead.

Arch-Lector Hans-Jorgen Gramm hunched over him, hands drenched from his efforts to staunch the flow. Konrad climbed onto the driver's bench, tried to make out the temple of Sigmar shown him in his dreams, but could not for the fog and drizzle.

'Men of Sigmar, blood of Magnus!'

A bounding horror galloped across the tenement tight to the wagon's right and leapt. Like a diving eagle, it plummeted for the fortified wagon. Coolly bringing his pistol to bear, Konrad blasted a hole through its chest. Its twitching corpse landed near the eviscerated horses, amidst the constricting circle of priests and peasants that were being pressed back towards the wagon. One of them righteously beheaded the thing with a hoe.

'Folk of Ostermark,' Konrad roared, fishing in his pouch for fresh shot and drawing up his powder horn, without pause for breath. 'If we die, then we die doing Sigmar's work. For von Kuber, for the Empire, and for Sigmar!'

The beleaguered men roared their love for the god of men and readied hooks and scythes for the daemonic harvest.

'Passable last words, my lord,' Gramm rasped. He tried to roll the driver's body from the forecastle but had not the strength in his arms, and settled instead for drawing up the man's mace for himself.

'I am no one's lord,' Konrad retorted, thumping the hammer talisman worn upon the heart of his mail. It rested upon the heraldic comet of von Kuber. 'I have two lords.'

The two men swayed as the wagon beneath them shook. Konrad leaned over the high walls of the forecastle, tracked his aim along its flanks, convinced they had just been rammed. But it was not just them.

The whole city was shaking.

The sky bled with colour, the blazing arc of sunlight beginning to fragment, to *constrict*. The entire sky phased in and out as if seeking some kind of equilibrium. Konrad's skin prickled and rose, every hair on his arms taut as though being drawn upward. As if Konrad himself was in some way responsible for reining the heavens into plane.

With a snarl he discharged his pistol into a daemon's back. He did not know what was happening and he did not care. With smooth precision, he reloaded. As Götz had always said, they were warriors, and they would see this end. One way or another.

The black horror shrieked, silver claws ripping for Felix's throat. Felix fended it off as best he could, but it was like trying to discourage a wolf with a stick. He jabbed for its face, seeking to exploit the superior reach of his weapon over the daemon's claws. It scuttled back, bunched its hindquarters, then lunged, spinning like a javelin through a blur of silver and black. Felix cried out, tried to slide clear, but a simian fist on an upward rise punched the wind from his chest and lifted him from his feet. The blow turned him over and he slammed face first into the ground.

For a split second he clung to the tremulous flagstones, then remembered himself and rolled to his right. A black fist crunched the stones where he had been. Propped up on his elbow, Felix's sword lashed out backhanded, severing the daemon's arm at the elbow. It howled, but did not bleed, flares of silver balefire streaming from the stump. Felix scrambled up. The black horror gnashed its fangs and flung itself forward. Felix braced and swung, a fencing school *mittlehaus* hewing its unguarded chest and cracking its ribcage like a conker. Felix dived aside before it landed. The body went skidding a dozen paces before flopping to a stop.

He just wished he had the opportunity to savour his triumph.

Everywhere he turned, faceless shades were being pressed into humanoid bundles and given form. Felix saw one ripped from the mind of a kneeling mutant only then to thrash and condense. The mutants' chant faltered, serried eyes blinking confusion before the newborn daemon tore its spine from its back and began to feast. Daemons freshly forced into physical form hooted and raged, feasting on corpses or bringing down uncaring mutants to slake their hunger. A monotonous whir sounded over the gibbering and shrieks. There was a crack like a pistol shot and the black horror that had been about to dive onto Brüder Nikolaus's back took a bullet in the side of the face and went down in a broken heap. The ratmen around him looked up to the slingers on the more distant galleries and hissed.

Uncaring, the sling-rats proceeded to rain missiles into the melee.

Caul grabbed one of his attackers by the throat and dragged its body over him. Bullets pulverised the dying creature and raked through those still standing. Hissing pain as his shield consumed itself in acid, Caul rolled clear, thick steam rising from his cloak to cover him as he scrambled behind a pillar. The others were not so quick-witted. Sling-fire mowed through man, ratman, and daemon alike. Nikolaus roared for the aid of Sigmar as all around him fell. The bloody-eared flagellant was struck in the collar, flipping him almost head over heels so his shoulders hit the ground before his feet. The one-legged sister crashed her stave across a skaven muzzle before she too was gunned down. Felix could do nothing but watch as Rudi caught a ricochet to the temple and went down under a mound of vermin. He staggered back, powerless to help.

From their vantages, the slingers shrieked and continued to pour down fire, widening their arc to cut a swathe through the kneeling mutants in case any man hid amongst them. Anything to ensure the ritual proceeded unhindered.

The ritual.

With an effort, Felix dragged his attention towards the altar and the sorcerers that surrounded it. They were the ones bringing these daemons into being. It was them that would break the daemon prince from its cage. Felix shielded his eyes, squinting directly into the aethyric glare.

The baleful light revealed a hulking silhouette. It grew large as Felix watched, like a body rising from the river's bottom until, in a ripple of silver fire, it broke the surface. Jolts of energy burst around its armoured bulk, writhing in the darkness that leeched from its unholy exoskeleton. Golkhan the Anointed clenched his fists and roared, leaping from the altar and ripping his claymore from its scabbard.

A second figure was already there waiting for him.

Hefting his axe, Gotrek charged.

Rudi gasped for air, overcome by the strongest sense that his spirit re-inhabited his body after a lengthy absence. Empty, foul-smelling cloth was draped over him and the only reasonable response his body could give to that first rush of breath was to vomit it back up. Spluttering on the bitter taste in his mouth, he rose, experienced a swirl of dizziness but managed to hold himself up.

Coloured lights jagged across the ceiling. The floor trembled. The air was thick and odorous, like pickled meats, and filled with howls as though he had been deposited on the threshold of hell. His heart stilled. What if he had? Had he not always been told that such was the fate of those who failed Sigmar?

He coughed, hawking a partially digested lump of gristle from the back of his throat and tried to calm down. He was not dead. His heart was beating too fast for that, and the difficulty he was having drawing in the sickly sweet air attested to the fact he was still breathing. The last thing he remembered with genuine clarity was the river, crossing that strange haunted battlefield with Caul Schlanger. And even that was muggy.

Rudi got feet beneath him and stood. He saw the corpses of two of Nikolaus's followers. He did not know how they had gotten there, but then he was not certain how he had gotten here. It looked like they had fallen well, heaped beneath Sigmar's enemies. From the fallen gear scattered around them it was not difficult to find a weapon, a short sword for his sword hand and a dagger for his left, as he had always favoured.

There was one thing Rudi still did know for certain. He was a man of Sigmar, blood of Magnus, and he had come here for a purpose.

He looked up, squinted. There was a star. A star in the centre of a fallen temple, as if the gods had torn away the sky and set it here that it might shine free.

A figure strode from the glare. For a moment it looked like von Kuber, but he had only seen the baron once before, and then from afar. He was clearly mistaken. This man was as tall as der Kreuzfahrer, but clad in bone-plaited black armour that shone with malice. His eyes glowed dully silver within the sockets of a horned skull. The Chaos warrior roared a challenge, thundering from the glare to engage another figure that, now Rudi's eyes had adapted, he saw was none other than Gotrek Gurnisson.

Staggering to the dwarf's aid like a dead man towards the light, Rudi paused.

The flagstones trembled, but it was due to something other than that which shook this chamber to its roots. Something was approaching, something big. A deep, animal roar sounded from a distant quarter. Turning slowly to face it, Rudi lowered his weapons. He exhaled a single word.

'No...'

Golkhan's blade met Gotrek's axe, hell-forged onyx and starmetal blue colliding in a prismatic hail of sparks. Gotrek ripped his axe back and smashed the haft sideways into the warrior's midriff. The champion retreated a pace, stealing the blow of strength, and thumped his pommel stone into the dwarf's chin. His jaw cracked, the blow spinning him, blood spraying. He swung a reversed blow to counterbalance, axe shearing for Golkhan's left knee joint. The Chaos warrior parried it.

'You're trying too hard,' the champion laughed. 'How like a dwarf.'

'I heard you used to be someone I'd feel bad about killing.' Gotrek scowled, rubbing his bearded chin and spitting a gobbet of blood. 'How like a man.'

Golkhan circled, ignoring the daemons that rampaged through his followers around him and the crackling energies at his back.

'Are you not going to ask me why? Is that not what heroes do?'

'I don't need to ask,' Gotrek growled. 'You were given a duty without end and you grew weary of the honour.' He pivoted on the spot to shadow the Chaos warrior's steps, spinning his axe in one fist until it hummed with menace. 'Your ancestors were of a nobler age. I send you to them with my apologies.'

'Evil begets evil, Slayer. The world is rotten. Be'lakor promises a clean end.'

'I make you no such pledge,' Gotrek growled. 'First I'll kill you, then that lot,' Gotrek pointed to the sorcerers concealed within their magical shield. 'And then, if he ever dares show himself, your daemon lord.'

Laughter, sonorous as a punch to the diaphragm, reverberated between column and stone. The sorcerous star rippled before its power like a soap bubble in a gale. Golkhan acclaimed his patron's voice with a grin.

'I am no one's subject. The Master is but the herald of he who is greater, tasked with crowning the Everchosen to lead the armies of the End Times. So you see he must be allowed to rise. Without him there can *be* no end.'

Gotrek drove a feint for Golkhan's left shoulder, forcing the warrior into a parry.

'Fight me already, you petty blowhard.'

The Chaos warrior stepped back, baring his armoured chest with a flourish. 'I was peerless before I was gloried. And look at me now! I will cut you into pieces, limb by limb. I will slave your soul to Be'lakor's will, that you might bear my banner to the Wastes. You will be at my side as I claim the crown of the Everchosen and bring about the end of days!'

Wielding his massive claymore one-handed, the Chaos warrior attacked with a scream. Gotrek blocked the first stroke, just barely, suffering a deep cut to his left bicep and supplying a vicious dent to the warrior's breastplate in kind. The champion retaliated with a torrent of blows that Gotrek matched, scowl fixed. The dwarf ducked a reaping swing, losing a scrap from his crest, then roared forwards, ramming the shoulder of his axe into the champion's armpit. The warrior grunted and stumbled. Gotrek's axe flashed across his pectoral plate, splitting a fragment of rib. Golkhan howled in agony as if it had been his own bones severed, clutching the break in one hand and sending a wild riposte that Gotrek blocked with ease. The champion came again, a maddened belly thrust that Gotrek batted down, his counter shearing a strip of bone from the warrior's vambrace and sending the great champion of Chaos into convulsions on the floor.

Gotrek circled around him and kicked him in the belly.

'Limb by limb, was it?'

'That axe,' Golkhan moaned, shoving himself back along the flagstones. Unsteadily he rose, using the horns of a kneeling mutant to haul himself up. He touched the shaven bone of his forearm and grimaced. 'The white witch warned me about that axe.'

Gotrek presented the blade like an oar to a drowning man. 'It's not done with you yet.'

Golkhan gripped his claymore in both hands and flew into the attack. His first blow hammered into Gotrek's guard like a tree striking a mountain. The claymore rebounded. The Chaos warrior hissed but came on, leading with his spiked spaulder to split Gotrek's cheek and spill him to the ground between the champion's legs. Golkan laughed, legs bestriding the recumbent dwarf, claymore upended for a killing drive. Gotrek's feet scissored through both of Golkan's feet, sending the warrior crashing to his back with an outraged roar. Both fighters grabbed for their weapons, rose as one, and struck blades with another furious spark.

Panting, Golkhan drew back. Gotrek began to chuckle, wiping a speck of blood from his eyebrow and rubbing it into his beard.

'You're bleeding,' the champion wheezed.

'I've suffered worse picking my nose.'

Golkhan snarled, but backed further, hand clutched to the broken rib.

I gift you an apportionment of my own might and still you fail me, Golkhan.

The disembodied voice rumbled over the anarchic bloodletting that filled its temple, impossible to ignore as a volcanic eruption in a thunder storm.

If becoming Everchosen of Chaos was nothing more than wearing a crown, then I could have chosen any mortal of a hundred thousand.

'Your champion is weak, like elven bladders,' Gotrek roared, lifting his face to seek the voice's source amidst the dark distortions and daemonic howls. 'Face me yourself. Unless your courage is better hidden even than your foul hide.'

Gotrek son of Gurni, you would challenge a god. Your audacity amuses.

'Stay away!' Golkhan shouted. 'I need no aid.'

A deep bellow sounded close by; the daemon's laughter boomed through it.

You forget yourself, vessel. There is but one Dark Master.

Across the tumult of shrieking ratmen, chanting mutants, rampaging daemons, the *whip-crack* of sling-fire and the shaking walls, one of the myriad portals rippled with energy.

A gigantic form emerged. Its muscular body was hunched, bound in dark rags. It turned in Gotrek's direction, lowered its hooded snout, flexed its fists and issued a titanic bellow every bit as mighty as the voice of Be'lakor.

'Grimnir's bloody crest,' Gotrek swore. 'I saw that monster downed by my own axe.'

The Beast was shoved aside to make way for an identical twin. The newcomer ignored the angry jaws of the first, cracking the twin tails of its rat-bone whip into the daemonic host.

They had wondered how it could be in two places at once.

What is death, Slayer, when time has no meaning? Be'lakor's laughter turned mocking. *Consider that, as you welcome death in my dominion.*

CHAPTER 21

The End Times

For centuries, the bitterness of the Damned had festered, been allowed to become fury. Now, by the power of the Dark Master, they had been granted form, powerful limbs and killing claws with which to vent that long-frustrated rage upon the living. All of the living. Alone or in rampant packs, they ripped into the surviving mutants, charging down the fusillades of the withdrawing skaven.

From the galleries, the skaven unleashed salvo after salvo onto any that approached too close. A pack of horrors overwhelmed one such position. The ratmen defended it with a fury and then, as scenting a signal, gave a collective squeal and broke, making the absurd leap from that gallery to the next. The black horrors bounded after them only for a hail of fire to beat their punished bodies back to the ground. Despite their efforts, their ferocity and their weapons, the skaven were pushed back, rallying at the last around the great bulwark of the Beast. Its bellows shook from column to column, its whip striking down black horrors with every stroke.

Felix had not the time, or the vaguest inkling of where to begin, to consider how that fallen monster had gotten here, nor how its mirror twin was even now crashing through the black horrors like a mounted Reiksguard through goblin bowmen.

It was charging towards Gotrek.

His companion saw the monster closing, thumped Golkhan off the shoulder of his axe, then swerved to avoid the swipe of its claws. The Beast hollered like a branded giant and struck again. Gotrek ducked under its arm, coming up to parry a tirade of blows from Golkhan's blade, then sent the champion reeling with a backhand blow in time to evade a punch from the Beast that would have taken the head off a troll.

Clearly, the Beast was not dead.

Felix had journeyed to the Chaos Wastes, been transported through daemon-infested pathways to mystical islands, but this was the first time that Gotrek's quest had taken them to a realm where time itself had no consequence. He took his sword in a hardened grip. Fluids he had no name for greased his face and gloves, threatening his sight and making his grip slippery. He closed with his companion.

By Sigmar, it would be the last.

A black horror skidded across his path. Felix hacked it down. A hand grabbed the back of his knee. Felix cried out, kicked back. The hand let go and a body fell. He spun round, lifting his sword two-handed to sever whatever came for him now.

A man lay before him. Two faces contested one head, both its mouths frozen in their repetitive cant. Its four eyes looked into Felix's two, and it shivered. The shiver became a twitch, then a spasm, and the mutant doubled over in agony. Fingers clawed at the black flagstones, shoulder blades rippling beneath flesh that was becoming harder and darker by the moment. Felix stepped around its grunting, half-made form and struck its head from its shoulders.

What insanity was this? Was this the reward these creatures had been expecting for their service to the daemon prince?

Somehow he doubted it.

Felix looked across the shaking chamber to see the same change being enacted over and over, flesh and shadow equivalent in their damnation. Even one of the fleeing ratmen shrieked and began to convulse before its comrades hacked it apart and tossed the pieces to the closing horrors. Felix felt an itch beneath his skin. Surely his imagination. There was no sign of hardening flesh or warping bone. But then he was not one of the Damned. He thought of the women and children of Die Körnung and his heart broke.

This was why Morschurle had been commanded to remain.

These people had been innocent, before corruption had warped their bodies and anger their minds. This madness had to be stopped. And it had to be done now.

The Beast bellowed, thumped its chest and threw a left hook. Gotrek's parry drew blood from its knuckles. The monster barked, then swung its right and missed, pulping a black horror that had been readying to pounce on the dwarf's back. Gotrek saw the daemon crash to earth, grinned, and grabbed the flapping end of a bandage from the Beast's snout. The Beast snorted as Gotrek yanked down its snout, cracking a clutch of teeth with a head butt that sent it sprawling. Gotrek cackled, but a second later was on the ground himself, the guard of Golkhan's claymore smashing into the base of his skull.

Felix accelerated into a run.

Golkhan pinned the dwarf beneath his boot, the tip of his sword parting the crusted beard like a beggar seeking bare flesh at a brothel. His gauntlets capped the pommel stone for a beheading drive.

Felix closed the remaining distance and then, with a yell, lunged into a flying tackle that ripped Golkhan from his feet and sent them both rolling across the floor.

By the twin virtues of luck and his foe's surprise, Felix came up on top and smashed the flat of blade into Golkhan's face. And again. Golkhan snarled, the shadow of a grin playing within his bone helm, and he punched up with an open fist. It caught Felix a glancing blow under the nose, but it jerked him back as though struck by a hammer. Black spots were summoned to his eyes, there to detonate with a force felt at the back of his skull.

Or was that his head striking the flagstones?

Had he really just seen Gotrek hit square in the head and get back up? Not for the first time, he marvelled at the thickness of his companion's skull.

'Peasant fool,' Golkhan bellowed, raising his sword for an over-arm slash. The sorcerous after-glare from the nearby Chaos star glittered across his armour. 'You could not best me before and you would try now? Fate will not spare you a second time.'

Felix clenched his eyes and waited for the cut of hell-steel to part lungs from liver.

Instead, there was a shiver of starmetal and a shriek of pain. Something heavy and metallic punched Felix in the belly and, on reflex, he curled into a ball. The object that had struck him rolled off him and onto the floor. He opened his eyes and touched it.

It was the right arm of Golkhan the Anointed. The Chaos warrior's claymore lay a few feet away. Black horrors clustered protectively over the severed pieces and snarled.

Gotrek stood over him, the silver-blue blade of his axe struck crimson with human blood. 'Carry your own bloody banner. I've been to the Wastes and returned. Twice.' And then, to Felix, as the champion continued to scream. 'Does like the sound of his own voice, doesn't he.' Felix offered his arm and Gotrek lifted him one-handed before shoving him on his way. 'Go, manling. Deal with the sorcerers. Leave this lot to me.'

Before Felix could protest, the Beast returned with a roar.

Gotrek's parry sheared a claw from its hand, but it did not feel it. Its fist impacted like a meteor, lifting the dwarf a foot from the ground and two dozen back. Somehow, he landed on his feet. He puffed out his cheeks and gave an ugly grin. The shaking ground made him sway but otherwise he kept his balance.

'The sorcerers,' Gotrek roared. 'Go.'

The Beast's rotten gaze rolled over Felix. There was no hint of recognition.

Finish the human, Be'lakor interceded. *Let him disturb the ritual and I promise your damnation will be eternal.*

The Beast grunted obeisance. It sniffed him, as if to get Felix's measure, then huffed with a fraught, wheezing laugh at the soft man it smelled. Felix backed off. With a deliberate flex of its claws, the Beast followed. He glanced to his left, expecting aid from that quarter, but none was forthcoming.

His companion's attention had been drawn elsewhere.

I will handle the dwarf myself.

Between the serried columns, air was flowing like oil, layered waves of quasi-reality rolling back to unveil a single point of elemental darkness. It was empty, like a hole, no larger than a nail. But it was widening, colours and sounds streaming into the vortex as it grew and stretched into a tear. Felix felt the unchained energies spilling from the void, heard and saw the reaction of the Chaos star to this new outpouring of power. The black horrors gibbered, prancing over only to bury their faces in their palms and look away. Their anarchic cries became shrieks as an arm drove through the tear. It was twice as long as a man's, musculature like a classical hero sculpted in black marble, and fingered with black talons that raked through the thickness of reality. Another set of claws forced their way beneath its triceps and, with the bellow of a god seeking escape from hell, it strained. The tear widened.

Felix caught glimpse of a face, of wings, of a black crown.

Gotrek cracked a smile and readied his axe, nothing but grim anticipation in his one good eye.

Wracked by a shuddering pain, Morzanna forced the ritual incantation through her teeth. She tasted blood. Her gums were bleeding. Be'lakor arose. Chaos streamed from the tear he had made. Morzanna gagged on its fury. It was like holding a leak only to be suddenly overwhelmed by a flood.

What could have driven one so all-powerful to do something so stupid?

Before she had been floundering, but now she drowned. Power within, power without. It was too much. She felt it rise above her neck, felt her mouth go under, the waters closing over the horns on her head.

It was the dwarf. The bane of the Master's kind.

'Hold,' she hissed aloud to the buckling sorcerers. 'Until the Master can seal the rift behind him.'

She groaned, gritting her teeth to resist, when a sudden shock to the barrier dashed her focus. Something had struck the warding lines and was trying to push through. An aethyric counterforce rippled across the point of intrusion. A heartless fiend like Golkhan could brave the raw essence of Chaos and hope to emerge unchanged, but otherwise the torment on a man's soul would be excruciating. She could not imagine the man who would be mad enough to try.

'Repent, schwester.' The burning silhouette of a one-armed man hammered against the wards, white fire and spears of warp-lightning flying from the blows. 'The Lord Sigmar longs to be gracious. He offers justice. Be purged in flesh and let your spirit meet him blessed.'

'Leave me,' Morzanna moaned, trying to concentrate on survival, but the pounding and prayers would not stop.

She knew well this man's monstrous dreams. It could be no

coincidence that he had come to this city, survived its horrors, and found his way to Morzanna's side. In a way she was glad.

Like Hurrlk, he felt almost like family.

Morzanna ground the hurt beneath bedevilled teeth. They had been a gift from Be'lakor, the one god that had yet to turn his back. Her master was near. It hurt now, but soon it would all be over.

For everyone.

Felix retreated from the advancing Beast, closer to the altar, pulling his sword and dodging back as the monster tested his reflexes with a sweep of its claws. It panted breathily, clearly finding them wanting.

'Gotrek!' Felix shouted, scrambling back as the Beast came again, this time for the kill, not even bothering to entertain the broken arm that a parry promised.

Felix pirouetted, the monster's fist breezing past his shoulder, and thrust back, but the creature's reach was long and his sword barely tapped its bone-plated belly. Snarling frustration he wove between the monster's fists, seeking in vain to strike a telling blow of his own.

An eruption of light from the direction of the altar suddenly seared his peripheral vision with gibbering pink lights. Unsighted, Felix retreated on instinct, feeling death streak past his burning eyes in the paw of the Beast. Blinking away colours, he rolled across the blow, coming in to hack an inch through the bandaged flesh of the monster's forearm. The Beast grunted and flung him off. Felix landed cleanly, leapt its scything tail and slipped around its back. Aiming for what he prayed was the twisted monster's heart he drove his sword into it. His rune-sword struck bone and bounced clear. Felix gave a disbelieving moan, then staggered back as a mace-like fist swung around.

Felix winced and lifted his arm to his brow. The Beast was hidden in the glare of the Chaos star. Something had happened to make it burn magnesium white. And from somewhere, he could hear a hymn.

The glowing monster growled, spreading its lumpen paws as if wanting Felix to observe the shadow of its bulk. And then, to Felix's horrified amazement, it spoke, issuing a rasping stream of words.

'See-smell, man-thing. Hear us, touch us. We are broken. Many times we die-die. Change bodies to burn and still back we come. Many times, again, and again, and again, forever-ever.' The Beast snapped for the tip of Karaghul that waved before its snout. Felix pulled back, eyes watering, and the Beast snarled. 'Never-not let you stop us. When this ends then we die-die.' The Beast drew up from its hunch, glaring over Felix's head to the emergent daemon prince. It released a sharp breath that sounded almost like a sob. 'We wish-ready to die.'

Felix crouched back, angling his sword into the glare, waiting for the animal bellow or the eruption of shadow that would betray an attack. Instead, it came slowly. It did not have to kill, only keep him from the sorcerers. Its bulk blocked the light, enough for Felix to see the broken intellect that glowed within its hood. A scabrous tongue flopped from its muzzle, licking across the teeth Gotrek had shattered.

Just as it withdrew the muscle, a short blade erupted from the front of its throat. For a moment the Beast just stood there, its tongue probing for the steel tip is if to taste it and judge it real. Then, with a grunt, the monster heaved forward.

Light seared again into Felix's eyes, leaving the redly glowing after-image of Rudi Hartmann clinging to the grip of the short sword like a climber to a piton. The young man lay amidst the monster's rags, feet lost somewhere in the folds that enwrapped its tail. He yanked on his buried short sword. There was a crunch of splitting vertebrae and a paltry spurt of thick, warpstone-flecked blood as the blade came loose.

'That was for my brother,' Rudi hissed. 'And this,' with his off-hand he rammed a knife into the orbit of the monster's left eye, 'is for my father. And this…' He stood, bent across the monster's giant back, shifted his grip on his sword and then buried it to the hilt in the Beast's black heart. Breathing hard, he pulled back. The dirty pommel stone quivered in place a clear foot to the left of where Felix had aimed his blow. Rudi regarded it appreciatively, signed the hammer with deliberate strokes across his breast, then brought the pewter talisman to his lips for a kiss. 'That was for almighty Sigmar, may He take pity on my unclean soul.'

Rudi cleaned his knife on his breeches, then looked up and shuddered, trying with all his might not to wilt before the dae-mon prince that inched his portal ever wider. The talisman did not leave his lips.

'Gotrek has it occupied,' said Felix, mouthing a 'thank Sigmar' as he felt out Rudi's trembling shoulders, expressing through touch the thanks that he could not, just then, put into words.

'We have to stop the sorcerers,' said Rudi. 'Can't you feel what they're doing?'

Felix could feel it.

It was like the earth was being lifted beneath his feet. Stone screamed with the conjoined voices of the Damned. This close to the Chaos star, the brightness was fierce, the heat punishing, the noise enough to make Felix want to tear off his ears and bury them under a rock. Blind as a beggar, gloved hands over closed eyes, Felix discovered what it was that made the power of Chaos rage and curse.

'Repent now and die early, for Sigmar is a god of vengeance…'

Felix opened his eye the narrowest split, peering between glowing fingers. The whole front of Nikolaus Straum's tat-tooed body was consumed in white fire. His one hand was crisp but continued to hammer at the unyielding barrier.

Whatever the flagellant had in mind was clearly not working.

'We need Gotrek for this,' Felix shouted. 'We need his axe.'

Rudi regarded him, eyes wide and uncowed by the nearness of Chaos. 'I have faith that Sigmar wouldn't have led us here for no reason. Don't you?'

Felix bit his lip, staring into the incandescent fury that burned right through his hands and gloves. He was not sure what he believed anymore.

Without waiting for him, Rudi hastened to Nikolaus's side. He squared his shoulders alongside the flagellant's, following the stream of verse until it neared a passage he knew. Adding his prayer to the prophet's, Rudi opened both palms, withholding a moment before the unholy fire, then turned his face away, clenched his eyes, lifted his voice that Sigmar himself might hear and plunged both hands into the barrier. His voice lifted into a wail, but he belted his hymn through the pain. Felix felt his respect for the flagellant's fortitude grow. Not a single tremor disturbed his faded tattoos, sea maidens and monsters unmoistened by so much as a bead of sweat.

Silvery balefire flared to white, energetic sparks jetting around the two men's hands. But the wards did not yield.

'Is this your plan?' Felix yelled, body shaking with frustration and guilt. 'We may as well battle the daemon prince!'

'Find strength and be faithful, Brüder Felix,' Nikolaus roared, not looking up. 'Even in this place, in the bowels of the daemon's own hell, we bring Sigmar with us.'

Felix bit back the angry retort that owed as much to fear as to faithlessness.

This chamber existed outside of time, and of space, a temple to a daemon that scorned the gods. A daemon whose laughter grew ever more real.

How could any being of light exist in such a place?

In a rush, he recalled his experience within the amphitheatre, an outpouring of remembered fervour so potent that it swept him back to another time no less dark. To the halls of Karag Dum, where he had felt the strength of the Heldenhammer flush his veins of doubt, replenished them with the strength to wield the Hammer of Fate and strike a blow upon a daemon of the Blood God.

What he would give for such a weapon now.

The hammer charm at Rudi's breast flashed silver.

Perhaps he did not need one. Forgoing hesitation lest zeal fade as swiftly as it had flared, Felix joined Nikolaus. Green-black chalk glittered by his toes, flames playing over his fingers as he raised them to the fire. He struggled to keep up with the flow of Nikolaus's words, but gave up.

Maybe Felix could not quote the teaching of each of Sigmar's carls as the hermit could, but Sigmar was a warrior and, much to Felix's ongoing dismay, so was he. He took a deep breath.

'Sigmar aid me!'

And thrust his palms into the fire.

Far beneath the black waves of Dhar, Morzanna perceived many untruths. Drowning in delirium, Morzanna saw images scatter like moonlight upon the ocean waves, lost lives and forsaken destines, fates worse than damnation.

She would have wept had she not already been subsumed by a sea of tears.

The chaotic spread of visions twisted before her eyes, showing nothing but herself in a million different ways. She was an old woman in bed; screaming in the embrace of a tattooed pirate; commanding the armies of Chaos across a misted isle; burning on a pyre before a triumphant mob; battling a handsome poet and a tattooed Slayer across a dozen battlefields; a mother of two boys; a child.

Were these illusions, possibilities, or were they memories? The last image lingered.

The child returned her stare. The eyes were the same as hers.

Had she really used to be so… *human*?

* * *

Felix's hands felt as though they were immersed in fire. The barrier was so bright that it was no different with eyes opened or closed. So he opened them. Lightning arced between eye lash and brow, painful flares earthing at his fingertips and sending glowing tracers spiralling the length of his arms. His reflective mail coat was as brilliant as the full face of Mannslieb.

The barrier held but he felt it waver. The roar was infernal, denying an audience for any sound but that of his own shouted oaths. The agony was indescribable, but in a strange way it helped. Pain tore through the corridors of his mind, slamming doorways as it went, cutting off sense from reason, instinct from purpose. There was nothing left but intent, the sense of something higher.

He had been purified in fire.

With the heightened awareness of near-death, Felix felt the malignant stain on the soul that was Be'lakor. He was not laughing now. Through a skein of magic and hate, he felt the daemon's panic, the fury of a demigod at the despoliation of its will. But the daemon seemed insignificant.

For there were others with him.

Rudi and Nikolaus yes, their pain incandescent as his own, but more besides. For a blessed instant it felt as though Sigmar had heeded his prayers and dispatched his legions to their aid. In that moment the pain was as nothing and, screaming the name of his god, he pushed.

The verse Be'lakor implanted into Morzanna's mind grew distant as she sank. She marshalled her strength, managing to grind out a syllable of the Master's incantation before her mouth filled with power. Three men grasped for her through the torrent of darkness, but they were not kind hands.

Fools, she thought. Did they not understand the balances they upset?

The three were close, forging deeper than she would have thought possible for so few. And then she saw why. They were *not* just three. They were hundreds. A hundred times a hundred.

Half seen, the expressionless shadows shoaled through the dark. Their faces were like smoke, bodies haloed in the silver witch-light of the grave. Even distant, so distant, she felt their wrath, the pound of their fists as they beat like solid silver upon the surface. Morzanna opened her mouth to cry out, felt her lungs flood with the seas of change.

The Damned had come as Be'lakor had said they would.

They had come *for her*.

Rudi could no longer see. All around him was blinding white. The heat was intense but he did not burn. These were the fires of the damned, that would torture for eternity and never consume.

He felt pain.

But also love. The fire scourged his flesh of sin.

It was as if he and his brother had burned alongside his mother after all. He felt their nearness, and that of others he knew. He saw comrades, childhood friends, and distant ancestors. They welcomed him home, celebrated him as one would a returning champion. They were dead, he remembered, but he was neither appalled by their unlife nor horrified by their approach.

They were damned. Sigmar had tested them harshly, but they had passed.

And he would not fail them now.

'Finish the stunted wretch!' Golkhan howled, clutching the stump of his arm.

A sea of black horror flowed and shrank around the spinning isle of death and ruin that was Gotrek Gurnisson. Charred black limbs scratched for his chest and arms, only to recoil

before the powerful warding runes of his axe and be parted
from their bodies in a sweep of super-sharp starmetal and an
arterial shower of daemonic essence. Limbs, teeth, heads and
foul blood flew up in a storm. The Slayer's back bled from
innumerable cuts, but still he stood, still he waited. The Chaos
warrior bellowed to be heard above their gibbering, resorting
at last to kicking one into Gotrek's path. It bounced to its feet
and reared, but the moment the red glow of the Slayer's axe
fell upon its face it hissed and shrunk back. Gotrek hacked
its head from its shoulders, then spun to split the jaw of an
opportunistic lurker with a gleaming uppercut.

Forget the Slayer, Be'lakor bellowed, straining to tear open the
streaming vortex to admit the spiked pinion of a bat-like wing.
Protect Morzanna.

'I serve neither her nor you,' Golkhan returned. Spittle flecked
his jaw. His chest heaved with agony. He thumped his cracked
set of second ribs, before returning the hand to his stump with
a grimace of pain. 'You serve me! I have what I need from you.'

*You have nothing! If I am not freed then the End Times will never
come. The world will linger. It will suffer and never die.'*

The stricken champion snarled, but the desperation in the
daemon prince's voice swayed him. With a stab of pain, he
removed his hand from his mangled shoulder. The black
armour of Be'lakor had sealed the wound in an agonising
mulch of curdled blood and hell-steel. There was little blood,
but it hurt like salt in an open wound. He swept his gaze across
the black hordes. The last of the mutants had been changed or
slain, the ratmen had fled for the portals. Even his own lieutenants were gone. He would have cursed Be'lakor for his foot
soldiers' indiscriminate bloodlust had he not known from
the beginning what would happen to the mutants once they
changed.

As he looked past one of the many silvery portals, he caught
a sweep of grey from behind a column.

One of his.

Golkhan gave a triumphal snarl. Men could always be trusted over beasts, rats, daemons, and witches. He lifted his arm, fist clenched in salute.

'You!' Get to the altar and deal with those thr–'

The thrown knife slammed between his eyes, near ripping his head from his shoulders but for the ungodly strength of his gorget and vertebral plates. His armoured body struck the ground, dead before it did so.

Be'lakor howled helpless fury, straining to tear the world apart with the power of his bare claws.

Across the chamber, from behind a trembling column of obsidian black, Caul Schlanger gave a thin smile, setting three more identical knives in parallel lines upon the floor. Satisfied with the ordered arrangement, he looked up towards the Chaos star. Before it had sparked with a periodic brilliance. Now it blazed like a bound star. And Caul had been schooled in magic well enough to recognise a misspell that had passed well the point of no return.

He threw a farewell salute to the screaming daemon prince and, whistling a dirge, turned back towards the portal for the city. Jaeger and his company had left him for dead in the house of Shallya.

It was only fair that he returned the favour.

'We rejoice in our sufferings,' Nikolaus intoned. His voice was level even as his body burned. 'Suffering brings endurance, endurance strength, strength triumph.'

His soul was being weighed by fire, cleansed, sins as kindling for the flames of judgement. And he had many sins. More than enough to consume his unworthy flesh. It was right the white lady should be here with him. She was not real, he knew. At least they had likely never met outside his dreams. It did not matter. Nor had he ever met Sigmar. It was what they represented; old lives and new, sin and salvation.

It was not just the white lady with him now. Here was Brüder Arnulf, all aggressive pride, and there strove Schwester Karolina. Her body was whole again, and she was beautiful. The realisation stirred nothing within him, his detumescence divine.

He had been purified.

His skin was blistering, peeling black, lead ink turning molten and dribbling over bare bone.

Like a man of Sigmar, he embraced the pain.

The war wagon of Baron Götz von Kuber rocked like a storm-tossed greatship between the black horrors that scaled its flanks. A sergeant of the moralpolizei struck down from the rearcastle with the butt of his Hochland long rifle. It cracked the daemon's jaw, shaking its grip and throwing it down amongst the unholy creatures that swarmed the wagon's iron-clad wheels. Another mounted the battlements, sunken face snarling before receiving the full fusillade of a pair of repeater handguns. Both weapons clicked to empty and the headless corpse fell. The men gasped in relief. Another horror scaled the sides behind them. One man spun, unloaded his emptied chamber point blank into its belly, then shrieked as the daemon ripped the guts from his still shuddering belly.

Konrad Seitz shouted for order, for the men of Sigmar to stand tall to the last. But there were too few left. The baronial banner had been trampled into the ash, the horn split, his musician slain. A handful of peasants could still be heard, fleeing for the river with a pack of horrors in loping pursuit. The rest lay dead in rings around the wagon, like the lines through a tree trunk marking an account of massacre and retreat. His own guard lay amongst them, men and boys, templar knights and warrior priests.

All dead.

A black horror sprung from the melee that consumed the wagon's rear and onto the high battlements of the forecastle. With a snarl, Konrad span, rammed his dragoon pistol halfway down the daemon's throat and pulled the trigger. The back of its skull blew back over the wagon in a sticky vapour.

'Men of Sigmar!' he bellowed, though he stood alone.

Hans-Jorgen's eyes stared wide and accusing to the heavens. A great tear split his vestments and coloured his pale chest red. Konrad holstered his pistol and drew his sword.

'Blood of Magnus!' he roared, climbing over his battlements to drop into the wagon's rear, hacking open a gibbering horror as he landed.

The handful of men parted without a word to admit him to their ranks. The daemons closed, but Konrad stood amongst equals and as equals they would perish. His heart swelled with courage and filled his veins with pride. Konrad clenched his sword and screamed. His comrades beside him did likewise.

And suddenly he did not feel nearly so alone.

Felix groaned. Rudi and Nikolaus were faltering, but the barrier was ready to give. He knew it. He had pushed it so far that the aethyric skin was bent around him, stretched so thin that he could see the agony on the sorcerers' faces. They had all to endure only a little longer. He ground his teeth and pushed hard. His muscles screamed from the effort. But where he pushed, the legions of the Damned pushed with him. They were innumerable, thousands upon thousands. There were farmers, fishwives, merchants and priests. And there were warriors. Felix saw the outline of armour and axes, Magnus's army, the shades of those that had once battled Chaos and would now battle it once more at Felix's side.

Had he really been so scornful of human nature that he could believe such men would fall to bitterness and rage, have thrown in their lot with the harbinger of the End Times?

He was a fool, but right now he was a glad and righteous fool.

Then, within the electric glare of power and fire, Felix caught sight of something that stole his breath.

He was tall, proud, armed and armoured like an emperor, silver smoke coiling within an open helm. Its wavering shield bore a griffon rampant, the heraldic mark of Magnus the Pious. Felix's heart swelled until it might burst.

All who ever lived. All who ever died.

That was what Caul had said. They were the Damned. Of course the Pious himself would be here amongst them. Amongst his own.

An electric shock bit his wrists, the vengeful strike of a dying serpent. He felt an end within his grasp. The flashes illuminated a faceless spectre at his side. It was a woman, wreathed in mistletoe and gowned in scorched taffeta. The faceless sister could not smile, but her warmth was comforting, and Felix felt her tenderness. She helped him, as she always had.

And together with a thousand others, they pushed through the last vestige of resistance.

Morzanna felt the commands of Be'lakor, shivering like a quake from the ocean's depths. The voice commanded, it threatened, it cajoled and it pleaded. But it only made it worse. It was hopeless. It was the daemon prince's own fault and it knew it. She smiled, as if the imminence of death gave her permission to be disobedient.

She had always known the Slayer would be the destroyer of them all.

'No, Morzanna. Fight. Do not believe that death can free yourself from me.'

Death.

The notion widened Morzanna's smile. Shadows crept from her eyes like tears, tenebrous threads coiling about her throat and enwrapping her arms in darkness. They pulled her down. Her chest burned, straining not for air but for a release from the power that filled them. One by one the sorcerers fell, blood streaming from their noses and eyes. They were envious, hateful, and treacherous. She despised them all, as much as she did herself. Ubek was the last, his lips parted in a hateful sneer that froze into a rictus as his blind eye blinked shut for the first and only time.

'Death,' she whispered, her flesh igniting with silver-black fire even as she drowned. She closed her eyes, unable to bear the empty faces of the Damned as they bore down.

'That would make a welcome...' she paused, smile spreading to her eyes as she felt the fires burn. '...*change*.'

CHAPTER 22

Salvation

The explosion was as brilliant as it was unexpected. No sooner had Felix felt the barrier give before him than he was lifted from his feet and flung across the chamber like a leaf on a gale. He saw Nikolaus fall to his knees, a prayer parting his lips as he was dashed to the ground and broken like a twig. The Damned were scattered, the shadowy beings dissolving before the wave of unleashed might.

Felix crashed into the side of a column, spun around its girth and sent tumbling along the ground until he hit another. Silver ringlets scattered from his battered mail like a trail of schillings, twitching across the flags as the chamber trembled before the strongest quake so far. Felix spread both hands to the floor for fear that it would drop away from under him.

Overcome by a sudden urge to be elsewhere, Felix pulled up his knees, winced as no man should ever have to, and got haltingly to his feet. His leg was numb from hitting the pillar, a bruise to his thigh the size and colour of a roggenbrot loaf.

The centre of the chamber had been scoured bare. The altar was gone. There was no sign of the sorcerers, the warpstone sigil, or anything else for that matter besides a hole in the ground. Power crackled across the chamber, incandescent flares licking the walls and causing stone to dribble like fat. Black horrors gambolled without purpose, slapping into columns and each other as the walls shook. And in the midst of their disarray, a dark angel wavered like smoke.

It was Be'lakor.

The daemon prince was almost as large as the Beast, larger still if one counted its leathery wingspan or the jagged height of its black crown. But where that degraded monster had been a rounded mass of malformed muscle and bone plates, Be'lakor was lithe, his powerful body sculpted in volcanic glass. That statuesque might was now hunched, as though wounded, bat wings cocooning its body. How it had come to be hurt, Felix could only hazard. Gotrek's axe passed through the daemon's leg trailing a wisp of black smog.

The daemon laughed coldly, the creak of glacial ice. 'You have taken my army, you have beaten my champion. My ritual has been spoiled but not ruined.' The daemon's voice was sonorous and smooth, but just a voice now that it did not cross planes. The chamber trembled, sending dust through the daemon's body. It chuckled darkly, as though tickled. 'I will be free. I may find myself five years past or five hundred. It is but a turning of the world to an immortal.'

'We're both here now, you sack of steam.' Gotrek made another swing. The runes of his axe flared with a frustrated brilliance as they clove through the smoke that was the daemon prince, Be'lakor. 'Fight me now and have done.'

Be'lakor continued to fade. Only an outline remained, shadow upon shadow, a hint of a crown. 'Your doom is coming. Trust that when it nears, it will be my hand that guides it.'

'When?' Gotrek roared, stamping through the fading shape.

He looked up, swung his axe and roared. 'Tell me who and I'll seek him out.'

Laughter echoed.

'You seek prophecy from a daemon king, son of Gurni. By thwarting me you assure only the crowning of another. The Everchosen of the four powers will march south and all will become darkness. If I must anoint their champion then I will see to it he has might enough to end you, Slayer.'

The voice faded to nothing. Gotrek growled and lowered his axe.

'I look forward to it.'

Cracks were spreading along the ceiling, the serried columns now looking decidedly unstable. Over shaking ground, Gotrek came running, snatched at Felix's arm and pulled him around before running past in that peculiarly dwarfen gait that looked as purposeful as an ox but without the grace.

'I told you this place wasn't sturdy,' he called over his shoulder. 'I give it five minutes before it comes down on our ears.'

Grunting through his pins and needles, Felix set off after him. His companion sounded remarkably buoyant considering he had once again been denied a doom. Felix could not keep the scowl from his face.

Probably because they were both about to get buried.

The black horrors of Be'lakor thrashed insubstantial fangs as they passed, following their master into oblivion as the power that sustained them waned. Some remained solid enough to fling themselves onto Gotrek's axe, and the Slayer was more than happy to oblige. Around the crumbling chamber, Felix saw a handful of ratmen and grey-cloaked soldiers still fleeing for the myriad silver-shimmering portals that led back to the city. He pointed to one.

'There. I'm certain that's the one we came through.'

'You sure? They all look alike to me and I don't want to

bump into myself coming the other way.' The dwarf suddenly chuckled, his errant good mood confirmed, and nuzzled his axe blade to his bearded chin as he ran. 'Now *there* would be a doom and a half!'

'Just take it,' Felix growled.

The portal shimmered as though it suffered. Its surface quavered before Gotrek's glowing axe, but the reaction was half-spirited. The dwarf was striding towards it, pinching his nose as if about to dive into deep water, when Felix saw the bloody pile of flayed corpses to his left shift. The body on top of the heap sat up and groaned. The young man's eyes narrowed as they sought focus.

'Did we win?' Rudi croaked. His skin was charred, his fringe and eyebrows completely burned away, and his woollen smock smouldering where it still clung to his flesh at all.

Felix wondered how *he* looked. He doubted his cloak could take that amount of darning.

'Aye, lad,' said Gotrek. 'You slew the Beast like a hero.' He stomped over to where the stricken boy lay, bent onto one knee and hoisted him up over one broad shoulder. As though bearing nothing but the weight of his own brawny bulk he rose again and turned back towards Felix, shifting the lad so he lay draped around his thick neck. Rudi said nothing. He was out cold. Gotrek gave him a congratulatory slap on the rump. 'When you come too we'll talk about thieving a dwarf's honest doom.'

The chamber shook as if to a blow. Felix started for the portal and waved to Gotrek to follow.

'What of Nikolaus?' he barked. 'And the lizard?'

Felix dropped his eyes. 'Nikolaus took the brunt of the blast. I didn't see Caul. He's probably gone too.'

'They will be remembered,' Gotrek said simply, then lumbered into a run that drove him through the mirror of the portal.

It rippled in torture. Felix took a deep breath, aware that it might well be his last, and jumped in after.

The transit was different this time.

It was briefer, for one, but empty. The voices were gone, replaced by a malignant presence that probed warily at the emptiness the Dark Master had left behind. Even other daemons, it seemed, shunned Be'lakor.

Felix was certain it was only that wariness that kept him alive long enough to burst out the other side. Sight, sound and smell returned in a bundle and, for a moment, it was difficult to extricate one from another. He heard Gotrek's roar, followed by a *whoosh* of starmetal and a bony crack, smelled a bitter musk, then his vision cleared enough to see the dwarf tug his axe from the skull of the Beast. The monster's eyes flickered red within its torn hood as it collapsed amidst a pile of vitrified rubble.

'Stay down this time,' Gotrek growled, smearing blood across his face with his bicep.

The pack of skaven that had followed their master back into the catacombs squawked and scattered, bounding over the blast debris and half-mechanical monstrosities for the exit.

The cavern trembled and Felix threw a hand to the nearest wall. He wished he had not. It groaned beneath his fingers, cracks splaying out from the surface and deep into the rock. The dwarf turned his blood-smeared eye to the ceiling, blinking away a trickle of grit that streamed from above. A tremor made his assorted chains and piercings chime, trembling pink in the strobing balefire.

'The rats have outdone themselves this time,' he said, lumbering into a run that took him after the fleeing ratmen.

Felix followed, running past the empty stares of the daemon machines. The abhorrent creations did not stir as the walls at their backs crumbled. Felix wondered if they were unaware, like golems awaiting their maker's command. But he knew that was not so. They knew what was coming and welcomed it.

They ran into the main chamber, Gotrek in the lead and pounding for the hall to the stairwell. Sheets of rock were cascading from ancillary shafts, spilling into the excavated chamber like avalanches and flooding the cavern with dust. A gang of daemon machines disappeared under a torrent of rock. Felix coughed and covered his mouth with his cloak. His feet were numb from the shaking and he could barely see ten feet through the dust. Incandescent flares lay within the shroud where torches had been torn from their corbels to blaze upon the ground.

The ground ahead crumbled into a crevasse. It was widening by the second.

Felix saw black cloaks leap over it and keep on running. He gave a cry of despair but Gotrek did not slow down. Rudi's face pounded into the small of the dwarf's back as he took the gap flat out, thumping into the far side without breaking stride. With a yell, Felix jumped after, the rock crumbling from his boot just as he cast off. His heart lurched as he smelled the dry reek of emptiness below, arms milling in a wild panic before he landed in a rough stumble that hysteria forced back into a run.

The acropolis trembled in its death throes. The ground behind him sheered back into the abyss.

Felix willed his legs to pump harder, but his bruised side was still numb. His unbalanced stride bounced him off the wall and scratched his arm, but at least he was heading forward. Gotrek was disappearing into the dust cloud, but there was only one way to go now. No chance of getting lost.

That at least was something.

Coughing and with chest burning for want of clean air, Felix staggered into the antechamber and through it to the stairwell just as the ceiling began to groan. Footsteps and distant squeals echoed from above the cry of tortured rock and Felix made after them as swiftly as his limp allowed. He had made a turn and a half when there came an earth-tearing crash. Rock dust erupted from the opening below, causing Felix to hack up what precious life his lungs had been holding onto. Grit flew into his eyes and he blundered on, not daring to open them. The walls shuddered in his hands, bleeding mortar, caving inch by inch. Felix pressed his hands to both walls, as if he supported them rather than the other way around. Eyes still shut and weeping rock dust, Felix took a step that was not there and fell heavily into the temple of Sigmar. He opened his eyes and blinked away the grit. His gloves were prickled with stained glass.

Gotrek was waiting for him.

'Up you get, manling. Dwarf-made it may be, but this place has stood up to about all it's going to.'

The windows had been shattered, throwing coloured glass like caltrops across the floor. Sturdy walls shook, the great silver hammer swinging so hard on its chain that cracks spread through the marble walls with each successive blow. The hammer whirred several feet above Felix's head but still he hunched under its swing as he limped after Gotrek and out into the open air of the acropolis.

Felix did not know what he had been expecting.

But not this.

The sky shuddered and stalled, one moment flickering black and white, then exploding through a mad spectrum of colour. The sun gave a fitful glow, spitting like a fire in the rain as it faded, shifted across the sky or simply vanished altogether only to bleed back a moment later. Felix felt rain on his face, but before he could catch glimpse of black clouds they had burst apart, descending on the city in a rain of ash. The city itself was just as maddening; piles of rubble, buildings, entire streets blinking in and out, falling into ruin and rebuilding as time's shackles were cast off and broken. Roads ripped themselves from the earth. Iron and brass screamed across the sky.

On the road towards the bridge, a row of houses sunk into the earth, the ground unable to support the mass as stone after stone after stone contested the single point in space. The buildings exploded. A mountain of stone and an iridescent storm of the eight colours of magic cascaded over neighbouring districts.

Felix ran to the edge, swaying with the shaking of the acropolis, and looked out into the wide bowl of the amphitheatre. Black-cloaked skaven were fleeing across the arena, sheltering in the open pit as the structure around them crumbled. The sand beneath their feet rippled like molten lead. Something was rising. Felix looked away, unable to stomach the short-lived screams as the space their bodies occupied was suddenly claimed by mortar and stone. The towering edifice of the Stadtverwaltung stormed up from the arena, barging aside the ramshackle terraces before both crumbled like ash before Felix's eyes.

Mordheim was tearing itself apart.

The river and the wall of fog that surrounded it were the only constants in sight. Fog lay over the eastern and southern walls of the city like extensions to its ramparts, obscuring his view of the stone beneath. They were much closer than the river, but he had no idea if the walls were gated or where a gate could be found if they existed. He did not even know if the mists *could* be crossed anywhere but the bridge. That left only one option, and Gotrek was already moving, his expression one of rigid determination as he pounded down the marble flight from the acropolis. The steps trembled underfoot, eventually giving way to a paved road. A wide avenue led through groaning ruins to the distantly glimpsed turrets of the bridge towers. The road was not twisting in on itself as it had before, which Felix supposed was something but, as he watched, weeds took root between the flagstones, flourished and then died, bursting apart in showers of jade to seed the earth with shivering motes of power.

Rudi stirred, blinking in confusion at the tattooed back that was his reward for regaining consciousness. Gotrek grumbled something dwarfish and set the boy down. Rudi stumbled, unready for the shaking ground. Gotrek watched him for a second then gave an approving grunt.

'I can't hear the voices,' Rudi mumbled, face awash with colour as he gawped at the sky.

'No,' said Felix, briefly smiling. He had not had chance to notice, but it was true.

Rudi turned back, looking up the steps to where the temple was slowly beginning to come apart. 'Brüder Nikolaus?'

'Talk later,' Gotrek growled. 'If you can flap your lips, you can move your legs.'

'Move?'

'That way,' said Felix, pointing across the tortured tenements towards the bridge. From the confused maze of streets ahead, there came the rumble of musket-fire. Gotrek started to move and Felix was right alongside him, turning back to shout. 'Quickly!'

'Quickly,' Rudi agreed, stumbling the first few steps but swiftly recovering the knack of it.

Together, the three of them tore down the ever-changing street, Felix and Rudi more than once relying upon the other to catch them as a weed materialised around their ankle to trip them or flagstones gave way to potholes. Gotrek ploughed through it all.

At a crossroads, they paused for a heartbeat.

Between the blinking of an eye, Felix saw that the torn ruin on the far right corner was packed with tattooed goblins. Their shrill war cries sounded in a sudden burst as they cavorted through the broken walls, feathered bandanas waving, slinging arrows into some *other* group of men that took cover behind a cart in the street and returned fire. Felix flinched. An arrow flew towards him. The next instant it was all gone. The ruin itself was heaving at its foundations as if it might rise up and crash through the streets to freedom.

It was as if the city's disparate times had been pressed into one place but not stuck, and it was uncertain which it was meant to occupy.

Felix blinked, still staring into the swelling building as Gotrek dragged him down the left-hand avenue. They cleared the crossroads just as the structure burst apart. The explosion annihilated the surrounding buildings, scouring the cross-roads with shrapnel while arcs of chromatic energy tore the air like lightning. Again, Felix and Rudi had each other to thank as the ground bucked and pitched them into each other's arms. A wave of ozone crashed over their heads. They kept running, turning another bend, trusting to Gotrek's instincts as the dwarf led them through an alley and onto another wide street.

The air reeked of blood, a cloud of gunpowder smoke prickling its way up Felix's nose and down his throat. He coughed, gripping his sword as Gotrek charged from the alley to behead a black horror that had been busy feasting on a corpse.

It was the corpse of a man.

His garb was plain, undyed woollen smock and breeches with a felt cap upon his bloodless head. A pitchfork lay beside him, broken at the haft and covered under the peasant's spilled guts. There were more of them, hundreds, torn open and lain out like crops before the changeling sky. Gotrek stepped over the body. The vanquished daemon was already beginning to fade.

The clangour of blades and human cries could be heard from ahead. Another musket round made the ash cloud quiver. Someone was clearly still alive. Felix ran into the open, avoiding treading on corpses where he could, squinting into the fog for signs of life. A pair of black horrors gibbered as they saw him, loping in from the right. Gotrek barked a laugh, swinging his axe as he spun away to face them. The daemons went for him, leaving Felix and Rudi to come upon the battered war wagon alone.

Felix had not seen the like in the Empire's armies for years. And this one would not be riding to war anytime soon. The horses had been butchered, the lamellar plates of their barding had been peeled back to expose the meat and were frothed with blood. The wagon itself looked as though it had been mauled. It had collapsed onto its rear axle, the wheels ripped clean off, its ablative flanks gouged to the wood beneath. But someone had hoisted a banner in the lee of the armoured forecastle. It was iron grey, emblazoned with the twin-tailed comet, and it was from there that the sounds of fighting came.

Felix and Rudi shared a look, then ran through the sulphurous murk to the savaged flanks of the wagon. Handholds were easy to find, and Felix hauled himself up, getting his fingers around the rim of a shield and pulling himself onto the wagon's ramparts.

The wagon's interior resembled a ghoul's abattoir. Bits and pieces that had once been living things lay everywhere, the battlements pasted with blood up to an inch thick. A black horror spun through the charnel reek and snarled, bunching as if to pounce.

Still straddling the rampart, Felix kicked it in the face. The daemon sprawled onto its back and Felix jumped into the wagon after it, moving to finish it off. He had taken one step and lifted his head when the daemon's chest erupted in a shower of black gristle and a crack like a splitting stone. Powder smoke rushed hungrily over the fading corpse, making Felix cough and his eyes sting.

A soldier in torn cloak and bloodied mail jumped over the body, swinging his pistol like a club. Felix cried out in alarm and ducked back. The gun stock struck the reinforced wood and split. The soldier snarled, tossing the ruined weapon aside and drew up his sword.

'Konrad,' Felix shouted, holding up a hand for peace.

The militia captain regarded him, confused. In his other hand, Felix tightened his grip around his weapon. The man's snarl slackened, some of the animal instinct passing from his eyes. He lowered his sword and, gladly, Felix eased his hold on his.

'Dwarf-friend,' Konrad breathed. He swallowed as if he had been waiting hours for the chance to do so. His horseshoe moustache clung to anaemic cheeks, adhered by his own blood to his flesh. 'Is this your doing? Did you and your companions unleash this hell on the city?'

'What?' Felix hissed, too thrown by the very idea to think what else to say.

'Where is von Kuber?' the man pressed.

Felix did not answer right away, time enough for Rudi to scale the wagon's sides behind him and drop down. Konrad's blade swept up to cover him. Blood loss and exhaustion made the steel shake.

Rudi faced the sword down, taking a step forward and palming the weapon gently to one side. Standing on the cusp of collapse, Konrad had not the strength left to try and stop him.

Felix had not noticed it before, but Rudi was three inches the taller.

'The baron was in the temple,' said Rudi. 'Along with others.' Something firmed within him as he looked past the soldier to where the acropolis lay hidden in the fog. 'He didn't make it out.'

Konrad's mask sublimed to one of grief. His eyes widened, his jaw softened, a tear moistened the jellied gore that caked the corner of his eyes. And then it was gone.

'His watch is over. There are no more von Kubers and the city must burn.'

As if choosing that moment to make its point, the fire-blackened tenement to the wagon's left side suddenly erupted. The three men ducked, shrapnel beating against the wagon's flanks.

'This city is doing a fine job on its own,' Felix shouted. 'The daemon has been banished, the curse is broken. There's no need to die here.'

'Broken?' said Konrad, incredulous, the *crack* of musket-fire from the direction of the forecastle a terse reminder that all was far from peaceful. 'The Damned haunt the streets in daemon form. A temple to blessed Sigmar is defiled and must be restored. Run you say?' The soldier chuckled darkly and turned his back. He gazed into the smog. 'I say no. The City of the Damned will be purged. It will be sanctified and then it will burn.'

Felix swallowed his rejoinder, shook his head angrily as he turned away and set foot to the rear ramparts to hoist himself up. Even after everything, he still felt the strongest urge to introduce Konrad Seitz to his fist. That was the problem with zealots.

They would never change.

'Come on, Rudi,' he called back, noticing that the man was not following.

The young man moved to Konrad's side and helped him stay upright. There was a determined set to his jaw, face turned back across the forecastle in the direction of the temple. 'Captain Seitz is right.'

'Rudi, don't be–'

'Go, Felix. This isn't your home, it's mine. My family. Many of the Damned have been freed but there's work still to be done here. I don't have Brüder Nikolaus to do it for me now.'

Held in the crook of Rudi's arm, Konrad gave a wolfish grin. 'We're sinning men of Ostermark, and there can be no more running. We'll save them all and burn the rest.'

Felix stared for a moment, a lump in his throat. Then, unable to think of a word to say, hauled himself over the wagon's rear. He landed on the bloodied flags with an almighty twinge in his bruised leg and started limping for the bridge.

'Where's the lad?' shouted Gotrek. His face and arms were black and glowed faintly with daemonic ichor. Somewhere underneath the belligerence and grime, Felix detected a trace of concern.

Felix looked back to the wagon, like a beached wreck in the gloom, unsure quite what answer to give. 'I think he always meant to die here.'

Gotrek nodded, understanding as only a Slayer could, then clapped his arm, leaving a bloody print on his sleeve. The pair of them ran, leaving the war wagon and its embattled men behind. Felix prayed for them.

To his surprise, he felt confident that someone listened.

The bridge was closer now, unchanging while earth, stone and sky shattered and blurred. It was like observing the accelerated passage of seasons; watching trees grow, flowers blossom and then die, creatures shifting too fast to be recognised except by a gut reaction to their presence, only the shape of the land itself to grant constancy.

Gotrek taking the lead, they emerged onto the courtyard.

The bridge reared vast from the fog, grey-stoned towers proud in spite of their ruination, the black claw-marks of the fire's touch at their throats. It was raining ash, but Felix ignored it, running ahead of Gotrek and charging for the bridge. A man was sat upon the steps in the ash snow like a hopeless paramour in the rain.

He had a knife.

'Only two?' said Caul Schlanger, turning the blade to clean soot from his fingernails. 'You do make a habit of this, Jaeger.' He did not look up as Felix marched towards him, lifting the four-fingered hand as if to inspect its cleanliness, then curling them down one by one, 'Ulisson, Straghov, Varigsson, Magdov–'

The last name turned into a blast of wind as Felix closed, planted his foot into the seated man's chest and slammed him back against the trembling steps. Caul snickered drily and set down the knife. Felix did not shift his boot.

'Bastard, Schlanger,' he hissed. 'You could have helped us!'

'You think I didn't?'

Felix levelled his runesword to the man's throat. 'Don't think I'll be unduly troubled to have a fifth name on my conscience.'

Caul winced at that.

'Where have we met, Schlanger? And if I think you're lying, I swear to Sigmar that I'll gizzard you like a fowl.'

The man's green eyes met his, each unmoved as a frozen lake.

'We have never met, Jaeger, but we share a mutual acquaintance.'

'Tell me,' Felix pressed, angered by the slow creep of the man's smile.

'We are members of a secret order, he and I, pledged to the understanding and eradication of Chaos. You will have heard of it. The Golden Brotherhood.'

'Max Schreiber,' Felix barked. '*You* know Max Schreiber.'

'Like the father I never had,' Caul smirked, a fastidious show of ordered enamel. 'He keeps well. In Altdorf, last I heard.'

Felix turned briefly to Gotrek before withdrawing his sword and sheathing it with a disgusted snort. He stepped back.

'I still don't know whether to believe a word from your mouth.'

Caul rubbed his throat, helped himself to his feet and mocked a hammer across the chest which he finished with a courtly bow and flourish. 'Like holy Sigmar, a liar is all things to all men.'

'Did Max send you here?'

'Men like Konrad and Gramm would burn us for the

knowledge we keep, but we knew something foul dwelt here. Something best left undisturbed. It was easy enough to bring myself to the baron's notice. He always had positions for killers.' He grinned, fondling his knife as though recalling something peculiarly delicious. Then he shrugged. 'I suppose now we know why.'

'You could have mentioned this before. How did you–'

Caul shook his head, lips tight as though something in this amused him. 'You can ask me every question you like Jaeger, why Herrcher Schreiber told me of his adventures, or how he knew you were in Osterwald and would come to me. But it won't matter.' He stepped back, up to the next step and into the mists, spreading his arm to the bridge. It trembled slightly and even the river, seen this close, bubbled as though it boiled. 'Because I very much doubt you will remember any of this.'

Gotrek strode past them, a dozen strides onto the bridge. At the point where the mist began to thicken, he held. His axe pulsed balefully, painting the grim dark red.

'Gotrek, wait,' Felix shouted, suddenly afraid. 'Even the daemon wasn't sure what time he would return to. How can we be?'

Gotrek chuckled, cold as the mists that pricked goose bumps from his arms. 'You have something to do tomorrow that can't wait?'

Felix blew an exasperated raspberry. His companion did have a point.

Gotrek clutched his axe in a strong grip, his one good eye glaring into the future.

'I've been promised a doom. And a dwarf never forgets.'

EPILOGUE

The sun touched hesitantly upon the ruins of Mordheim, edging the shadows from its jagged spires and down into the alleys, scattering gold upon where the autumnal warmth struck upon leaden frames, flagpoles, shards of glass. A cool breeze from the south pushed the fog from the River Stir and out onto the moors of Ostermark. The light wind made waves that caught the light at their crests, shimmering across its length and breadth, the earth affording an object lesson in beauty to the heavens. Clinging to its silver curve, Die Körnung sank ever so slightly into ruin. Its walls were shattered, its buildings ash and home to freshwater crabs and tough brown algae. The silted flats offered unconditional surrender to the water.

White hair scuffed like a dandelion clock, eyes dampened like crushed lavender, Mori sat amidst the burned, stake-like pilings of the jetty and stared across the water to the ruins of the other side. She sat with crossed legs, brown water halfway to submerging her knees. The sporadic sounds of musket-fire came from distant quarters, an occasional shriek to startle the circling gulls. She did not know how long she had been sitting there.

She gave a sniff and wiped a tear from her eye. Her sleeve was muddy. She did not care.

Watching the dappling brilliance arc subtly through the water to face the drifting sun, she gradually became aware that she was not alone. With a giddy rush she spun around. The crush of disappointment was instant. The beach was empty but for gulls.

But she felt something there.

'Hello?'

Her voice echoed back to her. Her heart knotted. It was as if she heard another's voice.

'Hello,' she called again, waiting for the echo.

Why do you weep, daughter?

Mori froze, splayed fingers sinking into the silt. 'F-father?'

Not yet.

'Sigmar?' she whispered, looking tentatively to the sky.

So much more.

Mori looked dubious, but she said nothing. It felt good just to be able to speak and have another reply in kind.

One fruit withers on the vine, while another will flourish. The forest burns to allow young saplings to cast their own darkness.

'I... I don't understand?'

Follow the river to the south gate, then take the Totenwald path to Drachenfels. There the barriers between worlds will be thin enough for me to speak with you again.

Joints cold and stiff, Mori stood, looking up the deserted beach to catch a glimpse of he who spoke. There was no one there. His words seemed to appear directly in her mind.

From there I will show you the Paths of the Old Ones. Mordheim has been denied me, but a fresh evil will soon arise on distant Albion. Damnation teaches nothing if not persistence.

'Why do you want me?'

The voice chuckled, like a winter chill on bleak scarp.

Dark Gods demand a high price, daughter. But they are fair.

ABOUT THE AUTHOR

David Guymer is no stranger to the worlds of Warhammer, with exciting stories in *Gotrek and Felix: The Anthology* and *Hammer and Bolter,* and much more on the way. He is a freelance writer and occasional scientist based in the East Riding. When not writing, David can be found exorcising his disappointment at the gaming table and preparing for the ascension of the children of the Horned Rat.

READ IT FIRST

EXCLUSIVE PRODUCTS | EARLY RELEASES | FREE DELIVERY

blacklibrary.com

Also available from

GAMES WORKSHOP®

and all good bookstores